PARIS REQUIEM

CHRIS LLOYD

PEGASUS CRIME

NEW YORK LONDON

PARIS REQUIEM

Pegasus Crime is an imprint of
Pegasus Books, Ltd.
148 West 37th Street, 13th Floor
New York, NY 10018

ISBN: 978-1-63936-266-0

0 9 8 7 6 5 4 3 2 1

Printed in the United States of America
Distributed by Simon & Schuster
www.pegasusbooks.com

For my mum and dad, Averil and Mervyn Lloyd.

'Hell is empty
And all the devils are here.'

William Shakespeare, *The Tempest*

November 1940

What is it with owls?

As if driving through endless kilometres of darkened forest with just a slit in the headlamps to guide your way wasn't enough, there was always some strigiform little bastard to remind you you were up to no good. That and the woods crawling with German soldiers who seemed to agree with them.

I froze half out of my car while the echo of the shriek died in the night. The echo in my bowels died with it. Listening intently, I waited while my eyes grew used to the dark. The blackness had rushed in to fill the void the moment I'd turned off the car's lights. This wasn't dark. This was an absence of light. I live in Paris under the Nazis, believe me, I know the difference.

I'd only just checked my stomach was back in place when the owl screeched again. A tortured sound shattering the louring silence of the night. I've heard Parisian pimps skewered by a rival make less of a song and dance.

As I gently closed the car door, another noise stopped me. A dog barking. Somewhere in the distance. A farmer's or a soldier's, I had no idea. I listened out but the beast remained silent. I could wish the owl would follow suit. Other animals joined in, this time with smell, not sound. Wafting on the changing breeze, the aroma of manure tickled my nose. I twisted my head involuntarily to get it out, like trying to kill a sneeze, but it clung on. Pigs. Why anyone would want to live in this wilderness was beyond me. I'd lived too long in the din and grime of Paris to appreciate the dung and grim of the country.

Feeling my way to the rear of the Citroën, I fumbled to open the boot in the dark. Another smell, faint this time, assailed me and I recoiled. Turning away for a moment, I took a deep breath and leaned inside. My hand touched a blanket and I pulled back hurriedly. I'd felt its contents give at my touch and I fought down a retch. More gingerly now, I reached back in, nudging the heavy weight under the blanket to one side to find what I was looking for. Feeling the coarse wood of the handle, I pulled a spade out, careful not to let it bang against the side of the car and ring out in the night.

Leaving the boot open rather than risk making any more noise, I hefted the spade on my shoulder and turned away, letting my peripheral vision try to focus on the edge of the forest. With another dog's bark in my ears and the cold and pungent air in my nostrils, I felt my path away from the safety of the car and into the darkness.

The owl spoke one more time.

Overture

September 1940

I

'I'd've been more than happy staying down south.' Boniface paused and took a delicate sip from his coffee. 'But the missus wanted to get back to Paris in time for my three girls to go to school.'

The other cops in the Bon Asile nodded sagely at Boniface's words, like it was the most natural thing in the world. Through the tobacco-brown café window, I saw a German jeep slowly cruise past. Paris was under the Nazis and Boniface was worried about his kids missing the start of the school term. He wasn't the only one. I watched two small boys follow in the wake of the German soldiers, dawdling to learning like it was any other September.

'And she missed the shops,' he added. 'Not that there's much in them.'

He had a voice like a Venus fly trap. Syrup-smooth behind sharp teeth, hiding a nectar-filled void. And like a carnivorous plant, form was everything with Boniface, substance a sugar-lined con. Some of the younger cops seated on smoke-stained chairs soaked up his every word. Others, not so much. Me, not at all.

Not bothering to stifle a sigh, I folded the newspaper and took my cup of coffee to the bar. The Bon Asile, a misnomer at any time, was a dingy temple to coffee and cigarette smoke in the narrow streets of the Île de la Cité behind Thirty-Six, our name for the police station on Quai des Orfèvres.

'Coffee,' I told Louis in a low voice, sloshing my nearly full cup on the counter. 'None of this ersatz rubbish.'

Behind his bar, Louis shrugged expansively. 'Rationing, Eddie. Can't get hold of the proper stuff.'

I glanced back at the other cops seated around the table, still enthralled by Boniface's stories, and turned to Louis. I pointed to the cupboard at the rear of the counter and spoke in a low voice. 'Real coffee, Louis. Or I'll tell your wife what you keep in that other cupboard.'

He blanched and made me a new cup. The smell alone left me swooning.

Back at the table, Boniface was still holding court. 'Dunno why you ever left the south, Giral,' he said to me when I sat down again. 'I found the chicks there very welcoming.'

'They must have been devastated when you left.' I took a sip of the strong coffee and forgot where I was for the moment.

'So why did you leave, Boniface?' one of the other cops who could be bothered asked him. 'You wouldn't have caught me coming back.'

'I was tempted,' he told them. 'Boy, was I tempted. Lie low in the sun down south and leave Paris and the Boches to you lot. But as I said, the missus wanted back. The kids, you know, school.'

'Which missus?' the first one asked, the ensuing laughter around the table raucous. Boniface was lauded among the more gullible cops for his boasts of having both a wife and a mistress in the city, each with a family spawned by him.

I picked up the paper again. I wanted to choose which lies I paid heed to. His voice washed over me. It was almost soothing when you didn't listen to what he was saying. He also had a habit of winking knowingly at his slightest utterance. And with his brilliantined hair with its tiny flourish above the right ear, he looked like he wished he was Maurice Chevalier. To me, he was more like a half-hearted Madame Pompadour.

'Surprised they had you back,' Barthe, one of the older cops, commented, knocking back his breakfast brandy.

Boniface laughed. 'Commissioner Dax nearly had my hand off, he was so eager for me to get back in the saddle. Spot of virile blood around here. Dax knows it wouldn't go amiss.'

'And because we're hopelessly undermanned, what with the war and everything,' I commented, without raising my eyes from the paper.

'But we've always got you, Eddie. You're part of the furniture.' I could hear the surprised annoyance in his voice.

I glanced up. The triumphant look on his face wavered as he noticed the other cops looking away, their expressions sheepish.

'Inspector Giral,' a voice broke the silence.

I turned to see a young uniformed cop had come into the café. The uniforms usually kept away, leaving this place to the detectives.

'What is it?'

'Commissioner Dax wants to see you. Says it's urgent.'

I got up and towered over the kid. He paled. 'Where were you ten minutes ago when I needed you?'

'You missed a trick there, Eddie,' Boniface told me. 'Should've made it back down to the wild south when you had a chance. Put your feet up with the other goat-eaters. No one in Paris to miss you.'

Bending down, I patted him heavily on the cheek. Everyone around the table looked everywhere but at us. His own look was one of growing surprise.

'You may have noticed the Germans in town,' I told him, my eyes staring intently into his. 'Well, they're not the only thing that's changed.'

'Take a seat, why don't you?' Commissioner Dax told me.

I already had. I leaned back in the chair opposite his desk and shrugged. Outside the window, a September sky failed to warm the morning air, hanging lifelessly over streets grey with uniforms and resignation. Even so, the room was stifling inside, a fly tapping constantly against the window. I knew how it felt.

Dax pulled two glasses and a bottle of whisky from a cupboard and poured us both a small tot. I looked at my watch. Barthe wasn't the only one to indulge in a working aperitif these days. He sat down heavily in his chair, the air from the cushion farting gently between us. He was still as gaunt as ever, his harsh horn-rimmed glasses nestling unsteadily on the narrow bridge of his nose, but his dietary choices were making up for lost time with his ever-increasing paunch. I wondered where he got the food from to grow it. And the whisky. He seemed to read my mind.

'Major Hochstetter,' he explained, brandishing the bottle.

Hochstetter was the German military intelligence officer assigned the job of making life difficult for me. I hadn't seen him for a few weeks now. Still didn't mean I wasn't hurt at not being on the free whisky list.

He clinked his glass against mine, which was still sitting on the desk between us, and took a drink. He looked tired. We all did. Hunger does that. So does having the Nazis coming to stay.

'Drink,' he urged me. 'We're all in this together.'

I picked up my glass. 'Except some of us are more in this together than others.'

It tasted good, I had to give Hochstetter that. He knew his whisky. The rare luxury of it almost hurt as it lit a path through my mouth and down my throat.

It was Dax's turn to shrug. 'Please yourself, Eddie. Hasn't stopped you drinking it.'

'What is it you wanted?' I asked.

'The Jazz Chaud. Body of a man found in suspicious circumstances.'

I looked pointedly at the whisky. 'So no rush, then?'

'Just trying to keep you sweet, Eddie. Remember that? Anyway, the stiff won't be going anywhere.' I watched him drain his glass and pour himself another two fingers. 'The place has been shut down by the Germans, but the caretaker found the body this morning when she went to check up on it. Looked like he'd been trying to rob the safe.'

'Rob the safe? With the place closed for business. Not the smartest suit in the club, then. What else do we know?'

'That's all, Eddie. Uniforms are there now, waiting for you to show up.'

I stood up. 'I'll apologise to them for being late, then, shall I?'

Dax wasn't taking Occupation well. Even just a couple of months ago, he'd have called me in to his office, told me about the suspicious death and shooed me on my way. 'Take Boniface with you. He's rusty after three months sunning himself down south.' He waved me away.

In reply, I poured myself another two fingers of the whisky and drained the glass before leaving his office.

Picking up Boniface from the detectives' room, we took his car from outside Thirty-Six and drove south across the river. I figured if Boniface was behind the wheel, he couldn't do much talking. I was wrong. He kept up a constant chatter, like rubber tyres on wet cobbles.

The Jazz Chaud was a jazz club in Montparnasse. We drove down wide boulevards into narrow streets to get there. The city was steadily refilling. All the people who'd fled in the weeks leading up to the invasion, terrified at the thought of what the Germans had in store for us, were now slowly coming back home. There was nothing like the bustle before the Nazis had decided to come and see us, but the city was yawning and stretching its arms, looking around itself in a daze and wondering what to do that day. The panic of the summer had proved false, the Germans treating us with a strange and polite formality. For now.

'It's as though we're all waiting like sacrificial lambs.'

I turned to see Boniface staring intently at me. 'What did you say?' I asked him.

He'd parked and was gesturing at the life around us. 'Us. In the city. One final fling before we queue blindly for our turn at the altar.'

He turned away and got out of the car. I could do nothing but stare after him for a few moments, the memory of his pomade still sweet in my nostrils, before following him.

The Jazz Chaud occupied the whole of a narrow building, a three-storey affair nestling amid a row of uneven buildings thrown up at random like damaged tombstones. I shivered despite the growing warmth of the day. This was a street the sun never troubled. Neither did the Germans, which was a relief. At least for the time being.

A uniformed cop on the door to the club looked green at the gills. He carried an aroma of vomit. For once, Boniface's hair odour was preferable. For the first time, I really wondered what awaited us inside.

In the entrance, I found Boniface bending over a middle-aged woman who was crying into a threadbare shawl, only occasionally coming up for air in racking gasps. She was clutching a tortoiseshell cat firmly to her breast. Mewing loudly, the creature was struggling to break free. Boniface touched the woman's face, his voice soft, soothing her, inviting her to say what she knew. I nodded at him and went on through the second set of doors into the club itself.

As a young cop in the twenties, I'd moonlighted in a similar club in Montmartre, knocking the heads of rowdies together on a Saturday night for money, but I hadn't set foot in a jazz club since. And I didn't know this place. In those days, I hadn't ventured this far south in the city for fun. I saw enough of it for work. In an instant, I recognised the underlying tang of alcohol and perfume from that time, the acrid smell of bleach and the sad sight of the stage silenced for the day. But all the aromas were weak, diluted. The club had closed before the Occupiers had got here and they'd banned it from reopening in one of their random acts of administrative zeal. The stage had been silent for months. Like every other fitting in the club, there was a fine coating of dust on it, covering the chairs and piano, the music stands and microphones. For the briefest of moments, I wondered what had become of all the musicians, both here and the ones I used to know, especially the African-Americans who'd stayed in Paris after the last war, not wanting to go back to the problems they'd face in America. I wondered if the Nazis had closed them down too.

A second uniformed cop was standing around inside, shuffling from one foot to the other and looking longingly at the empty bar. Older than his colleague at the door, he looked to be a hard man, of an age to have seen a lifetime of sights the last time we went toe-to-toe with the neighbours.

'What have we got?' I asked him.

'Bad, Inspector.' His voice was strangely light, discordant with his corpulent build and gimlet eyes. He nodded to a door. 'Through there.'

'The owner around?'

'Can't get hold of him. No one else here.'

I nodded and made for the door he'd indicated. When Dax had told me of the death at the club, I'd assumed an accident. A hapless safe-cracker who'd fallen from a window trying to get in. The two cops' attitudes told me I'd been wrong. Crossing the floor, my thoughts raced, trying to anticipate what I was about to find.

I couldn't have.

In an office, next to an open safe, a man was sitting on an ornate but faded captain's chair. He'd been tied to it, his wrists fastened with twine to the crafted wooden spindles supporting the leather-clad arms. Before approaching him, I instinctively checked the safe. It was empty, either because the place had been empty or because someone else had made off with whatever had been in it.

I turned my attention back to the man. The reports had been right about one thing. He was certainly dead. I heard a noise behind me and turned to see Boniface coming into the room, a look of horror on his face.

'Mother of God, I wasn't expecting that,' he said, his voice momentarily hoarse.

Looking back at the figure in the chair, I took in the eyes open in terror, the blood around the twine on his wrists where he'd struggled to get free, his legs stretched in front of him as he'd tried to push his head away from his attacker.

Someone had sewn his lips shut.

Crude thick stitches in the same rough twine, his mouth

puckered in a shocked kiss. A small beard of dried blood clung to his chin, a contrast to the colour drained from his lips.

'Neither was I,' I told Boniface. 'This is Julot le Bavard. He's supposed to be in prison.'

2

The skylight hadn't been forced.

I'd left Boniface downstairs talking to the caretaker – she seemed calmed by his scented charm, so I figured he'd learn more from her than I would – and I'd climbed the stairs to check on the roof. Julot was old school, he had habits he couldn't kick, tells that always gave him away. That was one of the reasons why he was in prison. Or should have been.

I looked in all the upstairs rooms. One of his habits was getting into the buildings he was burgling across the rooftops and through an upstairs window or – his favourite – a skylight. I checked them all, but none of them had been forced.

'So why change your MO?' I asked him in his essential absence. 'And why burgle somewhere that's closed?'

Julot wasn't the brightest of villains, but even he would know an empty club means an empty safe. Unless there was something else he knew. Which still wouldn't explain the change of MO. Shooting one last glance at the pristine twin skylights under the slope of the roof, I went back downstairs to find Boniface telling the caretaker she could go home now.

'You've been very helpful,' he assured her. In that voice. It worked. After the wailing of half an hour ago, she floated off like she'd just shed thirty years and spent the morning with her lover.

When she'd gone, I stood with Boniface in the alcohol-scented glow of the main room, not wanting to go back into the office just yet.

'Pretty much what we knew,' he told me, commenting on what the caretaker had told him. 'The club's been shut down by the Germans, so there wouldn't have been any money in the safe. She comes in every Monday morning to check up, but that's all. There's no one to clean the place because the owner can't afford to pay them anymore.'

'Did she say who the owner was?' I wondered if it was a face from my past.

'Jean Poquelin. He's away.' He recited from memory. '"With one of his lady friends." She doesn't know where he's gone, but he's due back tomorrow.'

'Take a look into him. We want a word with our Monsieur Poquelin as soon as he gets back.' It wasn't a name I knew. 'Does she know if he's been using the office, specifically the safe?'

'Not as far as she knows. I asked her.'

We went back to the room to check. The dust that lay in the bar didn't stretch to the office. The desk was clear, a blotter and ledger also free of the thin coating that covered every other surface. I ran a finger along the top of the green table lamp and it came up dirty. The office was in use but not being cleaned. It didn't tell us a thing.

Like me, Boniface was avoiding looking at the needlework sitting in the captain's chair. But I could still see it out of the corner of my eye.

'You don't do that to someone you simply catch robbing the safe,' I told Boniface. 'You shoot them or hit them. Or call us. Or both.'

'And if he's an experienced burglar, he wouldn't bother coming here in the first place anyway.'

I grunted an agreement. I'd never worked with Boniface before his Mediterranean jaunt and had always had him down as the froth, not the coffee, so his observation surprised me. I told him of Julot's usual MO. 'I don't think he came here of his own volition. And I certainly don't think he came here alone. Julot would only come in through the street door under duress. It's more than his pride would have allowed.'

'So someone got him to break in and then open the safe. And then they did this to him.'

'Why? Why not just kill him and dump the body?'

'Unless it's a warning.'

'Which makes me more eager than ever to see what this Jean Poquelin has to say. This has all the signs of a gang killing. If it is to set an example, it has to be aimed at him.' I forced myself to look at Julot. 'What none of it explains is how come Julot here is out of prison. He had at least another four years to run on his sentence.'

'How do you know?'

'I put him there.'

Boniface seemed to be on the point of replying when the door opened and the second uniformed cop showed someone in.

'Eddie, good morning.'

I turned to see Bouchard, the pathologist, take off his ancient Homburg hat and casually hang it on a stand in the corner of the room. He turned back to me and smiled, his eyes amplified through the semi-lunettes he always wore perched on his aquiline nose. With his speckled greying hair brushed back over his domed head, he conjured up an image of a nineteenth-century academic.

'Morning, Boniface,' he added. 'Surprised to see you back here. Too many angry husbands wherever it was you've been? Please don't answer, I'm not interested.'

I knew why I liked Bouchard. 'Morning, Doc.' I also liked calling him Doc. He hated it.

'So what have we got here?' Bouchard put his bag down on the floor at Julot's feet. He leaned forward at the waist to inspect the crude stitches used to sew his lips together. 'Well, we know at least that we're not looking for a surgeon.'

'Or a seamstress,' Boniface said, a smirk marring the mellifluous flow of his voice.

Bouchard glared at him. 'Have you got nowhere else to be?'

'Yes, you have,' I told Boniface. 'I want to know how come Julot's been released from Fresnes early. Go and see the judge and find out why he's been allowed out.'

He nodded his agreement. Not a greased hair fell out of place. That annoyed me.

Bouchard took some instruments out of his bag and turned back to Julot. I tried not to look, so I took a tour of the owner's office walls to distract me. It did, but not in the way I imagined. On the wall behind the desk, a group of four framed photos hanging in a quadrant stopped me in my tracks. In a moment, I forgot Julot and his *basse couture* lips, Bouchard and his nameless tools and Boniface and his stream of chatter and I stared at the pictures. Or, more precisely, the people in the pictures. Older than when I knew them, obviously, but I still knew them.

'So why's he called Julot le Bavard?' Boniface asked from over my shoulder, giving me a start. He still hadn't left. 'Julot the Gossip. Was he a snitch, then?'

I turned to face him full on. 'No, he wasn't a snitch. It was because he never fucking stopped talking.'

'Snitch?' Denise spat the word out along with the threads of tobacco sticking to her teeth. She tapped her cigarette angrily into the tin tray, the embers sizzling in a small puddle of cheap spilled cognac. 'Julot was a lot of things. Snitch wasn't one of them. You know that, Eddie.'

She turned to face me. The tears that had dried on her face, coarsened by years of smoking and the life Julot had led her, had been genuine. I'd been steeling myself to break the news about his death, but the Belleville street telegraph had got there first. When I'd found her, she was sitting in a café on Rue des Envierges, hugging herself and a brandy. Three other burglars' wives had been lending to the stunned warmth. They'd now retreated to the corner of the small café to give us some privacy, throwing cold and menacing glances my way. Belleville was Julot's home turf, a rundown district of twisting cobbled lanes and secretive corners on the Right Bank.

'Why would they do that to Julot, Eddie?' she asked in her shock for the dozenth time.

'That's what I wanted to ask you, Denise. Do you know of anyone who had that much of a grudge against Julot to do that to him?'

'Apart from me, you mean?' She laughed, a bitter rasp tinged with sadness. Denise was Julot's ex-wife, divorced after years of putting up with him spending over half their marriage in Fresnes and other homes from home. 'No one. And don't ask me again if he'd grassed on anyone. You know that wasn't Julot's style.'

I had to agree with her. I also had to ask the next couple of questions carefully. 'Could he have been talking too much about something? Do you know of anything he was involved in?'

I thought for a moment she was going to snarl at me, but she looked thoughtful. 'Nothing I know of, Eddie. But you know Julot, he liked to talk.'

'You could say that.' Compared with Julot, Boniface had taken a vow of silence.

'Bastard never shut up, if truth be told.' Again, the laugh. 'Mouth faster than a Longchamp winner. It was one of the reasons I ended up chucking him out.'

'Bit unfair, Denise. He was called Julot le Bavard. That should have been some sort of a clue.'

She shot me a glance but smiled ruefully, the corners of her eyes wrinkling deeply. 'Maybe you're right. I still loved the old so-and-so, even if I couldn't live with him. Harmless, wasn't he, Eddie? He wouldn't hurt a soul.'

I clinked my coffee cup against hers. 'One of the nicest people I ever arrested. Never any trouble.'

She raised her eyebrows at me. 'If only you could've seen your way to arresting him a bit less.'

We were both lost in thought a moment before I spoke again. Her friends in the corner were getting restless. 'When did he get out of prison? He still had time to run on his sentence.'

'I don't know. Today was the first I'd heard he was even out. Over a month, people are saying.'

'What else are they saying? How come he was released early?'

'You're the cop. You tell me.' She shook her head. 'He'd have been safe if he were still in Fresnes.'

'I don't know if I'd go that far.' It was my turn for the wry laugh.

'Safer than he was out here, anyway.' Her expression was bleak. 'It's all changed lately.'

'Since the Germans?' She shook her head but wouldn't answer. 'What is it, Denise?'

She laughed, stubbing out her cigarette, but her eyes hardened. 'I'm no snitch, either, Eddie.'

Her friends seemed to sense a shift in our conversation and came and sat down with us. The oldest of the trio, a chignoned harridan with bad teeth and breath to match, sat up close to me and stared into my eyes. I took the hint.

'If you hear anything, let me know,' I told Denise as I stood up to go.

'I'll tell you one thing, Eddie. Julot can count his blessings he's dead. If I'd known he was out of prison, I'd have killed the bastard myself.'

I left her and her three friends tending their cauldron and drove south from Belleville. I was learning the routes to take to avoid Adolf's marching bands and German patrols. If you closed your mind enough, you could almost forget the city was occupied. But then I crossed the Seine and was forced over by a motorbike and sidecar to wait for two staff cars to rumble past, the back seats glittering with oak leaves and shiny braid. I did say almost forget.

Bouchard was drinking bad coffee in the cutting room. He was sitting at a desk in a corner away from the slabs and skimming through a newspaper. I saw it was *L'Oeuvre*, a pacifist and left-wing paper before the war that had oddly become pro-Nazi now we had visitors. He threw it into a wastepaper basket, the distaste evident in his expression. A door banged somewhere along a corridor. A young guy came in and went out again without saying a word to either of us.

'Lively around here,' I told Bouchard.

'An uncommon quality in a mortuary.'

He got up and led me over to one of the slabs. A mound that was once a person lay under a white shroud. It never got easier. Bouchard pulled it back to reveal Julot. The stitches had been cut from his mouth.

'How did he die?' I asked him.

'In layman's terms, asphyxiation. Someone held his nostrils shut until he died.'

'And covered his mouth.'

Bouchard pulled the sheet back over Julot and shook his head.

'They didn't need to. His lips were sewn together ante mortem.'

3

Boniface was waiting for me outside my office.

'Just got here,' he told me. 'You wouldn't believe the time it took to cross the city.'

I checked my wrist. We'd been on German time since the start of the Occupation, one hour ahead of French, but I'd refused to change my watch. I'd soon learned to read the wrong time.

'What do you mean, cross the city? I only sent you to see the judge in the Palais de Justice. That's just around the corner.'

'All in good time, Eddie. All in good time.'

He did the wink. I groaned and led him into the office I shared with two other inspectors. One was out, the other had done a Boniface, only he hadn't returned from wherever it was he'd fled to.

'So what did you find out? You have been to see the judge, I take it?'

He nodded and smiled. One more wink and I swore I'd tip him out of the third-floor window. 'Had a word with Judge Clément. Man, he's got a real cutie of a secretary, hasn't he? The lovely Mathilde.' His eyes were moister than his hair.

'The judge, Boniface.'

'Right. Well, Judge Clément has got no record whatsoever

of Julot being paroled, released or on furlough. He says he's received no referral from Fresnes about him at all. No application from any lawyer. None from Julot himself. No compassionate grounds. As far as he's concerned, there's no reason for Julot to have been out.'

'So how come he was out?'

'There's more. So after that, I went out to Fresnes to see what was happening.'

'You did what?'

'Stonewalled, Eddie. No one would talk to me. Gave me the runaround when I asked about Julot. Told me he was still there but that I couldn't see him. When I insisted, they said it was because he was being refused visits and privileges. I told them I was a cop, I had the authority to see him. Told me to get a warrant from a judge.'

'That's bullshit. You think the prison's covering for him?'

'Seems more than that. I saw the governor, and there was a nervousness about him. Can't put my finger on it, but there was something not right.' He let his words sink in before carrying on. 'One other thing – they made me give up my gun when I went in.'

'Your gun? They can't do that. You're a cop, you can't be in Fresnes unarmed. I take it you held on to it.'

'I had to surrender it. They wouldn't have let me see the governor otherwise.' He leered triumphantly. 'So after I saw him, I had a chat with his secretary. Not a looker, but keen, you know.'

'The point, Boniface.'

'The point is she showed me the files in the governor's office. On the sly, without him knowing.' He suddenly flicked his fingers open, ostentatiously, like a cheap magician. '*Boof.* No record for Julot. Vanished.'

*

'All gone, Eddie. You need to get here in the morning if you want the best cut.'

'Best cut?'

'OK, a good cut.' Albert rocked his head from side to side and reconsidered. 'OK, a halfway decent cut.'

'Or something vaguely resembling the meat we used to get,' I clarified for him. He reluctantly nodded his agreement.

Albert was my butcher. And that's not as grand as it sounds. He was my butcher because the Germans had imposed even stricter rationing at the beginning of August, which meant that once you'd registered with the authorities, you then had to register with your local baker's and butcher's. After that, you could only buy from them. If they didn't have anything left by the time you got to the head of the queue or you got there late, you went hungry. Or you went to the black market, one of the city's growth industries under our new masters. I'd called in on my way home from Thirty-Six, knowing I was unlikely to find much. Even so, yet another meagre but imaginative supper beckoned.

'Just can't get the supplies, Eddie. It was bad enough before the Boches got here, but it's even worse now. I've got a piece of lamb neck if you want it.'

I nodded grudgingly and he took out a tiny piece of meat from behind the counter. Meagre didn't do it justice.

'It's all bone,' I complained. 'There'll hardly be any meat left on it.'

'Take it or leave it, Eddie, it's all I've got.'

I paid out the pre-war price of a small flat and watched him deftly wrap the lamb in paper.

'At least meat's not officially rationed yet,' I commented.

'Don't hold your breath. They're starting to ration it from

next month. You're going to need tickets to buy meat just like you do now with bread.'

'These really are the best of times.'

I picked up my bundle of joy and walked out into the remnants of the late summer's day. Outside in what should have been normal sunlight, I couldn't help looking at the package in my hand in disgust. In the phony war, before the Occupation, our own government had banned meat, sugar and alcohol on certain days – not that anyone had paid much attention to it – but it had got a whole lot worse since the Germans had come along to dip their bread in our sauce. For nearly two months now, we'd had to queue up at the local *mairie* to get tickets to buy bread at 350 grams a pop, sugar and rice. Now it looked like meat was going to be included. There were already rumours that cheese and coffee were going the same way. I thought again of the whisky in Dax's drawer with an absurd degree of longing.

I walked home slowly. Because we were on Berlin time, it felt like the sun was too high in the sky for the hour. I still hadn't got used to the different light. At times I felt like I was the only one. The streets were busy, busier than they'd been just a couple of weeks ago, and all the Parisians who'd returned from their bolt-holes were soaking up the extra hour's rays like nothing out of the ordinary had happened in their absence. I passed a queue outside a cinema and I wanted to grab them by the scruff of the neck and shake them until their eyes rattled and tell them to look around. To look at the grey uniforms striding through the streets, the German signs denoting places we were no longer allowed to go, the mountains of sandbags obscuring churches and monuments. And the blood-red banners with the swastikas at their core hanging from every official building.

Not yet ready for my empty flat, I took a detour through the Jardin du Luxembourg as it had become what passed for an oasis of hope these days. That was as long as you could avert your gaze from the red, white and black sentry boxes outside the palace and the huge Nazi flag cracking in the breeze from the rooftop. Goering's lot in the Luftwaffe had taken over the grand old building as their little Parisian pied-a-terre. Nowhere was safe from their depredations. Nowhere worth being, anyway.

As I dodged past two young families chatting, I recalled another day walking in the gardens just days after Adolf's acolytes had rolled into town. The park had been empty, save for a few soldiers sightseeing or checking people's papers. The Parisians who'd stayed in the city were few and far between, hurrying head down, avoiding one another's gaze, and I'd felt a sudden moment of loss. Anger at the death of the Paris I'd first come to as a convalescent in the last war. Despair at the thought of that city never returning. Of never walking again amid crowds in the sunshine. And now it was happening. Tempered, different, but happening. All around me, children ran and adults gossiped. German soldiers in groups laughed indulgently with infants and charmed young women and old men. And I felt an equal sense of anger and despair. But this time it was directed more at my fellow French than at the invader.

And at the same time, I reserved some of the annoyance for myself. For being unreasonable. The Germans were here. That wasn't changing any time soon. The exodus retracers could no more get rid of them than I could. And in the meantime, they still had to live, feed themselves, have a roof over their head, earn money, send their kids to school. It was a new normal, a tainted Chinese whisper of the old one, and it was the one we'd been given. The one we had to live with.

'So you deal with it or you don't,' I found myself saying out loud. I wasn't even sure what I meant by it.

At home, I put the meat into a pot of stock with a potato

and a tomato I had left over from last night's sumptuous banquet and left it all to reduce into something I hoped would be vaguely edible. I watched it for a few moments, planning how I'd go about syphoning off some of Dax's whisky, but went into my small living room the moment I realised I was starting to take the idea seriously.

Sitting on the more comfortable of my two ancient armchairs, I saw Julot's mouth again – the coarse stitches holding his lips tightly shut – and tried to imagine the fear and the terror he would have felt. I felt a moment's sorrow for him. I recalled a time nearly twenty years ago when I'd chased a burglar across the roofs in the Nineteenth until I fell and he got away. I didn't get a good view of him, but I knew it was Julot, even though I couldn't pin it on him. The thing was, he came and visited me in hospital. He brought me a bottle of expensive wine and sat for an hour and drank it with me. He'd nicked it, of course, but I kept quiet about it. Until the silly bastard got caught trying to sell the rest of the stash to the owner's restaurant and was given two years in Fresnes.

I smiled for a brief moment and raised a glass of wine I no longer had to him, and I puzzled at what it was that had led to him being out of Fresnes this time. Try as I might, I could see no explanation for that.

I thought too of Boniface. Just like Julot, he didn't stop talking, and he irritated the hell out of me, but one or two things about him had surprised me. Much as I hated to admit it, I had to admire his tenacity in going to Fresnes to dig deeper than his idle chatter would have led me to believe him capable of.

And I knew that all my thoughts were a diversion from the one consideration that was a constant in my unguarded moments. My son. Jean-Luc. Whom I'd walked out on when he was a child and who'd come – briefly – back into my life when the Nazis had come calling. My son, who'd been a soldier in the defeat on the Meuse in the fall of France and whom I'd helped escape from Paris under the Germans' noses. Whom I'd found and willingly lost again. But that was three months ago and I'd had no word of him since.

And that was why I sought distraction in thoughts of Julot and Boniface. And of Jean Poquelin, the owner of the jazz club, who I wanted to talk to. I glanced at the walls of my room and the shelves heavy with books and little else, save an old tin on the topmost shelf, out of easy reach. I had no photos of my son, or of me or of my past life. I couldn't bear seeing images of myself, which meant I also had none of others. The only memories saved were in my head, and there were times I could have them expunged from there too.

But right now, I wished I did have a few photos. But not of me.

I saw again the pictures on the walls of the office in the jazz club where Julot had been tortured and killed.

I saw the faces I'd known. They shouldn't have surprised me. I'd worked in a jazz club. They were all pictures from that time, people I once knew.

As the smell of burning from the kitchen lured me back to the present, I recalled the photo of the man I assumed must be Jean Poquelin.

Only that wasn't the name I knew him by.

4

'Watch your car for you, mister?'

I looked down to see a young kid barely up to my waist making me the offer. I'd parked on one of the wider streets in Belleville, not wanting to get snarled up among the cobbles of the narrow lanes. He held his hand out expectantly. His face was pale. It was the sort of neighbourhood where the light didn't dare set foot through the jumble of peeling buildings. He had a steady stream of snot from nose to lip and eyes like stolen dinner plates. He wore a threadbare tenth-hand jersey dirtier than the pavements that he had to keep tugging at so it wouldn't fall off his tiny body.

'It'll be fine, kid.' It had been a long morning.

'Your choice, cop.'

I looked at him a second time and handed over a five-centime coin. I figured it would be easier than trying to find four new tyres.

The patrons of Le Peloton fell silent the moment I walked in, the only sound a glass being replaced on a scuffed wooden table. The kid wasn't the only one to recognise a cop when he saw one.

'Am I in time for the Little Sisters of the Poor meeting?' I asked. No one answered.

I stood at the bar with my back to the zinc counter and gazed out over a dozen expressions. They ranged from morose to hostile. On every spare centimetre of wall, faded Tour de France posters of bygone heroes kissing trophies grinned in sepia. None of the clients looked like the sort ever to get on a bike. Not unless it was stolen. Behind me, I could feel Pottier, the owner, bristle at me from his pit.

'Now I'm sure you'll all sympathise,' I told the gathered throng, 'but I've had a tough morning and I'm just trying to do my job.'

'Up yours, cop,' someone grumbled.

A young punk out to prove a point came and stood menacingly half a centimetre in front of me. Holding his gaze, I cupped his face and kissed him on the forehead before calmly hitting his head against the counter. I watched him fall to the floor. A fraction of a second before I hit him, he'd said a word. One I didn't catch. I didn't think he'd be up to repeating it just yet. Even if I asked nicely.

'Unfortunate,' I announced. 'Anyone hear what he said?'

No one in the room moved or spoke. A couple of the younger cons exchanged surprised looks. It wasn't what they were used to from me. One of the time-served crims caught my gaze and looked away. He remembered the good old days.

'Ah well. As I was saying, it's been a bit of a morning and I'd just like some help. Julot le Bavard.'

At his name, a ripple of sympathy ran through the room. But I noticed something more, something I'd been seeing throughout Julot's old haunts for the past few hours. Fear.

'I liked Julot,' I carried on. 'I'd like to know who sewed his lips together and then held his nose while he struggled. Held his nose until he died. I'm sure a lot of you do too. So, I'm going to leave here now, but I'll be in the neighbourhood for a bit longer yet. If there are any of you who'd like to tell me what's going on, just come along and let me know. You won't be grassing, you'll be helping find Julot's killer.' I glanced down at the junior hard man. He wasn't going to awaken to a prince's gentle kiss any time soon, so I stepped over him and made my way to the door. 'I'm sure you'll know where to find me.'

I knew for certain they would. Belleville had war drums the way other parts of the city had water fountains. Where Belleville had water, it was running in dirty streams down the middle of the cobbled streets and grimy kids playing in the mud and filth it left in its wake. I skirted a group of them now, all dressed in over-sized and grubby hand-me-downs, and made my way to a spot I knew, away from prying eyes.

I couldn't help looking around me. My route meant I had to leave the safety of the narrow lanes and go out into the open streets. I say safety. It was all relative in Belleville.

I thought of the faces opposite me in Le Peloton. I felt the fear too.

And I felt like prey.

I descended the steps where Rue Piat met Rue Vilin and waited at the bottom. Everyone thinks that no one talks to cops. They do. To get one over on a rival, they'll talk to cops. To stay out of Fresnes, they'll talk to cops. For food on the table, they'll talk to the cops. They'll talk to anyone. Especially now, when food was getting harder to find than anyone to talk to me right now.

I knew that what I was doing was a last resort. I'd had a frustrating morning. I'd started the day at the Jazz Chaud in Montparnasse, looking for the man now calling himself Jean Poquelin, but he was nowhere to be found, the club locked up. From there, I'd driven across the river to where I was now – Belleville, a crooked and hilly outcrop on the Right Bank. A world away from the Paris that the Germans had come to plunder. I'd spent the morning trying in vain to get someone to talk. To give me some idea of who would have killed Julot. And why he wasn't in prison. I was beginning to realise that that question was becoming more important to me than Julot's death. I offered him a silent apology but didn't change how I felt.

There was one reason no one was talking to me. Fear. But it was stronger than fear. It was dread. I wanted to know why.

'I don't know anything, Eddie. Honest.' I recalled the words of just two hours ago said to me by Émile, one of Julot's thieving buddies. The dread was in his eyes. 'I don't know how come he was out of prison. He didn't say anything.'

'He didn't tell you?' Émile shook his head vigorously. 'Which is odd, don't you think? Julot le Bavard keeping his mouth shut. He must have said something to you.'

'I didn't even know he was out. I hadn't seen him.'

'But you saw him enough to know he didn't tell you anything.'

It was pointless. I let him go. He scurried away, nervously sucking his buck teeth, his ears pinned back in panic. And he wasn't the only one with the same scared look, the same anxious denials. That was why I'd gone to Le Peloton. To shake the tree and see what fell out.

Nothing did. The one thing I'd heard was a word said in bravado by a punk just before I clobbered him. And I hadn't heard that so I could understand it. Giving up, I climbed to the top of the steps but the street was empty, the doors all closed. Nobody wanted to talk about a chatterbox.

But they did want to write.

Daubed on the wall opposite, the white paint crying tears down the flaking plaster, was a single word. The whitewash was still wet. It hadn't been there when I'd arrived. It wasn't a word I knew.

I rejoined my car, where the skinny kid demanded another sou.

'A bonus,' he reasoned. 'For keeping it safe.'

I got in and turned the ignition on. It started without any problem.

'Not a chance, shortarse,' I told him and drove off.

'Capeluche?'

Down in the evidence room in the basement at Thirty-Six, I repeated the single word I'd seen daubed on the wall to Mayer.

'Not one I know, Eddie, sorry.'

'I figure it's either a name or some Parisian slang that's beneath the likes of us,' I told him, taking the paper back.

He gave a slight laugh. Like me, Mayer was another outsider. But where I was a southerner, he was a northerner, from the Alsace. A thoughtful, intelligent man with a nose for the truth and a tenacity to hunt it out, he was wasted down here.

'Looks like a nickname to me. Any news on Jean-Luc?'

His question alarmed me. He was one of the few cops who knew about my son. I was surprised by how much I didn't want to talk about it.

'None. How about you? Are you German yet?'

He looked shocked. 'Don't even joke about it, Eddie. I don't know what's happening, but I wouldn't put it past the Nazis. They're going to sneak up on all of us while we're looking elsewhere. By the time we do see them, we'll be screwed. That's the way they work.'

His vehemence took me aback, but I knew it was because the Germans coveted the Alsace and its people as their own. No formal mention of either Alsace or Lorraine had been made in the armistice we'd been forced to sign in June, but Adolf had pretty much annexed them in practice. Customs controls had gone up and *gauleiters*, German administrators, appointed. France ended at the Vosges again. If I were Mayer, I'd be worried at what the future – and the Nazis – held in store for me. I felt a momentary stab of guilt at making light of it to avoid talking about my own concerns.

'You're a cop, Mayer. It can't happen.'

His expression was bleak. 'And if it does? Who'll stand by me when they come calling?'

Annoyed with myself, I went looking for Barthe and Tavernier. I found them both on the third-floor landing, soaking up a sliver of sun. They were the two oldest detectives on the force, so I figured if anyone had heard of someone or something called Capeluche, it would most likely be them.

'Not a clue,' Barthe told me, shaking his head.

'Nothing,' Tavernier agreed.

Disappointed, I thanked them and watched them saunter back into the detectives' room. Barthe was steady on his feet. I have no idea how he did it. He began each day with a brandy and got progressively more hardcore as the hours wore on. It was a cycle of life counted out in sweetly scented bar glasses. Next to him, Tavernier walked with the weight of the world on his shoulders. He'd been counting down the days to his retirement, but any chance of that had evaporated with the arrival of the Germans. They were like old lags serving out their time by keeping their noses clean.

Dax just shrugged when I said the word.

'Probably nothing,' he said absently, adjusting his spectacles. 'Julot was a career criminal. He knew the risks. Don't get caught up with worrying what happened to him. Frankly, Eddie, I don't want you wasting too much time on this.'

Frankly, we both knew that was unlikely. 'I want to know

why he was out of prison. And why it was so savage a killing. We need to know what's going on.'

'What's going on?' He picked up a pile of German High Command orders and threw them up in the air. They fell heavily to his desk and floor, the swastikas like so many tiny but venomous spiders, infesting the expanse between us. 'This is what's going on, Eddie. Julot could have been released from Fresnes for dozens of reasons. And none of them are anything to do with us anymore.'

'I can't just wash my hands.'

'I know you can't. But you're going to have to learn when your hands have to stay dirty.'

I watched him tidy the papers together again. His expression was a cross of guilt and fear at being caught defiling the Nazis' bureaucracy.

'Quite apart from anything else, that doesn't make sense.'

'Don't try to be funny, Eddie, I don't have the time.'

I watched him try to put some order into the documents, his hands trembling slightly. I caught him glance a couple of times at the drawer with the whisky in. He was closer to the edge than I'd thought.

'The owner of the jazz club,' I persisted. 'Jean Poquelin.' Just in time, I stopped myself from telling Dax that that wasn't his real name. 'He's supposedly due back today, but I stopped by the club this morning and it looked very much closed up. I get the feeling he's not coming back.'

'Why?'

'Just a hunch.'

A knock on the door disturbed us. For the first time in my short acquaintance with him, Boniface made a welcome appearance. He leaned in through the door, and gave one of his winks. I didn't even mind that.

'Phone call just came through, Eddie. Jean Poquelin, the owner of the Jazz Chaud. He's rung to say he's back. We can go and see him whenever we want.'

He winked again and backed out.

I turned in surprise to Dax.

'So you got that one right, eh?' he said to me.

It was the happiest he'd looked all morning.

5

Jean Poquelin was waiting for me with a gun.

I circled his office warily, slowly approaching his desk on the balls of my feet. The captain's chair that Julot had been tortured in had been pushed to the far corner of the room, a trail of fingerprint powder in its wake. The room's owner had evidently been too squeamish to sit in it, preferring instead to have dragged over one of the four heavy armchairs positioned around a coffee table by the opposite wall.

I nodded at the weapon, an ancient and scarred revolver that looked like it had changed hands with many a dishonest master over the years.

'You won't be needing that.'

'You really think so?' His voice was neutral.

I was alone with him. Boniface had tried to insist on coming with me, but I hadn't wanted him there. Not this first time.

'Are you sure it's safe?' Boniface had asked me. His question had annoyed me at the time. I glanced at the gun and had to smile at the memory.

Looking at me from behind his fortress desk, Jean Poquelin had to struggle to force his chair back against the unwilling carpet to stand up. He eyed me up and down before walking equally cautiously round to the front. He took one more step towards me. As he leaned forward, I noticed he'd left the re-volver on the desk. He threw both arms around my chest.

'Christ, Eddie, am I glad to see you?'

I let him hug me for a moment before gently pushing him back.

'Jean Poquelin?'

He shrugged. 'It's my name.'

'No, it's not. You're Fran. Fran Aveyron. So why the false name?'

He laughed and stood in front of me, looking me up and down. It had been nearly fifteen years since he'd last seen me. Since I'd last seen him. 'It's not a false name, Eddie. No more than yours is. It was the American musicians that used to call you Eddie, wasn't it?'

I had to nod my agreement. 'They reckoned Édouard was too much of a mouthful.'

'Well, the same goes for me. My full name's Jean-François. You knew me as Fran because that's what everyone called me in those days. I'm a successful businessman now. I'm older. So people call me Jean. It's respect.'

'Successful?' I looked at the covering of dust that lay every-where on a landscape of faded tat.

'Hard times, Eddie. The Germans are in town, you might have heard.'

'So what's with the Poquelin?'

'Aveyron was my dad's name. Only I discovered he wasn't my dad, so I started using my mum's instead. Much more refined.'

I looked for a chair to sit on, I was suddenly tired. 'Very literary. Poquelin was Molière's real name.'

He followed me to join me on another of the chairs around the coffee table. 'Molière? Fancy that. Maybe I'm related. Me descended from a literary giant. Fuck me, wouldn't that be great?'

'Somehow I don't see it.'

I sat down and watched him take a seat at a right angle to me. I could see the captain's chair at the opposite end of the room, its arms opened out to me, as though beckoning. I noticed Fran had chosen a seat where it wasn't in his line of vision. But the door was. That was the Fran I remembered. Ever on the lookout. Either for a threat or for the main chance. I wondered which one he saw me as.

He'd been the barman in the jazz club in Montmartre where I'd moonlighted on the door when I was a young cop. He was seedy then, now he was down at heel with it. His hair was grey, lank. The widow's peak of his younger years, which had given him a piratical charm, had metamorphosed into two deep coves above each ear. His faded suit clung to him forlornly like an unwanted lover. He looked around his office, the fear briefly replaced with a sudden deep gloom.

'All gone now. The Boches. I left the city like everyone else did and came back last month, but they won't allow me to reopen. My livelihood's gone, the money running out. They say I'm morally unsound.'

'They got that one right then.'

'A joker now, Eddie? That's new.'

Glancing up, I saw the photos on the wall that had caught my eye the previous day. 'Do you still see any of the old crowd?'

He didn't even look over. 'No one. All moved on.'

'Not even Dominique?'

Fran met it with a leer. 'You were sweet on her, weren't you? I remember. Came to nothing, if I recall rightly.'

'Well?'

He leaped out of his chair. It was one of the traits I remembered about him. He could never be still for long. If I'd had any of the killer's twine, I'd have strapped him down with it to give me a moment's respite. He pulled one of the photos off the wall in a jerky movement and flopped down again.

'My, but she was a beauty, wasn't she?'

He put the photo in front of me and leaned back in his chair. Despite myself, I went silent. Dominique. A little older, but the same challenging expression, the same eyes that always saw through me. The image took my breath away. Between her and Fran in the photo was another figure. Joe. I felt a moment's guilt and had to look away. Dominique and Joe. Two people I'd failed in different ways. I turned the picture over and pushed it across the table.

'Well?' I insisted.

'Haven't seen her in years. I told you. All moved on.'

I gestured to the chair across the room. 'So what's going on, Fran? Why was Julot le Bavard tortured in your club?'

'I don't know. You've got to believe me. I don't even know who he is.' He corrected himself. 'Was.'

'What are you caught up in?'

'Nothing, I swear.'

'Don't forget I know you. I know you'll be caught up in something.'

He sighed heavily. 'I own a club now. It's all about the music, the jazz. It's legit. And it was a good club before the Boches came. Good musicians, good clientele. I didn't need to be into anything dodgy.'

'So why would Julot be burgling here? And why would someone kill him? And kill him the way they did?'

Fran shivered. 'I really don't know. Look around you. The place is empty. The safe is empty. There'd be nothing here to steal.'

'The safe may have been empty of money, but was there anything else in there worth stealing? You know what I mean.'

I saw in his eyes he knew what I was getting at. With a flourish reminiscent of the Fran I knew, he put his hand on his heart. 'Nothing, Eddie, on my mother's life. Those days are behind me now. I don't deal in drugs, I'm a serious business-man.'

'A serious businessman whose club is the scene of a vicious murder.' I nodded at the chair. 'This looks like a punishment or a warning, Fran. If it's a punishment for Julot, why choose your club? And if it's a warning, who for? It's got to be you.'

'I really can't tell you. I don't know anything about the guy. The other cop said he was from Belleville. I've got nothing to do with that part of town, this is Montparnasse. If it had been a local burglar, I might have seen some point to it, a warning to others to stay away. But not this guy, I've never seen him before.'

'Who'd be giving a warning like that? And why?'

'It's just a supposition.'

I changed tack to try and catch him on the hop. 'Where were you over the weekend?'

He leered. This was Fran, I recalled. He'd always been far too wily to be caught easily. 'Fun time. With a lady of my acquaint-ance. We made a weekend of it in Longchamp. At the races. A bit of horses and a bit of riding for afters. You get my drift?'

'Sadly, yes. So, let me get this straight. You happen to be away when your club is used as the scene for a petty criminal you don't know to be tortured and murdered, and his body is then left as an example. Which is it, Fran? You were away because you needed an alibi? Or you were away because you were afraid of someone?'

'Why would I need an alibi?'

'Which is a pretty interesting answer, don't you think? Because I don't think you need an alibi. Besides, why would you be involved in something like this in your own club? That would just be pissing on your own doorstep. That's not something you do.' I tapped the gun on the table. 'I think you're scared. That's why you went away. And why Julot was killed – to make you even more scared.'

He shook his head vigorously. 'Of course I'm scared. I am now. But I wasn't before. I had nothing to be scared of. I tell you, I haven't got a fucking clue what this is all about.'

'Who's sending you a message, Fran? What have you done to get Julot killed as a warning?'

'I told you, Eddie, I keep my nose clean these days.'

'Which is an unfortunate turn of phrase for a drug dealer to be using.'

'I'm not dealing. I've got nothing to do with any of that now.'

'Really?' I leaned forward and blew on the surface of the table. A fine cloud of white dust rose and hung in the air between us. 'So what's that? Stardust?'

For the first time, I saw him flounder, searching for words. He opened and closed his mouth without speaking. So it was lucky from his point of view that we both heard the door banging. The colour drained from his face.

'Is your lady acquaintance here with you?' I asked him.

He paused a heartbeat. 'It's just you and me.'

I went out into the main room to look. 'Stay here.'

'Not a chance.'

He stood up and followed me, almost snapping at my heels to keep up as I headed for the door into the main room.

The door banged again, a metallic sound that shuddered through the building. The big kettle drum on the stage echoed back to it in low complicity. I had to suppress a shiver as the bass ran through me. The original sound came from the rear of the club, so I followed it. A heavy security door stood at the end of a dark corridor.

'Where does it lead to?' I asked Fran.

'The alley behind the building. We keep the bins there.'

'Nice.'

I turned back to be hit by a scent. It stopped me in my tracks. I glanced at Fran but he didn't react to it. I don't think he'd noticed it. His addled nose wouldn't have been up to such refinements.

Reaching the door, I pushed against it. I'd expected it to be cold, but the metal was covered in green baize, no doubt to dampen the sound from the club. It felt oddly comforting. I opened it and emerged into the alleyway. It was as charming as Fran's description had led me to believe. Probably empty, with the club closed, the bins still gave off a smell of decay. I looked up and down the narrow lane, but there was no one in sight.

Pushing Fran, I went back into the club. I wanted to regain the scent I'd picked up on. It was one that I remembered from long ago. A perfume. One I hadn't sensed in years.

But it had already gone.

6

'I haven't got a ticket.'

'I told you. I can't sell you bread unless you got a ticket. Those are the rules.'

I glared at the baker behind his counter. He looked like someone had poured too much skin into the mix when they were baking him and he'd ended up with doughy cheeks and a crusty nose. Every part of his face moved when he spoke.

'Can't I pay for a baguette?'

'Sure you can. Provided you hand over a ticket with the money. Now, if you don't mind, I've got customers to serve.'

An elderly lady with horn-rimmed glasses and a lifetime of scowling behind her prodded me in the small of my back. 'I've been queuing for two hours.'

'I know. I was in front of you.' I turned back to the baker. I had one last card. 'I'm a cop.'

He smiled broadly. 'In that case, why don't you fuck off out and get your Boches friends to buy some bread for you?'

My stomach rumbled as I took the Metro to Montmartre. Breakfast had been a slice of bad cheese and a cup of worse coffee. And no bread. I'd used up all my tickets and had to wait a few days before I could get next month's batch. Opposite me, a German soldier in a group that had forgone their right to

44

their own carriage so they could ogle two young Frenchwomen belched quietly into his sleeve. My cheeks burned. Goebbels on a good day couldn't have come up with a more provocative fuck-you-we're-not-going-hungry propaganda campaign than that one small eructation. I bit my tongue. It was the only sustenance I was going to get.

Back up in the fresh air, I was surprised to find my footsteps faltering. I'd been to Montmartre countless times in my job, but this was the first day in nearly fifteen years I'd headed in this specific direction. My old jazz club. The one where I'd moonlighted as a doorman when I was a young cop. And the source of so much I'd done that I regretted. Well, maybe not the source, but a tributary that had fed into it.

I paused one last time before entering. The front entrance was smarter, the name changed, the walls and wood painted. It had moved on. So had I, I realised, only it had taken me a lot longer and cost me much more. But inside, the smell was as I'd remembered it. The same aroma I'd found in Fran's club that had awoken dark memories in me. A jazz club in abeyance, the daytime shift of bleach and stale tobacco momentarily taking over from the night-time lie of alcohol and sweet perfume. Only here it wasn't as final as it had been at the Jazz Chaud. Because this place hadn't been shut down, I was surprised to find.

But none of that was the point. It was a different scent that had brought me here.

'Claude?' the new owner repeated. 'No, he died years ago. Four or five at least. I bought the club from his widow.'

I nodded. I should have felt something but I didn't. It was too long ago. The new owner told me his name was Stéphane. He wasn't someone who'd been around in my day. I felt relieved not only that I didn't know him but that he didn't know me. There was no need for a clean slate.

'So how come you've been allowed to reopen? I thought the Nazis saw jazz as degenerate.'

He gave a slight laugh, quiet but genuine. He was of an age and of hollowed cheeks and dark, sad eyes that told me he'd served in the last war too. It was a look we all saw in each other and never mentioned. In that moment, I decided I liked him. 'They do,' he replied. 'In public. But secretly there's nothing the Nazis enjoy more than a good old bit of degeneracy.'

'Ain't it always the way?'

'The place is heaving with them most nights.' He surveyed the room and the stage I recognised so well. We were alone but for a cleaner slowly mopping the floor. 'Strange. We've been doing better since the Boches got here than we had been for years. Nothing like forbidden fruit to get the appetite flowing.'

'You're one of the lucky ones. The Jazz Chaud has been shut down.' For a brief moment, I wondered what it was that Stéphane was doing and that Fran wasn't that had led to their different fates.

'The Jazz Chaud? Poquelin? That petty crook. If the Germans have shut him down, it's the one good thing they have done.' I was taken aback by the contempt that crossed his face.

'You don't like him, I take it.'

'Small-time crook with delusions of grandeur. He'd sell his father for half a sou if he knew who his father was.'

That was the Fran I recognised. I filed it away and asked the question that had brought me to the club. 'I came to ask about a singer who used to work here. I don't know if she still does. Dominique Mendy.'

'Dominique? That's a voice from the past. Is she all right? She used to sing here, but that was some time ago.'

'You wouldn't have an address for her?'

'Sorry, I can't help you there.' He thought for a moment. 'If you know Dominique, you might know Joe too. American? A musician?'

Joe again. I tried to hide the guilt in my eyes.

'I know Joe. What about him?'

'He's been interned.'

'Why? He's a neutral.'

Stéphane pointed to our faces, to our skin. 'Not to the Nazis, he isn't.'

I closed my eyes for a moment. Joe had been a Harlem Hellfighter in the last war and had stayed on in Paris rather than face the bigots back home. Only now a worse version had caught up with him here.

'Where is he?'

'Les Tourelles. The Germans arrested him. At first, the Nazis started by banning concerts by black American musicians. "Degenerate Jewish-Negro jazz", they called it. But then Joe and all the other Americans in the band had to report to the police. Most of them were interned.'

'Just the black Americans?'

'The others were all right. They're free to carry on playing.'

'Even degenerate jazz?'

He nodded at the stage. 'They're still here, playing to a Boche audience every night.'

That struck a chord with my dealings with our occupiers ever since they'd got here. 'The Nazis are nothing if not selective. That's just one of the reasons they're so dangerous.'

Mayer was waiting for me when I returned to Thirty-Six. He led me downstairs, but not to the evidence room.

'Prisoner you should see,' he explained. 'Arrested last night in the Sixteenth.'

'He knows where the money is, then.'

'Wait and see.'

Intrigued, I followed the sergeant along the dingy corridor to a cell. He opened up and ushered me into the grim little home from home. At first, I didn't recognise the figure stretched out on the low ledge. But then he got up and twisted to face me, his thick legs bent in front of him, both feet planted firmly on the cold floor. His expression carried the sneer that gave him his nickname.

'Walter le Ricaneur.'

He stared at me coldly. The sneer wasn't entirely real. The left side of his face was frozen, the lip slightly raised, which gave him the appearance of constantly mocking you. The thing being, he usually was. His was a face that had grown into his attitude.

'Supposedly in Fresnes prison,' Mayer commented.

I went and hunkered down in front of him, my face centimetres from his.

'So why aren't you nicely tucked up in prison with all the other naughty children, Walter?'

'Good behaviour, Giral. Try not to slam the door on your way out.' He scratched his armpit and did another sneer on top of his original one.

'Impressive. You really must teach me how to do that one day.'

He held my gaze. 'I'd love a coffee. Plenty of milk, if you've got any.'

'Rationing, Walter. You'll have to make do with the charm of my company instead.'

He snorted. 'Rationing? That's only for the likes of you, Giral.'

I studied his face. He was a hardliner, but this was cocky even by his standards. I got the full blast of the double sneer again. 'So what is it that makes you think you're untouchable, Walter? And how come you're out of prison?'

The sneer turned into a smile. An evil one that would make his own mother leave home. 'See, that's the crying shame, Giral. You're going to find out soon enough. And you're not going to like it when you do.'

'Oh, Walter. You really don't do cryptic threats well, do you?'

The smile vanished. 'You'll be laughing on the other side of your face, Giral.'

'What, the frozen side?' I roughly prodded his cheek with my finger. If that didn't get a rise out of him, nothing would.

It did. Just not the one I expected. He laughed. A loud metallic sound that beat like an anvil in the confined space. The cold tone of it was made all the more harsh by the lopsided mouth it came from, the teeth crooked, the tongue red raw. I forced myself not to look away. Its echo died in the cell walls.

'You don't know what you're dealing with,' he murmured.

'Capeluche, you mean?'

I saw a moment's surprise in his eyes. I looked for more and found it. Behind the confidence was a fleeting scintilla of fear. Sensing an opening, I pressed onward.

'Capeluche,' I repeated.

Behind me, the door opened. 'Go away,' I shouted without looking back.

'You need to come,' a voice said.

I turned to see a cop in the doorway. Two German soldiers shouldered past him.

'Inspector Giral,' the first one said. 'You will come with us.'

To hide my anger, I turned away to face Walter. The sneer was back on his face, his eyes calm once more. Slowly, he raised his right hand and brought it between us, a heartbeat away from both our mouths.

Without a word, he mimed sewing his lips shut.

7

'Édouard, my friend.'

'Major Hochstetter, my German.'

'It feels like an age since last we met.'

'All good things must end, Major.'

Hochstetter was the German intelligence officer assigned to coordinate with my police department. More precisely, with me. It was just another of the gifts the Occupation kept on giving. He seemed to have just two ways of contacting me. One was to turn up unannounced in my office like a viral wraith. The other was to send for me. Today, he'd done the summoning thing. My annoyance had slowly simmered as the two cold-eyed soldiers had taken me from Thirty-Six to a bench under some trees in the Ménilmontant part of the city. It wasn't far from where I'd lived in my younger days as a married man with a young son. My ex-wife still lived here, although she'd left Paris in the exodus and I had no idea where she was. I also had no idea why Hochstetter should have brought me here. So far, I'd managed to keep my private life out of his scrutiny. And the fact that I had a son who'd escaped Paris when the Germans had first arrived. I racked my brains to anticipate what I was going to say. It was a trick you learned quickly with Hochstetter.

'You're probably wondering why I had you brought here.'

I shrugged, the Parisian way. 'No, not really.'

He turned to look at me. He had clipped cheekbones and dark, bottomless eyes that made you want to confess to things you hadn't done. He turned their full firepower on me now. 'I had forgotten your child-like insistence on being droll. Perhaps we may bypass that and get to the point.'

'You summoned me, Major. I'd say it was up to you to get to the point.'

'One thing, Édouard. I need hardly remind you of how inadvisable it is to be flippant with me. Your downfall is your choice. Until it becomes mine. Please remember that.'

I met his gaze. 'I'm droll, as you call it, to stop myself from saying something that would land me in greater trouble. Don't ever mistake it for flippancy.'

His cold look turned in an instant to laughter. 'Perhaps we should sit a while.'

On the other side of the road, a French paddy wagon had pulled up on the kerb. A second van pulled up behind, and a dozen uniformed cops piled out of it. They looked uncertain. Away to the right, I saw a German military vehicle, a heavy Horch staff car. An officer in the back seat spotted our little group of me and Hochstetter with the two soldiers loitering behind us. He gave a slight salute to Hochstetter, who returned it.

Under the orders of a police sergeant, the French cops entered one of the apartment blocks. Hochstetter casually lit a cigarette and flicked the match away, the flame dying in flight.

'So what is it you've brought me to see?' I asked Hochstetter.

In reply, he simply raised his hand to tell me to wait. Within moments, the cops came back out of the building, manhandling two middle-aged men and a younger guy, forcing them into the back of the paddy wagon. One of the older men spat at the ground at the sergeant's feet and got a slap across the head in reward. Even at this distance, his look of hatred at the police took me aback. There was a power and a venom in it that I hadn't seen since the political riots of the 1930s.

'Cops arresting criminals?' I said. 'You've brought me here to watch this?'

Hochstetter took a deep drag on his cigarette. They made me feel nauseous. I hadn't smoked since my time in the trenches at Verdun. It reminded me too much of the poisonous spirals of gas.

'Not criminals. Communists. Although most in Berlin would regard them as the same.'

'Communists?' I looked back in surprise at the cops closing the wagon doors. 'I thought you were leaving them alone for now.'

'Some we are, some we aren't. It's part of what you call a *razzia*, Édouard. A round-up of those who would disagree with Nazi rule. A delightfully operatic term for something so sinister, I always think.'

'Why the Communists? And why now?'

'To keep you all on your toes. What is the point of having power if you don't wield it once in a while? I would add that that is the attitude of the powers that be, not necessarily mine.'

I gazed along the street down which the convoy and its silent escort had vanished.

'Ain't that the way of all authoritarian regimes? Find some-one else to blame.'

'The Communists? They're hardly blameless.'

'I mean us. The cops. Get someone else to do your dirty work.' I recalled the look on the one man's face. 'Divert blame onto us. We shovel the shit, you smell of roses.'

'Surprisingly coarse in your summation, Édouard, but

unerringly accurate. That is why it is important that you work closely with us in the Abwehr. I can keep you unsullied by this sort of action. If I so choose.'

'You know, you could just as easily have come and threatened me in my own office. It would have saved us both a lot of time.'

'Put it down to my taste for the theatrical, if you wish, but it's an illustration. You are no doubt aware, although my superiors would try to deny it, that we lack the manpower to police even the Occupied Zone. I would hazard that this is partly the reason why we stopped where we did and sought an armistice with Marshal Pétain. Although we still pull the strings in the Unoccupied Zone, despite how much your countrymen like to fool themselves otherwise.'

'You seem happy to give all this away.'

'It is obvious, Édouard, don't try to say you are unaware. We are in power, but we need the French police and administration to help us wield that power. Without them, our task would be harder. And, I would add, a lot less pleasant for the average French person if such matters were left more to the machinery of the Nazi Party.'

'We work with you on our own demise so you don't make that demise even worse?'

He half-smiled at that. 'Others would see it as working on your new future.'

'Whether we want it or not.'

'Enough of this. You know where you stand, so now let me help you. Your current investigations. Are there any where you would require my assistance? I can open doors you no longer can. You would be advised to answer wisely.'

I thought of Julot in his chair and of the prisoners being spirited away from Fresnes.

'None.'

He concentrated for a moment on lighting another cigarette. We both watched the dead match spiral to the ground, a grey wake like that of a downed aircraft tracing its fall. In silence, he summoned the two soldiers with one finger.

'Well, pleasant as this has been, Édouard, it must come to an end.' He made to stand up, but leaned closer into me instead and gestured to the building where the three Communists had been seized. 'Like your colleagues, you will work with us. With me. Willingly or otherwise, but you will work with me.'

He stood up and was followed by the two soldiers away from the bench. A few moments later, his gleaming staff car emerged from a side street and glided regally away from the grime and poverty of one of Paris's poorest quarters. I watched it go. Looking back at the building opposite me, I saw again the three Communists being arrested.

'But that's not what made you bring me here, was it?' I asked in a low voice. 'Not these three.' I got up to leave. I'd have to find my way back to the centre by Metro, which irritated me as much as Hochstetter's fishing trip had done. 'So what was?'

I rode the Metro back to the Île de la Cité, but I was still hungry, so I went into a café and ordered a wine, which would have to do. It was about the only thing not yet rationed. I almost willed the Occupiers to ration it. That would be one way to make sure Parisians worked up enough rage to storm Adolf's Bastille. As I waited, two German officers got up and left. Behind them, they'd left some of cheese on a plate. I stared at two small, irregular chunks and checked the tables around me, deciding when to make a move. I could almost taste them, feel them crumble in my mouth. The owner brought my wine over and set the glass down on the table in front of me, blocking my view. When he'd gone, so had the cheese. The plate remained.

I looked around. A woman with a small child was nearest, her hand closing the clasp on her handbag. I couldn't blame her. But I could resent her. That's what we'd become.

I thought of Walter le Ricaneur in his cell at Thirty-Six. Of his fear at the mention of Capeluche. And of his mime act with the needle and thread. Hochstetter had stolen my advantage when he'd summoned me. That moment had gone, so now my best bet was to let Walter stew. Let his own dread loosen his tongue about what was going on with the prisoners at Fresnes. I pictured his perpetual sneer and I knew that that was an optimistic hope, but the panic I saw in his eyes had been real. Being left alone with that for long enough could do wonders for your desire to talk. With that thought, I finished my wine and ordered a coffee for dessert.

I walked the short distance to Thirty-Six. A German truck went past, the young soldiers staring bored out of the back at the city receding behind them. I looked away, ensuring I didn't make eye contact. It was something we'd all learned to do quickly, an uneasy edifice of a truce that you couldn't help thinking was built on sand. There were days you could almost imagine Paris without the Germans here. They seemed to be tiptoeing around us, told to be on their best behaviour, but then a military vehicle went past or you saw soldiers taking up seats on the Metro or a pushy NCO stopped you for your papers and the dream vanished.

At Thirty-Six, I went straight to the cells and found the duty sergeant stacking piles of paper neatly on his desk.

'Can you open Walter's cell for me?' I asked him.

'Can't, I'm sorry,' Eddie.'

He had a face that was paper thin, like a book turned spine out, and he spoke with a strong Breton accent. I smelt ham on his breath. Was everyone around here eating but me?

'What do you mean, you can't?'
He laid the papers down on his desk with a brusque finality.
'He's been released. Judge's orders.'

8

'Been talking to the lovely Mathilde.'

'Get to the point.'

For once, I was listening to Boniface.

'She doesn't know who authorised Walter's release,' he continued as I drove, 'but she says Judge Clément had to surrender a heap of files on other prisoners at Fresnes. All the ones on them held at the Palais de Justice.'

'Do you have the names?'

'Only Walter le Ricaneur's and we already knew about Julot. Mathilde's going to give me the rest when I see her.'

'Who did the judge have to give them to?' My money was on the Gestapo.

'A French guy.'

'French?'

'To quote Mathilde: "A seedy-looking gangster type". But he had authorisation from the Germans, which is why the judge had to go along with it.'

I drove deep in thought. I'd sent Boniface to the court to find out why Walter had been released. Losing prisoners from Fresnes was bad enough, but from our own cells at Thirty-Six was much more disturbing.

We reached our destination and I told him to get out of the car. 'Wait for me by the gate. I won't be a moment.'

Watching him walk away, I reached under the dashboard and felt for the small item I kept hidden on a clip behind a panel. I pulled it out and stuffed it into my sock before catching up with Boniface.

'Doesn't get any better, does it?' he commented.

I looked up at the huge doors set into their high arch in the squat square entrance to the building. To either side, a single storey of rough stone walls with barred windows emanated from it, seeming to stretch an eternity into the distance. We'd driven south of the city to the town of Fresnes. Home to Fresnes prison. But no longer to some of the city's leading lights, it would appear.

But for the imposing twin doors, it was almost anonymous, but as always, the knowledge that this ugly low entrance hid the real horror of the hectare after hectare of steep and terrifying barrack blocks inside seemed to make it even more sinister.

'You have to surrender your guns,' the warden at the gatehouse told us.

'No, we don't.'

I made to go past him, but four more wardens with batons stood in my way.

'Governor's orders,' he insisted.

'Since when? You can't make two cops go into Fresnes unarmed.'

'You want to come in, you leave your guns with me.'

I shared an annoyed look with Boniface. We had no choice. I signed a chit and watched the warden lock our guns away in a steel cabinet. I couldn't help feeling a sense of foreboding, and I had to hide a shiver as one of the wardens led us out of the gatehouse and into the beast's maw. Before reaching the low central building in front of the towering cell blocks, we passed a group of prisoners being held in a cluster in the open air. There was still a warmth clinging to the end of the month after the rain of past weeks.

Some of the inmates recognised me and muttered a greeting. 'Giral, you scum.'

'Ten months, Giral, then I'm out. I'll be looking for you.'

'And you, Boniface.'

Boniface looked back at them and grinned. 'Who's fucking your wives tonight, boys? I can't be everywhere at once.'

A handful of them surged at him but were beaten back by wardens with batons. The prisoners stared at us with a hatred you could feel on your scalp.

'You like to make yourself popular, don't you?' I told him.

In an office as grim as the exterior had promised, Ducousset the governor had the harassed look you'd expect of someone responsible for not letting some one and a half thousand of the country's worst criminals somehow get out. So I asked him why he had. Sighing heavily, he ran weathered hands through thinning grey hair and looked at me with open dislike. He seemed as pleased to see me as the prisoners in the courtyard had.

'I told your officer. There are no prisoners missing here. Every one of my inmates is accounted for.'

'Really?' I took out a photo of Julot tied to the captain's chair and put it on the desk in front of him. The black and white image didn't get across the red-rimmed horror of the original, but it was still stark enough to make Ducousset wince.

'That is not one of the inmates here.'

I took the photo back. 'Impressive. Best part of two thousand prisoners and you can recognise one enough from this photo to know he's not one of them. You evidently care for your charges.'

His look cooled down an ice age or two. 'You'd do well not to take that tone, Inspector Giral.'

'And you'd do well to stop pissing me about. If these prisoners haven't gone missing, you can no doubt bring them to me.'

'It isn't that they haven't gone missing. They're just not here. They never were.' His voice faltered slightly over the final words.

'Julot le Bavard and Walter le Ricaneur,' I recited. 'I know they're here because I put them here.'

'Maybe I could make a suggestion.' That was Boniface. 'Perhaps I could go into the secretary's office and run through the files with her. Just to check.'

I groaned silently. I assumed it was Boniface's over-active hormones getting the better of him as usual. But Ducousset backed away and studied him.

'No, you can stay here. I'll call my secretary and ask her to bring the list of inmates with her.'

He pressed a button on his intercom and gave her a terse order. He sat back and stared at the bars on his window until the door to the anteroom opened a few moments later. The secretary came in. I saw her glance at Boniface and blush, her left hand pushing her hair into place. I groaned again. With her right hand, she proffered a thick list of names to the governor, but Boniface stepped in before she could complete the action. Looking into her eyes, he gently lifted the sheaf of papers out of her hand.

'Thank you so much, Amélie.' I could see the moment's falter as he tried to recall her name. 'How can I repay you?'

If I groan any more, I'm going to be ill. Still, I had to admit that as a move, it was as slick as his hair.

'Look for Walter and Julot,' I told Boniface.

'They're not here.'

Ducousset stood up, his face red with rage, and he barked at Boniface. 'Hand that over.'

I thrust an arm out sideways and toppled him back into his

chair. The wind left his sails as quickly as it did his cushion. I thought of Walter and the people I knew to be his associates.

'Try Adrien Estébétéguy and André Girbes.' The governor stood up again and I pushed him back, pinning him to his chair. 'And Calais Jacques, while you're at it.'

'This is an outrage. Amélie, go and fetch someone to show these two out.'

I couldn't stop his secretary from leaving but I could turn to face Ducousset. There was rage on his face, but there was something else. It shocked me. It was the same fear, the same depth of barely suppressed terror that I'd seen in the cafés and streets of Belleville.

I stared into his eyes, but he turned away. 'You're not colluding,' I told him in sudden realisation. 'You're scared.'

'Not here,' Boniface interrupted. 'Not one of them. Are you sure you've got this right, Eddie?'

I looked askance at him the moment Amélie came back in with four sturdy wardens. Each with a sturdier baton. I stared at Boniface and thought I could have done with my own heavy stick right now. My hand on Ducousset's shirt front relaxed and he shook it off.

'See them out,' the governor told the newcomers. He straightened his jacket and brusquely shot his cuffs to recompose himself.

Boniface placed the list of names on the desk and stepped back. 'I can only apologise.'

Before I could batter Boniface charmless, the wardens herded the pair of us out of the governor's offices and led us along a corridor green with scuffed and peeling paint and mould.

'Apologise?' I stopped in front of Boniface and pushed him back against the drab wall. 'What the hell do you think you were playing at back there? I'm right about this.'

Out of the corner of my eye, I could see the wardens smirking at us. Boniface leaned forward and spoke in a low voice.

'I know you are. I checked a couple of names of my own and they weren't there when they should be.'

His words took me by surprise. 'So why?'

'Because we got what we wanted.' He glanced to his left to make sure the guards couldn't hear. 'We now know for certain that more than just a couple of prisoners have gone missing and we know it's being covered up. We weren't going to get any more out of Ducousset, it was pointless trying. It's up to us now to find out what's going on.'

I slowly took my hand away and studied his face. 'You know, when you're not talking bullshit, Boniface, you're not a bad cop.'

'Actually, I'm a very good one. I think that might be your problem. You know you're not the only one.'

'Come on, Abelard and Héloïse,' a surprisingly cultured warden commented, shooing us along. 'Keep your canoodling for outside.'

We walked on ahead of our four nursemaids. I, for one, was deep in thought, not too aware of our surroundings. The corridor seemed to stretch for an eternity through stifling damp.

'This isn't the way we came in,' Boniface suddenly turned and told the head Cerberus.

I looked up to see one of the wardens pass in front to open a steel-barred door and gesture us through. It led into a wider room with no furniture, just pale lights overhead and another locked door leading out the other side. I turned and waited, expecting to see the wardens follow us in and lock the gate behind them. They locked it, but they were still on the other side.

'What are you doing?' I demanded.

Behind me, I heard the door on the far side being unlocked and swinging open. I heard voices too.

'Oh shit,' Boniface muttered.

I turned to see about a dozen of the prisoners we'd seen in the yard being ushered into the room. Behind them, a couple of wardens, their caps pulled down low to obscure their faces, let the last of them in and locked the door behind them before disappearing along the corridor. We were alone and unarmed in a locked passageway with twelve men we'd helped put in Fresnes. And they weren't here to bring us posies of love-in-the-mist.

'You probably shouldn't have offered to fuck their wives,' I whispered to Boniface.

The self-appointed leader of the men, a two-metre Howitzer shell of muscle and attitude, rubbed a huge hand in glee over his bald head and leered at us. Zizi le Géant. A street-fighting man and fist for hire with the prostitution gangs in Montmartre. You knew you were in trouble when he spat on the floor. That was his signal to himself to attack.

'Going to enjoy this,' a voice at the back of the group said. Through the crowd, I saw it was Damascène, a bank clerk I'd put away for fraud a couple of years earlier. Too snivelling for a nickname, he was one of life's hecklers on the edge.

A shiver of anticipation ran through them.

Zizi spat on the floor.

'Oh, double shit,' Boniface swore.

'Not looking good, is it?' I admitted.

Zizi stepped forward and I crouched down. My movement made him stop in puzzlement. From my sock, I pulled out the object I'd taken from behind the dashboard in my car and stood up straight. It was my Manufrance, a small pistol that I had to hold up so they could see it. Oddly, it didn't stop them.

'Going to have to do better than that,' Damascène called from the back.

Despite the slow march forward, the group was starting to

break apart in hesitation. It gave me a clear view through to the bank runt, so I pointed and pulled the solid double-action trigger, which always made aiming a bit hit-or-miss. Damascène fell to the ground, screaming and clutching his foot. A thin fountain of blood arced through the air, splashing the others, who recoiled. Bit of a lucky shot, I had to admit. I only meant to shock them into stopping.

'Only seven bullets left, *poulet*,' Zizi commented. 'Not enough for all of us.'

'True. So if you'll just decide which seven of you want to die today, we'll get on with it.'

That did stop them.

That and the siren that suddenly threatened to split our eardrums. From either side, wardens unlocked the two end doors and streamed through. The ones at the front pointed their pistols at the men, the ones behind began belaying them with sticks. In the midst of falling bodies, Damascène lay screaming for attention. It was the most immensely satisfying moment I'd had all week.

'Heard a gunshot,' a senior warden explained as his men rounded the prisoners up. None of the guards who'd led us into the trap were among our rescuers.

'I want the names of the guards who left us here,' I told him.

He shrugged. 'Don't know who you mean. You can make an official complaint to the governor.'

Reluctantly, I put the Manufrance into my pocket. The warden took us back to the gatehouse, where we were handed back our service pistols. I'm not a lover of guns the way some of the other cops were – they're just a necessary evil of my job – but it felt good to be reunited.

'Neat trick,' Boniface told me as we walked back to my car.

'So, who do we think is behind the missing prisoners,

Boniface? Who has the authority to release the likes of Calais Jacques and Walter le Ricaneur from Fresnes?'

Boniface opened his door and leaned on the roof before getting in. He said two words.

'The Germans.'

Act I

October 1940

9

I had a visit to make. I dragged my heels.

I took the Metro to the Porte des Lilas. It went underground through Belleville, which, for my money, was by far the best way to see that part of town. Until a few years ago, the station had been the eastern edge of the underground railway system, but the line had been extended one more stop, so it didn't feel so much like travelling to the ends of the known world – or Paris as the Parisians called it. One good thing about the journey was that there were no German soldiers out this far, cluttering up the carriages, so you could almost forget they were here. You took your pleasures where you could these days.

I emerged from the hole in the ground and wished I'd stayed in it. Boulevard Mortier wasn't as grand as the first part of the name suggested, but it was certainly as bleak as its second part. It was named after the former Marshal of the Empire who'd been one of eighteen killed by Fieschi's *machine infernale* instead of its intended victim, King Louis-Philippe, proving we're all random targets of someone else's dreams.

A heavy rain had begun to fall while I'd been underground. One more annoyance. Sheltering a moment in a doorway, I saw a copy of *L'Oeuvre* lying in the gutter, its headline proclaiming DREAM THE FUTURE? NO, MAKE IT! I watched as the message steadily disintegrated in the rain, its false promise overtaken by a sodden reality. I found it strangely satisfying.

Les Tourelles had been a military barracks, but our visitors had turned it into an internment camp when they'd first come calling. I looked up at the squat complex of buildings hunkering to the side of the boulevard like it was taking a massive dump and I thought it had finally found its purpose in life.

Luckily for me, it was staffed by French wardens, so I just had to show my police ID to get past the boundary gate. I couldn't help shivering walking through the corridors. I'd spent part of the last war in a German prisoner-of-war camp that was even less salubrious than this one and the thought of not being able to get back out again still gave me the shakes.

One of the wardens guided me to a dingy room of institutional mould and left me to wait. The same smell of cabbage and urine lurked in the air. I had to fight an urge to get up and leave. It wasn't just because of the locked doors and barred windows. I heard a sound of a metal gate opening along a corridor and steeled myself.

The door slowly opened and I stifled a gasp. I didn't recognise him. The warden told him to sit down opposite me and went and stood by the far wall. We sat in silence for a moment, staring at each other across the scuffed wooden table.

'You're the last person I expected to see,' he said.

He looked like he'd been drained of muscle and fibre. His cheeks were gaunt, shoulders once the size of a doorway, with an enjoyment of life to match, were hunched and hollow. Faded clothes hung off him, his huge frame shrunken. I looked into his eyes. They were grey and shrivelled, like the tufts of hair clinging to the sides of his head. But worst of all was his voice. It rattled, a reedy shadow of the deep rumble I used to know. And that was my fault.

'Hello, Joe.'

'What brings you here, Eddie?'

'I don't know.' I didn't. I couldn't explain why I'd come to see him after all this time. What I'd hoped to achieve.

'You haven't changed,' he said.

'Is that a good or a bad thing?'

'You tell me. What is it you want? I've got a dinner date later and I want to look my best.'

That was the Joe I remembered, cocking a snook at life, even though I was having to get used to the change in voice. And the guilt that that punched into my soul with every word he spoke. I tried to laugh but couldn't.

'You haven't changed either.'

'Bullshit.' He did laugh. Not the deep river of sound I remembered from when we were both younger, but a trickle of water across worn stones. Like the old Joe, it was still melodious and captivating, but it had lost so much of the depth and syncopation of days past.

'Can I bring you food?' I asked him. I had no idea where I'd get it from, but he shook his head.

'They won't allow it.'

My feeling of guilt wouldn't go away, but it was tinged now with a regret. I'd lost a friend fifteen years ago through my own actions and I'd never once attempted to atone in all the years since.

'Is there anything I can get you, Joe?'

'Out.' There was a pain in that one word that I knew.

'I'll do what I can, I promise.'

He tipped his head to one side in a gesture I remembered and smiled, a low-wattage glow of melancholy that hinted at the Technicolor beam I once knew.

'Sure you will, Eddie.'

71

'I mean it, Joe. I promise.'

'Don't make promises you can't keep. Not again.' He shook his head at me. The certainty in his expression that I wouldn't or couldn't help him stung. I didn't pursue it.

'Have you heard from anyone? Have they come to see you?'

'Only Stéphane from the club. None of the guys in the band.' He gestured at his surroundings. 'They don't dare and I don't blame them.'

'And from the old days? Fran? Dominique?'

He shook his head. 'I saw them in the street a short while ago, though. They finally got together, I guess. Strange, you could've been the one to win Dominique over once.'

Past the barb in his words, I recalled Fran telling me he hadn't seen Dominique in years. The cop in me never went away. That was part of the problem. 'When was this?'

'This year. Just before the Nazis got here.' His voice sank to an almost trance-like quiet. 'That's really not that long ago, is it?'

He signalled to the warden he was ready to go.

'I'll come and see you again, Joe,' I told him.

We both stood up. In another age, another relationship, we would have embraced like brothers. He simply turned away from me and shuffled towards the door.

'Sure you will, Eddie,' he repeated.

The warden returned for me after handing Joe over to another guard outside the room and took me back to the main entrance.

'Friend of yours?' he asked me.

'He was once.'

We paused as he unlocked a gate. 'Bad business, this.'

'You could say that.'

'I sometimes wish I hadn't come back.'

'Come back?'

'I was evacuated at Dunkirk,' he told me. 'I was a reservist, in the 68th Infantry Division.'

'I thought most of your lot were captured.'

'They were. But some of us got away. For all the good it did us. I was back in France within the week. Dropped off by the Rosbifs in Brest. They told us to carry on fighting the Boches while they went back home and drank that stuff they call tea.'

'You don't like the British?'

He snorted. 'They're as bad as the Boches. They left us to our chances when we were supposed to be fighting together, ran off instead of rallying south of the coast. Don't get me wrong, I'm not pro-Boche by any means, but I'm not pro-Rosbif either. They're both out for what they can get, if you ask me.'

'So how come you're this side of the wire if you came back to fight the Germans?'

'I didn't. I was demobbed and told to go home. Didn't fight another day. So here I am, forgotten by the French army, sold out by the Rosbifs and now I'm in Paris scraping a living by doing the Boches' work for them in my own city. Try working that one out.'

I watched him shuffle back into the gloom of the internment camp and did just that. Outside, in the rain, I stared back at the ugly edifice in front of me. I relived the shock of seeing Joe and the little faith he had in me. And I recalled the warden's words. It felt like I'd been punched a second time in the stomach.

I didn't go home at the end of the day.

As I walked, I thought of Joe in his cell in Les Tourelles and I couldn't bear the thought of walls around me and a ceiling over my head. Instead, I sat on one of the metal chairs on a pathway in the Jardin du Luxembourg. In the days when the idea of swastikas hanging down like red and black tears from buildings and harshly striped sentry boxes louring in parks and gardens had seemed too remote to imagine, I used to come here to read. It had always been a respite from the fearfulness of my work and the tremors lying in wait in my lonely home. I'd spent many an evening among the trees alone with my friends Guy and Victor, André and Émile, Simone and Jean-Paul. Only today I didn't have a book to calm me. Not that I would have been able to concentrate on anything other than the sight of Julot sitting in a captain's chair. And the sound of Joe's voice and the change wrought in it. And the reason why.

I wished for a sound to take away the memory. There was the noise of people, the low growl of traffic beyond the trees and the high drone of military planes overhead. But there was one sound missing.

Birds.

There was not one note of birdsong in the garden. I listened carefully but heard nothing, just the sound of the wind soughing in the leaves and rats scurrying in the undergrowth. The rumour was that the birds had all died at the start of the Occupation when the fuel tanks outside Paris had been set alight, casting black clouds over the city and suffocating them. Others said they'd just left us, given up on humans too stupid to care for. Either way, like so much of the city, they were gone. They would come back, that I knew, but I felt their absence with a keenness that ached.

I sat in the garden until it grew dark. If I'd had a book, I'd have had to give up reading long before now. I stood up. It was time to go home. I recalled Joe in his metal cage and thought for a moment of the tin on the bookshelf in my flat. And of what lay in the tin. I sat down again. Home could wait.

10

The next morning was devoted to seeing my allotted butcher. The Occupation really was just one endless social whirl. If the rationing didn't kill us, the time spent on queuing would. And the bad food.

'If I could get better meat for my customers, I'd happily pay for it, Eddie. But this is what I've got.'

My new ration ticket for meat gripped in my hand like it was a winning ticket at Longchamp, I watched Albert carefully weigh out my bacon.

'So how would you get better meat?'

He spoke over his shoulder at me. 'Black market.'

'You do know I'm a cop?'

'Sure I know. I don't care. It's every man for himself now.'

He wrapped the meagre rashers up in paper and handed the parcel over. I handed him the ticket and the money. When rationing tickets had first come in, some people thought they were supposed to be used instead of money. There were big arguments in shops when people were told they had to pay too.

I dropped the food off in the cold box outside my kitchen window and went to work. If there was one thing I'd learnt, it was that being occupied took up serious amounts of time. I used to buy food on my way home from Thirty-Six. If I were to do that now, I'd go hungry. Well, even hungrier. I could already twist my trouser waistband from side to side. It was the latest dance craze in a city gone hollow.

I went looking for Boniface when I got to Thirty-Six. He was talking to one of the secretaries on the second floor, his voice drowning her in lustful sedation.

'Boniface, come with me. We're going to Montmartre.'

He smiled at the young woman and lifted himself slowly from her desk to follow me. She gave me a dirty look for taking him away from her.

'Why Montmartre?' he asked when he caught me up.

'It's where Walter le Ricaneur's from. I want to know where he's got to.'

On the way, Boniface told me one of the criminals he'd put away and who'd been spirited out of Fresnes was also from Montmartre.

'I'll go take a look for him,' he said.

'Good idea.' Not to mention a relief to my ears.

We left Boniface's car parked on Boulevard de Clichy outside the house where Degas had lived. Most of the arty crowd who'd moved into Montmartre at the beginning of the century had lived on the top of the mountain. The ones who were left still did. The bottom of the hill was very much the arse-end, the home of sleazy night spots, hookers and pimps. Climbing up Rue Houdon and turning down the third proposition in a row, I imagined old man Edgar would have been hard pushed to find any ballet dancers to daub today.

'Come on, Eddie, one last ride on the swings,' an ageing prostitute old enough for Degas to have painted tried to tempt me.

'I think the chain's long rusted,' I told her.

She cackled far too much. It wasn't that funny, but it was

nice to be popular for once. She cackled some more when a superannuated German staff sergeant, a feldwebel with a greying Kaiser moustache filling half his face, handed over a day's wages and disappeared into a shady doorway with her. The Nazi authorities had tried publishing a list of forbidden brothels in the early days of the Occupation, and soldiers weren't supposed to partake of the city's commercial carnality except in officially approved *maisons closes*, but even the powers that be knew it was a rule they were never going to even attempt to uphold.

The steep sides of the buildings would have made the day colder had it not been for the steady ascent up the narrow street. It was one of those roads that doesn't look like much of a climb until you start walking up it. At least the exertion was shutting Boniface up for once. It was quieter here, the only sound the rumble of military planes high overhead. There were days when that felt like it was all you heard, all other noises of Paris subjugated by the constant thrum of the Luftwaffe.

'My man's up this way,' Boniface suddenly told me. 'I'll peel off here.'

'Meet me back at chez Edgar.' He looked puzzled. 'By the car.'

He wasn't an art lover evidently. I watched him cut down the even narrower Rue Piémontési. I thought of telling him that Renoir had had a studio in the block behind me, but I didn't think he'd be interested. Turning back, I steeled myself for the last bit of my climb. I had the feeling my popularity was about to end. I was nowhere near the top of the mountain and I'd had enough.

'I'm too old for another war,' I muttered to a scrawny cat pawing at a drainpipe, no doubt smelling a rat. 'I know how you feel.'

Sophie Scipone worked in a café that had doggedly stayed

open throughout the early days of the Occupation. It wasn't out of defiance. The owner was just stingy.

'I don't know a thing,' she told me when I asked about Walter. The owner flicked his tea towel angrily at a table and glared at me. 'You know he'll dock my wages for this.'

'Outside,' the owner barked at me. 'Both of you. We don't want police in here.'

We went outside and I gave her a couple of notes to keep her sweet. And talking. She lit up a cigarette and blew out a stiletto of smoke from thin lips. She had eyes that would freeze Hell in a heatwave.

'I want to see him,' I told her. 'Is he at home now?'

She laughed scornfully at me. 'Home? Seriously? I chucked him out the last time he got put away.'

'Gave you a hard time, did he?' This is how I wanted her. Bitter and ready to squeal. They say justice is a noble cause.

'What do you think?'

'So have you seen him since he got out? Do you know where he hangs out?'

'Around Place Pigalle most nights. Flashing the cash. But that was a few weeks ago. I haven't seen him since.'

'Flashing the cash? Where's he getting it from?'

'I don't know, but he's getting plenty of it from somewhere.' She looked thoughtful. 'They're like kids in a sweetshop. Him and his new mates. There's a handful of them. Like they've found the keys to the cash box and they know you lot can't touch them. Cocky, like they're invincible or something.'

'New mates?'

'Not just from Pigalle. Or even Montmartre. From all over the city.'

'So who else is in this handful?'

'Like I'm going to tell you.'

She sounded more dismissive than afraid, but I sensed a quaver in her voice.

'What does Capeluche mean?'

She inhaled deeply, her eyes closed against the smoke. She was buying time to hide her response. She failed. The shake in her hand gave her away. She exhaled slowly.

'New one on me.'

'Is it a person? An organisation?'

'I told you. New one on me.'

'Do Walter and his new mates seem scared?'

My question took her by surprise. It was meant to.

'They're not the ones who are scared. Every other bastard around them is, but not them. They act like they're gods.' She threw her cigarette out into the gutter and looked directly at me. 'Because they know you lot are too much in the Boches' pockets to do anything about them.'

'We can if you tell me where I can find Walter.'

'Forget it, *poulet*, I don't go telling tales to the cops.'

She went inside and began mouthing off at the owner. I watched from outside the large pane of glass.

'You just did.'

'See the little piggy. See how he squeals. Pass me the needle. Pass me the thread. You can't squeal now, little piggy. You're stone cold dead.'

It was a child's voice. It was coming from around the corner by the café where Sophie worked. I followed the sound and came across a little kid playing in a puddle left by the rain over-night. He started singing it again.

'Where'd you learn that song?' I asked him.

He looked up and stared at me. He had eyelashes that a Le

Chat Noir vedette would have killed for and round cheeks as fulsome as any Renaissance cherub.

'Fuck you, *poulet.*'

He also had a mouth like the devil's arse. He jumped up from his murky puddle and ran off, stopping at the street corner to taunt me. He started singing again. I walked towards him and he ran off a second time, stopping at another corner further into the shadows of the peeling buildings.

I stopped some distance away. I knew I wouldn't catch him in the warren of alleyways. I wasn't sure I wanted to. He stopped singing and looked at me, his expression intense, unsettling.

'I just want to ask you about the song,' I told him.

He mouthed something, but he was too far away for me to hear it properly. I took a step forward and stopped.

'Say it again, I want to hear.'

He grinned, the cherubic face somehow demonic in the thin light. He whispered it again.

'Capeluche.'

'What does it mean?'

'He's coming to stitch you, *poulet,*' the kid said in a louder voice.

Before I could react, he'd disappeared into an alleyway between two buildings.

'You're not talking. Are you dead?'

I'd been in Boniface's car on Boulevard de Clichy a full minute and he hadn't opened his mouth once. Instead we both sat in silence watching what passed for traffic these days go by.

'Can we go for a pastis, Eddie?'

He looked spooked, his voice quiet. The change in him shocked me.

'No, you can't. No one can.'

He looked surprised at me and then grunted as he remembered. 'I'd forgotten.' The government in Vichy had banned pastis in August, along with every other drink over sixteen per cent proof. They really knew how to keep our spirits up. 'A wine, then?'

'We can try.'

This was a Boniface I'd never seen. We got back out of his car and went into the nearest café and ordered two glasses of red wine. It wasn't good wine, but then it wasn't a good café. I knew from old that the owner made most of his money passing punters onto the street's pimps. That and other equally unwholesome sidelines. He traded more in white powder than in red liquid. I felt the wine scratch my teeth as I drank it.

'So what is it?' I asked Boniface. 'What's got you spooked?'

He sipped from his glass thoughtfully and put it down. 'Does this feel different to you? I was too young for the last war. I wasn't in the trenches like you were, but I've heard the old soldiers talk about knowing when your time was up. A feeling they got.'

'It's just a myth. No one knew. You were surrounded by flying bullets. Your time was always going to be up.'

He shook his head. 'I felt something in there. It was like a thick fog in the streets, only you couldn't see it, you could only feel it. All around you, following you wherever you went. And the people. I've never seen fear like it. In everyone. Not an out-and-out fear, not a panic or a terror, but an underlying dread.'

I stayed silent. It felt uncomfortably like the way I'd been feeling the last few days.

'And I've never felt unease for myself like it,' he continued. 'It wasn't fear, it was a sense of something shifting.' He laughed, a remote, bitter sound. 'Even the kids felt menacing.'

I thought of the young child singing his song and his threat of Capeluche waiting for me and I shook it from my head. 'You're a cop, Boniface. You know this is fanciful. At least now we know Capeluche is a person.'

He faced me. 'He sews their lips up. He sits them down and looks into their eyes and sews their lips up.'

There was a look of such bleakness on his face that I called the owner over for two more glasses of mildew.

'Rationing,' he told me curtly, tutting.

'Since when has wine been rationed? Bring me two more glasses.'

'Who is this, Eddie? I've dealt with killers before, I've seen them carve each other up and slit a drunk's throat for ten sous, I've seen ten-day-old bodies fished out of the Seine and I've fought off gangsters coming at me with clubs and knives, but I've never seen anything like this. It's the silence. No one will talk, no one dares. The only ones talking are crowing, like they're part of the threat and we're next in line.'

The owner slopped the two glasses down on the creaky wooden table and sloped off. I watched him go before replying thoughtfully to Boniface. 'Sophie, Walter's old girlfriend, said the same thing. That there are those who are crowing, who are part of it. And that they're from all over the city.'

I watched his eyes focus. The cop in him overcoming the fear. 'All over the city? A gang of gangs.'

'What?'

'A gang of gangs. With the Nazis in town and our attention elsewhere half the time, they've come together to make a common stand. Christ, we'd never be able to keep on top of that, not now with everything else that's going on.'

'Walter from Montmartre, Julot from Belleville, the attack was in Montparnasse.' It was possible, I had to admit. 'But how come they were released from Fresnes? That can't be in spite of the Germans being in town. It has to be because of it. Surely, they're the only ones with the power just to go into a prison and have prisoners released. With no judge's orders, no passes, no furloughs.'

Boniface gave a low whistle that attracted the attention of two prostitutes at a nearby table. 'A gang of gangs sanctioned by the Nazis? Now we really are in the shit.'

'Which ones, though?' I asked. It was more to myself than to Boniface. I thought of Hochstetter and his fishing expedition, but this smacked more of the Gestapo. I hadn't had any contact with the cold men in black coats since the Germans had first arrived in town, but that had been more than enough to lead me to think that this was their sort of tactic.

'It still sounds fanciful,' Boniface commented. 'Why would the Germans need to work with French criminals?'

'The same reason they work with French cops. Because there aren't enough Germans to go around. Not while they're still fighting the British. And attacking Romania.'

'That still doesn't explain it. I understand needing to get the police on their side, but would they really work with a bunch of gangsters like this?'

'Work with them? The Nazis are made up almost entirely of thugs and gangsters. It's just that not all of them have a criminal record.'

He looked uncertain, but gestured towards the streets we'd both just left. 'It would explain why this lot feel so emboldened.'

We paused a moment to consider before I carried on. 'But the other question that's gnawing at me is, why kill Julot? Whoever it is that's behind what's going on? Why release him and then kill him? Especially the way they did.'

'He agreed to whatever it was and then tried to back out? He

was an example?' Boniface offered. 'Or he talked too much?'
Oh irony, where is thy sting?

'And who killed him? The French gang or whichever Germans
are involved in this. If they are involved in it, that is.'

'Would the Germans be having these people released from
prison so they can then kill them? Some sort of warning? I
couldn't find my guy. Walter's gone missing. Are we going to
find more bodies with sewn-up mouths?'

'Why would they bother? They're in charge. They'd just take
them out and shoot them?'

Boniface clicked his fingers. 'Unless we're looking at this
from the wrong angle. It's not the Germans emptying Fresnes.
It's the Free French. Recruiting from the prisons. And the
Germans have got wind of it.'

Now that really was fanciful. 'You've seen the names, Boniface.
Free French? These people would sell their own grandmothers
for a ride on a duck before giving themselves up for a cause.'

He paused and drank his wine, a small grimace at the taste
of it.

'This is evil, isn't it, Eddie? The Nazis controlling everything
from the shadows, leaving us to fight among ourselves. That's
all they have to do. Wind us up and set us off and we'll do their
job for them.'   .

Not for the first time, I looked at him in a different light. He
was a lot more than the froth he liked to present.

The two prostitutes got up to leave and passed our table. The
younger of the two, a gentle face hidden under a protective
patina of make-up, stopped in front of Boniface and smiled.
He winked back, the fear of a few minutes ago evaporated amid
his hormones.

'You just ruined it,' I told him.

II

Everyone stared at their feet and edged slowly forward. Me included. It was another of the season's new dances – the Paris breadline shimmy. The queue outside the baker's. A thin straggle of souls too exhausted for bitter conversation or gloomy gossip. Steadily shuffling along the mortal coil, each step on the way to the threshold of whatever delight rationing had in store for us, marked by a new crack in the pavement to reach. A playground game. Just not a very good one.

I shifted my gaze for a moment to my bread tickets. A virgin page of unsullied perforated lines. It was the first chance I'd had to buy bread since being issued with them – the first loaf I'd have had in over a week – and I just wanted to make sure I hadn't somehow lost them. They were wilting under my grip and I forced myself to relax my fingers.

I took one more step and inhaled deeply. Everyone in Paris had learned to anticipate this brief second. One moment there was no aroma, the next there was. The smell of freshly baked bread. A scent that filled your nose and danced its way through your mouth and down to the pit of your stomach, where a yawning hunger impatiently awaited it.

I was within sight of the entrance. I could see the golden baguettes stacked up behind the surly baker, their stock steadily diminishing. I calculated there'd still be enough left by the time it was my turn and I felt an improbable wave of relief. I closed my eyes and breathed in its promise. I imagined taking my bread home, fighting the temptation to break the end off and chew it as I walked. Instead, I pictured myself putting it in the canvas bag behind the kitchen door, looking at it longingly, knowing I had to go out to work. But I'd give in, I knew I would, and pull the end off, feeling the bread crack and tear in my fingers.

I heard a diesel engine slowly cruise past, so I turned my face to the wall to blot out the engine smell. I felt a shove in my back and opened my eyes. The elderly woman behind me had pushed me as the queue had drawn nearer still to the baker's. I found myself suddenly in the doorway. The aroma was almost overpowering.

I felt another nudge.

'Patience,' I told her.

Only it wasn't her.

A German officer, a hauptmann, was standing next to me, far too close, his hand firmly resting on my arm. I looked from him to the interior of the shop and back again.

'You can't be serious.'

'Please come with us, Inspector Giral.'

I pointed to the rows of bread behind the counter. 'No. You can wait.'

'Major Hochstetter cannot wait.'

I shut my eyes and silently cursed Hochstetter. And the hauptmann. And the two stabsgefreiters, or corporals, who had joined him. They were already firmly easing me from the queue.

'Seriously. Five minutes. That's all I need.' I tried to shake them off, but their grip grew stronger and they pulled me further away from the door. 'Two minutes.'

The old dear behind me in the queue prodded me along my way to help the German soldiers and quickly filled my place.

'Should be ashamed,' she said to the young woman behind her. 'Causing a fuss.'

I looked for someone I knew in the straggling line outside the shop to ask them to buy my bread for me, but there was no one I recognised. Hardly surprising, since I almost never spoke to any of my neighbours.

I pleaded again to the hauptmann's better nature but he'd given that up to join the Nazis. Inside, I saw the baker. He leered at me as he handed a baguette over to the shopper at the front of the queue and waved before I could turn away. It dripped sarcasm.

'Off with your friends, are you?' he called after me.

'Should be ashamed,' the old woman repeated, her elbows akimbo to stop anyone else getting past. 'Going on like that. Over a bit of bread.'

I sighed and gave up. 'Come on, then,' I told the hauptmann. He had a long, hooked nose and close-set eyes. Together, they looked like drooping facial genitalia. Not even that cheered me up.

I expected them to drive me from one side of the Left Bank to the other to the Hotel Lutétia, the Abwehr headquarters, but instead they took me across the river. For one moment, I thought I'd been tricked and they weren't Hochstetter's men, but we pulled up opposite the Palais Garnier and I saw the major standing at the foot of the opera house steps. Not for the first time, I had that strange blend of trepidation and relief at finding it was Hochstetter having me brought in.

He smiled and proffered his hand, like a praying mantis. 'Édouard, so glad you could come.'

I decided not to give him the satisfaction of complaining.

It only fed his habit. I was distracted by the sight of a small orchestra with a choir at the top of the steps.

'So why have I come?'

He gestured grandly to the ensemble above us. 'Opera.'

'Oh good.'

'I'm afraid I have a morning of carrot and stick lined up for you, as you will see. But I think it will be for your good.'

I gestured to the choir just as they started to chirrup. 'I can see the stick. Where's the carrot?'

He hushed me and turned to face the three rows of tonsils, his face a vision of rapture. He looked oddly human – that's not a trait I often associated with Hochstetter.

They finished. As usual, great music, dreadful noise.

'Marvellous, don't you think?' Hochstetter concluded. 'One of the free concerts the German people are offering to the people of Paris. In friendship.'

'We'd sooner have food.'

'This is food, Édouard. For the soul.'

'Yeah. Not quite as filling, is it?'

'I do not believe you are this much of a philistine.' He led me to the poster showing the season awaiting us. '*The Flying Dutchman*. Wouldn't you care to see that? You have heard of it, I take it?'

I considered his question. 'I enjoyed it when Marryat wrote about it, and I felt that both Ibsen's and Irving's use of the legend were interesting, but I particularly liked Heine's take on it.' I turned to look at him. 'It's when your lot started shouting to it that I lost interest.'

'I forget you are the son of a bookseller. Not the complete vulgarian. How about *Fidelio*? Would that suit?'

'*Fidelio*? No. Of course it wouldn't. What does it even mean?'

'You and your jazz. You have been ruined for culture. But

talking of jazz, I have heard tell of a rather gruesome murder. In a jazz club that is no longer allowed to operate.'

'How do you know about that?'

'I am a major in the Abwehr. My job is to gather information. My question is, how might I help you with your investigation into the circumstances? What do you think is the motive for such a brutal murder?'

I was taken aback but not surprised by the turn in conversation. This is what Hochstetter did. Alarmingly well. 'I really don't see how you can help. It has the signs of a gangland murder. Nothing to do with your lot, I'm sorry to say.'

'Is it something the German High Command should be concerned with? A problem of lawlessness, perhaps, in which we might need to take a hand?'

'Heaven forbid, Major.' And if Heaven doesn't, I will.

'Do you have any idea of the motive? Any suspects? I can use my men to support you in seeking out the culprits.'

'Motive? As I say, some gangland matter. Suspects? Half the gang members in Paris. It really isn't something for you to be worried about.'

'You don't see it as related to any other events? Any more significant matters?'

I thought of the missing prisoners. 'Not in the slightest.'

He studied me. 'No matter.'

'Can I go now? I have work to do.'

'You're forgetting the stick.'

He summoned the hauptmann, who led us to the car they'd brought me to the Palais Garnier in. We got in and drove off, but it was just a short drive, east from the opera house to the narrow streets of the Pletzel. The stabsgefreiter behind the wheel pulled over a short distance from a pair of police wagons. Hochstetter nodded once to the hauptmann, who got out of the car and walked towards a German car parked behind a French police wagon. He said something to the officer in the passenger seat, who gave a signal in turn to our cops. I watched in puzzled consternation as about eight French uniformed police emerged from the back of the wagon and entered an apartment block.

'What's going on?' I asked Hochstetter. 'More Communists?'

Instead of answering me, Hochstetter dismissed the two stabsgefreiters, so he and I were alone in the back of the car. He looked bored as we evidently waited for something to happen. Within just a few moments, the cops re-emerged from the building, dragging what looked to be three generations of a family out with them. One of the cops fetched a roundhouse slap to an elderly man, who looked to be the grandfather. He fell to the ground and the cop dragged him up roughly by the lapels.

He shook his head. 'Jews.'

We saw two small children being forced into the back of a paddy wagon. Their parents followed them in, their need to comfort them evident. I saw the expression on the mother's face. It was a fear the name Capeluche could only imagine summoning.

'Why have you brought me here?'

'The stick. These are Jews, but they aren't French Jews. Are you pleased we aren't using your police to arrest French citizens? That seemed to annoy you the other day.'

I turned to face him. 'What do you think?'

'It matters little. The Nazis aren't interested in French Jews. Not for the time being. For now, we are more interested in foreign Jews. Primarily German and Polish Jews.'

'Why are they being arrested?'

'They escaped justice. They fled their homes illegally.'

'You expected them to stay?'

'You are a policeman, aren't you? Surely that is of no concern when the law is broken. It's there to be upheld. By people like you.'

'Why have you brought me here?' I insisted.

'I feel you haven't quite understood the need to work with me.' He pointed at the wagon as the doors were slammed shut. The cries of the family could still be heard. 'I might be forced to request that you be seconded. I know how much that would dismay you.'

I was shocked. Not even I expected that from Hochstetter.

'That's not your decision. That's for the French police to decide.'

He laughed. I had never felt more like wiping it off his face and taking the consequences.

'You really think so? You might be a philistine, Édouard, but you are not a fool. Please don't behave like one. I'm afraid there are only so many warnings I can give.'

I did what I always used to do when I was angry. I went to the library. Not to calm myself down. To look. To learn.

After the anger I felt had abated, the morning's events stayed with me. While the sight of the family being led away haunted me – Hochstetter had understated it: involvement in that would more than dismay me – it was the name *Fidelio* that had piqued my curiosity. An opera. Capeluche had an operatic ring to it. Both the name and the way it was being used. So I'd come to the library at the Sorbonne to see if it came up in any of the books.

I hadn't come here with the intention of calming myself, but the smell of the ancient pages and leather, the rows of desks and lampshades, and the height of the walls as they flowed effortlessly into the ornate ceilings, soothed me. I felt at home in a way I rarely did elsewhere. I asked the librarian for some volumes and waited until she brought them over. I was alone as far as I could see, apart from two students at the far end and the librarian. I looked up artists and musicians, philosophers and orators, but found nothing.

'Excuse me,' a voice cut through my thoughts. It was the librarian, standing over me, holding another large tome. 'Capeluche, wasn't it?'

She handed me an ancient book on the history of Paris, opened on a page, and laid it flat on the desk in front of me. I saw the name and a plate with an engraving on it at the top of two columns of text.

'Thank you.'

I waited until she'd gone before starting to read. I'd set my sights too high, I learned.

Capeluche was an executioner.

He was the city executioner in the fifteenth century, I read, infamous for his cruelty. Where he largely achieved this infamy was in the Paris Massacres of 1418, during the civil war between the Armagnacs and the Burgundians – two factions in the same royal family fighting to be top dogs. Nothing changed.

He'd led a march on one prison, where a bunch of Armagnacs were being held, and he and his followers had dragged the prisoners out into the streets, where they executed the lot of them, including a pregnant woman. He then led the crowd on to the Bastille, where some of the higher-up Armagnacs were kept, and reneged on a deal he'd made to spare certain prisoners. Instead, he and his mob dragged them out of the prison and beheaded all of them except one outside.

I sat back and stared into space. There was nothing about sewing victims' mouths shut. That was a new refinement dreamed up by today's executioner. But there were the prisoners. Taken from their prison cells out into the streets. To be executed. Maybe Boniface and I weren't being so fanciful.

I was surprised to find I was alone in the vast reading room. Rain clouds had stolen over the city and little light came in through the windows. I shivered. I heard movement from the librarian's desk, but she was nowhere in sight. I looked to both sides of me. I saw no one.

Needing a pee, I took all the books but the history of Paris back to the librarian's desk and left them on the counter before going to the toilet. Returning, I still heard vague movements, their sound amplified but distorted in the high-ceilinged room. The darkness outside had closed in. Seeing no one still, I went back to where I'd been reading. The book was where I left it, but I saw something else on top of the open pages.

I stopped. Approaching slowly and looking around me, I went up to the desk. Sitting on the book was a child's toy. I could only stare. Dragging my gaze away, I glanced around me, but saw no movement.

Leaning forward, I picked up the toy.

It was a doll.

Its lips had been sewn together.

12

I took the doll to Thirty-Six and left it in my desk drawer. I took one last look at it – the dead painted eyes and cold red mouth. Whoever had left it was trying to rattle me. It was working. I slammed the drawer shut and went out.

'Capeluche?'

Fran stared at me and shrugged his shoulders. I'd left Thirty-Six and driven to the club in Montparnasse. We were sitting in his office and I was containing an anger that had been brewing since my meeting with Hochstetter and the discovery of the doll in the library.

'Who or what is Capeluche?' he asked me.

'Don't push me today, Fran. What do you know about Capeluche?'

Even in his self-adoration, he picked up on my mood. He held both hands up in placation. 'Hey, Eddie, it's the first I've ever heard of it. What is it?'

'You tell me.'

'I would if I could, believe me, but I haven't a clue what you're talking about.'

'Why was Julot killed in your club, Fran? What's it got to do with Capeluche?'

He looked perplexed. 'I've told you all this, Eddie, I have no idea, I never met the guy. And I don't know what Capeluche is.'

I studied Fran. He'd always been a conman, able to turn on the acting talent on the spin of a coin, but I really couldn't tell now which way up the coin had landed. I stared hard into his eyes. They gave nothing away, so I threw questions at him to try and catch him out in a lie.

'Why did you go and see Judge Clément?'

'Judge Clément? I've never even met him. What is all this, Eddie?'

I recalled the description of the 'seedy-looking gangster type' that the judge's secretary had given Boniface. 'Who gave you the authority to have the judge hand over the prisoners' records to you?'

Fran looked at me mystified. 'I don't know what you've been taking, my friend, but either I'm seriously missing something here or you're not making any sense.'

We were disturbed by a figure at the door, who walked in and quickly backed out.

'Oh, I'm sorry, I didn't realise you had visitors, Monsieur Poquelin. Don't mind me, I'll just get on with my things.'

It was the caretaker that Boniface had charmed on the day we found Julot. Middle-aged and slight, she wore a thin brown coat and flat shoes. She took off a headscarf to reveal short brown hair with clumps that stuck out in spikes, like she'd tried patting it down with wet hands and left it to dry. Fran waved her away.

'Have you had any contact with the Germans?' I asked him. 'Have they come here to see you?'

'The Boches? Why would I have any contact with the Boches?'

'I don't know, Fran, you tell me.'

'I haven't. The only dealings I've had are when they refused to let me open my place up when I came back to Paris. I've been trying to get my local *mairie* to let me open again, but they're afraid to go against what the Boches said.'

'And the Gestapo? Have they come calling?'

He made a big show of counting his testicles through his trousers. 'No. No Gestapo here, Eddie. I've still got everything I should have.' I didn't comment or react, so he'd feel the need to carry on talking. My incipient anger was like any drug I'd ever taken. Addictive and potentially self-destructive. But it was getting results. Fran was rattled and giving up answers that I was sure were as straight as anything I'd ever be likely to get out of him. 'Anyway, why would they come to see me? My club's shut. I'm not even in their gun sights.'

I heard the caretaker pottering about in the main room. I didn't let up. 'Why did you lie about Dominique?'

'Dominique? Christ, Eddie, what is this? I haven't lied about her.'

'You said you hadn't seen her for years. But you were together earlier this year.'

'All right, I saw her maybe.'

I shook my head, my anger bubbling over. 'It was more than just seeing her, though, wasn't it?'

He sat back and looked at me. A leer spread across his face. 'So that's it. You're still sweet on her.' He nodded slowly. I could have happily knocked it off his shoulders. 'Hey, I was just sparing your feelings. I knew you liked her, so I didn't want to brag about, you know, enjoying her.'

'You always could be a shit.'

I made to stand up but the caretaker came back into the room. She was carrying a tray with two cups on it.

'A lovely cup of coffee,' she announced, setting them down on the table. 'I thought you could both do with one.'

She smiled shyly, not making eye contact, and left. I breathed in the aroma of the coffee. It was real and strangely soothing. I could feel my anger seep away. I picked up my cup, unable to resist, and drank it slowly.

'So you've caught up with the lovely Dominique, have you, Eddie?' Fran asked me, his voice gentler, without any of his usual wheedling.

I shook my head. 'Joe.'

He gave a low whistle. 'How did that go? I thought you two ...'

'Why did you lie?'

'I told you, to spare your feelings. Believe me, I have no idea what's going on here, with this Julot guy and the prisoners. It's got nothing to do with me or my business. There's nothing sinister about keeping Dominique a secret from you. I just wasn't sure how you'd react. You were always a scary guy, Eddie, unpredictable. I didn't know if you'd break down if I told you about me and Dominique or shoot me.' He paused. 'Hey, how's that kid of yours? How old must he be now? Eighteen? Nineteen?'

The question took me by surprise. I thought of Jean-Luc. 'Nineteen.'

'He all right? A soldier, I heard. If there's ever anything I can do to help, you've only got to ask.'

I recalled Joe's words to me. 'Sure I will, Fran.' The sarcasm was lost on him.

'And if he is in any trouble, you can trust me to keep my mouth shut, you know that. And any help I can give you, Eddie, of course. You just say the word. These are tough times for you, I get that. They're tough times for us all.'

I could feel his voice pulling me in, its grip as strong as the coffee's. He'd always known how to score a direct hit on me.

'I don't need your help, Fran.'

He pulled an ornate wooden box out of a drawer and opened it. Inside, it was divided into smaller compartments, each one containing white powder. Cocaine. I had to tear my eyes away from the sight.

'And you can help me. You're a cop. You can put in a word, get the Boches to let me open up again.' He tapped his nose. 'I'll see you sorted.'

'Not again, Fran.' For the first time in years, I recalled the high the first time he gave me cocaine and I got up. I knew I had to leave before he wormed his way back into my head.

'Any time you want, Eddie. You know where I am. It'll be like old times.'

'I know.'

I sensed the perfume on the staircase when I got home. It had the same effect on me as it had had in Fran's club, a mix of longing and regret, only now it was tinged with the fear of Julot's lips sewn together and the vision of a doll's mouth on a story of an executioner.

Gun in hand, I tentatively opened the door to my apartment and toured the rooms. It didn't take long. Mine was not a palatial residence. A living room with two armchairs, bookshelves and a fireplace. A kitchen with two chairs, a table, a stove and a sink. My bedroom with a bed, a wardrobe and a cupboard. And a spare bedroom with much the same, along with a memory of my son's brief and difficult stay at the start of the summer. So much for the grand tour. The one thing it had going for it right now was that it was also a scent-free paradise. Whoever had worn the perfume on the landing hadn't made it past the front door.

I went into the kitchen but kept the gun to hand, visions of unease topmost in my mind. It struck me that that was precisely what the person who had killed Julot had wanted.

Rooting around in the cold box outside the kitchen window and through all the cupboards, I rustled up some tired old Brie that had reduced to mush, some green beans and a potato. I boiled up the veg and mixed it all with some old mustard and called it a cheese surprise. The surprise is that I kept it down. And I had no bread to ease the pain, thanks to Hochstetter. I drank some water from the tap to take the taste away and went into my living room.

I suppose it was inevitable, but I pulled the tin box down from the topmost bookshelf and sat down, staring at it, unopened in my lap. The scratched and faded illustration of long-forgotten biscuits on the lid danced in front of my eyes as I thought of Fran. He had been the one at a low ebb in my life who'd got me hooked on cocaine, one of the reasons I'd given up so much and lost so much in turn. I thought of him and Dominique together. Despite the distance in time, I felt a bitter pang of jealousy.

The tin felt uncomfortable on my thighs, but I couldn't put it back on its shelf. Not yet. Neither did I dare open it. The last time I had done that was when my son had been here with me, the week the Germans had entered Paris and awoken so much of what was wrong with me. Seeing my son for the first time after I'd walked out on him and his mother fifteen years earlier, for their own safety and mine, had helped put the contents of the tin to rest.

But then the words spoken by the guard at Les Tourelles had partially lifted a lid in my mind. I'd failed my son again. I'd sent Jean-Luc away from Paris, fearful of what the Germans might do if they found him, a French soldier on the run. My mind had thought of prison, of forced conscription into the German army, of execution even. I'd thought at the time I'd been doing the right thing.

The guard had told me of being sent back from Britain after evacuation at Dunkirk. Of thinking he was going to be sent to fight again, but of being demobbed instead and sent home to his family. Of getting a job and being as safe as anyone could be under Nazi rule. And I knew my son could have had the same. Once again, I'd done the wrong thing for Jean-Luc. And for me.

Steeling myself, I stood up and carefully put the tin back in its place. I hadn't opened it, one temptation I'd resisted.

At first I thought the sound was the echo of the box on the shelf, but it happened a second time. A knock on the door.

I'd left my gun on the kitchen table and went to retrieve it. At the front door, I looked through the spyhole, but the landing was in darkness. Holding the pistol by my side, I opened the door the moment I registered the aroma coming from outside. It was the perfume I'd noticed earlier.

I opened the door wider. A triangle of light quickly spread out of my small hallway, casting its glow on a figure standing outside, steadily bringing their features into view. My breath caught in my throat.

'Well, Eddie? Are you going to ask me in?'

13

Everyone had tired eyes these days.

I looked closely at my half-unexpected visitor. It wasn't just the intervening years that was the cause. It was the lack of good food, the disruption to normal life, the imperfect present and tense future that faced us. And the fear that one day our entirely predictable visitors would slowly start to turn on us far more virulently than they had so far.

'You going to offer me a drink, Eddie?'

She still had a voice that was infinitely more addictive than anything Fran could ever hope to peddle. If only he could package that in a twist of paper, he wouldn't have to live his days scurrying around the back streets of Montparnasse in search of his next main chance.

'What would you like? Water or water?'

Frankly I was drunk on her perfume.

'Make mine a water.' She smiled, a sleek panther of a gaze that enticed before pouncing.

Dominique.

A love I never had and one I hadn't seen in fifteen years. And you can make of that statement what you will.

I went to the kitchen to get us both a glass of water in my two cleanest dirty glasses and slowly returned to the living room. She had my good chair. Surprising how the few visitors who ever came calling always went for that one. I sat down in the unfamiliar grip of the other one and studied her. She drank water from a murky tumbler with the sophistication of a literary circle hostess holding a coupe of champagne. She'd been a singer back in the day, a beacon that had illuminated the sleaziest of clubs and who'd once almost threatened to enlighten my life. Only I'd managed to screw that one up too. That and the fact we'd both been married to other people at the time.

She looked curiously at her glass and set it down amid the stained rings on the low table. 'Eddie without whisky. Never thought I'd see that.'

'Just passing, were you?'

The tiredness was back in her eyes. There was something more. Her gaze alternated between feigned interest in my coffee table and a faux-amused aloofness at me.

'You've been asking after me, Eddie.'

'How do you know?'

She gave me the sort of smile you'd give to a simple child. Even that thrilled me. 'Montmartre. And jazz. Two of the tightest worlds known. That's how I know. You should remember that. So why are you wanting to see me after all this time?'

'Police business.'

This time her smile was fake disappointment. 'Story of my life.'

'Were you with Fran at Longchamp last weekend?'

The gently mocking smile was back for a moment. 'He's still using Longchamp, is he? Some things never change. Not even with the Germans here.'

'What do you mean?'

'Longchamp was Fran's seduction promise. A weekend of horses, champagne and gambling to entice you to his bedroom.'

'And it worked for him?'

She studied me. 'For a time.'

'And last weekend?'

'Not me, Eddie. One of his employees, I imagine. It was one of the job requirements of working with Fran.'

'I smelt your perfume at his club.'

She shook her head slowly. 'Again, not me.'

'I remembered it from before. It was always your perfume.'

'That's very flattering, Eddie. But I'm afraid it's not exclusive to me. Fran buys it for all his conquests. He has a friend who supplies it.'

'Even all those years ago?'

'No. It was my wearing it that gave him the idea. You know Fran. He leeches off others.'

'But you were still with him. A few months ago. You were seen.'

'"You were seen"? Christ, Eddie, could you sound any more like a cop? Or a jealous ex-lover?'

That stung. I drank my water to hide it and recoiled. My mind had led me to expect whisky. That stung a second time.

'So who was I seen by?' The playful flutter at the edges of her mouth was back.

I hesitated before answering. 'Joe.'

She looked shocked. 'Joe? You saw Joe?'

'He's been interned.'

'I know. I just never thought you'd have the nerve to see him again. Not after what you did. Did he see you?'

'He did.'

She took a sip of water to compose herself. 'God, I wish this was whisky. OK, so I was seen. And that's why Fran stopped seeing me when the Germans showed up. I don't think he was too comfortable being seen, as you call it, with an African woman. Saved me the hassle of telling him to get lost.'

'But you were still at his club the other day.'

She grinned. 'Not falling for it, Eddie. I told you, it wasn't me.'

She didn't falter, but something didn't gel. Somewhere in her words, she was lying. I just didn't know where.

'So if you're not here to confess to anything, and I don't think you suddenly had an urge to pay me a social call, what is it you want from me, Dominique?'

'Always the cop, Eddie.' Despite her flippancy, her voice gave an emotion away. A fear. I thought it was going to be about Julot. I was right that she'd been lying to me. I was wrong about Julot.

'My son. You remember him?'

'Your son? I know you had one. I never met him, remember.' I recalled that he was about a year or so older than Jean-Luc. I scoured my memory for a name but none came.

'Fabrice.' She helped me out. 'He's a soldier now.'

I felt a moment's sadness. 'Aren't they all?'

She carried on like she hadn't heard. 'With the Tirailleurs Sénégalais. The 24th Regiment. The last I heard from him was in April – he was stationed on the Maginot Line – but I know from parents of other soldiers that his regiment was fighting the Germans around the Somme after that, in early June.'

The Somme. Echoes of the past. 'Why are you telling me this?'

'He's missing.'

Her eyes were suddenly red, the tears not far away, but she visibly steeled herself. The Dominique I remembered always had to stay in control, keep calm no matter what. I thought of my own son and knew the need to close off parts of my mind, to slow down the fears, the need not to dwell. I saw the same in her now.

'Has he been taken prisoner?'

'It's been three months, Eddie. The German authorities have released the names of prisoners. Fabrice's name isn't among them.'

'They won't have released all the names. I know how long this takes, how much confusion there is.'

She looked angrily at me. 'His name isn't among the captured. He's not a prisoner.'

'So what do you want me to do about it?' There was another obvious option, but she wouldn't want to hear that. She would have thought of it too. A lot of dead soldiers were still missing.

'I want you to find out what happened to him.'

'There's nothing I can do, Dominique. You need to talk to the military.'

'You think I haven't tried.'

'I'm just a cop. I can't do anything.'

'Can't or won't?'

'Come on, Dominique. This is nothing to do with me. He's a missing soldier. One of thousands. He's another victim of war.'

She stood up and shouted my words back at me. 'Victim of war? I thought you were the only victim of war, Eddie. The only one ever to have existed. You always behaved like you were.'

'Please sit down. I'm sorry.'

She walked towards the door.

'Sorry? You'd be able to do something if it were your son.'

She slammed the door as she left. The echo of it reverberated around my head. I stared at the corridor after her.

'I can't do anything for my own son, either,' I murmured into the empty hallway.

14

'Lying on the book?' Boniface asked.

We were sitting in my office, the doll on the desk between us. He picked it up again and examined it. I'd already had it checked for fingerprints. It had been clean. Turning it over and over in his hands, he stared at it intently. I'd explained to him what I'd found out about Capeluche and about the doll being left for me. He put it back down.

'City executioner,' he repeated.

'The problem now is that since the real Capeluche took prisoners out of prison and executed them, is that what we're dealing with?'

'We'd thought of that,' he reminded me. 'Julot's dead, we can't find Walter or the prisoner in Montmartre I put away. Are they being released to be killed?'

'Still doesn't make much sense. Why go to all that trouble just to kill them?'

'Or one of them is the executioner. Capeluche. Walter or any of the others released. And he's then killing the others.' He shook his head. 'But that still doesn't make any sense.'

I had to agree with him. 'The problem being that we now don't know if Walter is missing because he's a victim or a suspect. Or neither.'

Boniface nodded at the typed list of some thirty names of missing prisoners that we'd drawn up. 'That goes for all of them. So what do we do now?'

'We go to Montparnasse,' I told him.

'Why Montparnasse? I thought we were seeing this as Paris-wide. Not a local gang thing.'

'We are. And I still think something bigger is going on than Julot getting himself tortured and killed in a sleazy jazz club in Montparnasse. But I also think the whole Fresnes and are-the-Germans-involved thing has become a diversion. It's stopping us from paying enough attention to the basics. The specific Montparnasse aspect of the murder and the disappearances.'

'Get the smaller picture to see the bigger picture, in other words.'

'Exactly. And we're unlikely to see the bigger picture if we just keep going at it like this. We need to break it down and find a chink in the armour.'

'And you reckon Montparnasse will give us that?'

'We've tried looking for Walter and others in Montmartre and drawn a blank. I say we now try Montparnasse. And Calais Jacques. Look at the names on the list. There has to be a weak link somewhere, and Calais Jacques would be my choice.'

He looked out of the window and back at me. I could see he got the connection. 'Calais Jacques is a Montparnasse boy.'

'If he's out of Fresnes, the most likely place he'd go would be his old stamping ground. That's where he'll have friends, where he operates. We know his usual haunts. Nothing happens in Montparnasse without Jacques knowing. We find him, we stand a chance of getting a toe in the door of finding out what it is that's going on across the city.'

'Makes sense.'

'I know it does. Get your car.'

I let him talk and drive. I was learning not to listen. I found I could blot him out for the moments I spent cooped up with his incessant blather. It was a lot like the way Parisians viewed the Germans. Because they didn't view them. They didn't see them. Out of the car window, I watched a middle-aged couple walk past three Wehrmacht officers on the pavement. Their ignorance of the soldiers was total. They'd have paid more attention to a dead rat on the ground than they did to the three tall men. I saw it everywhere. It was a sort of absurd refusal. A denial that we'd lost and that the city was occupied by foreign troops. If you didn't look at them, they weren't there. Only they were.

Switching off from the chatter that echoed like twisting the dial on a radio, I could concentrate on other things. Oddly, the steady flow of white noise underlying all the other sounds helped me focus.

Calais Jacques. He was called that because he was from Calais and his name was Jacques. There were times when the Paris underworld's talent for colourful nicknames failed it. Thickset and bluff, with arms hairier than the cheese in a Montparnasse café, Calais Jacques was an enforcer. For a brief moment, I'd wondered if he could have been behind Julot's death, but I'd dismissed the idea immediately. Such an imaginative punishment would never have occurred to our Jacques – he was the classic knuckleduster and hit-people-with-a-big-stick sort of a villain. Besides, his blunt fingers would never have been able to thread the needle. Although he might have been one of the gang helping subdue Julot while someone else did it.

The drone stopped and with it the car engine. I checked to see where we were. Boniface had parked to the west of the cemetery, on Rue de la Gaité, near the Bobino music hall. I'd seen a young kid, Édith Piaf, sing here not long before the war had started. She was good. She could sing a song as powerfully as Josephine Baker could. And Dominique. I was surprised that that last thought had strayed into my mind. It seemed a lifetime ago.

'You take north of Boulevard du Montparnasse,' I told Boniface. 'I'll take these streets.'

'You reckon it's safe to split up?'

Safer on my ears, I thought. 'Quicker,' I told him.

He set off along the street, which had been a home to theatres and music halls for years in the *années folles* of the 1920s. I decided to take my chances on the street I was on and up as far as the old Vavin crossroads, where the artists and writers had settled in the twenties and thirties. They weren't there now. Cocteau had once said poverty was a luxury in Montparnasse. Cocteau was an optimist. The area had gone badly downhill since those heady days.

I sensed a presence the moment Boniface disappeared from view. Scanning the street around me, I headed for the Rue Delambre, knowing a few places where Calais Jacques could normally be found. Someone was following me, of that I was certain, but every time I stopped or waited in a doorway, no one appeared. I thought of Boniface and his fog. I could see what he'd been getting at.

I double-checked everyone I saw, in case they were appearing more than once in my peripheral vision. A line of women were still queuing outside a baker in vain. An elderly couple stood in their midst, slighter, smaller than the rest, a product of another age of shortages. Two schoolkids on bikes raced along the road, late for class or bunking off school.

At the top of the street, a German patrol car went past, two feldwebels in the rear like low-grade officers being cavalcaded around the city. The two gefreiters in front, snot-nosed privates fresh out of shorts, looked bored and miserable in the cold air.

There were no French cars, not even the ones with the precarious top hat of gas cylinders on the roof that were popping up on the streets since petrol had become so scarce. We'd become a city of walkers and cyclists.

I heard a child singing.

It stopped me where I stood. It was the song I'd heard in Montmartre. I looked all around me. I half-expected to see the cadaverous child from the day before, but he wasn't to be seen. I turned a full three hundred and sixty degrees, searching for the source of the singing, but it receded and approached constantly as I spun.

'Come out,' I shouted.

The singing stopped.

The silence was worse. If I'd had no idea where the sound was coming from before, I had even less now. I instantly felt exposed. I could almost sense a rifle pointing at me. I looked up and around, but there was no one at a window, no one in a doorway.

I carried on to where I was heading, but the moment I reached the end of the street, the singing started again. It was from my right. I followed the road, tracking the cemetery wall. The song was louder. I could make out the words more clearly. Moving along, I realised it was coming from the other side of the wall. Whoever was singing was in the cemetery.

Hurrying along the road, I got to the main gate and ran in. A silence hit me, more powerful and foreboding than the endless, horrible moment in the trenches when the artillery stopped and the order to charge was about to be given. It brought me to a standstill. Ahead of me lay avenues amid the ornate tombs and I had no idea which direction I was to take.

Pulling my gun, I turned along one of the paths that ran under the trees between the huge rectangular islands of graves and mausoleums and slowly made my way to the east side of the cemetery. A noise to my left startled me and I raised my gun. An elderly man stood in front of me, a small bunch of flowers in his hand and tears in his eyes. He looked suddenly afraid, shocked out of his grief.

'I'm sorry,' I told him.

Leaving him behind, I carried on my way. I got to the far wall without hearing a sound. Not knowing what to do, I re-traced my steps. Cutting in among the gravestones, I walked through them, some of them taller than me and capable of hiding anyone, but I heard nothing.

I headed for the central part of the cemetery and the Genius of Eternal Sleep statue. Crossing the circle of grass, I stood on the middle and scanned the rows of stones and trees, listening.

I heard it. Finally. Borne on a low breeze. The song.

It was leading me away from where I'd first heard it, growing louder. I broke into a trot and then a run, my head darting this way and that to hunt for the source. At last, it was ahead of me. A stone scraped on a paving stone to the right of me. I turned towards it, but another sound of twigs snapping to the left brought me back. The trees around me joined in, moaning quietly as the wind picked up. I revolved on my own axis again, unable to pinpoint a sound that would tell me who or what I was supposed to be following and where.

Stopping, I took a deep breath. The sweat coursed down my face and back and chest. I could feel the heat come off me.

'Where are you?' I shouted.

It felt wrong among the dead.

'Where are you?' I repeated, this time a whisper.

Ahead of me, distant, the song began. I ran towards it and found myself racing along a dead-end path towards the wall where it met Rue Émile Richard. If my persecutor was there, he wouldn't have a way out, I realised with a sense of triumph. I picked up speed and came to the wall just as the song came to an end. I was by the cenotaph to Baudelaire. I revolved first one way, then the other, but there wasn't a single person apart from me standing among the dead.

More slowly now, I searched. The monument to the poet loomed in front of me. The creator of 'The Flowers of Evil' and translator of Edgar Allan Poe had a cenotaph that was in keeping with the man. An unsettling stone mummy over an empty tomb that lay at the foot of another yet more disturbing figure standing at a right angle to it, almost hovering over it. Supposedly a pillar, the second figure resembled an elongated demonic skeleton, evil angel wings folded either side, ready for flight. At the top, a figure of a man emerged from the stone to stare down at you, his chin resting on his clenched fists, his eyes probing. It had always been controversial. The tomb was empty as Baudelaire was buried in a family plot on the other side of the cemetery, supposedly against his wishes.

I noticed that the leaves that had fallen to the cenotaph had been brushed off the stone mummy. They lay in small heaps to either side and at the foot of it. Concentrating more on the reclining figure itself, I saw a pair of objects placed on the mummy's chest, like offerings. Approaching cautiously, all the while glancing to the right and left, I saw what had been left on the monument. My breath caught in my throat.

Lying side by side and glinting sharply in the meagre sun was a large needle and a length of twine, the same type that had been used to kill Julot.

The one raven left in Paris crowed from a nearby tree.

15

I thought the twine and the needle were supposed to be message enough, but by the time I was approaching the gate leading out of the cemetery, I already had the sensation of being watched again. For an agonising moment, I thought that I could hear the song once more, but it was simply the breeze washing through the trees surrounding me. Stopping by Saint-Saëns' tomb, I listened out, straining to hear any voice under the sound of the trees. I rotated again, like I had before, but I saw no one, just the crouched figure of an elderly lady in the distance picking her way carefully through the tombs.

A Peugeot 202 with German military plates was parked outside the cemetery, some metres from the entrance. Idling at first, the engine was turned off, but the doors remained closed. Warily, I watched it. This wasn't the area I'd have expected our visitors to be frequenting. Unless, they had a burning desire to see more French graves.

'Édouard, you look pale.'

The voice startled me and I jumped, despite myself. Without realising, I'd been focusing so much on the car that I hadn't spotted Hochstetter sitting on a bench outside the gate.

'So you've taken to meeting me on benches, now?' I couldn't keep the annoyance out of my voice.

He smirked and patted the seat next to him. 'You look like you've seen a ghost.'

Pausing a moment, I sat down. I looked at my hands in my lap. They were still trembling slightly from my guided mystery tour of the cemetery. I placed them either side of my thighs to try and hide the sight from Hochstetter.

'So how did you know I was here?'

'I have people keeping an eye on you. You know I do.'

'Any reason in particular you're having me followed?'

'No. Should there be? And before you object, it's for your own safety.'

'Who from?'

'Yourself, mostly.'

'Now who's being droll?'

'I'm simply being pragmatic. I'm a very busy man, I don't have the time to train another French police officer.'

'You think I'm trained?'

'You think you're not?'

We stared in silence for a few moments at the few cars going past. The city had filled, but the fuel tanks hadn't. Petrol was scarce, and so many French cars had been requisitioned by the Occupiers anyway.

'So is this carrot or stick?' I asked him.

'I'm simply here to look after your best interests. So please ask for anything you want.'

'There is one thing you can help me with. You've been sitting here waiting for me. Did you see anyone coming out of the cemetery just before I did?'

He lit a cigarette, wafting the match to extinguish it before dropping it to one side. He was meticulous in every movement. It was a timely reminder that he left nothing to chance, missed nothing.

'Intriguing. But no, I'm afraid I saw no one.'

I hadn't expected him to. Whoever had been taunting me was possibly still inside the park or, more likely, had left through another entrance. A French car with new German plates, showing it had been commandeered, went past, the tyres swooshing through the fallen leaves.

'So why are you here really?'

He slowly inhaled on his cigarette before delicately tapping the ash onto the ground. I was suddenly irritated by the way he used it to delay speaking, to make me wait and wonder what he was about to say. It was the most absolute display of his superiority.

'You evidently remember our little discussion regarding the carrot and the stick. And the need for you to work with me. My being here is just a little reminder. Take your sidearm, for instance. The French police are allowed them to maintain that control, but in strictly regulated quantity. Were you to lose that right to hold a gun, your effectiveness would be severely limited.'

'Are we talking us in general or me in particular?'

'Oh, you in particular, Édouard. If I feel I don't get a commensurate level of cooperation from you, it is in my gift to have your right to carry a gun removed. You might do well to remember that.'

I looked away a moment to hide my anger. 'So which of my investigations is it that you're interested in? Because that's what this is about.'

'All of them. None of them in particular. That is for you to decide. Remember, I'm here to help. Your Marshal Pétain said there was to be collaboration between our two nations. You can see it as our collaboration.'

I chose my words. 'I will tell you everything that I know will help with my investigations.'

'Very good, Édouard, you're coming along just fine. We will make a Pétain of you yet. Collaboration.' He rolled the word around his tongue. I was already disliking it intensely. 'A curious term. Vichy is a temporary solution, I'm afraid. A way of relieving the strain on our own resources by placing our trust in a people we have subjugated. Our lack of manpower makes this idea of collaboration a necessity. But it is curious to what extent the subjugated people will accept that. Take our relationship. We are cordial enough, but it is not a frictionless relationship. That is why it is imperative to gain your cooperation – which is, perhaps, a more pleasing word – so that you are strong enough to maintain control over your countrymen, but not so strong that you pose a threat.'

I was spared having to reply by a man walking towards us along the pavement. He was carrying two fishing rods over his shoulder. On edge, I tensed but immediately relaxed. I watched the man, a thin middle-aged guy in trousers and a grey cardigan showing through an old overcoat, but he kept his face averted from us. Hochstetter stared at him idly as he went past.

'He's a long way from the Seine, wouldn't you say?' he asked me.

'It's a bit of a walk,' I agreed.

'I must say I have seen a few fishermen recently. It does seem to me to be rather optimistic to try and catch fish that would be edible in your Paris river.'

I looked at Hochstetter as he spoke, but there was no hint of understanding in his eyes, just a faint smirk at the oddity of the French. Looking past him, my gaze followed the two fishing rods swaying as they receded into the distance. My companion had lost interest in them completely. I looked down and hid a smile, my first that day. Two fishing rods. Our word for a rod was a *gaule*. Two fishing rods were *deux gaules*, which sounded a lot like De Gaulle. They weren't fishermen on their way to the river. They were a silent protest, a display of support for De Gaulle in London and his calls to resist the Occupier. Cocking a snook at the Germans right under their noses. And if Hochstetter was anything to go by, they hadn't yet sussed what it was all about.

'It's about political freedom.'

His words shocked me. Had he worked it out? 'What is?'

'*Fidelio*. Beethoven's only opera.'

I felt a sense of relief that he hadn't got the meaning of the fishing rods. It showed he was fallible. 'Either you are the least self-aware colonialists in history, or someone at the opera house has a very dark sense of humour.'

He flicked the end of his cigarette into a puddle, where it quickly fizzled out.

'And political prisoners.'

I let his words sink in.

'There is one thing you can help me with,' I told him. 'An American. A musician. He's been interned.'

'And how do you think I can help?'

'Pull some strings. Get him released, so he can go home.'

For a brief moment, I imagined the idea of Joe wanting to go home and almost laughed. The Joe I knew would have been joining in with the fishing-rod man. And more. Especially after the experience of internment.

'This is a jazz musician, I take it. Am I to assume, then, that he's also a black American musician? Because if that is the case, I really wouldn't waste your time or mine trying to help. I doubt there's little that either of us can do to remedy the situation.'

'He's American. A neutral.'

'I'm afraid that's not what our friends in the Nazi party see when they look at him.' He got up, his audience with me at an end. 'You really are going to have to learn to choose the battles you intend to fight.'

'I don't choose my battles, they tend to choose me.'

He laughed and started to walk away. 'That is so predictably true.'

From the bench, I watched a plain-clothes agent get out and open the Peugeot door for Hochstetter to get in. It drove off, sending the leaves in its wake swirling an autumn wake in the road.

'But I choose how I fight them,' I added.

16

When I got back to Rue de la Gaité, Boniface was embracing a short blonde woman in high heels that made her almost as tall as he was. As I watched, they planted a big kiss on each other's lips before he finally put her down. She turned to wave at him as she hurried away along the narrow pavement. I walked up behind him and tapped him on the shoulder.

'So what the hell was that all about?'

He made to wink but thought better of it. I had hopes he'd found a cure. It still didn't quell my annoyance. Without a word, he beckoned me over to the car and indicated that I should get in.

'Got some news, Eddie,' he told me.

'You've got an erection?' I asked him. 'You've found yourself another wife? What the hell do you think you're playing at? You're supposed to be looking for Calais Jacques.'

'Police work.' He tapped the side of his nose. I got an urge to tap him there too, just a bit harder.

'I think your idea of police work differs from mine.'

'That,' he said, gesturing along the street in the same direction as the woman had disappeared, 'was Mireille Gourdon. She's one of Calais Jacques' ex-girlfriends.'

'That still doesn't mean you had to kiss her.'

'Whatever it takes, Eddie, whatever it takes.'

'So what's the news?'

'She says Jacques has been around the neighbourhood. The difference is he was spending money big-time. In the clubs, on clothes, jewellery. The sort of money he's never had before.'

'Where does she say he's getting it from?'

'Drugs. Dealing in them, she reckons. Selling them in the clubs the Boches have allowed to stay open.'

'Drugs? Jacques has never dealt in drugs in his life. He's an enforcer. He might work for others selling drugs, but he's never been part of selling them.'

'That's what she says. He's the one doing the dealing. Not alone, either, although she wouldn't say who he's working with. I don't think she knew who it was, but I can't be sure.'

Another one with money to burn, I thought. Exactly the same as Sophie Scipone had told me about Walter le Ricaneur.

'We need to know where all this newfound money is coming from.'

'She thinks he's enforcing too. Protection.'

'That sounds more like the Jacques I know. Does she say who for?'

He shook his head. 'Doesn't know or won't say. That's when people start to clam up. Whoever it is has got people scared.'

I said it was time we left, but he shook his head a second time and carried on talking. 'I've got other news. Walter le Ricaneur. He has an ex-wife. Here in Montparnasse.'

'Have you found her?'

'I haven't looked for her yet.'

His answer irritated me again. 'Of course not. You were too busy munching on the mouth of Jacques' ex-girlfriend. Instead of that, go and find her, see what she has to say. For Christ's sake, Boniface, get a grip.'

'That's not the news. The news is that she left Walter after she had an affair with someone else. Your friend, Poquelin.'

'Poquelin?' It was a moment before I realised he was referring to Fran. Another Lothario for me to get angry with.

'Still want me to look for Walter's ex-wife?'

'Yes, I do. But first you can drive me over to the other side of the cemetery. I'll go and see Poquelin.'

He shrugged and started the car. 'Sure. But it's pretty strange that you never seem to want anyone with you when you question this Poquelin guy.'

I calmed myself a moment before answering.

'Just drive. And learn when to shut up.'

'Why didn't you tell me you had an affair?'

'Christ, Eddie.' Fran poured himself a glass of unlabelled whisky. He didn't offer me one. Beneath his nose, a tell-tale sprinkle of white powder clung to the bristles he'd missed when shaving. 'I didn't think it was important, all right?'

'You had an affair with the wife of a criminal and you didn't think it was worth mentioning?'

'He's dead. I didn't think it mattered.'

'What do you mean, he's dead?'

I thought of Walter going missing and my mind raced. Calais Jacques too. Both of them fallen out of sight.

Fran looked mystified. 'You know he's dead. You found him.' He patted the arms of his chair. 'Here, in this chair.'

I was stunned. 'Julot? You had an affair with Julot's wife?'

'Isn't that who you meant?'

'Hell, Fran, I meant Walter le Ricaneur. How many other gangsters' wives have you been screwing?'

He took a long drink of the whisky and coughed. 'It's no big deal, Eddie. I own a jazz club, I take my pick of the women I want. It's just part of the scene.'

'And what do their husbands have to say about it? More precisely, Julot. Did he see it as just part of the scene?'

'You've got it all wrong, Eddie. I had a fling with Julot's wife years ago. They weren't even together. He was in prison.'

'Is that why Julot was killed? He was getting heavy when he got out of Fresnes?'

'Now hold on.' He patted the chair again. 'This was nothing to do with me. OK, I had his wife, but I never met the guy. It was years ago. If he'd been that worried, he'd have come looking for me way back.'

I studied his face. Even through the fug in his eyes, he seemed genuine. Nothing like a liar aggrieved of being accused the one time they're telling the truth. 'So what about Walter's wife?'

'What about her? I had her when her old man was in prison. If you don't want your wife messing around, don't get caught. That's the moral I see.'

'I love the word "moral" on your lips.' I had to admit to myself that there were years of resentment at Fran's part in my troubled past that hadn't gone away. 'Do any of these women have names to you?'

'I got morals, Eddie. Take this Julot's death. If I ever find who did it, I wouldn't sew their lips together. I'd stitch their fucking hands tight so they could pray when I did to them what they did to this guy. It's ruining what business I've got left.'

'Yeah, I guess you're right, Fran. You've got morals all right.'

He saw through the sarcasm. 'You're not one to lecture me.'

I reached over and drank from Fran's glass. I saw why I'd abstained in the past. It would have melted the moustache off Adolf. It served to calm us both, though, which is what I wanted.

'So why do you think Julot was killed here, Fran? And not you? Was it a warning to you?'

'I told you I don't know.'

'I know you did, but I don't believe you. Who've you been getting on the wrong side of? Why's your club not been allowed to reopen? There's something going on here that you're not telling me.'

The door to the office banged open and a young woman walked in. She looked startled to see me.

'Hi, Jean,' she greeted Fran. 'Who's your friend?'

'This is Eddie, Paulette. He's an old friend.' He looked pointedly at her. 'A cop.'

'Nice to meet you, Eddie,' she said in a tone that said otherwise.

She had a voice that sounded like gravel being scraped over sandpaper. But that evidently wasn't what Fran sought in her. She was tall and willowy, with long legs encased in a tight blue dress and a gentle face that was at odds with the sounds that came from her mouth. She could have done a whole lot better for herself.

She sat down on Fran's lap and they started kissing. It made Boniface's earlier effort with Mireille look like a schoolboy kissing a dusty old great-aunt. The sounds coming from Paulette's mouth were even less enticing than the original ones. Fran tore himself away and leered at me.

'Ain't she sweet, Eddie? Want to join in?'

He pushed Paulette's thighs apart. She smiled at me and beckoned with a long-nailed finger.

'No thanks,' I told them.

I got up and left them to their meal.

I watched Paulette's bright red nails dig into Fran's cheek.

But there was one other thing I noticed about her. Something

I registered the moment she walked in and that overrode everything else about her.

And it was the reason there was someone else I had to go back and talk to.

17

Boniface and I had one other place to call on in Montparnasse, but that was the following night. And it almost made Fran's club look like the bar at the Ritz.

'I like what you've done with the place, Luigi,' I told the owner.

With a face hidden behind a massive moustache and a nose that pointed in several directions at once, Luigi had left his native Naples after getting into trouble with not just the city's cops but its gangs too. For a break, he'd come to Paris and carried on where he'd left off at home, getting on the wrong side of their Parisian counterparts.

With a grimace and a grim warning not to do any damage, he'd pulled aside the thick black curtain behind the door and reluctantly let us in.

'This is Boniface,' I'd told him. 'He's a little more house-trained than I am, but don't let that fool you.'

'Please, Eddie, I swear, don't cause any problems. I don't need it.'

The world before us opened up into a darkened bar full of pimps, prostitutes, criminals and German soldiers. Two gefreiters in the corner were fighting over some slight while others looked on and encouraged them.

'Worried we'll give the place a bad name, Luigi?'

He led us to the bar, as far away from other punters as possible, and installed us in our own little corner of heaven out of sight of disreputable company. He needn't have worried. His French patrons all knew us and sidled away as stealthily as they could.

'Some place,' Boniface muttered. It was his first time.

I hadn't been back since the early days of the Occupation. Then, the bar had been the chosen hotspot for the officer classes, but they'd obviously moved on to fresher pastures. Luigi's was now firmly the domain of the lower ranks. Instead of majors and hauptmanns discussing the finer points of Lohengrin and blitzkrieg, earthy feldwebels and strutting stabsgefreiters mingled with the crème de la crème of Montparnasse low society and did deals for perfunctory sex and other less licit pleasures. These weren't the model soldiers the city saw on the street during daylight hours.

Luigi flicked a tea towel ineffectually at the grime of the counter and served us both a red wine. From the good cupboard, as I'd insisted, not the Occupation brew concocted in Satan's bowels. I took a drink. It was almost worth putting up with the surroundings for. I put my glass down and spoke to Luigi.

'Go and get Pepe for me.'

He looked mystified. 'Pepe? I haven't seen him for months. He doesn't come here anymore.'

I looked frankly at a point above his jigsaw nose and between his dark bagatelle eyes. 'Go and get Pepe for me. I won't ask a third time.'

Sniffing, he walked off and came back a few minutes later. He was alone.

'Pepe asks if you can see him at the back of the bar.' Luigi shrugged sheepishly. 'He's got his reputation to worry about.'

I glanced at Boniface and we picked up our glasses. Police work was police work but good wine under an Occupation was something to be cherished. We walked through a waxworks of averted heads to a small room at the back of the bar.

'Thanks for seeing me here, Eddie.'

'No problem, Pepe. Hearing you worry about your reputation has been the first thing to cheer me up all day.'

He smiled at that. Some people really don't get it. A scrappy little figure to begin with, Pepe had certainly not filled out on rationed food. Not that I imagined he paid much attention to the idea of ration tickets and allocated bakers. He still wore the same and probably unwashed uniform of wing-collared shirt and black tie over trousers in a coarse workman's fabric. He normally wore a cap at a carefully jaunty angle, but he'd removed it for the evening's social gathering. He was bald underneath. I don't think I'd ever known that. A lookout for street gamblers, he was on the edges of the city's underworld, but he occasionally came good with the information he sold me in exchange for a few francs and not getting arrested.

I introduced Boniface. 'He's a nasty bastard, not the sweetness and light you see in me, so careful how you go with him.'

To his credit, Boniface turned on the bored killer stare for Pepe's benefit.

'What is it you want to know, Eddie? I don't know much.'

'I know, Pepe, but you're all I've got. Calais Jacques.'

He looked like he'd been poked with a cattle prod.

'I haven't seen him.'

I rocked my head from side to side. 'Now, you see, you said that much too quickly. So, let's just get past all the crappy bits where you deny everything and I tell you I'm going to arrest you and you deny some more and I threaten you with violence and you deny a bit more still, so I offer to pull your balls off, and we get to where you tell me what it is I want to know and we can all enjoy the rest of this pleasant soirée. What do you say?'

'He hasn't been in here, Eddie. I haven't seen him.'

I took one step closer. 'You see, Pepe, we've been told that Jacques has been throwing the money around as well as himself. And for one of those reasons or the other, you're bound to have come across him in the last few weeks. So let's try again. Where is Calais Jacques?'

You could always tell with Pepe when he was looking for an easy answer he could give you to avoid a more difficult one. It was like a little whirring that was audible outside his head.

'He's been in. But not for a couple of weeks at least. He had lots of cash.'

'I just told you that. Give me more.'

His eyes darted from side to side and suddenly he looked scared. 'Please don't ask me, Eddie. I only know what I've just told you.'

I picked up the end of his thin tie and pulled on it. It tightened around his throat. His gaunt face began to turn red and his eyes bulged in growing panic. 'Try and know a bit more.'

'He's been selling drugs for someone. I don't know who, Eddie, I swear, but it's big.'

I loosened his tie a little and he sucked air into his lungs. 'Is it another gang? Is someone else moving into Montparnasse?'

For once, he looked thoughtful. 'Yes, but no. I haven't heard of any gangs from other parts of town getting stronger. Or of any new gangs. I don't know what it is, you have to believe me. And it's not just happening here. It's all over. Belleville, Montmartre, Ménilmontant. It's big, Eddie, bigger than anything I've seen.'

I loosened his tie completely and smartened it up. Looking longingly at the good wine in my glass, I handed it over to him. 'You've done well, Pepe. But I'll need to know more. Keep your eyes and ears open. Do you know anything about Julot's killing?'

He handed the wine back untouched. 'No, Eddie, don't ask. I really know nothing about that. It's got everybody spooked. No one knows what's going on with that.'

'Have you ever heard of a killer sewing victims' lips together before?'

'Never.'

I nodded. Neither had I. 'If you do hear anything, you know what to do.'

We were interrupted by a couple of German NCOs walking in on us.

'You can go now,' the bigger of the two told us. 'We need this place.'

I stood in front of him. 'We're just finishing. What do you need it for? I might be able to help.'

He laughed and showed me what looked like a shotgun cartridge. He pulled the top off to reveal round disks inside. 'Maybe you want to buy.'

'Not me,' I told him.

His friend tapped him on the shoulder and signalled that they should leave.

'Come and see me if you do,' the first one told me before they left.

I watched the pair walk up to a group of three pimps at a table and I turned back to Pepe.

'What was that about? What was in the tube?'

'Vitamins, I think.'

'Vitamins? Right.'

'That's what I've been told.'

I waggled my finger at him. 'You know what to do if you hear anything, Pepe. Understood?'

He nodded and Boniface and I went back to our place at the bar to finish our drinks. The spot was empty, like we'd tainted it and no one would stand there. Boniface was silent for once. I turned to him.

'I know I'm going to regret this, but what is it?'

'I've never seen you like that before. The way you were with the little guy. And the German. You were always famous at Thirty-Six for being calm, unworried. A bit of a pushover even, according to some people. Why's that, Eddie? Why the change?'

'The Germans came to town. The rules changed.'

'Except the older cops. They reckon you weren't as easy-going as you made out.'

'You do like to talk, don't you? I was a young cop once, I was vigorous. Then I got older, that's all.'

'And now with the Boches in town, you've got young again.'

'Something like that.'

Except that wasn't the case either, I had to admit. This was a version of myself that had always been there. I'd just suppressed it. There were times I worried it was the real me, not the calm old Eddie most people thought they knew, but an unpredictable creation, even to myself. I'd been forged in the last war. In the trenches and in a German prison camp. Moulded in the political extremes and the robust responses to them of the thirties and the choices I'd taken that had hurt others almost as much as they'd hurt me. And now, to survive Hochstetter and the Gestapo and the Occupation, I was having to let the old version loose again. I didn't necessarily like it, but I didn't see any other choice.

'Drink up,' I told him. 'I've had enough of this place.'

*

The next day, I went calling. On the Gestapo. There are times you get these ideas that turn out never to be as good as you think they are.

And while we're on the subject, I've no doubt that Hochstetter would have corrected me when I said Gestapo. To them, they were the SD or the SiPo or the RSHA or the Gestapo or whatever names and initials they wanted to give themselves. But to us, to the French who had to put up with them, they were all the Gestapo. Ultimately, one thug with a swastika looks much the same as any other thug with a swastika.

The last time I'd had dealings with them, they were at the Hotel du Louvre. They weren't supposed to be there. They weren't even supposed to be in Paris, since Adolf had listened to the Wehrmacht and forbade them from coming to the party, but they'd gatecrashed in a couple of jeeps and found themselves a place to stay. And stay they had.

Now, they'd gone even higher up in the world than the sumptuous Hotel du Louvre and found a place to park their Aryan arses on Avenue Foch. Except that wasn't really the Gestapo, but the SD. As I said, they all looked the same to me. And since the address I got for the Gestapo was on Rue des Saussaies, that's where I went.

'French police,' I announced myself at the door. 'Liaising with the German authorities.'

It worked. They let me in. I almost wished it hadn't, but if you're going to shake a few branches, you have to expect one or two to fall on you.

There were two men in the entrance talking when I was shown in. From the shiny bits and bobs on their uniforms and the deference paid to them by the officer who'd invited me in, they were obviously on the top of the mountain, pissing down on those below. Instinctively I turned to the older of the two, a powerful-looking man in his mid-fifties, especially since it was him that my host approached.

'What is it about?' he asked me. We moved no further than the lobby, which was a relief.

'I'm here to request a list of the French prisoners that have been released from Fresnes prison.'

He looked mystified. 'That is a matter for your French police. Or a French judge. Ask them.'

'I mean the prisoners who have been released prematurely. Without our participation.'

The younger one, also tall, and clean-cut with hair swept back from his forehead and temples and a hard line for a mouth, joined in. I figured I might get more out of him. Which only goes to show.

'What prisoners?' he asked.

'The prisoners whose early release the Gestapo authorised. I've been sent here by my superiors for a complete list of those released.'

He shook his head in disbelief and looked quizzically at the first man.

'I have already said that we have no idea what this is about,' the older one repeated.

'I suggest you take this matter back to your superiors,' the young one added.

'You can confirm that prisoners were released on your orders, though?' I insisted.

'What is your name?' the older one asked. He held out his hand for my ID, so I had no choice but to hand it over. 'Inspector Giral,' he read. He nodded to the officer on the door, who made a note of my name.

'You are labouring under a misapprehension, Inspector Giral,' the young one told me. Without another look at me, he began to walk towards the staircase and spoke to the officer who'd opened the door to me. 'Remove him.'

Which is not what you want to hear from the Gestapo. But he just meant to have me ejected, which was the second relief in as many minutes.

Outside, I walked quickly to the end of the street and stopped. I leaned against a wall and shook. I knew when to be afraid, and the two men in uniforms in the hallway made me feel almost as scared as a length of twine and a needle had. I gathered myself and carried on to retrieve my car.

'You've done it now,' I told myself. 'All that's left is to see how they react.'

As I said, there are some things you think afterwards might not have been as good an idea as you'd first thought.

18

Probably the one good idea I had that day was not to mention my visit to the Gestapo to Dax. I don't think he would have got it. I was still trying to understand why I'd done it myself.

We were sitting at the small dining table in his apartment on the Right Bank. It was a rather more luxurious place than mine. I still wondered if it was entirely the fruits of an honest career. There was a bottle of whisky on the table and two glasses, another gift from Hochstetter. When Dax went for a pee, I picked the bottle up to look at the label. It was good stuff. A stamp on the bottom-right corner of the label with the imperial eagle and some other abstract symbol told me it was the property of some semi-official German company. They all were. The city had been inundated with businesses coming in, borne on the tide of the military success, here to make a killing of a different sort. Official and semi-official central buying offices snapping up everything we had to offer at cut-price rates. And it was all going back to the Reich. All the money and all the products we could no longer find for ourselves or were banned from having. The Germans had set an exchange rate of one Reichsmark to twenty francs, which meant that not just the Nazi authorities, but German soldiers and traders could buy everything up cheaply and ship them back home, while we went without. And if you were wondering why they'd set the exchange rate so high, it was because we were expected to pay for the costs they were accruing by occupying us. To the tune of twenty million Reichsmarks a day. Call me picky if you like, but that didn't seem right to me.

I put the bottle down. And worst of all right now was that there was one cop in this room who wasn't even getting free whisky out of them. I wondered what Dax was doing right that I wasn't. Quite a lot, probably. The man himself came back into the room and sat down opposite me. I tried telling him of the notion that Boniface and I had had about a gang of gangs, possibly with Nazi collusion, but he just waved the idea away and took another long sip of his drink.

'I'm not interested, Eddie. No need to see conspiracies that aren't there.'

My frustration bubbled over. 'What is wrong with you?'

He looked surprised. 'What do you mean?'

'Come on.' I tapped the bottle. 'This stuff. The one you keep in your desk at Thirty-Six. You're screwing up too much. One day you're on the ball, the next you're too drunk by breakfast to care.'

'These are tough times. I've got the Boches on my back.'

'So have I, Dax. So has everyone. We need you to pull yourself together.'

He sat and stared at his glass, his expression maudlin. 'We killed someone, Eddie. You and me.'

'What? That's ancient history.' That took me by surprise. My immediate shocked reaction to his remark was oddly and instantly replaced by a cool calm. For the first time since I'd dropped in unannounced on him, my voice was gentler, more considered. 'It was fifteen years ago. It was a mistake.'

'Don't you ever think of it? Wonder what happened to that man's family?'

'Every day. But we can't change it. Why would you bring it up now? We've both more than made up for it.'

Despite my words, I knew what he meant. When the Germans had first arrived, it had opened up old scars in me. I'd had my own crisis about what we'd done. The tin on the shelf at home bore witness to that. Dax and I had never been friends, but we'd been united by a single action. We'd accidentally shot an innocent man one night when we were both younger cops. A mistake. But one we'd covered up, forever making us co-conspirators, each reliant on the other. I looked at Dax. He wasn't to be calmed.

'We killed him.'

'You killed him.' My voice took on a sterner note.

'And you helped me cover it up. We're both as guilty as the other. We've always admitted to that. To ourselves at least.'

It was my turn to stare at the bottle. He picked it up and poured us both another shot.

'And that's what has to give us strength,' I told him. 'We know we did something wrong. But it ended there. We atoned. We atone every day in our work. This isn't going to change anything. It can only make it worse.'

With a sigh, he nodded. 'You're right. I still don't like it, but you're right.'

'Neither do I.'

And I had an extra cross to bear, I thought, an extra level of guilt Dax knew nothing about. As I'd been able to do for so many years, I filed it away in the recesses of my mind. I didn't need Dax dredging it up now.

He seemed to pick himself up. 'You are right, Eddie. About work. There are days it gets too much.'

'But you'll get back on top of things again?'

'I will.' His eyes glinted through his glasses. 'Back on top and keeping an eye on you.'

'Oh, great.'

He topped up our glasses again. This was someone who didn't have to ration.

'Heard the news? From Vichy?'

I groaned. Another area where he and I agreed to disagree. Ever since Marshal Pétain had set up the puppet government in Vichy under the terms of the armistice, the country had found yet two more camps to divide ourselves into. Those who thought he'd done the right thing and that the Vichy government would solve the problem of Occupation, and those who had more than two brain cells to rub together. As I said, we weren't friends, we were just thrown together by a single act that had determined so much of both our lives.

'What have they done now?'

'Statute for Jews. All Jews banned from high public office. They reckon it's only the first of many.'

'Is this the Nazis or Vichy?'

'Vichy. They've done it off their own bat.'

'And you agree with it?'

He shook his head. It was an almost sad gesture. 'But I agree with Pétain. He did the right thing for France. It was the only course the country could have taken at the time. And, anyway, I think he's got a plan. He hasn't really capitulated. He's a wily old fox is the marshal, he's got something in mind.'

'And persecuting the Jews to appease the Nazis is part of the plan, is it?'

'No. I don't go along with this. This is just doing the Nazis' work for them.'

'We finally agree on something,' I said, draining my glass. 'Pétain hasn't got a plan. He sold us, gave us away to the neighbourhood bully. We're screwed. All of us, especially the Jews. And this statute is only the start of it.'

'Pétain knows what he's doing, he'll come good in the end.'

'So all the Jews who fled to the Unoccupied Zone now find themselves facing the same problems as the ones here. And you call that coming good?'

'They can't come back here, anyway. The Boches banned them from returning to the Occupied Zone.'

'Who in hell's name would want to?'

Outside Dax's apartment, even though it was gone nine o'clock, I was surprised to see the streets relatively busy. Just a month ago, they would have been deserted. But just a month ago, the curfew would have started an hour earlier. At the end of September, the Germans had extended it by an hour to midnight. I walked by the river, looking at the people around me. It was like attending your own funeral. Or the trial to decide your own execution. I had the feeling of being lulled. All of us. Groomed for an evil that was being brewed in Berlin and the Hotel Majestic, where the German High Command had installed themselves in our luxury. People were getting used to being occupied. That was the danger. I found it almost as disturbing as I'd felt walking into Gestapo headquarters earlier.

Amid the crowds, I walked past a poster announcing the new opera season and I thought of the jazz club. And of the absurdity of concerts in the midst of war and occupation. It made no sense and it made every sense. No sense in that no one in their right mind would want to go and sit in a theatre, surrounded by grey uniforms, when young men were dead and missing in their thousands. And every sense in the Occupiers' use of it to quell the people. Opera for the elite, theatre and cinema for the masses. Beer and circuses. Fiddle while Paris slowly burns. All of it designed to make sure we held our gaze elsewhere. Looking at the Parisians around me, I saw that I was no different from them. If we were being invited to our own funeral, we might as well make the most of the wake.

On impulse, I descended the steps to the Metro and got on a train. It took me to Montmartre. At the end of the ride, the walk through the darkened blackout streets of an area I'd once known so well was unsettling. Landmarks that should have been familiar took on an unknown edge, a sense of straying into a false memory. All around were noises that were unfamiliar, strange susurrations in the shadows, the sound of scavengers who had been around for much longer than we had and who would long outlive us. It was a world on borrowed time.

And beneath it all, the fear. The dread I'd felt the last time I'd come to Montmartre. The sound of a child singing. I heard noises and voices, sounds that resonated and that struggled to make themselves understood. I stopped on a street corner shortly before the haven I was seeking. There was no child singing. It was in my head. Where fear lies.

Stéphane greeted me with a warm handshake. He was dressed for the evening in a black tuxedo and bow tie, impeccably fastened and cut to impress. I suddenly felt poor in my cop's suit, shabby and ill-fitting and fraying at the edges. It had been a long day. They all were now.

'Good to see you, Eddie.'

He clapped me on the back and led me to a table. I'd be sharing it with a young couple drinking champagne. It never ceased to strike me as odd that even in the most challenging of times, there were people who seemed to be above it. They were the scavengers who would survive the rest of us. On my other side, and closer than I would have wanted, was a table of German officers. This is where the ruling classes were now, not the Luigis of the city. It almost had an air of the Paris I once knew, if only you could blot out the grey uniforms and guttural voices.

Stéphane took my drink order. Wine this time. 'I think you'll find a pleasant surprise this evening,' he concluded before walking off. I wondered what he meant.

I looked around me at the clientele and hoped he was right. Only then did it strike me that this was the first time I'd been back to the club at night after I'd left my moonlight job here as a doorman the best part of fifteen years ago. Everything was in exactly the same place, but it was entirely different. The stage was where it always was, the bar was too, the tables and chairs laid out in the same semi-circle facing the stage, the balcony overlooking the floor below just as it was. But it was transformed. Even with the uniforms of Occupation and the vultures that had descended to feed off it, there wasn't the air of sleaze and decay that there had been in my day. I found it vaguely depressing. Maybe there was a reason we'd lost the war. Perhaps we'd been losing for years, we just didn't know it.

I felt a tap on my shoulder. One of the German officers. I prepared for fight since flight would have been hopeless in a crowd like this, but he simply made a gesture to ask for a light for his cigarette. I spoke to him in German, forgetting myself.

'I'm afraid I don't smoke.'

He looked surprised. 'Strange to find a Frenchman who speaks our language.'

He had a cultured voice. In a fluid movement, he put his cigarette back in its packet and put it down on the table. He looked like every other officer I'd ever known, but with an air of compassion underlying the self-confidence. His cap was on the table and I could see that his hair was slightly longer than as worn by his companions, his features fine and clean-shaven, his eyes blue. He could have been on every Wehrmacht recruitment poster.

'I spent the last war in a prison camp in Germany,' I explained.

'Ah, I apologise. Let us hope that all of that is behind us now.'

I tried not to stare. He genuinely felt what he'd just said. It threw me. Fortunately, I didn't have to reply as the opening beats of the music on stage sounded and the lights dimmed. I stole a last surreptitious look at him. His eyes shone in anticipation of the first song. But for age and fate, I could have once found myself in a similar situation. A soldier in an occupied land. France had occupied the Ruhr in the 1920s after the last war. Our behaviour there wasn't always as it should have been. Because of that war, I'd changed the life and career I'd had mapped out for me – taking over my parents' bookshop. Maybe that was no bad thing, but it hadn't been my choice. I wondered what my companion might have done had the Nazis not come to power.

I concentrated on the music. The bars settled into *De Temps en Temps*, a song by Josephine Baker that I'd loved since the first moment I saw her sing it on stage. I almost felt disappointed. I didn't want to hear someone else perform it. In the moment of wondering who would be singing it and if they'd possibly live up to Josephine, Stéphane's promised surprise became apparent. Dominique walked out onto the stage and the room was enchanted with the quality of her voice. For five minutes the war went away. So did the last fifteen years.

At the end, I noticed a small ruckus on the table of Germans next to me. The one next to me tried to calm it down.

'I'm going to complain,' I heard one of the officers say.

With a click of his fingers, he called Stéphane over and spoke to him in heavily accented French.

'This woman is banned from singing here. I will report this club to the High Command unless you take her off stage.'

To his credit, Stéphane stayed calm but in control. 'She isn't banned. She has a right to perform here.'

'Black Americans are forbidden to perform. You should know that.'

'She's not American. She's a French citizen. From Senegal. She is allowed to sing.'

My companion spoke to his friend in German. 'Please, Heinrich, don't make a fuss. Let her sing. She has a beautiful voice.'

Heinrich wasn't to be swayed. 'It is not right.'

'But it is not wrong either. Here, I'll call for another bottle of champagne if you'll just enjoy the show.'

Our Heinrich was all right with that, it seemed. He calmed down and turned to talk to the officers the other side of him, his outrage forgotten. My companion winked at me with a charm that Boniface could never have achieved.

'My name is Peter, by the way,' he introduced himself to me and twisted to shake my hand.

'Eddie.'

'I'm sorry about this.'

He spoke in a low voice not to antagonise Heinrich. I looked from one to the other and couldn't help seeing them as symbolic of the slow but inexorable change in behaviour we were witnessing as a whole. Peter was the blond and courteous German soldier we'd got used to in the early weeks of the Occupation, the pacifier easing the path. Heinrich was the officious and vindictive new face that was creeping in, the demand for a new order whether we liked it or not. I had an awful idea which one would win.

'I thought jazz was supposed to be degenerate,' I told him.

'Only to those who don't love it.'

'But doesn't that put you at odds with the Nazis?'

He smiled and shrugged. 'You fought in the last war. Does that mean you agreed with everything your government did? I'm a soldier, I'm serving my country. You did the same.'

I responded with my own smile. 'Yes, I did. And I probably will again.'

He laughed. 'Just don't let me hear you saying that.'

I couldn't help joining in with him. There are few things as frustrating as liking your enemy.

'So why are some clubs closed down?' I asked him. 'If one's degenerate, surely they all are.' I still wanted to know what it was that singled Fran's place out.

Peter leaned in towards me so his companions wouldn't hear. 'Consistency is rarely the hallmark of authoritarian governments.'

'Better not let your friends hear you saying that.'

He was about to reply when Stéphane came over to talk to me.

'Can you come with me, Eddie?'

As we walked away from my table, he told me he thought I might have wanted saving.

'No, it was oddly pleasant,' I told him. Strange how we clutch at goodness in the middle of the dark. 'By the way, is Dominique really allowed to sing?'

'Not a clue. I hope so. That's why I only dare let her sing one song.'

He led me to one of the dressing rooms behind the stage. I remembered the warren of corridors from my time here. Dominique was waiting for me, seated in front of an ancient dressing table. She was alone in the room.

'I wanted to see you,' I told her after Stéphane had left us alone.

'And I wanted to see you. Are you going to look for Fabrice?'

I sat down on the edge of a faded chintz armchair. None of the pieces of furniture in the room matched any of the others.

'No.'

'Then you can go,' she told me, a look of unfettered anger on her face.

'I'm afraid I can't, Dominique. I want to know why you lied to me.'

'Lied to you?'

'About the perfume. I've met Fran's latest lady friend. Her perfume was completely different from the one you wear.' I noticed it again now, just as I had the moment Stéphane had opened the door. 'You were the one at his club the day I went there.'

She looked at me like she was deciding what to say.

'OK, I was there.'

'So why did you lie? And why did you hide from me that day?'

She lit up a cigarette. I was surprised at first, but then I remembered her once telling me that she smoked for her voice, to give it an extra timbre. She blew out a stream of smoke at her reflection in the mirror.

'Hide from you? That's the self-centred arrogant Eddie I remember. I didn't hide from you. I just left without seeing you. I'm allowed that right, surely?'

'So why lie?'

'Because I didn't want to have to explain why I was seeing Fran. About having had a relationship with him. You don't have a right to my private life.'

'You think I'd care? Are you still having a relationship with him? Is that why you were there?'

'You see what I mean? No, I'm not. I just went there to ask

him for help in looking for Fabrice. He was as unhelpful as you are.'

'Why Fran?'

'Because I'd tried everyone else.'

'And then you tried me. As a last resort.'

'Christ, Eddie, that's not why. I hadn't seen you or heard from you for years. You were long out of my life. Why would I ask you for help?'

'Why did you?'

'Because I'd heard you'd been asking about me. I'm desperate. I thought it was worth a try. I was evidently wrong.'

'Desperate?'

She cocked her head to one side. 'You've hardly shone like a beacon when it comes to helping, have you, Eddie? Just ask Joe. So now you know the truth, are you going to help me find my son?'

'Take one guess.' I instantly regretted my answer, born of anger at her remark about Joe. I let out a deep sigh. 'I can't, Dominique. Even if I wanted to. It's a German military matter. There's nothing I can do about it.'

'Even if you wanted to? That says it all, Eddie.' She wrote something down on a piece of paper on the dressing table and gestured for me to take it. 'My address. For when you decide to join the human race, so you know where to find me. Now just go.'

I took the paper and left. She'd already turned away from me by the time I closed the door.

Instead of taking a left and heading back to the main room, I went right towards the door leading out into the alley behind the building. Countless times in the past, I'd stood out here talking to Dominique in between her sets on stage. She'd smoke like she had done just now, the zip at the back of her dress pulled down a few centimetres to let the cool air get to her back. I had never wanted to be with anyone so much. I hadn't since.

Outside it was darker than I'd remembered it. It was the blackout, throwing the narrow lane into impenetrable shadow. Closing the door to behind me, I leaned back against the wall and felt an enormous sadness wash over me. I'd never meant to argue with Dominique. I recalled her barb about Joe. The implication I was unreliable. Sadness gave way to anger. An anger I'd learned to contain. I struggled with it now.

I heard a sound next to me. A click. Turning, I saw that the door had been closed by someone on the inside. It had no handle on the outside, so I had no way of getting back in. I banged on the door and shouted, but no one opened it.

Muttering a curse, I felt my way in the dark towards the end of the alley. It would bring me out into the street next to the club and I'd just have to take a first and a second left and I'd be back at the main entrance. That was easier said than done in the blackout. I heard sounds all around me. Shuffling and scratching noises. Rats. Or so I thought.

A torch suddenly shone in my face and I felt hands grab my arms from behind and pin them to my sides.

'Hands together, Eddie,' a voice from behind me said. I recognised it as Calais Jacques's. Even as he tied my wrists roughly together, I registered surprise. It was unusual for a Montparnasse villain to be in Montmartre after dark.

'Got him?' another voice asked. Walter. A local gangster working with one from outside. I had an odd moment of triumph in realising we'd been right in our theory of a gang of gangs.

But then a coarse sacking bag, the inside smelling of sweat and tobacco, was pulled roughly over my head and I entered a greater darkness.

19

The stench of sweat and the smell of tobacco from the sack over my head was overpowering, but what made me shake was wondering how many others had been made to wear this bag. Julot maybe. On the day he'd died.

My arms were gathered tightly behind my back, my muscles aching with the unnatural angle. I was on a straight-backed chair, my hands tied to the wood. I tried moving my legs, but they were securely fastened. Whoever had done it knew what they were doing. I recalled the image of Julot in the captain's chair. My last resting place was evidently a lot less sumptuous.

I heard footsteps behind me and I braced myself for a blow, but none came. Instead, the sack was pulled roughly off my head and the footsteps receded. I thought my eyes weren't used to the light, but I realised I was in darkness. There were the sounds of traffic. Not heavy, but enough to surprise me, given how few vehicles there were on the road. It sounded like trucks. Military, I wondered. But then the sounds stopped, no more lorries revving their engines outside. Other than that, I heard nothing. A table leg scraped somewhere, making me jump, but then silence again.

I found the idea of the table scarier than any other sound. It had the feel of office, of bureaucracy, of a department devoted to fear and terror. I recalled the two faces of the Gestapo men I saw the previous day and thought I'd shaken the wrong tree. Or the right tree too much. A gang of gangs. With Gestapo backing.

A light went on, blinding me for an instant. I closed my eyes, and slowly opened them to get used to it.

That was another in a litany of bad decisions.

Instead of the room bathed in light as I'd expected, there was just one ray shining down from what looked like a low ceiling onto a table just a metre in front of me and to my right. My eyes slowly adjusted. Not as slowly as I'd have liked, I discovered.

On the table were two objects.

A needle and a length of twine.

Despite myself, I struggled, hoping to topple the chair over in case I could slip the ties off the ends of the legs. I felt the skin on my hands and legs tear. It sent waves of pain through me. And hopelessness. I realised that I wasn't being held by rope but by more of the twine. I remembered that that was how Julot had been tied down and I stopped struggling. I'd never shake the twine off, and the chair was too heavy to overturn. There was nothing I could do but wait. And hope I found a chance to do something to escape my fate when the time came.

My head hanging as I regained my breath, I heard voices. I looked up and tried to scan the darkness outside the pool of light on the table. I saw nothing and no one. I listened more intently and realised something I hadn't registered. It surprised me.

The voices were talking in French. I'd expected to hear German. While I was trying to make out exact words, one voice finally spoke out loud and clear. I realised it was directed at me.

'You should have taken the warning.'

I heard more sounds. A door banging open, the sound deafening in the room I was in. It had to be some sort of warehouse or huge shed. Strange the thoughts that come to you at these times. There were more voices and the sack was suddenly placed over my head again. I waited for what was to happen to me. At least it wouldn't be the needle and twine, I hoped.

Instead, there were hurried voices in the distance, obviously in the far corners of the room. I couldn't make out words or individual tones. After a time, the footsteps came back. I waved my head from side to side, this time hoping the bag wouldn't come off. But instead, I felt a knife prick my left hand as a blade cut through the twine holding me down. The same was done to my legs and I let my feet spread out in front of me. If I'd hoped to do any jumping up and overpowering of attackers, that idea soon vanished. It was all I could do to rub the pain out of my limbs and the life back into them. Before I could even do that, my hands were thrust behind my back again and tied once more. Other hands grabbed my arm and led me away. I had no idea what was happening or where I was being taken.

More importantly, I had no idea what had just happened. Someone had come in, that much I could work out. And, if my luck were to hold, that someone had put a stop to the thing with the twine and the needle. Whoever they were, I could have kissed them. The question was what was to happen to me now. Never satisfied.

I felt myself pushed into the back seat of a car. Someone began to speak in French, but another voice told them quickly to shut up. They weren't voices I recognised. All I knew was that Calais Jacques's and Walter's weren't among them. I wondered at the part they'd been about to play.

After what seemed an age of twists and turns and toppling over in the back of the car, unable to support myself with my hands tied behind my back, the car stopped. And with it, my fear started up again.

I heard a front car door slam shut and then the air hit me as the back door was jerked open. Hands dragged me along the back seat and out of the vehicle. I stood in the cold air, waiting for what was going to happen to me. I heard the car door open and close again. I waited for whoever had got out to come over to me, but no one came. Instead, the engine revved and it raced off, leaving me in the darkness, the sack over my head and my hands tied with twine.

I waited, expecting a blow or a gunshot, or someone else to come and take me, but there was nothing. I listened intently. No sounds of engines, no voices, just a silence as black as the darkness inside the sack. Finally, the panic of the smell of tobacco began in me. It was almost a relief. That was all I had to worry about, not a needle and a length of twine.

Except I was somewhere I didn't know and I had a sack over my head and my hands were tied. The rosiness of the situation changed by the minute. I called out in case anyone was nearby, but no one came. I had no idea what time it was. The middle of the night, I reckoned, deep in the heart of curfew.

Moving very carefully, I found myself up against a stone wall. A building. Feeling along it with my hands behind my back, I located a metal grille. It felt like a door into the building. Inching along the wall, I came to the corner. My luck was in still. It was at the end of the street. Leaning back against the wall, I began to rub the twine up and down the stone edge. I thought it would take an age to wear through, but it snapped surprisingly quickly. Almost too quickly. I was still trying to work out what I'd do once I finally got free.

Shaking my hands out, I ripped the sack off my head and spat the taste of the tobacco out of my mouth. I blinked at my surroundings. It took me a moment to get used to the dark.

And to my surprise. I dropped to my knees at the corner of the block and leaned in against the wall.

I was outside the building where I lived, just a few metres from my front door. I could have wept. Never had it seemed so like home.

I was ravenous. Except I wasn't. It was just something to be doing to fill my mind. To try and expunge the smell of tobacco inside the sack and the sight of a needle and twine taking centre stage under a spotlight on a small table.

While the bacon fried, I sliced the baguette that I'd finally managed to buy that morning. As thinly as possible, the way we'd all learned, to make it last as long as you could. The slice was uneven where my hand had shaken cutting it. The texture was so unlike the bread we used to get, more a collection of crumbs held together in hope.

The aroma of the bacon almost made me sick. I knew I was simply diverting my attention. I checked my watch. It was a little before two in the morning. The sack held over my head could only have been less than an hour ago. I'd climbed the stairs from the street to my apartment, although now I had no recall of actually doing it, and gone straight to the bathroom where I'd been sick. Staring at my reflection in the mirror, I remembered that I hadn't eaten since lunchtime and I was instantly starving. Except I wasn't. It was my mind distracting me for its own good.

I put the food together on the plate, looked at it and left it there. It would keep until breakfast. I couldn't afford to waste it. I went through into my living room. There was something I shouldn't do but that I knew I had to.

Reaching for the tin on the shelf, I took it down and sat on my armchair with it. I lifted the lid, the first time in months.

Inside, nestling amid old letters and postcards were my son's first shoes. I held them. They were so small I could have wept. I remembered showing them to Jean-Luc in the summer. Reluctant at first, he'd finally picked them up and shared a brief smile with me before handing them back.

I replaced them. Sadly, they weren't the reason I'd opened the tin. That was a bullet. Dull and tarnished, it was like a malevolent acorn, ready to take seed once more. I took a deep breath and took it out. I felt again the small indentation in it.

Quickly, without thinking, I went to the bathroom and took an old German Luger from its hiding place behind the tiles above the sink. Back in my chair, I reunited it with its bullet. They had come into my life as a pair. In fact, they had almost come together to cause the end of my life when a German officer in the last war had held it to my head and pulled the trigger. The gun had jammed and I had killed the German instead of him killing me.

I picked the bullet up. I'd never known if the indentation in it had been caused by the gun misfiring or if the misfiring itself had deformed the bullet. It was one of those moments of cause and effect over which you have no control but that determine a moment that in turn determines a life. I recalled Dominique accusing me of thinking I was the only victim of war. Of course I wasn't. But I was a victim. And that had left me as tarnished and warped as the bullet and had altered my north ever since.

I loaded the bullet into the magazine and cocked the pistol. Looking down the barrel, I thought of my son. I had no idea if he was still alive. If he were, I had something to live for. I felt the cold metal of the gun against my forehead and saw again the needle and twine on the table. For years, I'd been afraid to live. My compass gone, the decisions I'd taken warping and misshaping my life since. Now, though, I knew I was more afraid to die.

I lowered the gun. For as long as there was doubt, I had my son. I had someone who needed me even if he wasn't aware that he did. I also had a vision of Dominique. Her expression when she first told me of her son missing.

I pulled the trigger one last time. Pointing away from me, harmlessly. It clicked. I always knew it clicked. All it had ever proved was that I wasn't afraid of feigning dying. This night had shown me that I was afraid of actually dying.

Standing up, I turned the lamp off in the room and walked to the double windows leading out onto a tiny balcony, little more than a ledge with a railing. I pulled the heavy blackout curtain aside and leaned out. Removing the magazine from the gun, I took the bullet out and felt it in the dark, my fingers seeking the cold comfort of the indentation. I decided it would be the last time. Looking to the street to my left, with the Boulevard Saint-Germain at the end, I hurled the bullet as far as I could, trying to reach the crossroads. In the dark, I heard it clatter to the ground. I had no idea where. It was gone. I breathed the night air. It felt fresh.

Back inside, I turned the lamp on again and picked up the tin. My son's baby shoes were now the most important items in there. They always should have been. I closed it and replaced it on the shelf.

I felt nothing but a sense of relief. And resignation.

20

My eyes were shut, my head in my hands, trying to rub the tiredness out of them. Rain was rattling against the windows of my room at Thirty-Six. A draught always blew in on blustery days and I pulled my jacket tighter around me and shivered. I'd barely slept. If Fran were to walk in now with a bag full of white powder, I couldn't promise I wouldn't do something stupid. Just to get through the day.

I kept the elements out with my eyes tightly shut. The visions in my head were of last night in the darkened room. The sounds of the voices speaking in French, the words they said indeterminate.

I opened my eyes. On the desk in front of me was a cruel echo of the night. Side by side were the needle and the twine from the cemetery in Montparnasse. I grimaced at the sight. It wasn't like images of them hadn't swirled around my dreams in the rare moments of sleep I'd managed to catch last night.

Despite the shock of finding the two objects on Baudelaire's cenotaph, I'd remembered to take them with me. I'd just learned this morning that it was a sort of twine used by anglers. I closed my eyes again. The image I had was of sitting on the bench with Hochstetter and the man with the two rods walking past. I struggled to recall his features. I could see him walking past, but my memory, like my thoughts at the time, was relentlessly focused on the two rods swaying over the man's shoulders, not his face. Reason told me that if he were someone I knew, that at least would have got through to me at the time. The fact I didn't know him meant nothing. I had no idea even if he was anything to do with the taunting of me in the cemetery. Fishing twine was hardly a rarity, even now in rationed Paris.

I opened my desk drawer to put them away and gasped at the sight of the doll inside. In all that had happened, I'd let it slip from my mind. Seeing the sightless eyes and sewn lips, I slammed the drawer shut and got up. I needed to get away.

I took the same Metro line to Les Tourelles as before, not knowing what I was hoping to achieve once I got there. I just knew I had to be doing something. The same warden who'd told me about Dunkirk led me to the room where I'd seen Joe last time.

'You'll see a change in him,' he warned me. 'He's going downhill.'

'I should have brought some food with me.' I was angry with myself for not thinking, but the warden shook his head.

'Least of his worries. He's one of the ones down for transfer. We're to hand him over to the Germans.'

'Why?'

He shrugged. 'Orders. That's all we've been told.'

'When?'

'Month at most. If he's lucky, he'll be dead by then.'

I couldn't get his words out of my head when they brought Joe in. He had deteriorated, worse than I'd thought. He didn't react when he saw me, not even anger or disappointment.

'What is it, Eddie?'

'I've come to see you, Joe.'

He stared at me across the table, his eyes sunken. I could hear a rattle in his chest and pulled my own jacket tighter against the damp. His expression changed the longer the silence continued. He looked at me quizzically. I had no idea what to say to him.

'Have you got any news for me, Eddie?' I heard no hope or expectation in his voice. 'Are the police going to help me?'

In desperation, I recalled talking to Hochstetter about him. 'I've asked the Germans for help.'

'And?'

I grasped for something to say. I knew I'd made a mistake in coming. 'These are difficult times, Joe.'

'You haven't done anything, have you?'

He looked up to the warden and signalled that he wanted to go. I tried to find words as he walked slowly away from me towards the door.

'I'm trying, Joe.'

He stopped and turned to face me. 'This is worse than doing nothing, Eddie. I didn't expect much from you, but this false hope is the worst thing you could have done.'

He turned away again. He didn't even look angry or surprised. He stopped once more in the doorway and spoke again.

'Please don't come back.'

I'd sat in the room in Les Tourelles before plucking up the energy to leave. Despite my fear of being locked up, I could have stayed alone in that room, hidden from everything I was facing outside. Joe's cold acceptance of my worthlessness had cut me to the quick. I felt lethargic, reluctant to go when the warden came to fetch me.

Outside in the persistent drizzle, I stood with my eyes closed and let the rainwater wash over me. I have no idea how long I stayed there, but I was drenched through. Finally, I opened my eyes. Despite the grey and the damp, the colours around me seemed more vivid. I felt alive again. More alive than I had since someone had placed a sack over my head and threatened me with needle and twine. I took a decision. Catching the Metro, my mood steadily lifted, I felt stronger. Not even the dark of the tunnels could disturb my sense of purpose. I'd return to Thirty-Six, but there was something I had to try first.

I went to the Hotel Bristol. That's where the US embassy staff and journalists had based themselves when the Germans had first come to Paris. The journalists were still there. The diplomats had gone.

'Where can I find them?' I asked a journalist in the hotel bar, my voice more confident. Thin as rationed bacon, he had thick horn-rimmed glasses and a receding hairline. I could smell the hotel's red wine in his glass. It was better than the stuff we were getting.

'Why do you want to know?'

'Journalists and cops. Twice as inquisitive as the other and half as honest. I'll let you decide which is which.'

He laughed at that and invited me to a glass of wine. I checked my watch and said yes. I'd had worse breakfasts.

'I don't normally drink this early in the day,' he told me, 'but these are tough times. You see things you don't want to see.'

'I understand.'

I took a drink of the wine. I'd drink it any time of the day. I all but fainted with the taste. He waited and I told him about Joe. I hoped he'd see a story in it and help get the musician out. He didn't.

'Black American, you say?' He turned back to the bar. 'Good luck with that, buddy. The consulates haven't been too helpful with their cases.'

'That's why Joe stayed here after the last war.'

'Château de Candé. That's where some of the embassy staff are. Try there.'

Another American journalist sitting nearby came over to us. 'No, they've gone. Left last month. You've got to try the embassy in Vichy.'

He was younger, energetic. Wavy hair over an angular face and a Clark Gable moustache. Everyone wanted to look like someone else. I hoped he might help at least. He didn't.

'Sorry. But I've got a telephone number if you want it.'

I took it. It was the best I was going to get.

'Good luck,' the first journalist called after me when I left. 'You're going to need it.'

I went back to Thirty-Six and climbed the stairs to the third floor. Intent as I was on my desire to help Joe, I didn't even jump out of my skin when a mop and bucket that a cleaner had left on the landing toppled over as I walked past.

One phone call later and I could see the two journalists had been right. Sitting at my desk in Thirty-Six, I'd been passed from phone to phone until I'd ended up with some junior official who had a voice like he'd shaved twice in his life. He made up for it with a level of self-importance a French functionary would have killed for.

'A jazz musician, you say? Negro, I take it?'

'American,' I added for his benefit. 'Like you.'

'He should have left the country sooner.'

He hung up. I tried ringing back but couldn't get through. Evidently, the brightest and the best of both our countries had found their way to Vichy. I finally put the phone down and stared at it in its cradle. I recalled the look on Joe's face and his words and I knew I'd have to find another way.

I went for a pee and got back to my office to find Boniface

walking in ahead of me. I got past him to find the doll lying on my desk.

'For Christ's sake, Boniface, leave things in my drawer.'

He looked surprised. 'I haven't opened your drawer, Eddie.'

'Well, who took this out, then?'

I picked up the doll with my fingertips, not wanting to touch it. Its sightless eyes and sewn lips repulsed me. Needing to get it out of my sight, I jerked the drawer open to hide it inside as quickly as I could.

Only there was a doll in there already. I dropped the new one on my desk and sat down heavily.

'What is it, Eddie?'

I took the original doll out and laid it side by side with the new doll. They were identical. Down to the three stitches in the mouth.

'Did you see anyone in my office?' I asked him.

'No one.'

I stared in dismay at the two dolls. Someone had been in my office. I jumped up and went out into the detectives' room.

'Has anyone been in my office?' I shouted.

All the heads turned, and all of them shook a negative.

'Did you see anyone, Barthe?'

'No one, Eddie. I've been here all morning.'

'I've only been gone five minutes. Someone must have seen something.'

The detectives looked at each other. Their expressions were half-quizzical, half-embarrassed.

'Nothing, Eddie,' another replied.

I went back into my room and sat down. Boniface took the seat opposite. He picked up my phone and rang the front desk to ask if anyone had been in the building. He hung up.

'Nothing, Eddie.'

Without a word, I picked up the two dolls and locked them away in my drawer. I gathered my thoughts for a moment before looking up at Boniface.

'What was it you wanted?' I asked him.

'Estranged son.'

It was possibly the shortest sentence he'd ever uttered. My thoughts immediately turned to Jean-Luc.

'What?'

'I've found out something pretty interesting.'

'Have you found Walter le Ricaneur's ex-wife?'

I was stalling him, I knew, while I could think of an answer that would put him off. The idea horrified me almost as much as the dolls did. If Boniface knew about Jean-Luc, the whole of Thirty-Six would know by now. And God only knew who else.

'It's Walter. He has an estranged son.'

I had an odd feeling like I had the moment the person came into the room last night and prevented my torturer from giving me a sewing lesson. Another reprieve.

I nodded to hide my relief. 'Is that right?'

'Walter ran out on his wife and kid years ago. Imagine that. What sort of a man does that to his own kid?'

'So how does this help us?'

'The kid's not a kid, he's twenty. His name's Dédé Malin, the same surname as his mother, not his father. And he's just been released from Fresnes.'

That made me sit up. 'Seriously? Released from Fresnes as in he's served his time? Or released from Fresnes as in he's another prisoner gone missing?'

'No, Eddie, this is genuine. I got it from the lovely Mathilde, Judge Clément's secretary. He was due for release. He got out yesterday.'

'So he and Walter were in Fresnes at the same time? Hell,

that must have made for some uncomfortable shower times.'

Boniface waggled his finger to stress his point. 'No. I've asked a few questions. From what I can gather, Walter doesn't know who he is. He left before Dédé was even born, so he's never known him. Dédé's mother moved to Montparnasse while she was still pregnant.'

'To get away from Walter, no doubt. Does Dédé know who Walter is?'

'Yes. And he hates him.'

'And if anyone's going to be willing to talk about how come Walter left Fresnes before his time, it would be a son who hates him.'

'Precisely.'

'So what's the kid got to say?'

'That's the problem, Eddie. He's gone missing.'

21

I told Boniface to try and find Walter's ex-wife to see if she knew where Dédé was and I got ready to go out myself. Last night's experience had wrought a few changes in me. One of them meant I had to go and see someone.

I glanced out of my window. The sky was overcast but it wasn't raining for once. Down below, on the opposite pavement, I saw a Peugeot 202. I knew instinctively it was Hochstetter's Abwehr vehicle, the same car as the other day, keeping track of me.

'Nice to know you care,' I said.

Looking to the right and left, I spotted a Citroën Traction Avant parked a short distance away, almost by the Pont Saint-Michel. I felt an immediate tremor. The Traction Avant was the car of choice of the Gestapo.

'Pity you do too,' I added.

I went downstairs and out into the street. Heading for my car, I saw the Gestapo car slowly start to move forward. I stopped momentarily before picking up my pace. Unfortunately, the Traction Avant did likewise. It soon became evident that it would catch up with me before I got to the safety of my own humbler Citroën.

I made my choice and changed course. I opened the rear door of the Peugeot 202 and sat down in the back seat. The passenger turned around to face me.

'The Lutétia, please,' I told him. 'As quickly as you like.'

'This isn't a taxi, Inspector Giral.'

'You won't be wanting a tip, then.'

'We're not taking you to the Lutétia.'

I pointed to my car. The Gestapomobile had stopped some metres behind us. 'That's my car over there, as you know. I'm about to drive to the Lutétia to see Major Hochstetter. If you don't take me, you'll just have to follow me. And we'll all still end up in the Lutétia anyway. My way's so much easier.'

The passenger and the driver had a brief discussion while I kept a wary eye on the men in black. The two Abwehr men glanced in their direction from time to time too. In the end, they went with my idea.

'Well done, boys,' I told them. 'You just can't get the petrol these days.'

I sat back and enjoyed the ride. The person I'd intended to see would have to wait a while. Glancing back, I noticed that the Traction Avant hadn't followed. No worry, they'd be back.

My drivers let me off outside the front entrance to the Hotel Lutétia. I hadn't been summoned to the place for some time, but whenever I did come, the undulating balconies on the façade always made me feel like the building was raising its eyebrows at me in reproval. For once, it felt good to be coming here of my own accord.

'Édouard, my friend, how may I help you?'

'For once, I hope you might.'

Not even rudeness fazed our Major Hochstetter. I would have felt bad about it but it felt too good. In a plush suite of rooms converted into an office, I waited while he did officer-y things and gave a bunch of orders to a young adjutant.

'And fetch coffee for both of us, please,' the major told the junior officer. 'I'm sure Inspector Giral would appreciate it. He looks rather the worse for wear.'

Feel free to discuss me, I thought. I took a seat. I had a sudden tremor of fear. I was riding on adrenaline, but the events of the previous night had left their mark. I did my best to hide it from Hochstetter.

'Now how may I help you?' he asked me when we were alone.

Where to begin. 'My investigation.' It seemed as good a place as any. 'You offered help.'

'If it is within my power.'

'The Gestapo. Do you think they might be involved in the death of Julot la Bavard, the man killed in the jazz club in Montparnasse?'

He looked mildly surprised at my question, but not at all discomfited. He wasn't Hochstetter for nothing.

'I would agree that our friends in the Gestapo are remarkably imaginative in their cruelty, but I would say that what happened to this criminal is not how they tend to operate. If they'd had anything to ask him, they would simply have taken him to the Rue des Saussaies. Done it officially, so to speak, insofar as anything they do is ever done officially. For that reason alone, I would be surprised if they were involved in this matter. Unless there's something else you haven't revealed to me.'

'There is one thing. Some prisoners have gone missing from Fresnes prison.'

'I know. I was wondering when you were finally going to mention it.'

I kicked myself. I should have known he'd know. 'I feel that only the German authorities would have the power to have prisoners released from a French prison like this.'

'And why would they do that?'

'That's what I don't know. But I think it has to be related to Julot's death.'

Coffee arrived and the adjutant poured us both a cup. I spent a full ten seconds breathing in the aroma and letting my adrenaline calm.

'Perhaps you should tell me what you know.'

I took a long drink before taking the leap. With the Gestapo on my back, I knew I needed help, even from this quarter.

'About thirty prisoners have gone missing from Fresnes. Not all from the same gang, or even members of a gang at all. All of them from different parts of the city. All in prison for a range of crimes, although most of them were there for serious offences. All are career criminals.'

'Intriguing. Go on.'

'Pressure was brought to bear on the French judiciary to have them released. Their files have also gone missing from both the prison and the courts. We know it was a Frenchman who took the court records, but he had authorisation from the German authorities. We assume it's one of the various agencies of your lot squabbling over who's top dog.'

I stopped. I figured that what I'd just told Hochstetter was pretty much everything that he could have learned for himself. Any omission or lie here would be pointless as he'd latch onto it immediately.

'Do you know who the Frenchman is?'

'No. And no one is willing to talk. There's a general sense of fear among the people we ask.'

'And you feel the German institution involved is the Gestapo, I gather. As I say, I'm not convinced I see Gestapo involvement in the death of the burglar, and as for their involvement in the release of prisoners, I don't see what they stand to gain from it. Although I will say that war – and Occupation – make for some strange bedfellows. Either way, Édouard, I would strongly advise against accusing them of anything.'

'That might be a little late. I went to see them at the Rue des Saussaies.'

'Why?'

'To see what their reaction to my questions would be.'

'Do you know, Édouard, we in the Abwehr were only discussing recently the apathy of the French population. You seem to be a people defeated. You are, of course, but you have taken defeat so very much to heart. It is just such a pity that you in particular appear unable to adopt the same level of apathy. It would make your life so much easier. And mine, if you have indeed come here to ask for my help in defusing matters with the Gestapo. Out of interest, what has their reaction been?'

I told him about my being abducted the previous night. And about the needle and twine. And about this morning's little escapade with the Abwehr taxi service.

'And you think last night's incident was the Gestapo?'

I had to admit I didn't know. 'Whoever took me spoke French. I heard no German. But it all smacks of them. And I was taken not long after going to see them.'

That merited a cigarette. I looked away as he lit up. 'This is most intriguing. And appallingly stupid on your part. I'm afraid that once the Gestapo take an interest in a matter, there's very little anyone else can do to deter them.'

'Can you find out if they're involved?'

'I can try. Leave it with me, I shall see what I can turn up.' He took a deep drag on his cigarette, the leaves crackling in the glow. 'I gather you are also here to seek my protection against our friends in black coats.'

'Yes.'

'And I trust you are aware of the price of that?'

I finished my coffee. 'Only too well.'

22

I still had someone to see but it would have to wait until I'd finished washing my mouth out with a glass of wine in a nearby café.

As I stood at the counter, two gefreiters studied a young woman's papers. I'm sure it was coincidence that she was attractive and alone. I showed them my police ID.

'She's with me,' I told them. 'Assisting me.'

The taller of the two looked back at me, sizing me up. 'This is none of your business.'

'Yes, it is.'

'Leave it,' his companion murmured to him.

I could see him wrestle with a natural inclination to make something of it. His hard blue eyes flickered from my brown ones to the pink scar on my top lip. For some reason, those few centimetres of puckered skin often put pocket toughs off trying their luck.

'He's police,' his friend added.

I beamed at the tall soldier broadly. He hesitated for a moment before backing off, although I don't think it was my rugged charm that won him over, but the orders he'd no doubt received to win Parisian hearts and minds. He could have done with a refresher. With a sullen glare, he handed the woman's papers back to her. She put them away without raising her eyes from the table, not even to watch the two soldiers leave the café to a silence as cold as the coffee in her cup.

When they'd gone, she glanced up at me and I smiled at her. She simply glowered back.

'Get lost, cop.'

I left too, without a word. I wondered how I'd react to me if I weren't a cop. If I were in her position. One more joy the Occupation has brought.

Boniface was waiting for me outside in his car. I'd called him at Thirty-Six from the café phone the moment I'd got there to get him to come and pick me up. I didn't fancy walking the streets with the Gestapo wanting to say hello.

'I've found Walter's ex-wife,' he told me. 'She owns a haberdasher's not far from the Jazz Chaud. I'm going to see her now. You coming?'

I looked at my watch. The next tick on my list would have to wait.

We found Madeleine, Walter's ex, closing the shop for lunch. A timeless haberdashery with dark wooden drawers from floor to ceiling and a counter stacked head high with trays selling cotton reels, coloured thread and bright ribbons, it was faintly incongruous in a street of seedy cafés and carnality hidden for the day. Recognising me, she let us both in before locking the door behind her and flipping the CLOSED sign. Thin, like everyone else these days, she had long prematurely greying hair wrapped around her head in a plait and lines around her eyes and mouth.

'I don't care where that useless bastard is,' she told Boniface when he asked after Walter. 'It's my son I'm worried about.'

'Is this Dédé?' I asked her.

'You know perfectly well it is. He's fresh out of Fresnes and all you can do is harass him.'

'So why are you worried about him?'

She folded a length of material with an irritation that made the fabric make a noise like a whip cracking. For a moment, I thought she was going to blank us, but she suddenly opened up. Like a flood gate.

'I don't know where he is.' Boniface and I exchanged a glance. She put the fabric down and leaned heavily against the counter. She held back tears as she spoke. 'You know Dédé was in prison the same time as Walter? I was terrified the whole time he was going to do something. Dédé, I mean. He's very protective of me, and he's always hated his father for what he did.'

'Abandoning you?' Boniface asked.

'And the rest,' she told him bitterly. 'So when I heard the rumours that Walter was out, I felt such a relief. But now Dédé's been released and I should be happy, but I almost wish he were back in jail. He's been talking, you see. About his father.'

'What exactly?' I asked her.

'About how come he was let out of Fresnes. And all those others.'

I tried to hide my eagerness. People only help the cops when they think you don't need it. 'What's he been saying?'

'Oh, he didn't actually say what happened. Just that he knew what was what. And that he was threatening to tell. And then that thing with Julot le Bavard happened and Dédé's gone missing and I'm so terrified what might happen to him.'

'You have no idea what he knows?' Boniface asked her. She just looked annoyed at him.

'Do you have any idea where he might be?' I asked.

'No, he's nowhere I can think of.'

'We'll make sure he's all right,' Boniface promised.

Instead of answering him, she turned to me, her voice taking on an anger to replace the worry. 'Oh, you'll make sure he's all right, Eddie Giral, I promise you that.'

'We'll find him,' Boniface said.

'That's one promise you'll keep,' she warned me. 'Or else.'

She shooed us out of the shop and locked up to hurry upstairs for her lunch.

'Find him, Eddie,' she said as we parted, the worry once more back in her voice.

I told Boniface to drive across the river and head for Montmartre. After meeting Dédé's mother, my task seemed more urgent than it had before.

'And then?'

'And then we go back to Montparnasse to find Dédé. And hope we find him before his father does. But first, there's something I've got to do.'

I checked again the piece of paper I had in my wallet and directed him to an address near the top of the mountain. He parked at the foot of a steep flight of steps and made to get out of the car with me, but I told him to stay put.

'Wait for me here. And if you hear a kid singing, arrest the little bastard.'

I started up the steps. Very pretty but a pain in the arse when you want to get anywhere in a hurry. By the second flight, I was singing the praises of my lovely flat street in the Fifth.

'They have invented the lift, for Christ's sake,' I said by the third.

The building I wanted was on the landing between the third and the fourth flight. I stopped to get my breath back and turned to look over the city. The view told me why anyone would want to live there. Even in the gloom of an autumn day living under foreign rule, the old girl looked a city of light. For one brief moment, I recalled the excitement I'd felt at coming to live here after the last war, at losing myself in the beautiful anonymity of it all. I turned to go in.

Inside, there were more stairs. At least the person I wanted to see was in. She stood in the doorway, her arms folded, steadfastly refusing to invite me in.

'What do you want?' Dominique asked me.

An elderly man shuffled past us on the stairs. He greeted her warmly as he went by. In my building, I only knew one of my neighbours well and I tried to avoid him at all costs for the sake of my sanity.

'Can I come in, Dominique? There's something I want to say.'

'We said all we had to say the other day, Eddie.'

I looked at her. Her expression was implacable, her slender frame seeming to fill the entrance to her home like the toughest of barriers. I glanced down the stairs I'd just climbed. I wasn't going to have a wasted journey.

'I'll do what I can to find Fabrice,' I told her.

She looked shocked and asked me to repeat what I'd said.

'Why the change of mind?' Her voice was still harsh. I wasn't forgiven.

I cast around for a reason to give her. I decided the truth would have to do.

'I thought I was going to die last night. I think I would have but for someone stopping it from happening. And I thought of my son and what would happen to him.'

Her arms remained folded. 'And what's that got to do with Fabrice?'

I was lost for the right thing to say. 'I need to find him, I suppose. I can't find my own son right now, so I need to find yours. I can't explain why.'

'I can, Eddie. It's for your sake, not mine. As always.'

'Just let me help you, Dominique. I will, anyway, no matter what you say.'

Her arms slowly loosened and she clasped her hands together lightly in front of her. Her voice was still cool. 'All right. Thank you.'

With nothing more to say, I nodded once at her and set off down the stairs. On the first turn, her voice called after me.

'Please don't let me down, Eddie.'

'Glad I inspire confidence,' I murmured, although I waited until I was at the bottom before I said it.

'Any luck?' I asked Boniface, but his face gave me the answer.

'Does anyone actually walk around this city with their eyes open?' he demanded with an expression of disgust. 'No one knows anything, no one sees anything.'

We'd spent a few hours treading the streets of Montparnasse, each one separately, shaking up all the contacts we knew, but he'd obviously come across the same reaction I had. The same reaction we'd been getting ever since Julot sat in a captain's chair. A CLOSED sign bigger than the one on Madeleine's shop.

There was one thing I had learned.

'Come on,' I told him. 'I've got a treat for you.'

'Dancing girls? Chilled champagne?'

'Better than that. You've been so eager to see our friend Fr—, our friend Poquelin, well now's your chance.' I glanced quickly at him to see if he'd caught my mistake.

'You mean you're not keeping him to yourself for once?'

Fran wasn't in his club when we got there. It was Paulette who opened the door for us. A smell of bleach cut the air, making my eyes water.

'So it's true,' I said to her. 'The club's reopening.'

She nodded. 'He heard today. The Boches have allowed the local *mairie* to grant him a licence. He's out celebrating now.'

I nosed around the place as I spoke to her. The stage had been cleaned, the stands and drums gleaming, and the bar looked like it had been given a good rubdown. Only the tables and chairs in front of the stage were left to do. They looked even seedier in contrast to the glitz of the rest of the place.

'You not celebrating with him?'

She stopped and looked at me. A bitter laugh emerged from her lips, a sound like fingernails on a blackboard. 'I'm surplus to requirements. He hears he's reopening and he tells me I'm not up to the standards of the new club. So I'm out.'

'But you're still here?'

'He's got me doing the cleaning. I don't do it, I don't get paid the money he owes me. Bastard.'

'When's he coming back?'

'That's anyone's guess. He's gone with one of his low-life friends. They won't be back until he's drugged to the arse and wants to screw me one last time.'

'So not bitter then?'

Waiting in the wings, Boniface turned on the full wattage of his electric charm for her benefit. 'No one should treat a lovely lady like that,' he told her.

'Too fucking right,' she replied. Heaven smiled the moment these two met. 'Soon as I get my money, I'm out of here.'

'Where is he now?'

'Luigi's. You know the place?' Her voice took on even more of a rasping tone. 'And he says I'm not classy enough. Arsehole.'

She found a bundle of notes in a drawer under the bar and hurriedly put them back, hoping we hadn't seen. I knew the moment we were gone, so were they and so was she. I didn't blame her.

'I guess you found the money he owes you,' I told her.

'Twice in one week, Eddie. This is an honour.'

'Knock it off, Luigi. And get us two red wines. The good stuff.'

A guy at a piano was playing *De Temps en Temps*. He really shouldn't have. It sounded like he'd only just discovered he had hands and was beating the keyboard with them to see what they could do. I recalled Dominique singing it. That was only last night, I was shocked to realise. The piano was what was left of Luigi's attempts at high culture when the Germans had first got into town, but since that meant a woman stripping while singing, I reckon he had a skewed idea of what culture was, like someone had explained it to him once while he wasn't listening.

'Looking for Jean Poquelin,' I told him when he served us. 'Been told he's in tonight.'

'I don't want trouble, Eddie.'

'Then you should have taken up the priesthood, like your mother told you. Where is he?'

He hung his head in resignation before giving the subtlest of nods towards the rear, where we'd found Pepe the other day. It all went on in Luigi's back room.

Boniface and I drained our glasses and went in search. We found him. And he wasn't alone.

'Calais Jacques,' Boniface muttered in disbelief.

The two men looked up at us and quickly scrabbled something away into their jacket pockets.

'Now that didn't look suspicious,' I told them.

They were with two German soldiers, a stabsgefreiter and a gefreiter – a corporal and a private – who had the same look you saw the world over. Two small-time crooks caught up in a war and a uniform, seeing it as an opportunity to carry on where they left off. They were dealing in something and Fran and Jacques were buying. The stabsgefreiter got up and came over to me, the swagger one I'd seen a million times. He prodded me with his forefinger.

'We are soldiers of the Third Reich,' he said in faltering French. I smelt the cheap beer on his breath.

I leaned forward and whispered to him in German. 'And I am seconded to the Gestapo. I work out of 11, Rue des Saussaies. How much further do you want to go with this?'

For a moment, I saw the power that the name gave you and I had a brief flash of understanding of what that power could do to you. He instantly backed away from me and signalled to the gefreiter to get out of there, almost stumbling over a table. In his stupor, he saluted me, one of Adolf's cheery waves.

'Something we said?' I asked the two men left in the room with us.

Boniface closed the door and I stood over Fran and Jacques. The latter tried getting up, but I restrained him, using my height and standing position to stop him. I knew that if Calais Jacques did get up, he was more than a handful for me and Boniface in a brawl, especially with Fran floating around the edges.

'You've got nothing on us, Eddie,' Fran told me.

'Aw, Fran. We just came to congratulate you on the club re-opening. And to ask what you had to do to get that to happen.'

'All above board, Eddie.'

'Indeed. Just like the company you keep.' I turned to Calais Jacques. 'Long time, no see, Jacques.'

'You can't touch me, Giral,' he replied. 'You don't dare.'

'So what did you get up to last night?'

He grinned at me, an evil and toothless leer. 'Wouldn't you like to know?'

'Who was it in the warehouse?' I couldn't help feeling an

edge of anger in my voice. It was born of the fear I'd felt last night. 'What about you, Fran? Were you there too?'

'I haven't got a clue what you're talking about, Eddie. I was with Paulette last night. You can ask her.'

'I'd love to, but she's gone. And she's taken her money with her.'

I saw a moment of realisation on his face. 'The little bitch.'

'I've got nothing on you, Fran, so you can go. But you, Jacques, I'm afraid you're coming with us.'

'What for?'

'Absconding from Fresnes. Assault. Kidnap. Being a pile of shit. Anything else I can think of.'

He laughed. 'You can try, Giral, but you won't get far.'

From his seat, he did the mime Walter had done, pretending to sew his lips shut, his eyes on me all the time.

'Not going to work this time,' I told him.

He stopped and laughed again, an evil cackle, his mouth open, his eyes shut.

And that's when I hit him.

23

'You're wasting your time, Giral. I'll be out by lunchtime.'

Calais Jacques was sitting on the bench in his cell at Thirty-Six. With his shirt off and stripped down to his string vest despite the cold, he looked like someone had wrestled an ape into a shopping bag. His jaw was red and swollen where I'd hit him. It was an improvement.

'I was going to ask you what you knew, but I guess that would be a waste of time. You must be pretty near the bottom of the tree.'

'Nice try, *poulet*, but it's not going to work. I may be big but I'm not as dumb as I look.'

'Got yourself caught, Jacques. Sounds pretty dumb to me. Tell me what's going on and I might put in a good word for you with the judge.'

'I already told you, Giral, I'll be gone by lunchtime. Now off you trot and see if you can find someone to bring me my breakfast before I have to go.'

I was on a hiding to nothing. Outside the cell, I told the Breton sergeant to tell me if anyone came with a warrant to have Jacques released. I had to admit I had the feeling he was probably right about being gone by lunchtime.

'Don't let him out until you've seen me,' I warned him.

I began the walk back up the three flights to my office deep in thought. This wasn't the Calais Jacques I knew. The old one was a pro, a time-served villain who took arrest and imprisonment in his stride. It was all just part of the job to him. The attitude, the entitlement, this was all new. He'd never answered me back like that before. I hadn't even known he had the vocabulary to do it.

I had visitors. My initial instinct was that it was Hochstetter back to his old ways, but he seemed to have eschewed the visit to Thirty-Six for a random bench somewhere in the city. Besides, these visitors were in a different uniform. Opening my door, I found two green uniforms infesting my office like mould. I didn't recognise either of them, but I knew what they were.

'Sicherheitsdienst,' one of them said to me. He was sitting at my desk, casually opening and closing the drawers.

'Make yourself at home,' I told him.

I left the door open behind me and went in. I'd already suppressed an urge to turn tail and run, so I figured that leaving an escape route was the next best thing.

I trod warily in my own room, watching them watching me. The Sicherheitsdienst. The SD. I was never sure which lot fitted in where, but what I did know was that they were the intelligence service for the Nazi Party and as such scarier than a table full of fishing twine. As far as I could work out, the SD and the Gestapo were sister organisations in the RSHA, the Reich Main Security Office. And if you need to know any more than that, you're really not paying attention. I also knew that as the Party's intelligence service, the SD was a rival to Hochstetter's Abwehr, the equivalent for the Wehrmacht. A sort of Cain to his Abel.

'We have been looking for you,' the one behind the desk continued.

Both men had a diamond-shaped patch with SD in it on their sleeve and a skull as a cap badge. Someone really ought to tell them. The one who spoke had three square flowers on one side of his collar. The other one had to make do with two. I reckon the extra flower made all the difference. So did the man behind the desk. So far, he'd done all the talking. He closed the drawer.

'Well, you won't find me in there.' Another thing I'd learned was that I talked too much when I was scared. The state of my panic right now, I'd be giving Boniface a run for his money.

He stood up suddenly and came round to the front of the desk, where I was standing. Thin and angular, with a long nose and small mouth that together looked like an exclamation mark, he moved in a jerky, aggressive motion that was unsettling. I found myself instinctively tensing up to fend off a punch should one come.

'We wish you to come with us.'

'Where?'

'SD headquarters.'

'Sorry. Been there. I'm hoping to try Corfu this year.'

He looked nonplussed at my reply but recovered. 'You will come with us.'

He nodded at his companion and walked out of the room in his odd, jumpy walk. As tall and as broad as me, but with a scar on his right cheek as opposed to mine on my top lip, two-flowers looked impassively at me and held his hands out to usher me out of the room. I accepted the invitation.

Outside, they drove me across the Seine and up the Champs-Élysées, now just a sad, leaf-strewn road in a city gone grey. I expected them to take a right in the gardens along Avenue de Marigny, which is how I'd have gone to Rue des Saussaies, but instead they carried on. Startled at first, I even wondered if someone had told them I'd impersonated a Gestapo agent the previous night, but they eventually turned left onto Avenue Foch and I realised my mistake. I said I got confused between the SD and the Gestapo. All I knew was the SD did the thinking, the Gestapo did the thumping. Since these were SD, my hope was I wasn't going to be getting a battering. Then I remembered the twine on the table and I started to get scared again. We pulled up outside one of the plush buildings on Avenue Foch and they signalled to me to get out.

'You're not ones for roughing it, are you?' I told you I was scared.

They made me wait in a corridor the colour of jaundice and left me in the care of two uniformed kids with rifles and a clerk at a desk. Make people wait. It's an old trick but it works. My imagination at what the SD might want me for roamed the inside of my skull like a nightmare seeking a home.

They called me through into an office before I was ready. Sitting behind a grand desk in a room the size of the detectives' room at Thirty-Six was the younger of the two men I'd spoken to at Gestapo headquarters. He looked like a bureaucrat with a uniform and a gun. The nightmare found its home.

'Inspector Giral,' he greeted me.

'And you are?'

'Of no matter to you. For the time being. Please, take a seat.'

I sat down opposite him and he offered me a cigarette from a wooden box on the desk, which I refused.

'Why have you brought me here?'

'Your request for this list of prisoners released from Fresnes prison. What do you know about this matter?'

His tone was cold, but polite. It took me by surprise, but made me wary. I had a feeling that my best course was to stay as near to the truth as possible. Just not all of it.

'Simply that a number of prisoners have been released from the prison before the end of their sentences. It appears that the German authorities took this decision.'

'And you know this, how?'

'The governor of the prison.' I didn't mention Judge Clément. If I was going to land anyone in it, it would be Ducousset, the governor, who I still suspected of setting me and Boniface up.

He wrote something down and looked up at me when he'd finished. 'I'm afraid we have no record of any of this, Inspector Giral. Were you advised by anyone to request this information of us?'

Hardly. Before I could think of an answer, he carried on talking.

'Major Hochstetter of the Abwehr, perhaps? I know you work closely with him.'

'No, no one advised me. I'm a police inspector, my job is to follow up all possible avenues. This is just one of them.'

He studied me for a long and uncomfortable moment. 'Leave this with me, Inspector. But I would ask that if you do learn of any development, or of any action taken by the Abwehr, that you pass it on to the SD. I'm afraid I would have to insist on it.'

'I assure you I will. The moment I know what Major Hochstetter is doing, you will be the first to know.'

It was a dangerous game. Split up into their factions and offices and departments, the Germans often seemed even more divided than we were. My mistake would be in thinking that that weakened them. If anything, the rivalry between them, and the use they made of me in waging that internal war, made me more vulnerable, not less. Hochstetter was unpredictable, but I was beginning to get a handle on how to work him – as far as that would ever be possible with someone like him. But add the

SD and Gestapo and whoever else to the mix, stir in the un-predictability inherent in each of them and in their relationship with each other, and I just had the feeling that I'd be the one picking up the broken eggs at the end of it.

'You may leave,' he told me.

I sat and waited until he looked up to see why I wasn't going. He finally did.

'Capeluche.'

His face was blank. 'I beg your pardon?'

'Capeluche.'

'Is this the person who advised you to request information from the Gestapo?'

'I'm sorry, I thought they were part of your organisation.'

'You thought wrong.'

I left and breathed in a huge lungful of autumn Paris air once I was back out in the avenue. The name hadn't registered, but that didn't mean I was any the wiser.

Walking deep in thought past the fine buildings on Avenue Foch, many of them inexorably yielding to the Nazi edifice, I suddenly remembered Calais Jacques in the cells at Thirty-Six. With a renewed determination, I quickened my pace.

I was too late. The Breton sergeant was very apologetic.

'Gone, Eddie, I'm sorry. I came to see you but no one knew where you were.'

I hid my frustration. 'Who came for him?'

'Lawyer. With a court order from the judge. It was all above board, Eddie, there was nothing I could do.'

'See anyone else with the lawyer? Any German soldiers?'

He shook his head, so I left and made my way upstairs, where I had another visitor, a woman. She wore a thick brown coat and her short hair stood up in clumps. It took me a moment to place her.

'The caretaker from Jazz Chaud,' I said. I didn't know her name. 'Is this about Jean Poquelin?'

'Not entirely. May I take my coat off and sit down?'

'Of course.' I closed my office door and pulled the chair out for her. I waited for her to remove her coat and fold it neatly on the other chair next to her and try unsuccessfully to smooth her hair. Once she was primly in place on the edge of the hard seat, I went round behind the desk and sat down. I wondered what it was that she wanted. 'How may I help you?'

'I think you've been looking for me.'

'I have?'

'Yes, only I'm probably not what you're expecting.'

24

'To your credit, Eddie, you haven't laughed at me.'

She looked at me intensely. Gone was the rather unassuming middle-aged woman in a shabby coat, the unruly hair and the mousy manner. In her place was a controlled woman with a confident but cool expression and a voice that was gentle but firm.

'Are you from Capeluche?'

She tutted theatrically at me. 'Oh dear, you've just lost the credit you earned. I am Capeluche.'

I shook my head, but a closer look at her eyes slowly made me stop. 'Why should I believe you?'

'Why shouldn't you?'

She left the question hanging in the air, daring me to respond. I didn't. I was trying to reconcile the mild-looking person in front of me with the vision of Julot struggling in a chair while she sewed his lips shut and held his nose.

'You made me coffee. You have a cat.' Which were probably the dumbest comments I could have made. In my defence, I was just playing for time while deciding what to do. I believed her. I just knew that if I called any of the detectives in from the outer room while I arrested her, they'd be the ones to laugh in my face.

'Not my cat. Just a stray, I'm afraid. I picked it up the day you found poor Julot because you'd never suspect a middle-aged woman with a tortoiseshell cat.'

Every word she said punched a hole in me. Every word was true. 'Why were you there that day?'

'I wanted to see what I was dealing with. You're good. Both of you. You and the other guy. You're both better than you think you are. I've heard about you, Eddie. I've heard what you were like back in the day and what you're like now.'

'Please don't say I intrigue you.'

'You don't. But you interest me. Although in one way, you do disappoint me.'

'What's that?'

'You didn't see me. I mean, *see* me. You saw a woman, and not a young woman at that, and you didn't even rule me out. By that, I mean you didn't even consider me. To rule me out as your killer, you had to consider me a suspect in the first place. And you didn't. Why? Admit it. At no point, did it ever occur to you to question me. Because of who I was.'

'So is this your reason for killing Julot?'

She laughed. It surprised me. It was a bright laugh, with no hint of cruelty or bitterness. It was the laugh of someone who once had the gift of laughter but who lost it a long time ago. She shook her head. Her hair still stood on end in places, but it no longer looked unkempt. It looked individual, unique. I was annoyed with myself for noticing it.

'My employers are the reason for my killing Julot.'

'So you did kill him?'

'Please, Eddie, don't go patting yourself on the back thinking you've tricked me into a confession. I came here today to tell you I killed Julot. That's not the point.'

'Who are your employers?'

'That's something I'm not at liberty to tell you. And if you have any sense, you won't persist in trying to find out. You see, I've been sent here to ask you to stop your investigation. You can carry on looking like you're investigating if you wish, but that's all you'll be doing. I would recommend you accept my employers' request. You've seen what they're capable of, what I'm capable of.'

'You want me to sabotage my own investigation into Julot's death?'

'No. Your investigation into the prisoners who have been released from Fresnes.'

'And if I don't?'

She shrugged. 'That's your choice. It's not one I'd recommend.'

'You've tried to kill me once and failed. Last night. The needle and twine in the warehouse.'

'I didn't fail. My orders were changed. At the last minute. You're a lucky man, Eddie. You got a reprieve. Until new orders. I wouldn't waste it if I were you. The people I work for would snuff you out like a candle. You've seen that.'

'Why did they kill Julot?'

'An example. He talks too much. Personally, I think they released him all along with the plan to have me kill him. To encourage their other employees to toe the line. That's how serious they are.'

'How many employees have they got?'

'How many prisoners have you counted gone missing? Just subtract one.'

'Was there a reason it was in the Jazz Chaud?'

'Also an example. If Poquelin wanted his club reopened, he had to understand the rules.'

'So if your employers managed to get his club opened, that would make them the German authorities.'

She shook her head and smiled ruefully. 'Nice try. But no, there's more than one way to convince a local *mairie*. So, unless you have any other questions, I'll be taking my leave.'

'Aren't you forgetting something? I'm a cop. You're in a police station. You know what that means. I'm arresting you.'

She picked up her handbag from the floor at her feet and started rummaging around inside. 'You're right, there is something I'm forgetting.'

She pulled out a piece of paper and leaned forward. Turning it over, she let it float to the desk, where it landed in front of me. It was a photograph, the quality of the image clear. I couldn't help gasping.

'The Pyrenees,' Capeluche said. 'A small town near the border with Spain. But unfortunately on the wrong side of the border from your point of view. Which is why the place is crawling with Gestapo.'

'How did you get this?'

She turned the photo around so she could see it. 'And that is your son, Jean-Luc. He's looking well, I'm told.'

I took the photo back and turned it to face me. Sure enough, it was a photo of Jean-Luc. Taken recently. He was wearing the jacket he'd been wearing the day he left Paris. Lost to all else, I examined the photo closely. He was talking to another man I didn't recognise. Behind them I saw mountains. I looked up at her questioningly.

'Where is it?'

'I'm afraid I can't say. Keep it, if you want. I have more.'

It took me everything I had not to reach across the desk and strangle her until she told me where my son was. 'What do you want?'

'Your son is waiting to be taken across the border. Whether that happens or not, whether he finds himself in a Gestapo cell or not, now depends on you.' I could see her watching me clench my fists. 'I really wouldn't try to take your anger out on me. For one thing, you really would not get far. For another, the people he's paid to take him over the border are expecting to hear from me. When they do, your son remains safe. For the time being.'

I looked beyond her to see what was going on outside my office. Through the glass pane in the closed door, I saw the world carry on as normal out there. Boniface was talking to a group of cops. Nothing had changed. Not outside this room, anyway.

'What can I do to ensure his safety?'

'I told you. Stop your investigation into the missing prisoners. I will give you a choice, though. If you do fail to do as I ask, I will either tell my employers, who will in turn inform the Gestapo, or I will tell your Major Hochstetter. I'll give that choice to you.'

She got up and put her overcoat on. In an instant, she was the unassuming middle-aged woman I'd found waiting for me in my office.

'I don't have a choice, do I?' I told her.

She stopped to look at me before opening the door.

'You always have a choice.'

25

I still argued with the baker, I still told Boniface to shut up, I still queued for meat.

'Can't get good lamb or beef anywhere, Eddie,' Albert my butcher told me. 'While the Boches are busy with their snouts in the trough, there's no pork to be had for the likes of us.' He laughed at his own joke.

I nodded and picked up my package, exchanging it for my ticket and a handful of francs. I looked at the flimsy sheet of coloured stamps in my hand. They looked insipid and hopeless, like our existence had been reduced to scrappy little squares of blandly coloured paper.

'Are you all right, Eddie?' he carried on. 'You've not been yourself these days. It's hunger causing that. Anything worth having, the Boches take it straight from us and send it back home. At a fraction of the price we're expected to pay. The scraps they leave for us. Bastards.'

'Bye, Albert.'

I took my parcel home and left it in the cold box outside my kitchen window. I no longer cared about the inconvenience of queuing early to buy food before going to work. The picture of Jean-Luc that Capeluche had given me was on my bookshelf, as far away from the tin as I could place it. I looked at it before going back out. It was strangely comforting, the only photo of him that I had.

'Bank hold-up,' Dax told me when I got to Thirty-Six. 'Local bank branch robbed at gunpoint, a cashier badly beaten, the whole neighbourhood's shop takings and wages taken.'

Dax at least had found a new sense of purpose. We were taking turns these days. I tried not to let my lack of it show.

'I'm on it,' I told him.

'Take Boniface.'

I shrugged and fetched talking-boy. I let him drive us to Boulevard Voltaire in the Eleventh. It was a broadish, tree-lined street roughly midway between Place des Vosges and the Père Lachaise cemetery, but it was by no means a wealthy part of town. A few days ago, that fact would have angered me. Now it left me numb. Boniface talked all the way. Not even that annoyed me. Except for one comment he made when we parked outside the bank. He got out of the car and looked at the fine wooden doors leading into the building.

'Like things aren't bad enough without our own villains making it worse.'

It annoyed me because I should have said it. Before Capeluche had come calling with a photo of my son, I would have said it. But now I found I couldn't.

'Talk to the other cashier,' I told him instead. 'I'll have a word with the manager.'

But before I got to the manager's office, a uniformed cop beckoned me over and pointed to a woman sitting on a chair inside. For a moment, I thought it was Capeluche. My heart raced for a brief second until I realised it wasn't her.

'She got a good view of one of the robbers,' the cop told me.

I pulled up a chair and sat down. She was a customer, who just happened to have been in the bank at the time it was held up.

'There were two of them,' she told me. 'I didn't see the one. They both had scarves over their faces and his didn't fall off. But the other man's did. Just for a second. I saw him.'

'Can you describe him?'

'Horrible. Like he was grinning. On one side of his face.'

I quickly looked around to make sure Boniface was nowhere near, and I told the uniformed cop to go and stand by the door.

'Did you hear a name?'

She shook her head apologetically. 'But he was big, muscular. And that face. It was the left side, like it was stuck like that. It sent shivers through me.'

She was describing Walter le Ricaneur.

'OK, you go home now,' I told her. 'And I'll come and see you if we need any more. Don't talk to anyone else about what you saw.'

Nodding, she picked up her shopping and hurried out of the bank. I watched her go and carried on to the manager's office. He was standing by a safe, its door open, the contents gone.

'They made me open it,' he told me in a shaky voice. 'They hit Guy, one of my cashiers, with a gun until I opened it.'

With wispy blond hair and a round face, he was pale by nature, but the experience had brought out an even more pallid shade in him. I asked him if he wanted to sit down, but he was too on edge.

'Did you see either of the two men?' I asked him.

'No.' I hid my relief. 'But they dropped this. I don't understand. It was on my desk.'

He held out a piece of paper to me and I took it. I nearly let it drop from my fingers. It was the photo taken of my son in the Pyrenees. At least, it was half the photo. The other man was in it, but the side with Jean-Luc on had been ripped away. I knew it was a message from Capeluche. A warning to look the other way. This was a job by the people she worked for.

'Have you shown this to anyone else?'

'No. I was too shaken by what happened. I've only just noticed it now.'

'And you're sure it was left by the robbers?' I know I was.

'I don't know. It must have been.'

I placed it in my jacket pocket. 'It's probably nothing.'

I turned to find Boniface in the doorway. He was looking intently at me.

'Have you finished interviewing the witnesses?' I asked him.

'Twice in one week, Édouard, this is an honour.'

Another officer was just leaving Hochstetter's office when I got there. He had the same whistles and flutes on his uniform as Hochstetter did, so I assumed he was a major too.

'Thank you, Major Kraus, we will carry on with this later.' Thought so.

Switching his attention to me, Hochstetter asked the adjutant for coffee for us both and turned back to the high window in his office. In ancient times, the coffee alone would have been worth the discomfort of visiting the Abwehr at home. Ancient times was three days ago.

When I spoke, I had to shout above the din of a gramophone record that Hochstetter was listening to. Heavy-duty trilling that seemed to entrance him. He stood at the window with his eyes shut.

'Have you heard anything?' I called. I wasn't in the mood for the usual jockeying for position with him. 'About the Gestapo?'

He turned to face me.

'*Fidelio.*'

'What?'

'On the gramophone. This is *Fidelio*. Beautiful, don't you think?'

'The Gestapo,' I reminded him.

He turned back to the window. The music had changed. 'It is the story of Leonore, who disguises herself as a man – Fidelio. This way, she can pass herself off as a guard to secure the release of Florestan, her husband, a political prisoner.' His head rocked gently in time to the choral dirge. 'This scene is the "Prisoners' Chorus". The prisoners have been let out of their cells in the belief that they are to be freed. It is extraordinarily uplifting one moment only for their hopes to be profoundly dashed the next.'

Angrily, I lifted the needle off the disc and set it down.

'What have you learned? About the Gestapo?'

He was taken aback by my bluntness. His voice was cool. 'I take it you mean their involvement in the missing prisoners. I'm afraid I've so far been unable to unearth any conspiracy involving them. But that doesn't necessarily mean anything. People who are so adept at getting the information they want from others are invariably the hardest at giving up their own.'

'I know that. I need you to tell me something I don't know.'

He studied me closely, uncomfortably. 'I must say, there appears to be some urgency about your enquiry, why is that?'

I couldn't help pacing as I spoke. 'The Gestapo came to see me. Or rather, they took me to their headquarters, and they asked me about the prisoners. They claimed they knew nothing. They also wanted to know how much you knew of what was going on.'

The adjutant came in with the coffee and Hochstetter invited me to sit down. He sat opposite me.

'What did you tell them?'

'I said you knew nothing.'

'Please keep it that way. I would ask you also not to make any noises about the matter until I have more news for you. Or to attract the Gestapo's attention.' He stirred his coffee thoughtfully. 'So you returned to the Rue des Saussaies?'

'No. Avenue Foch.'

He looked nonplussed. 'Let me get this straight. You were taken to Avenue Foch to be questioned. In that case, that would not have been the Gestapo. That was the SD, the Sicherheitsdienst.'

'They're the same thing. One works for the other.'

He laughed. 'Not quite. Very crudely, the SD is the information-gathering service, the Gestapo the executive, rather like your police.'

'Entirely unlike our police,' I commented. I still had some teeth left.

'Perhaps. Although the Gestapo don't always rely on their friends in the SD for their information. They prefer to acquire it first-hand, as you've experienced. Anyway, you're right in that they are both part of the RSHA, the main security office, but within that, they have fairly clearly defined demarcations of duty. There's by no means the enmity that exists between them both and the Abwehr, but that is not to say that there still isn't some internal rivalry between the SD and the Gestapo. Although they might claim otherwise, you can't always assume that if the SD know something, the Gestapo know it too. To put it in a way you might understand, the SD regards itself as the grand opera, whereas it sees the Gestapo as your low jazz. The Gestapo, in turn, often sees the SD as rather elitist. In a nutshell, we need to be looking not only at the Gestapo, but at the SD as separate entities in this.'

'What have you heard? Do you think either are involved in this?'

'My, my, we are tetchy today.' He looked at me over the cloud of steam rising from his cup. 'I know I made the observation the other day that I didn't think that this was the way either the Gestapo or the SD would go about matters, but the evidence of their interest in talking to you would seem to contradict that. I have attempted to ascertain what I can, but as you are aware, there is a degree of rivalry between the Abwehr and the RSHA agencies, so I am finding myself coming up against a similar wall of silence that you are finding.'

I slowly stirred my coffee and shook my head. 'Do any of you actually get on?'

He laughed a second time. 'I don't even like the people in the room next to me.'

26

'I've found Walter le Ricaneur.'

'You've what?'

Half an hour after I got back to Thirty-Six from seeing Hochstetter at the Lutétia, the phone on my desk rang. It was Boniface, calling from a café in Montparnasse. His voice was muffled, like he was trying not to be overheard where he was.

'Walter le Ricaneur. He's here, having a drink.'

My mind raced, trying to recall if Boniface had heard any of my interview with the witness at the bank robbery. I remembered him looking curiously at me after I'd put the torn photo in my pocket. I had no idea if he'd seen me do it.

'What were you doing looking for Walter?'

'I wasn't. I'm looking for Dédé. I was drawing a blank, but then Mireille Gourdon, Calais Jacques's ex-girlfriend, gave me a lead. She told me of this place as one of Walter le Ricaneur's hangouts. I figured that if he came here, Dédé might come too if he's got a grudge against his father.'

It was good work by Boniface. I could have throttled him.

'Has he seen you?'

'No. He's in the back room. But I think the kid's here too. There's a young guy in the front near the door who answers Dédé's description.'

I had to think quickly what to do. I couldn't tell Boniface

to forget Walter, but neither could I antagonise Capeluche by going for him. There was a risk his involvement in the bank job would come out. And my covering it up. I reasoned that it was Dédé who was more important for us to get hold of, but I had to make sure that Walter didn't get wind of what was going on and report back to Capeluche.

'Go back outside the café, Boniface. Don't approach either of them. If they leave, stick with Dédé. I'll be there as quickly as I can.'

'I'll be outside in my car. What about Walter?'

'Leave him. We're not interested in him for now.'

I hung up and hurried out of the office. I took my car. It would be quicker now than the Metro. I never thought I'd live to say that about Paris. I parked behind Boniface's car – another first for the city – and got into his car next to him.

'They're both still in there,' he told me. 'Now you're here, we can take one each. Which one do you want me to go with? Walter or Dédé?'

I studied the front of the café. Through the large window to the left of the door, I could see a young guy in a brown leather jacket sitting there. Like Boniface had said, he looked like the description we had of Walter's estranged son.

'It's Dédé we want. I don't want to lose him. We'll both stick with him.'

'Let Walter go? There's no need. You go and talk to Dédé. I'll follow Walter.'

I tried not to let my frustration show. 'We've already had Walter in custody and we got nothing from him. It's pointless. If we arrest him again, he'll be out within the day. We go for Dédé.'

It was another ten minutes before there was any movement. Neither of us had dared go back into the café in case Walter saw us and recognised us. The door opened and Walter himself came out. I had to put my hand on Boniface's arm to stop him from opening his door too soon.

'If Dédé's here to do something about Walter,' I told him, 'he'll follow him out in a few moments. That's when we move. We need to get hold of Dédé before he catches up with Walter at the first corner. But we also need to let Walter get out of sight before we can do anything.'

He nodded his agreement. Less than a minute later, the young guy in the window went to the bar to pay and then came out. Boniface and I got out of the car and hurried over to him. We caught up with him when he was just a few metres from the corner. Walter was already out of view.

'Dédé,' I called in a low voice.

Boniface stood in front of him, stopping him from running.

'What do you want? I'm clean.'

'I'm Inspector Giral.'

'I know who you are, cop. And this one. I saw him in the café.'

We edged him back towards Boniface's car, away from the street corner. 'Your mother's worried about you, Dédé. She asked us to look for you.'

The sullen look from his thin face vanished in a moment and he was a kid. 'Mum? Is she all right?'

'As I said, she's worried about you. Why don't you come with us and we'll take you to her?'

He looked warily at the car. 'I'm not getting in that. Not with you.'

'Come with us to the station. You'll be safe there.'

'No. No way.' He looked around in panic. 'They'll kill me.'

'Who will?'

'You know who.'

'No, we don't, Dédé,' Boniface joined in. 'We need your help with that. Your mother said you had some information about what was going on.'

'I'm not a grass.'

'Fair enough,' I told him. 'If you're happy for your father to get away with whatever it is he's doing, don't tell us anything.'

'They'll kill me.'

'From what I hear, Dédé, they're going to kill you anyway if you don't let us stop them.'

He gulped, the prominent Adam's apple in his narrow neck bobbing up and down like a target at a funfair.

'Talk to us, Dédé,' Boniface told him.

The kid looked around uncertainly. 'Can we go somewhere else? Around here? Somewhere I know?'

We let him take us to a café a few streets away. The owner and a couple of the patrons in there greeted him warmly by name. It was a young crowd, nearer Dédé's age. The two people behind the bar were a mother and son by the look of them, the boy of a similar age to Dédé. I saw why he felt safer in here. We sat at a table and the mother brought us a coffee each.

'I understand you won't know much,' I told him when she'd gone, 'but anything you can tell us will be useful.'

'I know plenty.' He had the bravado of his age. I'd been counting on that. The leather jacket he was wearing was slightly too large for him. A hand-me-down, second-hand or stolen, I decided. It made him look more of a kid.

Boniface sat back and folded his arms, his gaze challenging. Damn, he was a good cop. 'Such as?'

'I know who it was had them released.'

'Who was it?'

'A French guy. A criminal.'

'French?'

'I told you I knew. He just walked through Fresnes, pointing to the people he wanted released. And the governor allowed him.'

'Who was he, Dédé? His name?' Boniface asked him.

He suddenly looked scared.

'Were there any Germans with him?' I asked.

He nodded. 'One, but I didn't see him. I just know there was a Boche with him.'

'Do you know who the French guy was?'

He looked from me to Boniface and slowly nodded. He looked terrified.

'I need a pee.'

I could have sworn. I smiled softly at him. 'You go pee, Dédé. We'll be here.'

He stood up, but instead of heading for the back of the café, he ran out of the front door. One of the other people had opened it ready for him, I saw, and by the time Boniface and I were up to follow him, they'd closed the door and were standing three deep in front of it.

'Out of the way,' I shouted at them, but they wouldn't budge. Through the window, I saw Dédé vanish into a street off the road we were on. I fought down an urge to thump the kid nearest to me. 'Well done,' I told them. 'You probably just got him killed.'

27

The opening notes of *J'attendrai*' played and the audience drowned them out in dewy-eyed applause. I liked the song. It wasn't normally my sort and it had been seized on by a sort of sentimental patriotism, but it was still a good song. Curiously, the German soldiers in the audience loved it too. It had also been recorded in Germany, as *'Zurück'*, and appealed to the same longing. I looked at the heads, both civil and military, bobbing appreciatively in time to the melody and wished our similarities could outweigh our differences. In the lights, I caught the flash of a swastika on an arm and a jagged double-S on a collar and I knew they never would.

I turned away from the stage and scanned the room. I couldn't help the automatic actions I'd had when I worked in the jazz club in Montmartre – surveying the room for trouble, looking for wrongdoing, making sure everyone did as they were meant to. It was no different from policing under the Occupation.

Fran's club on its grand reopening night. The man himself, or Poquelin, as I had to remember to call him, was standing by the bar, black-market champagne in one hand, Paulette's replacement in the other, both of them commodities to him for which he would never pay the full price. Looking around, I saw the place had more than its fair share of local criminals, and not a few Germans – some officers, some lower ranks – but I was surprised to see the place well-stocked with what passed for a jazz crowd these days. My prejudice when Fran had asked me to come to the first night had been to assume it would be little better than Luigi's with a band.

The song finished and Fran waved me over. He weaved towards me, meeting me halfway. He still held on to his two temporary possessions.

'Eddie, Cosette. Cosette, Eddie,' he introduced me to his new 'lady friend'. I had the sudden memory of Boniface quoting who I now knew to be Capeluche using that description a lifetime ago. Fran let go of Cosette and slapped her on the arse, shoving her back in the direction of the bar. 'Off you go.' He watched her freshly smacked bottom sashay through the crowd.

'Classy, Fran.'

'Isn't she just?'

'I meant you.'

He raised his glass to me. 'Thank you, Eddie.'

I raised my own wine glass back without smiling. 'I want a word.'

The only problem was that Fran had been enjoying substances besides the one in his champagne glass and wasn't up to listening.

'I gotta thank you for this, Eddie.' He waved his glass around, splashing his drink over a couple of jazz-lovers nearby. They laughed indulgently. 'It's thanks to you the Boches allowed me to reopen. I was going under, Eddie, I don't mind telling you.'

He took three attempts to get out the words he didn't mind telling.

'It was nothing.' I recalled Capeluche's comment about getting the club reopened. I was telling the truth, it was nothing to do with me.

He patted me on the chest. 'Thank you, Eddie.'

'Don't mention it, Fran. Maybe you can do something for me one day.'

'You name it.'

'But right now, I want a word.'

He looked doubtfully and pointed to his office, but before we could make our way over, a couple of German officers came and started talking to him. They wanted him to get the band to play *'Zurück'* again.

'Sorry, Eddie,' he said, leading them to the stage.

'Catch you later,' I told him.

I did. But only after the band played *'J'attendrai'* two more times.

'Have you seen Jean?' I asked Cosette, remembering Fran's current name in time.

'In the office,' she replied without looking at me.

I knocked quietly and went in before he could have a chance to stop me. He was sitting at his desk. He'd sobered up a little. What surprised me were two German soldiers – NCOs – on the two sofas by the door. They looked up as I went in but lost interest in me immediately.

'Sorry about the other night,' he told me. 'I didn't know you were after Calais Jacques. I'd have told you where he was if you'd asked.'

'Of course you would.' I nodded to the Germans. 'What's that about?'

He tapped the side of his nose. 'Business.' He pointed to two tubes on his desk. They were the same as the ones I'd seen the Germans dealing in Luigi's. I remembered what Pepe had thought they were.

'Vitamins, Fran?'

He laughed and nodded too long. He'd sobered, but not much. 'They sort of are, in a way. Vitamins.'

He picked one up and handed it to me. It was a reddish-brown cylinder roughly the size of a shotgun cartridge and had the word 'Pervitin' down the side in blue on a white label. I took the cap off and shook out a round, flat tablet into my palm.

'Try one,' Fran said, leering intently at me.

I shook my head, more for my benefit than his. 'What is it?'

'Pervitin. The Nazis developed it for their soldiers. Or pilots. Something like that. It's methamphetamine. Take one of those beauties and you won't come down for days. Just what you need to keep you going through tough times, eh, Eddie?'

I put the tablet back in the tube and dropped it on his desk. 'No thanks.' I nodded to the two Germans. 'I take it they're your supplier.'

He gave a wolfish grin. 'Got a never-ending supply, courtesy of the German military. Those two work in the quartermaster's store.'

'And you don't reckon there's anything wrong with it?'

'What? Dealing drugs or dealing with the Germans? On the first, I never heard you complain all those years ago. As for the second, I'm a businessman. We've all got to make a living.'

I looked from the Germans to him. 'Nice.'

'Don't tell me you wouldn't do the same. Work with the Germans if you had to.'

'You got your employee records, Fran? I need to take a look.'

'What are you on about? Employee records?' He laughed. 'What sort of guy do you think I am?'

'You really don't want to know. Your caretaker. What's her name?' I saw again Capeluche in this same room, serving us coffee. Pottering. Listening.

'Given up with Dominique, eh? Setting your sights a bit lower there, aren't you?'

'Just give me her name.'

He shrugged. 'I don't know. She's the caretaker. She takes care.'

It struck me again just how smart Capeluche was. 'What do you call her when you speak to her? You must have a name?'

He looked thoughtful for a moment. 'I don't speak to her. She's just there. Anyway, she's not my type.' He saw something funny in that. I let his amusement subside.

'And I take it you won't know where she lives?' His look confirmed that. 'How long has she been working for you?'

'She doesn't work for me. She just turned up one day. Said she worked for the landlord and she'd come to look after the place.'

'And you didn't think to check?'

'Christ, Eddie, I can't be bothered with any of that shit. I've got a club to run. Anyway, why are you so interested in the caretaker? I can get you any woman you want.'

'Yeah, because that's how it works, isn't it, Fran?'

Looking at me, he took a bottle of good whisky out of his drawer and poured us both a glass. He clinked my glass and took a sip. I remembered Dax's secret stash. For something the Vichy government had banned, a surprising number of people were able to get their hands on it. I hesitated for a moment but then drank from the glass. I stared at Fran and recalled his comment of a moment ago about working with the Germans. It depressed me to think that we really weren't that different.

'Listen,' he told me, his tone conciliatory. 'To show there's no hard feelings, I'll introduce you to my two friends over there. They were telling me something earlier that you might find interesting.'

I glanced over at the pair. They looked just like any Parisian mulchbag that I'd arrested every Saturday night for a decade, only in uniform. They did little to inspire confidence, so I couldn't imagine they'd have anything of interest to say.

'I don't think so, Fran.'

'Come on, Eddie. I'm serious.'

I allowed him to lead me over to the sofas and we sat down. He introduced me in clearly enunciated French and told them to tell me what they'd told him. The first one began in faltering French, which was going to take an age, so I told them to tell it to me in German. They looked relieved.

Their voices slurred, they told me of the fight through France. From the Belgian border to Paris. They'd followed the front line, witnessing the aftermath of the march on the city.

'Run, Frenchies, run,' one of them said. He mimed someone running in panic and dissolved into laughter. He was worse for wear than his companion, but it was a close-fought race.

I glanced at Fran, irritated, and made ready to get up and leave. 'Seriously?'

'You need to listen to this, Eddie.'

'We were spending the night in some village,' the other one took up the story, 'when some of the old hands started telling us a story.'

'Blacks,' the first one butted in.

'What do you mean?'

'Black soldiers,' the first one carried on. He was marginally more educated than his companion. 'There were African soldiers fighting with the French.'

'Where was this?'

'The Bois something. The Bois d'Eraine.'

'Where's that?' I asked Fran.

'Just south of the Somme,' he told me.

It took a moment for the name to register. The Somme was where Dominique had last had news of Fabrice, her son, fighting with a Senegalese regiment.

'What happened?' I asked the more coherent of the German soldiers.

'So when the French surrendered ...'

'... there were no more black soldiers,' his friend finished, with a high-pitched laugh.

It took me all my effort not to reach over and punch him in his high-pitched mouth.

'What do you mean? What happened?' I demanded.

'They were separated from the white French soldiers and taken away,' the second one explained.

'Where were they taken?'

'I don't know. Away.'

'Where?' I repeated. I wanted to grab him by the collar to insist, but didn't dare.

His friend started laughing again, the drug misting his eyes.

'No more black soldiers,' he repeated. He said it again. And again. Endlessly until he dissolved into laughter. 'No more black soldiers.'

28

I was sitting in front of my fourth official of the morning. This one at least showed signs of life, if not interest. A Hauptmann Schnabel in the German military administration, he was busy talking on the phone to someone somewhere else in the same building while I waited patiently for an answer. I think he was the highest rank the other three had dared pass me on to.

I'd come to the Hotel Majestic first thing in the morning after a troubled night's sleep. All I could think of while I waited was the temptation of taking some of Fran's Pervitin to keep me awake. The story the two German NCOs told me had been fizzing around my brain all night, depriving me of sleep. African soldiers. In the Bois d'Eraine, south of the Somme.

Which is why I was listening to the hauptmann harry the person at the other end of the line. He had one of those military haircuts like someone had put a bowl on his head and cut round it and a vein that stood out alarmingly on his neck as he spoke. I'd been passed from one office to the next, and I still wasn't even sure I was in the right place.

'I'm looking for information about a missing soldier called Fabrice Mendy,' I'd repeated for the fourth time to my hauptmann. 'I want to know if he's been taken prisoner or if he's a casualty.'

That had been all right.

'He was with the 24th Regiment of the Tirailleurs Sénégalais. He went missing in the Somme.'

That hadn't.

'I'm afraid I don't have that information,' he'd told me.

'The family need to know. They want reassurance he's alive, even if he is a prisoner in Germany.'

Which is when young Schnabel got on the phone. I took it from his reaction he was surprised by what he heard. He hung up and straightened some papers on his desk.

'It appears that French colonial soldiers were separated,' he told me.

'Separated? Why?' I could feel myself shake.

'All I know is that they haven't been sent to prison camps in Germany like the other French prisoners.'

'But they have been taken prisoner?'

'Yes, they have. I can assure you of that.'

'So where have they been sent if not to Germany?'

'I'm afraid I don't have precise information about individual prisoners. The administration is different from prisoners sent to Germany. Had your Fabrice Mendy been sent there, I would have been able to verify his whereabouts and inform the family.'

'Had he been killed, would his family have been informed?'

'Yes, his next of kin would have been informed by now.'

'So, if that's not the case, it's possible he is a prisoner?'

'In all likelihood, yes, he is.'

'But let me get this straight. Because he's an African prisoner, he wasn't sent to Germany? But you don't know where he has been imprisoned?'

He had the grace to look sheepish. 'It appears that that is the case, yes.'

'When will you know? So I can tell the family?'

'I am sure that this information will be made known to the family in due course.'

'In due course?'

I left the hotel, not entirely satisfied. I had to hope that since Schnabel had told me the family would be informed by now if Fabrice had been killed, that that meant he'd been taken prisoner. But if he was a prisoner, I had a feeling that that meant I'd be beating my head against Nazi bureaucracy to get any answers about exactly where he was being held.

At least I now had something to tell Dominique, even if it wasn't his exact whereabouts yet. Thinking of it again made me consider my own son. And of how I was deliberately prevaricating in the bank case after finding the torn photo to protect him. Capeluche had told me to stop looking into the prisoners missing from Fresnes. I hadn't stopped. I couldn't. Even though Dax wasn't convinced of the need to investigate, if I were to suddenly drop it, it would lead to questions. And I wanted to know what was going on. But the truth is, I hadn't perhaps looked as diligently as I otherwise would have.

In my tiredness, a blur at the corner of my vision as I passed a building startled me. A flash of blue to my right. Only it wasn't my tiredness.

Taking a left before I reached my car, I stopped in a doorway and waited. A man in a blue coat walked slowly past. I stepped out behind him and tapped him on the shoulder. He looked startled but quickly recovered. He didn't try to run or take a swing at me. He was short and muscular, with a pock-marked face running to fat, like someone had squeezed an over-ripe melon into a condom.

'Anything I can help you with?' I asked him.

He looked for a moment like he was going to try and talk his way out of it but changed his mind. 'Just doing my job.'

'Who for?'

He looked sympathetically at me like it was the most simple question I could have asked. It probably was. I considered the likely candidates. There were too many – the SD, Hochstetter, the Gestapo, Capeluche's employers, as she called them, my own police, any one of the other German agencies in the city or any one of the countless other groups I'd not yet heard of. They all used informants. It was the city's one growth industry. These days, there were more different kinds of grass on the streets than there were in the Bois de Boulogne. As for my choice of which one of them I wanted paying attention to what I was up to, none of them appealed to me.

'I wouldn't try finding out, if I were you,' he told me. He pointed to a black Peugeot 202 over the road from us. 'You're a popular boy.'

'Aren't I just? I could arrest you if you don't tell me.' I said it but my heart wasn't in it.

'Sure you could. But how far d'you reckon you'd get with it?' That was why.

'Did Hochstetter send you?'

He laughed, but that was the only reaction. I'd hoped it had been Hochstetter as he was the least scary option. And that says a lot for the atmosphere in the city these days. In my part of the city, anyway. In the end, I had no idea who he was working for and no realistic way of finding out, short of battering him and I was too tired to try. He was a bit too big for me on my current diet. So I let him go.

'Don't let me see you again,' I warned him.

'I won't. But it doesn't mean I won't be there.'

I watched him go and thought of Pepe, my main informant, whining every time I asked him a question. I was really going to have to get a better class of snitch if I was to survive the new reality.

I had thought of going to see Dominique to tell her what I'd learned, but I decided against it now. With half the city hanging onto my shirt tails, I reckoned it was probably best not to draw attention to her.

Ten minutes with Dax and I wished I had. I also wished I hadn't put him straight the other day in his apartment. There are times when your actions come back and bite you on the arse. This was one of them.

'The Boulevard Voltaire job,' he'd assailed me with the moment I got into Thirty-Six. I had to fight down the absurd notion of telling him that it would make a great name for a jazz band. I told you I was tired. 'Where are you on it?'

That was the bit that went well. It was all downhill after that. 'Making enquiries,' I told him. It was suitably vague.

'Boniface tells me there was a witness who saw one of the robbers, did you talk to her?'

I recalled the witness's description of Walter le Ricaneur. 'She only got a vague glimpse of him. It could be anyone.'

'Talk to her again. She would have been emotional and confused when you interviewed her. You know that.'

'I'll do it.'

'No, send Boniface to talk to her instead.'

'There's no need,' I argued. 'I'll go and see her. But we won't get much more out of her.'

He opened his office door and called Boniface in. I tried to put my sleep-deprived mind into gear.

'Anyone but Boniface,' I insisted. 'He talks too fucking much.'

Dax turned on me. 'Go easy on Boniface. He's a good cop, he does his job properly. You're going to turn him into one that doesn't care. I won't tell you again.'

Boniface came in and Dax told him what he wanted him to do before turning back to me. 'What about the manager? What did he have to say?'

'He was too shaken. He just said he was forced to open the safe because the robbers were attacking one of his staff.'

'Have you seen the staff member who was attacked? Where are they?'

'In hospital.'

'Well, when were you planning on seeing them? What are you playing at, Eddie? I don't see any progress on this.'

'It only happened yesterday.'

'Oh, I'm so sorry, Eddie, was I supposed to make an appointment so you could do your job? What do you mean, it only happened yesterday? For Christ's sake. Boniface, you check up on the manager. Eddie here will see the injured cashier when he can spare us a moment.'

'The manager?' I said. I recalled the torn photo he'd given to me and that I'd kept secret. 'That's my job. I spoke to him at the scene, I know what's what.'

He looked angry but calmed slightly. 'All right. But I want Boniface to speak to the witness.'

Boniface looked for a moment like he was about to say something, but for once, he kept his mouth shut. It was more disconcerting than his prattle. He looked oddly at me and then back at Dax, his expression blank.

Dax finally dismissed us and Boniface followed me to my office.

'Have you got the witness's address, Eddie? I'll go and see her now.'

'You won't go and see anyone until I tell you to. I'm in charge of this investigation.'

'What do you want me to do, then? In this investigation?'

I thought for a moment. I couldn't tell him to do nothing. 'Go and see how the cashier in hospital is. Find out what they know.' I had to hope he hadn't seen too much.

I left after he did. Dax cornered me again as I was going.

'This is priority, Eddie. I want some answers today.'

So do I, I thought. Just not the ones Dax wanted.

It was a morning of looking for everyone's son but my own.

I parked in Montparnasse, a short walk from the haberdashery where Madeleine, Dédé's mother, worked. I went in and waited while she finished serving a customer.

'I found Dédé, but he ran,' I told her. 'As far as I know, he's still safe, but I can't help him if he won't let me.'

'I know. He's been to see me since. I made him see sense and he says he's willing to talk to you. But only you.'

'Didn't he tell you what he knows? I need a name.'

'He won't tell me. Only you. That other cop, Boniface, he came by earlier, but Dédé will only talk to you. I need you to look after him, Eddie, make sure he's safe.'

'I'll see him, but tell him not to pull a stunt like the last one. This is my only offer.'

The bell above the door rang as someone opened it. Madeleine looked up briefly and then back at me.

'I'll make sure he comes to see you.' She turned to the customer. 'How can I help you?'

A woman in a brown coat and spiky hair came and stood next to me at the counter. My mouth almost fell open. It was Capeluche. She smiled at me and at Madeleine.

'I really don't want to jump in front of this gentleman,' she said. Her voice was the same timid tone she adopted as Fran's caretaker.

'You won't be,' Madeleine assured her.

'Thank you. I wonder if you can help me. I'm looking for a needle. It's got to be heavy-duty. The material it's got to go through is quite thick, you see. Not very giving.'

Madeleine turned away to look through the thin wooden drawers on the wall behind the counter while Capeluche twisted her head to face me. She unleashed the full wattage of a smile at me and turned back, recomposing her face in time to answer Dédé's mother.

Madeleine showed her a selection of needles. Capeluche picked up a long one and tested the tip. 'Oh, this should do the job perfectly. Now, I'm also looking for twine, would you have any?'

I backed away while they did their business, having to keep a lid on an anger in me that was as fearful as Capeluche's innocent act. She bought the two items she wanted and turned to leave. Before she did, she spoke to me.

'Thank you so much. I hope I may repay your kindness one day.'

I waited until she'd closed the door behind her before going back to the counter. Madeleine was impatient to ask me her question.

'When can you see Dédé?'

With the echo from the bell over the door still ringing, I shook my head. Capeluche was lost from sight but not my visions. 'I can't, Madeleine.'

Her expression was one of disbelief. 'What do you mean?'

'I mean I can't. It's not safe for me to see Dédé.'

'You said you'd protect him. You promised to. Only a moment ago. He's only come out of hiding because I told him you'd make sure he was safe.'

I turned to leave. 'I'm sorry, Madeleine, I just can't.'

'You're a disgrace, Eddie Giral,' she shouted after me.

'It's for his own safety,' I tried to convince her from the open door.

'A disgrace. You won't hear the end of this.'

She broke down in tears. I almost went back in to try and say something that would calm her, but I knew that there was nothing I could offer. Outside, I'd half expected Capeluche to be waiting to talk to me, but I couldn't see her anywhere. I could hear Madeleine's sobbing from the other side of the door and I cursed Capeluche and her torn photo of my son.

Retrieving my car, I considered my options. I had no intention of seeing the Voltaire bank manager or of returning to Thirty-Six. I had nothing to tell Dominique and I couldn't face home. I realised I didn't want to be in Paris, either, so I took a decision on the spur of the moment.

Checking all around me, I slowly drove away, taking the road south out of the city before turning east and then north. It would have played hell with my petrol ration, but I saw no choice. I also saw no one following me. Opening the throttle, I set off along the Lille road, feeling a greater sense of relief at leaving Paris behind me. It was almost a feeling of euphoria, like I used to get from the stuff Fran peddled. And just like the stuff Fran peddled, it didn't last long. The further behind me I left Paris, the more I questioned what I was doing. The doubts started jumbling my brain. My speed reduced without me realising. I'd acted entirely on impulse, a desire to get out of the city and away from the scrutiny of the people following me and the pressure of pretence. I pulled off the road by a row of trees and threw up into a ditch, the bile sharp and foul in my mouth. There was little to spew.

'Wait until they ration that,' I told myself, my throat aching.

For some absurd reason, the thought made me laugh. Loud and hard like a false friend, until tears came. Silent now, and gulping in breaths of air, I sat down on the ground with my back to the car and stared out at a barren field, the crop either harvested or destroyed. I considered what I was doing, the calm of release from the city marshalling my ideas. By the time I stood up again and got behind the wheel, my thoughts were clearer.

Instead of turning back, though, I carried on my way. Leaving Paris further behind, my speed was now as steady and as constant as my determination. Not even a German patrol, on the outskirts of Senlis, could deter me. A jumpy stabsgefreiter in a forage cap and acne examined my police ID closely, but eventually waved me through. It was the brush with reality that I needed.

Checking my surroundings after the patrol, I realised I had to take it carefully from here to make sure I didn't stray too far north. The Germans had designated a Forbidden Zone from the Swiss border stretching round in an arc to the Somme – the North-East Line, they called it – and I didn't want to get too near and draw attention to myself. I doubted my police ID would do much to keep me out of trouble were I to cross it. I was crossing too many lines lately. I started looking for signs. There were none. I suppose I'd expected a big friendly billboard telling me I was on the right road. I had no idea what I was supposed to be looking for. I'd had to look it up the night before in my old school atlas. It wasn't that helpful. Like it was a secret to be kept.

Plumping for a road that looked like it would lead me to where I wanted to go, I turned off the main road and found myself in a little place the size of a small street in Paris called Bailleul-le-Soc. At least there were trees.

I assumed it had to be the Bois d'Eraine.

29

I'd lived in Paris for too long. I was surrounded by farms and I had no idea what they farmed or what sort of thing they'd be doing this time of year. I stuck out like a pimp in a church hall. My hands were clean for one thing. Literally, at least, if not metaphorically.

Two houses stood together in their own tiny row separate from any other buildings. I saw no reason for their being there. I knocked on the door of the one on the right. It was opened by a wizened old guy with no teeth and a face tanned like an old chair. But then this was the country. He was probably younger than me.

'Is this the Bois d'Eraine?' I asked him.

He spat on the ground outside his front door and nodded. I shifted position just in case.

'Is there a German garrison near here?' I asked again. Just as well to get that out of the way.

That earned another spit on the ground, this one more emphatic.

'Who wants to know?' he asked me. I love country folk with their simple questions.

'I do.'

'You a *flic*? Or a German?'

'Do I look German?'

'A *flic*. What is it you want to know?'

This is where I had to start treading carefully.

'Were you here when the fighting was on?'

'Where else would I have been? Lived here all my life. Not moving now. Not for the Boches. Not for the Ministry.'

The way he said it, he obviously saw the Ministry, whichever one it was, as the greater enemy. I chose my words. 'Were there any African troops here? In May or June?'

He spat a third time. It was getting tiresome. I longed for the mugs and thugs of Paris.

'It's young Fernand you want. Over that way. Two kilometres. Pig farm. Red roof.' He spoke like he spat, a sort of scattergun eruption.

I returned to my car with a sense of eyes on me. The door to another house slammed shut as I drove past. The curtains in another twitched.

I found young Fernand without any trouble. It was a pig farm after all. I saw the red roofs at the end of a long lane long after the smell had lured me into its embrace.

Young Fernand opened the door before I was out of my car. 'Young' was evidently a relative term in these parts. He watched impassively as I trod warily through the steaming piles in his yard. The stench was overwhelming. I bet myself that the likelihood of my ruining my shoes was in direct proportion to footwear being the next thing to be rationed.

He gave me the country nod. It was used instead of wasteful luxuries like words to greet people. Just a single nod upwards, that was my lot.

'You from the Ministry?' he asked me.

'Cop.' I showed him my ID. 'I take it the Ministry's not

popular around here?' I still wondered which precise Ministry kept these people enraged at night.

'You could say that.'

'Can I come inside?' I was trying to talk without opening my mouth to stop even more of the smell from getting in.

In response, he turned away, leaving the door open. I followed him into the kitchen. The warmth of the stove reminded me how cold the day had become outside. I stood by it, warming my hands. Next to the stove, a plate stood on the sink with a slice of ham on it that would have taken five hours to queue for in Paris. I'd never felt so tempted, not even by Fran's cocaine back in the day.

'Rain's stopped,' he told me. 'Been shit all month.'

He sat down at the table. The parts of a shotgun lay on a cloth in front of him, with oil and rags to clean them. He wore blue work trousers with a check shirt over the top. A blue jacket hung from a hook on the back door. His stomach was held in place by thick braces to keep his trousers up. He was unshaven, his cheeks and chin a darker blue than his clothes.

I joined him at the table. 'Been bad here, has it?'

'Told you. Been shit all month.' Good to get that out of the way. 'You asking about the Boches.'

Through the back window, I could see the sheds where I assumed the pigs lived. Beyond it, the trees stood in a line like an army in formation, threatening to overrun the farm. The sun was already sinking behind them. Young Fernand picked up a rag and gun part and started polishing it.

'You were here when the fighting was on, I take it?' He nodded. 'What about our army? What do you remember of them?'

'What do you mean? There was fighting. Our boys lost.'

'Do you remember any African troops here?'

'Some.'

'Do you know what happened to them? After we lost? They were separated and taken prisoner. Do you know where they were taken?'

He waited before answering, concentrating on cleaning the locking pin on the shotgun. I thought for a moment he wasn't going to say anything. I saw a flicker in his eyes.

'Is that what you heard?'

'What do you mean?'

The problem was the next thing we both heard was a banging on his front door. He jumped up, startled, his quick movement at odds with his bearing. In the same moment, two German soldiers appeared at the back door. They banged on it and demanded we open. The farmer looked angrily at me and went to open the front door. I let the two soldiers at the back door in. They pointed their rifles at me and made me back away.

Fernand reappeared in the kitchen, followed by a gefreiter and an officer, a hauptmann. The three soldiers looked through the kitchen and examined the shotgun parts on the table. Short and bespectacled, with the air of a city librarian, the hauptmann looked quizzically at me. By my clothes, it was obvious I wasn't a farmer.

'Papers,' he ordered.

I handed him my police ID, which took him by surprise. 'A Paris police officer. You are a long way from home. What are you doing here?'

'I'm looking for a prisoner. He absconded from Paris. We had reports that he'd been seen here.'

'In this farmhouse?'

'No. In the area. I'm simply asking the local residents if they've seen anyone suspicious hanging around or if they've noticed anything stolen lately.'

The hauptmann turned to Fernand. 'And have you?'

The farmer blanched. 'No. I told him.'

'You will come with us.' That was in my direction.

They took me in their car while one of the gefreiters drove behind in mine. I sat next to the hauptmann, who told me his name was Prochnow, in the back of the big Horch vehicle. It was one of those high-sided jobs that made you feel like a kid in an over-sized sweater. It felt just as sweltering. A trickle of sweat ran down my back. I looked out at the trees darkening in the dusk, my mood matching the gathering darkness.

'Where are you taking me?'

'Compiègne.'

At the Wehrmacht garrison, they sat me down in a grey corridor outside Prochnow's office and left me there to wait until a gefreiter finally took me in and sat me down opposite Prochnow. Without a word, he picked up my ID from his desk and studied it. I had no idea what he hoped to find on it that he hadn't already discovered.

'I'm a French policeman,' I reminded him. 'I demand to be allowed to return to Paris.' I felt a lot less confident than I sounded.

He ignored my demand and laid the ID down on his desk with deliberate movements. 'A missing prisoner, you say?'

I kicked myself for having used the word 'prisoner'. I couldn't change it now. 'Yes. He was in our cells awaiting trial and he escaped when he was being taken to court. He's dangerous, so I've been sent to find him. As you'll appreciate, it's difficult these days coordinating with local police officers.'

He called a clerk in and told them to look for the phone number of the police station in Paris.

'I can give it to you,' I told him.

He smiled. 'I would prefer to find it for ourselves.'

After a few minutes, the phone on his desk rang to tell him the call had been put through. He eventually got through to someone in authority and asked who he was talking to. I was already working out how I was going to argue my way out of it, preparing myself for when whoever it was at the other end told Prochnow I wasn't supposed to be there.

'Detective Boniface,' the hauptmann repeated.

I cursed silently. Prochnow explained very carefully that I was in Compiègne and asked if I was there to catch a missing prisoner. I waited on tenterhooks, wishing the call wouldn't end, so I'd have time to come up with something.

It ended almost immediately. Boniface for once not talking as much as he should. Prochnow looked pleased.

'Well, Inspector Giral, that all appears to be in order.'

'It is?'

'Yes. Your Detective Boniface was most helpful. He informed me that you have indeed been sent here to look for a missing criminal. I apologise for any inconvenience.'

I could only stare at him. Boniface's ability to surprise yet again.

'If that's all, might I be allowed to leave now? It's a two-hour drive to Paris.'

They let me go after another half-hour of taking down my details and filing them away in an ancient wooden filing cabinet.

'The next time you come here, please inform the German authorities first. It will save a lot of trouble.'

'I'll be sure to do that,' I promised.

One of the soldiers from the farm showed me to my car. I got in under his gaze and turned the ignition, trying to make a hurried job look natural and carefree. I fully expected a soldier to come running from the building to haul me back in before I'd got the chance to get away.

Outside Compiègne, I pulled over and sat in my car for a few moments, deep in thought about young Fernand and the trees beyond his farm. Despite the cold, I felt the sweat run down my back. Night had fallen, but provided I had a clear road, I'd be in good time to be back in Paris before the curfew. I wasn't worried about Paris, I just didn't want to be on the road after hours.

From my inside pocket, I took out the slice of ham from young Fernand's kitchen. It had been sitting in there ever since I'd pinched it from his plate before the Germans had got there. Picking the fluff off it, I sat and ate it slowly. It tasted like nothing I'd experienced in at least a year.

30

I should have been worried about Paris.

Not Paris as such. She's big enough to take care of herself. Most of the time. I meant the bit of Paris that had me in it. Especially since it seemed that everyone else was unduly worried about that bit too.

I picked up my first follower the moment I crossed the Seine and headed the short distance for home through the streets of the Fifth. It was a Peugeot, so I reckoned it was Hochstetter's proxy fairy godmothers making sure I didn't turn into a pumpkin. I let them be. There were still two hours to go until curfew but I was hungry and wanted to get home and they were unlikely to stop me. The drive back to the city from the Bois d'Eraine had been slow and mercifully uneventful, but the ham I'd borrowed from young Fernand had only kept off the pangs for about fifty kilometres, and right now I was ravenous. There was half a baguette with my name on it in the linen bag on the back of the kitchen door and a rasher of bacon in the cold box, so I wasn't going to let the small matter of being followed by German military intelligence put me off my supper. My stomach rumbled as I recalled the taste of the ham in the woods outside Compiègne and my foot involuntarily pressed harder on the accelerator.

That's when I got my second guard of honour. A Traction Avant. No fairy godmothers this time. It was waiting for me in my street, so I carried on driving, working out my next move and quelling my hunger pains. The Gestapo driver pulled out sharply in front of the Peugeot, so they were directly behind me, with the Abwehr reluctantly bringing up the rear. We made a fine caravan. My stomach growled noisily. Right now it was a caravanserai I needed. I looked in the mirror at the heavy cars trundling along behind me and pitied my poor little street. It wasn't big enough for three cars at once. I was worried it'd sink under the weight.

I turned onto the Boulevard Saint-Germain and checked myself. Instinctively, I'd found myself heading for Rue Saint-Séverin and the narrow lane leading to the street behind my apartment block, but I'd stopped myself in time. It was my secret parking place, something I'd learned to do quite quickly after the start of the Occupation. I didn't want to give that little hidey-hole away, and I'd nearly led them directly to it.

The Traction Avant was close enough behind me that I imagined I could hear its occupants' breath. I checked the mirror. It seemed to me to be filled with the rugged acne of a hard man intent on catching up with me. I slowed at a junction and it bumped slightly into the back of me.

'Touch my bottom again and I shall scream and scream,' I mouthed at the driver in my mirror. Luckily, I don't think he could reverse lip-read French.

I hung a right and entered the narrow streets behind the Sorbonne. I was moving further and further away from home. A few more right and left turns and I was on the incline leading up to the Panthéon. Not sure that was what I intended. I changed down a gear. More petrol I couldn't afford. That and my own need for fuel were beginning to annoy me.

Another vehicle pulled out in front of me from a side road and stopped. I hadn't seen it coming and had to brake hard to avoid hitting it. A German patrol car. I stopped and checked in my mirror, expecting my retinue to get out and come towards me. Instead, they waited patiently behind me in their cars. A feldwebel got out of the patrol car and flagged me down. A stabsgefreiter in the driver's seat kept the motor running. I realised then it was just a routine patrol stopping me at random, nothing to do with my various devoted followers.

'Well, I'm not going anywhere with you in the way, am I, sunbeam?' I told him while he was still out of earshot.

He walked up to me and demanded to see my papers. I handed them to him through the open window and he looked closely at them. He had the myopic squint of a man too vain for glasses and a sharp lantern jaw you could slice ham with.

'A policeman?' he asked. 'What is your business?'

'On my way to see Major Hochstetter of the Abwehr.' That seemed to impress him. I gestured surreptitiously at the cars behind me. 'You might want to check up on those two. Been following me since my meeting with the SD.'

After a moment's thought, he nodded and gave my ID a second examination before signalling to the patrol car. The stabsgefreiter moved it out of my way. The feldwebel gave my papers back and told me to move along. Not quite believing it, I started off up the road towards the Panthéon. As I passed, I saw the patrol car reverse back into the way of the Gestapo car. As calmly as I could, I accelerated away and turned down the first street to the right that I found. Before turning, I looked back at the Traction Avant being flagged down and grinned. I didn't wave. Not even I'm that cocky.

I sped up and hurried through the small streets to the main road. Once the patrol realised the men in the car were Gestapo, they'd be out of their path faster than I could eat stolen ham, so I knew I didn't have long to put any distance between me and them. I made it count, racing across junctions and cutting down the narrowest alleys the car would fit. Not for the first time, I thanked the lack of cars on the city streets.

Except now I was further away from home than ever. Cruising through Montparnasse, I realised my followers would simply go back to wait for me at my apartment building, so it was pointless trying to beat them to it. And if they really wanted to see me, they'd come knocking anyway. Not even the prospect of a measly rasher of bacon and day-old bread was going to make up for that.

'I need to eat something,' I told myself. And for some reason, mainly because it was nearby, I parked up in the street near Luigi's and made my way there on foot. I still had good time before the curfew. I was able to be out after midnight, anyway, because of my police ID, but I still preferred to keep out of the blackout limelight as much as I could.

'We don't want any trouble,' Luigi told me through his moustache after he'd pulled the black drape covering the door aside.

'I want food,' I told him. 'We can save the trouble for another day.'

He didn't understand what I meant, but let me in nonetheless.

'We don't serve food,' he told me from behind his bar.

He'd done the usual thing of parking me well away from his usual punters. I didn't mind. I looked around. It was hardly the caravanserai I'd been hoping for, but it would have to do. The two German soldiers who'd told me about the Bois d'Eraine – the ones I'd met at Fran's club – were selling their Pervitin to an unsavoury brace of scrawny French pimps. At another table, a bunch of soldiers with a single star on their sleeves were playing cards, their voices raucous with Luigi's gutrot. The star said they were oberschützes, privates not good enough to become gefreiters. This place really attracted the best and the brightest. And here I was.

'Nice crowd in tonight,' I told Luigi. 'Food.'

'I don't serve food, Eddie, you know that.'

'I don't mind what you've got, Luigi. Bit of ham, some cheese, bread, anything.'

He dropped his cloth on the counter in exasperation. 'I told you, Eddie, I don't do food.'

'You've got to eat, haven't you, Luigi? When you're here working?'

He looked doubtful. 'Yeah.'

'That's fine then. I'll have some of that.' He stared back at me in consternation. 'Well, off you go. And I'll have some whisky too.'

'I can't serve whisky. Vichy rules.'

'The good stuff.'

I held his gaze until he finally gave in and disappeared behind the curtain at the back of the bar. He came back out two minutes later with a small plate with a slice of ham and a sliver of cheese on it. The bread was see-through, but it looked as tempting as anything I'd eaten in the last year.

'That was my supper,' Luigi told me.

I finished the last of the ham and wiped the crumbs off the plate with the bread. 'You're going to be pretty hungry come morning, then, aren't you?' I didn't believe him for one minute.

He took the plate back with a grunt and placed an opaque glass on the counter with whisky in it. I breathed in the aroma. It wasn't good, but it was as good as it got when you weren't supposed to have it. Rumour had it there were illegal ware-houses of the stuff being hoarded to sell to the Germans at their usual rock-bottom rates. Or to people like Luigi willing to turn a blind eye to the contents. And where they came from. I took a sip. It hurt, but in a good way.

'I hear you've been looking for Dédé Malin,' a voice wheedled at my shoulder.

I nearly spat the liquid heaven out in my shock. I turned to see Pepe's weasel features sidling up to me. More panicked than I would have admitted, I looked over his head to make sure Capeluche was nowhere in sight. I knew she wouldn't be, this wasn't her sort of place, but Calais Jacques might have been in earshot. I scanned the room and was relieved not to see him anywhere. I recalled Capeluche buying needle and twine from Dédé's mother earlier that day and hid a shiver. I turned back to face the bar and calmed.

'You heard wrong,' I told him.

'Pity. I know where you can find him.'

I stared at the bottom of the glass, my mind working quickly to work out where this was coming from. 'So do I.'

He came closer. 'Sure? I can tell you.'

That settled it. Pepe was way too eager to give me information I hadn't asked for. I turned to face him. 'Only I don't need to know, Pepe.'

His look turned instantly to disappointment. 'I thought you did.'

I smiled at him. That should have warned him. 'I can see that.' I reached over and pulled his tie, dragging him closer still. His face was centimetres from mine. 'But what I would like to know is who it is who told you to come and tell me you have information about Dédé.'

I tightened my hold and his face grew redder. 'I was just trying to help, Eddie.'

'Yes, but who?'

Through his puffing crimson panic, I could see a greater fear. He shook his head but wouldn't open his mouth. Luigi came across and tried to grab my arm, but I swatted him away with my other hand.

'Tell me, Pepe, and I'll let you go.'

'I can't.'

I released him and helped him dust himself down and get his breath.

'Well done, Pepe, you just did.'

His expression of fear before was nothing compared with the look of terror now. I almost felt sorry for him. Almost. I drank up my whisky and put some money on the counter for Luigi.

'You won't be wanting any ration tickets, I take it?' I asked him and left.

Walking through the darkened and near-deserted streets to my car, I wondered what it was that had just happened. A cat miaowed loudly in anger somewhere in the darkness and the thought struck me. It had been a test. Capeluche testing me to see if I'd take the bait to defy her and look for Dédé.

'That should satisfy you,' I said in a low voice. I wondered if it would.

I neared home in my car to find a third fairy godmother had joined in the fun. A second Traction Avant. The SD, I wondered. That was in addition to the man standing in a doorway opposite my flat, the cigarette stubs at his feet giving him away. Another nail in the coffin for reasons to smoke. Either way, I sighed heavily and began the second convoy of the night through the streets of the Fifth. I wasn't going home tonight. I made a similar journey, this time into the narrow roads of the neighbouring Sixth.

'Never a German patrol when you need one,' I muttered.

What I did find was a pair of German trucks trundling slowly along the Boulevard Saint-Germain. I got in line behind them, wondering how I could use them. My three bridesmaids tucked neatly in behind me, each at a respectable distance. We drove east a few blocks in a stalemate train. I was tempted to duck down any of the narrow streets leading off the main road, but I knew the others would have no problem in coming after me.

I suddenly saw that the first of the lorries was making to turn into Rue Bonaparte, its movements laborious given its size. Without hesitation, I gunned my engine and pulled out in front of both lorries and squeezed past them to get onto the side road before they did. I heard the squeal of brakes behind me as the first truck juddered to slow down, but I ignored it and cut right in front. I missed it by a coat of paint and accelerated along the road. Behind me, I saw that I was the only one who'd pulled the stunt. The lorries were behind me, quickly receding in the distance, and none of the three cars was anywhere in view, blocked by the trucks in the narrow street. I let my breath out in a sibilant cheer. I hadn't realised I'd been holding it. Rue Bonaparte, I thought. Fitting that a street of booksellers should be the one to save me. I turned off immediately and weaved through the streets, crossing the river to put as much of a gap between me and my pursuers as I could.

Just a short walk from Thirty-Six, I pulled up and turned my engine off. I couldn't keep driving around the night-time city. I'd be too easy to find. I sat in my car and considered my options. It didn't take long. I wasn't so far from where Dax lived, but I knew I didn't want to bring him into all this. He'd ask too many questions. I thought of Boniface. I didn't know where he lived. And he'd talk too much for my state of mind. Fran wasn't an option. It would be one more thing he had to use against me. With a touch of sadness, I realised that the one person I could have counted on once, long ago, was Joe.

Getting out of the car, I checked my watch. The Metro would still be running, but only for half an hour, until curfew started. I hurried to the nearest station and got on the first train that came in. The carriage was empty except for four revellers on their way home after a night out. The idea of it shocked me. I wondered with a mild anger if anyone had told them we'd been occupied.

I got out and climbed through the streets. The last haul was the killer. My calves ached and the hunger assuaged by Luigi's light supper was making a comeback. I found the building I wanted and climbed the stairs. Hesitating a few moments at the apartment door, I finally knocked. Only no one answered. I knocked again, louder this time, and heard a shuffling inside, but still no one opened the door. I knocked a third time. Quieter again, not forceful, but there was no response. I put my mouth up to the door and spoke in a low voice.

'It's Eddie.'

Again there was silence, but eventually I heard the chain slide on the door and the bolt being opened.

'Jesus, Eddie, you terrified me.'

She looked worried at first, but I could see it quickly being replaced by anger. She pulled her cardigan tighter across her chest.

'I'm sorry, Dominique. I had nowhere else to go.'

31

There was a week-old newspaper on the bedside table. I picked it up and scanned the front page. Apparently, we were all very happy under German rule and the economy was picking up nicely. Three cheers for that.

In the midst of the propaganda dreck, I came across a story I'd been aware of but missed. The floods in Perpignan, my home town. The whole of the country, not just young Fernand in the Bois d'Eraine, had been suffering torrential rain and storms on and off for the whole of the month. The ones down south were worse than I'd realised. About a hundred people had died in a landslide in the Pyrenees. Because the newspapers and radio were too intent on telling us how well off we all were, real news was sketchy at best. As a result, I found I switched off from much of what we were told.

I put the paper back on the table. It's odd, but with all the man-made stuff going on around us, it took me by surprise for some reason to find natural disasters still happening. I imagine I expected nature to behave while we humans did our best to destroy everything else.

I thought of my parents. I had to assume they were all right as the area of flooding wasn't near where they lived. I could write to them, now that post was getting through in some form, but I had no way of telephoning them. They used to have a phone in the bookshop, but ever since they'd retired, they hadn't had one at home. The bookshop. Where I was supposed to have taken over, even though I'd wanted to go to university to follow my brother Charles and his dashed destiny to be a teacher. None of it had happened. The last time we got into an argument with the neighbours saw to that. Charles was buried on the Somme and I came home damaged and with the idea of being a cop to see if I could undamage everything. Including myself. That had worked, I thought wryly. I made a quick calculation. I hadn't heard from my parents for two years. The gulf widens when you keep staring at it.

Lying back, I felt my head sink into the unfamiliar comfort of the soft pillow. The light was different, falling in thin strips down the wall to my left, the negative of the shadow cast by the blinds. The cracks in the ceiling followed another pattern. The feel of the sheets, the smell of the air in the room, they were all new.

And I knew I was evading the issue. The sheets, the pillow, the bed. The paper, the floods, my parents. All a diversion to hide from the thoughts that should have been running around my head.

The door opened and the diversion ended. Dominique walked in. She was wearing a silk dressing gown. Pre-war clothing, my mind instantly decided, the bizarre thoughts born of surprise at finding myself in this situation. And yet another distraction.

She got back into bed beside me, her gown still on. I sensed she felt the same embarrassment and the same surprise that I did. But by the same token, it felt natural, something that should have happened all those years ago. Except neither of us knew what to say. We lay side-by-side in silence. I tried to think of the least trite thing I could possibly utter and gave up.

'You'll be wanting a wash,' she finally said, adding in embarrassment: 'After the day you had yesterday.'

'Right.'

It felt a relief. Only I was naked in her bed. She realised and got out again. 'I'll leave you to it. I'll be in the kitchen.'

I hurriedly washed and dressed and went through to the living room.

'Breakfast,' Dominique sang from the kitchen. 'I'm just making coffee.'

She'd laid the small table with two plates of thinly sliced bread and jam. The economics of lust under the Occupation, I thought. Spend the night with someone and you or they had to give up some of the breakfast that you'd queued for hours to buy at prices you couldn't afford.

'Not real coffee,' she called again from the kitchen.

'It'll be fine.'

As I waited for her, I took a look around the room. No books on shelves, but a gramophone player with a neat row of jazz records. I tried to work out how that made me feel. I had no idea how any of this made me feel. Except for a surprising sense of calm I'd rarely felt in years, mixed with a warm excitement I'd probably never known. I looked again at the records and had a sudden odd vision of them being a complement to my books, not a substitute for them.

She came in, carrying a tray with two cups of coffee. The steam rose from them in narrow tendrils. I watched her as she carefully added the cups to the bounty already waiting on the table. She was concentrating on not spilling the coffee and I felt an immediate sense of guilt. This wasn't lust. I was momentarily lost in the contours of her face, the darkness of her eyes, the slenderness of her neck and I had to turn away. She didn't know I was watching her and I felt like an intruder.

'Not much, I'm afraid,' she apologised now, breaking into my thoughts.

'It's a feast,' I told her.

She smiled and gestured to me to sit down. We sat at right angles to each other. It created an intimacy that the confrontation of facing each other would never have produced. It felt like we'd sat like this together for years. But we hadn't.

'That's all the bread,' she said.

'It's hard to get,' I agreed.

'No butter, I'm sorry.'

'Good coffee.'

'I can put a record on.'

I shook my head. 'No need.'

It was the small talk of two people with too much to say to each other.

Instead, we sat and ate in silence. She caught me looking at her and smiled again. A gaze from both of us that lingered. A greater intimacy than any words could ever have given us. She put some jam on a slice of bread and handed it to me. I took it, my fingers touching hers.

It was too soon for words, I realised. She didn't.

'I would have left my husband for you,' she suddenly confessed. 'All those years ago.'

I took a bite out of the bread to avoid having to answer. Her words surprised me. Not the sentiment but the fact. It was clumsy. That should have been my role in this. I was the awkward one. My silence lingered that moment too long. She looked at me expectantly, waiting for me to speak.

'I'll try and talk to the local police,' I finally told her. 'Next time I go back to the Bois d'Eraine.'

My sharp shift in the conversation shocked her. I saw a slight flare of anger in her eyes.

'You heard what I said?' she asked.

'And I'll try the German authorities again.'

She looked away. 'Did you hear what I just told you, Eddie?'

'Only I can't do any of it officially.'

She turned to face me again. 'You can't do what officially?' she demanded.

'Look for Fabrice.'

I fidgeted with the slice of bread on my plate. Thankfully, my words seemed to annoy her more than my silence at her admission. All I felt was relief. She picked up the last piece of bread and angrily spread a thin layer of jam on it. This time she didn't give it to me. 'What about Jean-Luc? You said you couldn't find anything out about where he was either. Have you tried again?'

I took a bite from the bread. I was on safer ground, despite her growing annoyance with me. 'I have to be careful, Dominique. Very few people at work know I have a son. And I don't want the Germans to find out.' I explained to her who Hochstetter was and my relationship with him.

'Why haven't you asked him about Fabrice? That wouldn't be giving anything away about Jean-Luc.'

'I don't know. It's not as easy as that. I don't want to give too much away to Hochstetter. He'd use it as an extra hold over me.'

'This is my son.' She tugged the gown tightly around her in an abrupt expression of rejection. 'What about Joe, Eddie? Have you done anything to help him?'

'I'm trying, Dominique.'

She sipped her coffee, her anger simmering in time with her drink. 'That's you, Eddie, through and through. You forget about people too easily when they're not around. No one exists to you unless you see them. Joe, Fabrice, your own son, me. I bet you've barely thought of any of us.'

'I have.'

I had. I knew I had. But perhaps not enough. Not consistently. My mind ran to Capeluche and Hochstetter and tried to give me a justification I couldn't share with her. But I knew there was a truth in what she said. I'd always been able to shut people out without a second thought. I'd thought of it in the past as a positive, an ability to move forward at a time when I didn't dare look back. But to others, I could see it was a weapon that cut both ways. It was a self-centredness born of self-loathing.

Only now I sensed that Dominique loathed me too. I drank my coffee in a gulf that separated us like a photo torn in two.

'I did leave my wife,' I suddenly said.

'For me?' My silence said too much and she stood up. 'Maybe you should go, Eddie.'

I got up and looked at her, but she was avoiding my gaze. I'd never felt such longing to do the right thing. I just didn't know what that was. Wanting to say something but unable to, I put my jacket on. She followed me to her front door.

'Will I see you again?' I asked her.

She studied my face. I'd never felt so alone.

'Yes. Just not now.'

She closed the door. I gazed at the dark wood for a moment or two, hoping she'd open it. She didn't and I turned away.

Wearily going down the stairs inside her building, I noticed something in my side jacket pocket bump gently against my hip. It was a pocket I never used. Reaching in, I found a tube. I took it out and saw that it was a packet of Pervitin, the methamphetamine that Fran had been dealing in his club.

'You bastard, Fran,' I muttered.

I knew he'd left it in there as a temptation for me, a pathway to the addiction he'd caused back in my younger days. I looked at the tube a moment longer than I should and shoved it back in my pocket.

32

There was more music to be faced. I knew I couldn't put it off much longer. Taking the Metro to Thirty-Six, I looked around me and went in. I seemed to be safe from pursuers for the time being, even though 'safe' was a relative term as neither inside nor outside the police station offered any great measure of security. For once I was relieved to find Boniface heading me off before Dax saw me.

'I've spoken to the witness,' he told me. 'In the Boulevard Voltaire job.'

'You were only supposed to speak to the cashier.'

'I thought I'd save you some time.'

Hiding my panic, I called him into my office. 'What's she got to say? She was very upset, I seem to remember. I don't know how much store we can put by what she thinks she saw.'

'I agree.' He took a seat, so he didn't see the look of relief I was convinced must have crossed my face. 'She says she thinks the robber had a moustache now and was foreign. I spoke to the uniform who spoke to her first, and he says she said something about a smile.'

I feigned irritation. 'I thought as much.'

'What did she tell you when you spoke to her?' he asked me.

I thought on my feet. 'Clean-shaven, French, nothing about

a smile.' Different enough to discredit her account, not so different Boniface would question it.

'Back to square one, then. You were right.'

'Where's Dax?' I asked him.

'He's out. Some meeting with the Germans, I think. He should be back soon.' He turned to look over his shoulder at the detectives' room outside. 'So they caught you, then?'

'Beg your pardon.'

'The Germans. Up in the Oise.'

I recalled Prochnow, the German officer, talking to Boniface on the phone the previous night. So much had happened since that it had gone from my mind. It put me in a tight spot. I couldn't let him know about my investigation into Dominique's missing son, but with Capeluche on my back, I couldn't fob him off either with the story I'd told the Germans that I'd been pursuing the missing prisoners investigation. I couldn't let it get out that I was still on that case, especially when I hadn't been.

As it was, he took up his own reins. 'They said you were after one of the missing prisoners. So I played along with it. I thought it would be better to tell the Germans what they wanted to hear.'

I knew I should thank him for it, but I was too on edge. 'Not the Fresnes prisoners. The description the Boulevard Voltaire witness gave me put me in mind of one of the Montmartre crowd I arrested once.'

'What was he doing all the way up in Compiègne?'

'My grass, Pepe, you met him, he told me he'd been seen up there.'

'Who is it? I'll put my feelers out.'

'No need. Wild goose chase. Couldn't have been him.'

'So who was it?'

I was exhausted. There's nothing more tiring than keeping on top of the lies you tell to cover up other lies.

'Just forget, it, Boniface. I told you it was nothing.'

He held his hands up to placate me. 'OK, OK, I get the message.'

'Is that all?'

I expected him to take the hint and go. But this was Boniface.

'Dédé. He's willing to talk.' I remembered Madeleine telling me that Boniface had been to see her.

'I know. I've seen his mother.'

'So when are we seeing him?'

'We're not. He'll only talk to me.'

'So when are you seeing him?'

'Christ, Boniface, have you got nothing better to do than pester me? I'll see him if I think it's safe. There's no point en- dangering his life for a name.'

An odd look went across his features, one I hadn't seen before. He didn't believe me. Despite my anger and the irritation he aroused in me, the knowledge cut me. I didn't like Boniface, but he was a good cop. I didn't want him to think I wasn't. He got up to go.

'Sure, Eddie. What do you want me to say the next time the Germans call?'

I left Thirty-Six to retrieve my car. I also wanted to be out when Dax got back.

I scanned all around me as I walked a roundabout route through the streets on the Île de la Cité to get to my Citroën. I couldn't help feeling jumpy, but oddly, the pursuers so keen on knowing what I was up to last night seemed to have lost interest. Or I just couldn't spot them. That was more likely.

My mind occupied, I only saw the figure leaning against my

car when I was almost upon it. With her brown coat and scarf, she looked like any other shopper tired at returning from the morning queue for food.

'Good morning, Eddie,' Capeluche greeted me. Gone was the caretaker voice. In its place was the quiet authority I'd heard in my office, but with a spring in its step.

'What do you want?'

I stood in front of her, my size looming over her. Lifting her weight from my car and moving towards me, she reached up and stroked my cheek.

'Oh, Eddie, you look tired.'

I had the strange feeling of something blocking the vision in my left eye. I refocused and saw that something thin and pointed was just centimetres in front of my face. Capeluche's hand rested on my cheek. She pulled it away slowly and I saw that she was holding a stiletto, a killer's weapon, to my eye.

'I'm impressed.'

'You were meant to be.'

'Is that it?'

'I do like you, you know.' She pulled her hand away, but stayed close to me. She examined my face, her gaze flickering back and forth between my eyes. It was one of the most disconcerting experiences I'd known. 'No. I actually have a couple of requests for you. Your friend Poquelin, or Fran, as you call him. We'd like you to spend less time at his club now that it's reopened. It's bad for business. We feel he's more our concern, especially since you now know he's innocent of any involvement in Julot's death.'

'I do?'

'Of course you do. I told you so. Poquelin's only involvement was that he knew that if he wanted his club to reopen, he had to do as he was told and go away for the weekend.'

'But I take it he is part of your little set-up.'

'Good God, no. Even my employers draw a line somewhere. Not for his morality, but for his ability. No, your man Poquelin is as scared of us as the next man. We just got his club reopened so he can pay us not to have it closed again. Or worse. A club's no good to my employers if the Nazis won't allow it to open. It doesn't make them any money. So, no need for you to fall out with him. But also no need to pursue him any further.'

'Is that what you came to see me about?'

All the time, she stood up close to me. Even if I had contemplated trying to overpower her, I wouldn't have had a chance. She knew that the shorter the distance between us, the greater the threat she and her stiletto posed to me. I was struck by the contrast between the danger she represented and the middle-aged woman in a mousy coat that she displayed to the world. I was intimidated by one metre fifty of invisibility. That was her strength.

'I'm afraid not, Eddie. I'm a little disappointed with you. I did ask you not to pursue your investigation into the prisoners.'

'I'm not.'

'I think we'll have to disagree on that. Which is a pity for your son, wouldn't you say? He's never really been able to rely on you, has he?'

My hands balled into fists at my sides, but I stayed calm. 'If you look properly, I'm not investigating. I'm going through the motions. If I don't, my employers will want to know what's going on. I know the Boulevard Voltaire job was your lot. I looked the other way with that. If I did the same with the prisoners, I'd be facing too many questions.'

She bit her lip. 'I want to believe you, Eddie, really I do.'

'I make a big deal about the prisoners without getting anywhere. That way, I can brush the bank job under the carpet while

I'm making it look like I'm focusing on the Fresnes problem. If I'm really investigating, what progress have you seen me make?'

'Oh, Eddie, I know you're trying to speak to this Dédé boy.'

I shook my head. 'If I were trying to speak to him, I would have by now. You know that. The fact I'm still supposedly looking for him when I know perfectly well how to get hold of him shows I've got no intention whatsoever of seeing him.'

'You talk well, I have to admit that. OK, I'll give you a little longer. But don't forget about your son. I can tell my employers about him any time I want.'

'They don't know?'

She laughed. It was such a gentle sound to convey a cold cruelty. 'I'm not owned by my employers. I keep other irons in the fire. One of them is your son. That whole business is nothing to do with them.'

I had to ask despite my pride. 'What do you know about Jean-Luc?'

Oddly, she seemed to soften for a fraction of a second. 'He's safe. For now. He's trying to cross the Pyrenees into Spain. You see, I also work with people who do that, who get runaways and refugees out of the country. For money, of course, but perhaps a nobler service than my other work. We all have our lines that we draw.'

'I wish I could believe that.'

'You'd do well to.' A car drew up on the other side of the road, a Citroën Traction Avant, the Gestapo's vehicle of choice in Paris. And of countless others. Including some of the city's more affluent organised criminals. She glanced over to it. She took a step closer to me and spoke in a low voice. 'Don't make me come and see you again.'

Act II

November 1940

33

'If you won't come to see me, I suppose I'll just have to come and see you.'

It was Dominique at my door. I took a step back.

'You'd better come in.'

She gave me a wry smile and wafted into my tiny hallway. I closed my eyes as her perfume left a temptation in passing. By the time I'd followed her in, she was sitting on my good armchair. She patted the other chair and I sat down.

'So what's it to be, Eddie? I had to be the one to come to see you. Why's that?'

I searched for the right thing to say.

'Would you like to go for a walk? In the gardens? It's not raining.'

Her gaze lingered on me and she gave a small nod.

Outside, it hadn't rained all day. For the first time in many days, I saw couples walking in the Jardin du Luxembourg. Or perhaps I just saw them now. I breathed in the air. The scent of the grass and trees was heightened by her perfume.

'Are you a good cop, Eddie?' she asked me. 'Because you're hopeless with women.'

'Not all women.'

She laughed. A warm sound that made summer of autumn. 'Hopeless.'

Another couple walked past us, holding hands, like the city wasn't just hours away from the curfew imposed on us by an invading army. They irritated me, but that was perhaps also because I couldn't take Dominique's hand.

'Do you want me to stay the night?' she suddenly asked me as we walked in the Jardin du Luxembourg.

'Yes.'

'There. That wasn't too difficult, was it?'

We passed the bandstand. A quartet was playing *J'attendrai* to a small crowd of French civilians and German soldiers. Dominique began to sing, almost under her breath, but I could hear the extraordinary beauty of her voice, the depth she put into each word. I remembered another voice from long ago, a very different one.

'Would you like a coffee?' I suggested. 'We could go somewhere.'

It was warm inside the small café opposite the gardens where I used to come for Sunday coffee. I hadn't noticed the air turning chilly outside. I heard a table of four people, two men and two women, discussing in hushed voices the new Vichy Statute for Jews. They showed a sense of disbelief that I'd noticed in others since the news had come out, a perplexity at what our supposed representatives were doing in our name. They shared the same horror I did. I smiled at them but they quickly stopped speaking the moment they saw me. Distrust spread like an illness.

I recalled her singing and that of another voice. 'I don't know what to do about Joe,' I told her.

She sipped her coffee. You couldn't enjoy it, it wasn't real. 'What have you tried?'

I told her about talking to Hochstetter and the US embassy and how I was getting nowhere. 'And he's going to be moved. Handed over to the Germans.'

'You have to do something, Eddie.'

'I know. But I don't know what. I should go and see him but I've got nothing new I can tell him.'

'You can't let him down again.' Her words hung between us. I changed the subject.

'I'm going to go back to the Bois d'Eraine. Talk to the Germans there to find out where Fabrice and the other Senegalese soldiers are being kept.'

'I want to come with you.'

I shook my head. 'You can't. It's too risky. It's bad enough for a Paris cop to be there asking questions.'

'Without an African woman tagging along for the ride, you mean?'

'No, I'm sure the Nazis will fall over themselves to help.'

She gave one of the most melancholy laughs I'd ever heard. 'Let's go home,' she said.

'Whose home?'

'Yours.'

She went on outside while I paid for the two drinks. Leaving the deceptive warmth of the bar, I saw her waiting for me at the corner, some ten metres from where I was. I began towards her when I saw a figure come up behind her. A woman in a brown coat over dark trousers, her hair in clumps at right angles to her head.

As I watched in horror, quickening my pace, Capeluche stopped walking and waited beyond Dominique. She looked at me expectantly. I passed Dominique without a word, avoiding making eye contact, as though I didn't know her. I tried to shake my head at her as imperceptibly as I could as I went by, but all I saw from her was a look of not understanding giving way to one of anger. I prayed she wouldn't say anything.

'Good evening, Eddie,' Capeluche said when I was almost upon her.

I stopped, trying to see what Dominique's reaction was, but I couldn't twist around innocently enough to see. Capeluche suddenly let out a small laugh.

'She's gone,' she said. 'Your friend. You do like to create problems for yourself, don't you? Seeing a Senegalese woman under Nazi rule. Maybe not the wisest of moves. But that's love. Or attraction or whatever you like to call it.'

I wanted to tell her to shut up. I was surprised to realise that I wanted to kill her. I turned to see Dominique disappear around the corner at the opposite end of the street. In trying not to give her away to Capeluche and keep her out of danger, all I'd achieved was to upset her. And for nothing.

'Is there anything about me you don't know?' I asked her.

'I know you'd like to kill me right now.' She stood close in front of me. 'But that's probably not a very good idea.'

I felt a pinprick in my stomach. She pulled back and I saw she was holding the stiletto in her hand. I had no idea how she'd managed to pull it on me again without me seeing. I felt my stomach under my shirt. She'd simply punctured the skin, a tiny wound that stopped bleeding the moment I put my finger on it.

'I'm impressed. Again.'

'You were meant to be. Again.'

With her left hand, she pushed the stiletto back up her right sleeve. She flexed and it flicked out again, the hilt sitting poised in her right hand, the thin blade under my throat. It was on a spring action arm, released by a movement of her wrist. I'd seen a Pigalle pimp in the past keep a Derringer on a similar contraption. She'd gauged the distance to perfection, the tip licking my skin without piercing it. Another deft movement and the knife was gone.

'I know it's a bit ostentatious,' she said, 'but I think I've made my point. Would you like to come with me? There's someone I want you to see.'

'No. You can say what you want to say to me here.'

'I'm afraid my invitation to come with me was actually not an invitation. You see those two cars over there?' She pointed to a brace of Citroën Traction Avant cars parked by the gardens and signalled to one of them, which drove off. 'That one is now following your friend, so I suggest you do as I ask.'

With no choice, I let her lead me to the second of the cars and we got in. 'Where are we going?'

'I want you to understand a little bit about me, Eddie.'

We drove in silence to a narrow street in the Folie-Méricourt part of town. For once, there wasn't the high-pitched whining sound of sheared metal from the small ironworking businesses, shut down and quiet for the weekend. She let us into an apartment block, but instead of climbing the stairs as I'd expected, we went through to the rear of the ground floor where she unlocked a door into what I thought would be a metal workshop. I tensed, not knowing what to expect.

'Hervé,' she called. 'I'm home. I have a visitor.'

Increasingly mystified, I allowed her to usher me into what would have been a comfortably furnished apartment in old business premises had there been any walls. Instead, the one large room was divided by the furniture into the different areas of a home – a kitchen, a living room and a bedroom, all open to each other. The only internal wall was at the far end, probably the bathroom. Still taking in my surroundings, I heard the sound of something scraping on the tiled floor and a man around my age in a wheelchair came into view. Capeluche went over to him and kissed him.

'This is Eddie,' she told him. 'I wanted him to meet you.'

Her voice was different again, softer than the killer but more confident than the caretaker. She turned his chair around and pushed him into the living-room area, with two mismatched armchairs opposite each other and a space in between where I imagined his wheelchair normally sat. She parked him where I thought she would and gestured me to sit down on one of the armchairs. We were in a horseshoe around a low table.

Hervé had no legs. But that wasn't what I saw. It was his face, his expression. I stared into his eyes. He gazed back at me. He turned once to Capeluche for reassurance and then back to me.

'You understand,' she told me.

'Shell shock,' I replied, my voice low.

'Hello, Eddie,' he said to me, a small smile on his face.

'Hello, Hervé.'

I looked from one to the other, unsure of what I was supposed to do. My eyes kept returning to the man. Shell shock. I knew what that was. That was what had first brought me to Paris in 1915, to an institute in the Fifth Arrondissement. Where I'd met a nurse called Sylvie, Jean-Luc's mother, and fallen in love with her before they'd sent me back to the front, deemed fit to face more shells.

Capeluche kissed him again and sat down on the other armchair. She looked at him for a few moments in silence. Her expression was gentle, her spiked hair somehow softer, her hands no longer a killer's.

'Why have you brought me here?' I asked her.

Seeming to tear her gaze away from Hervé, she turned to face me. 'I lent my handsome, funny husband to the government so he could play in the war they wanted. And they sent him back to me like this. With no money, no compensation and a pension a mouse couldn't live on.'

'I'm sorry. But I don't see what that justifies.'

She looked frankly at me. 'Do you know what they told me to do? To make ends meet? Take in sewing. That's what they said. Take in sewing. "You're a woman, you can take in sewing."'

She turned back to Hervé, her face filled with a latent fury that was almost as shocking as the coldness I'd seen in her eyes before. Watching the husband and wife stare without comprehension at each other, I saw again Julot's mouth and understood where it came from. I closed my eyes and sighed. What do I say to an uncontained anger and grief like that? Especially when I'd felt it too.

'Why throw your lot in with criminals?'

'You need to ask? They're all criminals. The government that did this to Hervé were all criminals.' She paused. 'Every single one of them.'

'So why join them?'

'Because there are times when to survive, all that's left to you is to join them. You just have to choose the gang of criminals you think is going to win.'

'You have a choice.'

'Do you? You might have. I didn't. But you have a choice now.'

'What's that?'

'Join me. Your police aren't going to go anywhere, not with the Nazis in power.'

'They won't be in power forever.'

'How do you know that? And then what are you going to do? I know you, Eddie. I know what you're capable of. I see it in you.'

'What am I capable of?'

'The same as I am.'

'I'm not.'

She gestured to Hervé and put her head to one side and asked,

'Are you sure of that? Just how well are you doing these days? With your cop's salary? At the beck and call of the Boches? Join me and you won't ever have to do that again. Join me and you won't go hungry again.'

'I'm a cop.'

'And? Where's it getting you? You have a choice which way you go in this war. The choice is yours to make.'

'Is it?'

We sat in silence for a moment, all the words said. The still was broken by the sound of Hervé humming gently, a tune we used to sing in the trenches.

'What's your real name?' I asked her.

She shook her head. 'The only name you need to know is Capeluche.'

'An executioner.'

'Well done, Eddie, you've done your homework. I thought a bookish man like you would get to the bottom of it.'

'What happened to him? The real one?'

'He led a revolt.' She laughed, the first time I'd heard a bitter note under the rage in her voice. 'It failed.'

'You don't think that's an omen?'

She shook her head. 'He was a revolutionary. They always end badly. I'm a pragmatist. I recommend you be the same.'

'Believe me, I am.'

'I'll remember that. I have another name for you. Henri Lafont.'

I was puzzled. It wasn't a name I knew. 'Who's that?'

'That's for you to find out.'

Hervé ceased humming for a moment and made a small noise at the back of his throat. She reached across to stroke his head with an affection that was painful to watch. He began to hum again. She smiled at him and I had to look away.

'I need to go now.'

She gestured to the door. 'You're free to go any time you want, Eddie.'

'One thing I don't understand. You're killing anyone who threatens to say anything about who's behind this, but here you are, telling me this.'

'Nearly everything,' she corrected me. She soothed Hervé as his humming became more agitated. 'That's where you just lost the choice, Eddie. Now you know, you either join me or I kill you.'

34

'New one on me.'

I turned to Boniface and asked him if he'd heard of a villain called Henri Lafont, but he denied any knowledge either, only he took longer to say it than Dax had.

'What's it to do with?' Dax wanted to know.

'The Boulevard Voltaire robbery.' Well, it was in a very circuitous away, I argued to myself.

'Good to see you making some progress on this,' Dax grumbled.

'Isn't it?'

I also tried asking Barthe and Tavernier as they were the old-timers and Mayer as he knew what he was talking about. I even tried the rest of the detectives and put a phone call through to Judge Clément. Not one of them had heard of the name that Capeluche had given me the previous day. I checked such records as we had since the turmoil of the Nazis hitting town and our bosses floating all the papers down the Seine in a barge. We'd got them back, more or less, but they were all over the place. I drew a blank everywhere.

I waited until Boniface left the detectives' room before going to tell Dax that I'd be out all day working on the Boulevard Voltaire robbery.

'Take Boniface with you,' he told me.

'Will do.' Won't do.

My first job was to pay another visit to the library at the Sorbonne. I reckoned that if Capeluche was a reference to the city's history, Henri Lafont might be too. He wasn't. The same librarian as the other day brought me the big old history of Paris where I'd found Capeluche. Not a Henri Lafont in sight. I asked the librarian if the name rang a bell, but she was as mystified as everyone else I'd asked. Closing the large tome gently, I cursed Capeluche and her cryptic 'help'.

I'd been followed by Hochstetter's men on the way from Thirty-Six to the Sorbonne, which hadn't worried me, but I had no intention of having their company for the second part of the day. Outside the library, I picked up my car and finally lost the Peugeot 202 tailing me with the old drive-out-in-front-of-a-German-lorry-at-a-junction ruse. It was only going to be a matter of time before a German lorry stopped me or crushed me under its wheels, but it worked again now. Checking behind me, I took a roundabout route to the road north out of the city and opened up.

Hauptmann Prochnow checked my ID again and compared it with the record he'd kept in the big old cabinet in the corner of the room.

'No change since the last time you looked at it,' I told him.

He thanked me. The day the Germans get my sarcasm, I'm really in the *scheisse*. I'd got past the same checkpoint at Senlis and parked as near the Wehrmacht garrison in Compiègne as they'd allowed me to. A clerk in a uniform had made me wait in the same corridor where I'd waited last time, before Prochnow had invited me into his office. I'd decided to do things officially this time. Provided your definition of official meant not telling Dax where I was and lying to the German army.

'What is your purpose for coming here?' he asked me after handing me back my ID. 'Is this related to the prisoner you were looking for the other day?'

I kicked myself again for having used that as a reason. 'Yes, we have further information. The miscreant we're looking for has a brother who was in the French army. We believe that the brother was taken prisoner in the fighting in May and is in a prison camp somewhere near here. We think our missing prisoner will be trying to make contact with his brother, or even attempt to free him from prison. We want to apprehend him before he can do that.'

It had taken me from Paris to Compiègne to come up with that story. I maybe should have taken the scenic route.

Prochnow just looked puzzled. 'There are no French prisoners here. All captives taken were sent to camps in Germany.'

'That is strange. We'd been informed that the brother was in prison here.' We hadn't, but it was worth a shot. 'He served with the 24th regiment of the Tirailleurs Sénégalais.'

Prochnow looked like he'd been stung. 'A colonial regiment?'

'In the French army.'

Prochnow didn't do the uncomfortable look that Hauptmann Schnabel in Paris had. 'That is a different proposition.'

'Why?'

Not even that one word discomfited him. 'You are certain that this man's brother was taken prisoner?'

'Definitely. The brother's name is Fabrice Mendy.'

'And you were told that he was being kept prisoner here in Compiègne?'

'I might have misinterpreted that information, but that is what I understood. Do you know where he would be?'

'So you can apprehend the criminal from Paris?'

'Exactly.' I'd almost forgotten that part of the lie.

'I'm afraid you are only partially well-informed. The treatment afforded to colonial soldiers was different from their white counterparts. They were separated from the other soldiers.'

'In what way?'

'African and Arab captives have not been sent to prison camps in Germany like the other French prisoners.'

'Where have they been sent?'

'They are here in France. The order was taken to keep them in France.'

'So you should be able to find this prisoner?'

He shook his head. 'That is not to say that these soldiers are here in Compiègne.'

'So where are they?'

'They are in *Frontstalags* throughout the Occupied Zone. But I'm afraid I wouldn't have access to precise information about individuals. The administration is different from prisoners sent to Germany. Had your Fabrice Mendy been sent to Germany, I would have been able to verify his whereabouts and tell you where he was.'

I shook my head and wondered where to go next with my questions. 'Why have they been kept in France?'

He looked at me challengingly. 'To stop the spread of tropical diseases to Germany.'

'I beg your pardon?'

'Although the most important reason for keeping these people here is to prevent the racial defilement of women in Germany.'

They kept me in a cell.

Except it wasn't a cell but a room with two soldiers outside with Mauser submachine guns, so these four walls definitely did a prison make.

They'd put me in here because I might just have made a lunge across Prochnow's desk for his throat. On hearing his words, I'd had a vision of Dominique. I hadn't attempted to go and see her after last night's encounter with Capeluche. She hadn't called me either and she didn't have a telephone at home, so that looked like stalemate for the time being. I thought of her fears for her son, and I lost my usual good reason and common sense and decided I'd try to force Prochnow's head into the old wooden filing cabinet.

My hearing now was like listening underwater. A couple of soldiers had come in at the commotion before I could reach Prochnow and one of them had fetched me a blow to the ear that was still ringing an hour later. Through the ocean mist, I heard the door open and turned to see Prochnow come in. He was flanked by the Mauser twins.

'You are very lucky you didn't manage to assault me,' he told me. 'Or you would be facing a German military court. But as you are a policeman, I will give you the benefit of the doubt. You will return to Paris now.'

He handed me my police ID and told the soldiers to accompany me to my car.

'As I'm a policeman, I will continue with my investigation.'

He stood centimetres from my face. 'You do not understand. You will return to Paris now.'

They followed me all the way to the checkpoint in Senlis. Muttering unseemly words under my breath, I drove on until I'd gone a good way past the control and stopped at a crossroads. I turned right. I was busy looking for the smallest possible roads I could find. And for a way back to the Bois d'Eraine that took me nowhere near Senlis or Compiègne.

'I will return to Paris,' I said out loud, looking for somewhere to hole up off the road and wait until dusk fell, 'when I'm ready.'

35

Remembering my route from the other day, I drove through the dark to Bailleul-le-Soc and found the long road leading to young Fernand's pig farm. The aroma would have guided my way even on the foggiest of nights, headlamps or no. The farmer didn't look too pleased to see me.

'I don't want trouble with the Boches,' he told me.

He'd loosened the braces over his shoulders until they were hanging down round his arse. His trousers were staying up by gravity alone.

'There won't be,' I assured him.

He grunted and let me in. I followed him into the kitchen. A door from it was open, leading into a pantry. He shut it quickly, but not before I saw sides of pork and ham as rich as a villa on Avenue Foch hanging inside. My mouth salivated at the sight and smell of it as my mind tried to reconcile how a stench like the one outside could be part of the process to produce an aroma such as the one just snatched away from me.

Sitting down at the table, he picked up the last piece of ham from his plate and put it in his mouth. Looking at me, he chewed it noisily.

'Got any of that to spare?' I asked him.

'Nope.'

I nodded at the pantry. 'Looked like you did.'

'You want it, you buy it.'

'How much?'

He named a price.

'I want some ham,' I told him, 'not your first-born.'

'Take it or leave it.'

He belched. That would have to do for me.

'We were interrupted last time,' I told him. 'You were about to tell me something.'

He shook his head. 'I can't help you.'

I leaned conspiratorially towards him on the table. 'You were complaining about the Ministry. I've got a friend there, I can put in a good word for you.'

'Have you?'

'Of course I fucking haven't. But if you don't tell me what you know, I'll make sure I do get a friend there and I'll have them come after you with every fucking thing they've got. Taxes, black market, permits, swine fever, you name it.'

'You couldn't.' His voice was unsure.

'Try me.'

He got up and cut another slice from a ham on the sink and sat down with it. This is my sort of bribe, I thought, but young Fernand looked me in the eyes and slowly ate it.

'The African soldiers were separated from the French ones.'

I stared at him. 'I could have told you that.' My frustration shone through. I listened to him chomp on his ham. 'What else do you know?'

'That's it.'

Fighting down a desire to grab the ham off him and scoff the lot, I had to turn away. I looked outside, through a chink in the blackout and thought of the forest beyond the darkness of the farmhouse.

'The forest. Do you see much in the way of comings and goings in there?'

'Some. Germans mainly.'

'What are they doing?'

'Don't know. Most of us locals won't go in there now. Not with them here.'

Instinctively, I looked at the chink in the blackouts again and thought of Prochnow and his *Frontstalags*, the prison camps where the African soldiers were being kept. Would there be room for one in there? And if so, could they keep it secret? As to why, that was obvious. The Nazis obviously had no intention of extending the prisoner-of-war niceties to all of their captives.

'You got a torch?' I asked him.

The light from Fernand's torch was weak, which was no surprise but probably a blessing. He'd only lent it to me because the glass was cracked. At least it wouldn't be a beacon pointing the way to me as I set off for the woods. Young Fernand had told me that I'd be better entering the tree line a few kilometres further to the west, as that's where he'd seen most activity. Taking his advice, I'd driven away from his farm and parked off the road. I'd left my Citroën protected as much as possible by a small clump of trees and set off on foot into the woods. With a temperamental torch and the sounds of animals and who knew what else scurrying among the undergrowth, the forest was scarier than a Pigalle backstreet on payday.

'Have you got a spade I can borrow too?' I'd asked him before leaving.

'Nope.'

'I thought not.'

I wished now I had one. Not to unearth anything I might find but as a weapon. The country and me weren't made for each other. There were too many sounds. To support that argument, a soul-rending scream split the night. A barn owl. I dropped the torch and had to scrabble around in the dark to find it again. The fall had turned it off. I found it and switched it on as quickly as my numb fingers would allow.

Young Fernand had told me the likely places I should go looking, but in this dark and with this fog, that was entirely academic. Simply retracing my steps to where I'd left my car was going to be enough of a challenge. All the while, I had to hold the torch in one hand and wave my other hand from side to side in front of me to avoid walking into a tree. Every now and then I came across a clearing, the lack of trees a brief respite from the worry of knocking myself unconscious.

It was these open areas that the farmer had told me would be the logical place for any camps to be located. I'd check one, obvious even in this dark mist that there was no camp, before moving on to try and find the next. But it was slow and I could be missing clearings completely in the night. Knowing it was going to be an impossible task, I began to wonder if I dared come back in the morning and search in daylight. I had no idea how frequently the Germans patrolled the woods, especially if they had something to hide in them.

It was as I was considering my options that I saw a light flash by to my right. I stopped and turned my torch off. The darkness closing in on me almost made me turn the thing back on again, but I knew that would be even more dangerous than any fear of the night.

I saw it a second time. This time, I heard voices too. They stopped. Straining to hear them again, I heard the sound of something heavy falling, this time in front of me. Over the noise of twigs snapping and leaves rustling, I heard a single word. A swear word. It was in German.

Another light shone somewhere in front of me, near where the sound of swearing had come from. There was a hushed order in German not to make a noise. It was much nearer to me than the first voice had been. I froze. I had to hope they'd be as blinded by the reflection by the fog on their lights as I had been.

A light picked me out, just for a moment, but it shone on me. I jumped to one side and dropped to the ground, watching the beam swing back to where I'd been standing just a moment ago. I heard a shout in German, and another beam of light began to search the clearing where I was.

Dragging myself along the ground towards the trees, I thought the only route open to me was to my left. I hadn't heard any sound from that direction. A third light shone on the patch among the trees and I risked it. I got to my feet and ran for a path between two trees that I'd spied in the brief instant one of the torches shone on the area. I had no idea what lay beyond the wall of fog cast by the lamp behind the trees, but it was my only chance.

I heard more shouting as I burst through the trees, the noise I was making more frightful to my ears than the barn owl. One of the soldiers shouted at me to stop and a gunshot sounded. No bullet came near. A warning shot. I had a feeling the second round of gunfire wouldn't be.

One arm protecting my face, I ran. I came up against a tree, bouncing back off it, but was able to keep on running. Another shot was fired. I heard it zing through the trees to my right. I think it must have been shot by the man behind me, but he'd done it more in hope than confidence. It helped me quicken my pace, aided by the lack of trees as I found myself in another clearing.

Suddenly, my foot gave way and I stumbled and fell. I got

up gingerly, feeling a sharp pain in my ankle. My foot sank slightly in the earth. It was softer where I'd tripped. Biting my tongue against the soreness, I felt around for harder ground. There was a sizeable area of softer earth, but I finally found a solid footing and was able to support my weight. I'd lost time, but the pursuer behind me seemed to have gone astray in the trees before the clearing and I saw the torch beam shine away to my right.

Turning left, I hobbled through the woods. Another barn owl screeched and one of the Germans fired off a shot in reflex. Another shouted at them angrily to stop wasting time. I hoped I wasn't imagining it, but the sound of the chase seemed very slightly to have diminished. Another beam cut through the fog as much as it could. This time it was weak and I could barely see it. Through the pain, I was as near rejoicing as I'd ever been. My pursuers were losing me. Perhaps misled by the owl and the confusion of the fog, they'd taken a path that was moving them further away from me.

Listening all the time, I slowed down to make sure I didn't fall again and do more damage to my ankle. Stopping for a moment, I rotated my foot. It turned fully, if with some pain, but it didn't seem broken. The sound of crashing in the trees receded. I could sense they were more half-hearted. I hoped they'd think I was some poacher out in the night. I also hoped they wouldn't find my car. I certainly knew I had no chance of finding it.

Walking slowly now but not daring to turn my torch on, I came to another clearing that seemed larger than the others. The fog was swirling now, and in a moment of slightly greater clarity, I sensed a change in the shadows ahead of me. It was something that was breaking up the horizon between the trees.

Warier than ever, I approached it. My eyes darted from one

side to the other, in front of me and behind. For all the good it did. I could still see very little. The one thing I could make out and that was pulling me towards it was the shape before me. I could see now that it was a building. A house by the size of it.

It was in darkness, not a light seeping out through blackout curtains or under a door or window frame. Standing stock still on the stone porch, I turned back to face the woods and waited and watched in the darkness. I saw no torchlight, heard no voices, felt no movement. Turning back to the house, I got the same feeling. No house that was occupied – by prisoners or just by a family – was this dark, not even in a blackout.

The door was locked. Trying to make as little noise as possible, I heaved against it with my shoulder until I felt it give. Not wanting to kick it because of the noise that would make, I pushed harder until eventually I was able to break the lock. Checking again for sound, I pushed it open and went in. I was right. It had the smell of absence. No one was living here. Turning my torch on for the briefest of moments, I mapped out the room in my mind and turned it off again. Next to me, I'd seen a heavy dresser, which I dragged away from the wall and pushed in front of the door to slow down any searchers. I assumed there'd be a back door if I needed to get away. A barn owl screeched in the night. The pain in my ankle made me immune.

'Nice try, arsehole,' I muttered.

What little light there was outside came in through a pair of small windows. I hurried over and pulled the curtains tightly shut. Searching deeper into the house, I discovered there were only two rooms downstairs – a living room and a kitchen, each the same size as the other. Closing the curtains in the kitchen and checking the back door was locked, I went upstairs. Just two bedrooms. I closed the curtains in both and turned my torch on for a second to check what was there. It was more frightening having that brief moment of weak light in which I needed to see everything in the room followed by a blacker darkness than no light at all. The bed in the bigger bedroom was made and looked horribly welcoming, but I knew I didn't dare fall asleep here, just in case the Germans decided to search the area in the night or early in the morning.

Hobbling down the stairs, I went back into the kitchen and sat down at the table. Shining the torch on my foot, I saw that it was swollen, but I'd been right that nothing was broken. Leaving the torch on for a moment, I checked that the curtains were tightly shut and found some sheets in a cupboard to pack around the door and the window frames. The dark was getting to me and I wanted to be able to see. Hanging from a hook, I saw a hurricane lamp. Checking, I saw that there were no light switches on the walls. The house didn't have any electricity. Finding matches in a drawer, I pumped the kerosene into the lamp and lit it, double-checking the doors and windows again for any chinks in them.

With the lamp on the table, I sat back and closed my eyes. The bed upstairs beckoned, but I knew I was right that it would be too dangerous to sleep. I looked at my watch. I reckoned there'd be about four hours until the sun started coming up. I'd have to stay here until that time and then go and look for my car, hoping the Germans hadn't found it in the meantime. Or this house.

Getting up to ward off sleep, I went in search of food. There was nothing. The house had been inhabited until recently, but whoever had lived here had gone. It clicked. They'd most likely left in the tide of refugees when the country had fallen to the Germans in the spring and hadn't yet come back. I wondered where they were. I wondered who they were. Spaces on the wall showed where pictures had hung. Family photos, I guessed, some of the possessions that were too valuable to leave behind. It felt remarkably sad.

My eyes fluttered and I realised that I'd dropped off. I looked at my watch and saw that it had only been a few minutes, but I didn't dare let it happen again.

I remembered something. In my jacket pocket, I found the tube that Fran had placed there without my knowing. The Pervitin. The methamphetamine that the Germans had given their troops to keep them going. Even with all the stumbling and running through the woods, it hadn't fallen out. Yawning so much, my jaw made a cracking noise, I knew I had to take a decision. Opening the tube, I shook out one of the white tablets. Taking a deep breath, I put it in my mouth and swallowed and waited.

Looking at the simplicity of the kitchen around me, I was surprised to find my thoughts going back to Dax's apartment on the Right Bank. It was a world away from this. It was also a world away from other cops' homes. I knew he turned a blind eye to things. That was our mutual insurance policy, we had that on each other. But he always swore blind that he wasn't on the take. As the meth kicked in and the thoughts in my head became wilder and more disjointed, I pictured again the relative opulence of his flat and I heard Boniface telling me that Dax had a meeting with the Germans. I heard Dax himself telling me countless times that he didn't want me wasting my time on the missing prisoners. And I heard Capeluche talk about her employers and the power they wielded and the information they had on me.

Which was when the thoughts in my head began to stumble over themselves, the randomness and clarity of them picking up a pace I remembered from a lifetime ago. Just as I used to, I felt a carousel of excitement and fear in my brain that I thought I'd lost. My eyes opened on a spring lock. I wished the merry-go-round of thoughts would vanish in the darkness beyond the abandoned room.

36

I found my car after two hours. It was less than a kilometre from the house where I'd spent the night, but I'd set off in the wrong direction at first light and only found it after sweeping back and forth across the woods searching for the clump of trees by the road where I'd left it. The Pervitin was buzzing through me, overriding the pain in my ankle. It felt good but even under its influence, I knew from past days that it was false, that the release would be a greater descent than the ascent had been. That's why you kept going back to it.

For my part, I went back to Paris. This time, I had to nego-tiate a German patrol almost immediately after finding the Lille road. I was much too close for comfort to Compiègne. My right leg jiggled uncontrollably as I waited in my car for a feldwebel to take a thorough look at my police ID. He took it with him into a small hut and wrote my details down on a piece of paper. I cursed and then prayed he wouldn't ring through to the garrison in Compiègne. If he did, Hauptmann Prochnow would be sure to demand that I be arrested. The feldwebel came back and handed my papers over with a terse order to carry on my way. I almost mashed my foot down on the accelerator in my relief, but managed to control myself and drive off sedately.

There was no escaping Dax in Paris. As sorely tempted as

I was to go straight home and let the Pervitin wear off, I had to face him. He called me in the moment I got up to the third floor.

'Boulevard Voltaire, Eddie. What in God's name is going on? Where the hell have you been?'

The drug gave me a confidence it really shouldn't have.

'I'm more interested in missing prisoners, Commissioner. I've been following that up.'

'You and these prisoners. For Christ's sake, Giral, what are you playing at? I told you I don't want you wasting time on them.'

'And why's that, Dax?'

'Because it'll be the Germans doing it for whatever fucking reason they want, Eddie, that's why. They're the only ones with the authority to get prisoners released from Fresnes. The sooner you understand that and leave it alone, the better for all of us.'

'We've got an interview with the manager of the bank,' Boniface said. 'Me and Eddie.'

I saw him for the first time. I'd had no idea he was in the room. His words placated Dax.

'Good. Tell me what you learn.' Dax had one last word for me. 'I'm warning you, Eddie. I want results on this robbery. Forget the missing prisoners, we can't do anything about that.'

I was about to reply, but Boniface almost physically pulled me out of the office. We walked downstairs to look for his car, but Boniface stopped the moment we were outside.

'Go home, Eddie. I don't know what you've taken, but if you stay here, you're going to do something you regret. I can't keep saving your bacon for much longer.'

'What does that mean?'

'Just go home.'

I watched him get into his car. The drug showed no signs of

abating, but I knew that he was right. I needed to be where I could do no harm, mainly to myself. Remembering to park in the street behind my block, I had no desire to check on possible informants looking out for me, so I just went in through the building on Rue de la Parcheminerie, at a right angle to my own street and hidden from view, and crossed from one roof to the other. It was an escape route I'd learned years ago when I'd first moved into my flat. With the Pervitin racing through me, I even ran up the stairs in the first building and leapt the low wall between the two roofs. That was a first.

My small flat felt strange. I'd spent a night away and my racing mind took an age to get used to the topography of it again. I moved my armchair to nearer the window and sat in it, looking out. I'd never done that in the fifteen years I'd lived here. The chair had been where it now stood from the moment I'd rented the apartment after leaving Jean-Luc and his mother.

I jumped up again. It felt wrong and I had to move it back to where it was. I checked my watch after what seemed like five minutes and saw that I'd spent over two hours adjusting my armchair to find its original position. I was ravenous. Going into the kitchen, I cooked the remains of the bacon and finished off the whole of the baguette from the bag behind the door. In a brief moment of insight, I saw that a drug addiction these days would play merry hell with rationing. For some reason, the thought made me laugh.

Needing noise, I turned the radio on. A man told me that Laval had been made Vichy Foreign Minister. In the space of just a few days the previous week, both Laval and Marshal Pétain, the head of the Vichy government, had met Hitler in Montoire, near Tours, in an unequivocal display of our decline.

'Foreign Minister,' I told the radio. 'If that doesn't win us any friends, I don't know what will.'

A rogue in an affected white cravat, Laval was right-wing pro-German and thought by many of us as one of the architects of the demise of the Third Republic. A lawyer and politician who'd jumped ship more often than a privateer, he boasted of his peasant origins while rubbing the vast wealth he'd amassed in the face of the country.

And to cap it all, Pétain had shaken Hitler's hand. In Montoire. He'd shaken the monster's hand and spoken of collaboration, just as Hochstetter had taunted me with. In my frenetic mist, I even rang Thirty-Six and asked to be put through to Dax. I was going to ask him if he still thought Pétain was the wily old fox biding his time before turning the tables on Adolf. Or if he was just another politician willing to ally with the devil to save his own career. The officer who answered wouldn't put me through. I was disappointed and about to try again, but a sudden hunger overtook me and I left the phone off its cradle. The man on the radio was still talking.

'What a time,' I shouted at him.

In one of those moments of clarity when you start to come down from an artificial high, I hurled insult after insult at the propaganda spewing from the radio. An authoritarian regime that had done away with many of the liberal policies we'd fought so hard and so long to achieve, under the dictatorial powers given to Pétain, Vichy was little more than Nazi fascism, I told the man. They'd even taken our old revolutionary motto of 'Liberty, Equality, Fraternity' and replaced them with 'Work, Family, Fatherland'. It was the corruption of an ideal.

'What are we? Soup kitchen Nazis? Ersatz copies of Adolf's dream?' I screeched.

I devoured my bread and bacon while I shouted. Crumbs and gristle sprayed onto the radio but I didn't care. I picked the bits off with my fingers and put them in my mouth a second time.

Like Laval, many of the Vichy appointments made no bones about such niceties as ability or integrity. We were ruled by a clique of incompetents and yes-men, out for what they could get and willing to toe whatever line it took for their own personal gain. And in the meantime, the rest of us were powerless.

Another word sprang unbidden into my mind. One that was gaining ground slowly, a whisper in the corner of a café, a secret word among friends under a tree in the park. Said once by De Gaulle and always spoken since, never written. Not that I'd seen. The word was resistance. I had no idea what it meant, not in real terms, I'm sure no one did fully, but I shouted it at the man on the radio, who seemed impervious to my arguments.

I was in my armchair. I hadn't slept but I hadn't been awake either. It was still dark outside and I was by the window. The radio was on, but music was playing. Opera. A baritone. I jumped up and turned it off. It was too painful. I sat back down again and thought of another baritone a lifetime ago. Not opera. Jazz. Joe.

He was a drummer but he also sang. A reverberating counterpoint to Dominique's lyrical perfection. I remember him singing 'Avalon' many years ago, his voice deep and rumbling with an aching sensitivity, like a soldier laying flowers at a friend's grave.

Until fifteen years ago. When I ended it. And ended our friendship.

He and Dominique had pleaded with me but I hadn't listened, too drugged to care about what they said. Joe had been paying protection money to a Corsican gang operating in Montmartre. I'd only just learnt. Much of the little he earned went to them. I saw red when I found out. He asked me not to get involved, to let things be. But I hadn't. I'd gone for the gang. Told him I'd protect him. He'd told me I couldn't. Dominique had echoed him. And they'd been right.

And the Corsicans had taken it out on Joe.

They'd smashed a metal pipe into his throat and damaged his vocal cords forever. Ended his singing forever.

And our friendship. Only I was the one to do that.

I was in my chair but it was back in its place in the middle of the room. I watched in fascination as the Pervitin made my fingers jerk uncontrollably. Focusing beyond my hand, I saw the low table in front of me. I was shocked to see the Luger on it. The ritual. Where I feigned shooting myself. I had no recall of re-enacting it.

Which was when I remembered I no longer had the dud bullet.

37

Boniface was talking to me. It was over thirty-six hours since I'd taken the Pervitin and its effects were lingering. I'd spent a second night without sleep and I didn't feel it. I'd given up on my armchair and moved it back to the window. With the lights off and the curtain open, I'd sat through the hours, staring out at the buildings opposite and the night sky. I'd finally felt a calm I hadn't in days. That was the danger, I knew. The temptation of the drug that could pull me back in.

I felt in my pocket now, in my office at Thirty-Six. I hadn't got rid of the tube. I knew I ought to. It was afternoon, I'd lost almost the whole day. I told Dax I'd been chasing up the witnesses in the bank robbery. I hadn't. I'd spent the morning finding the right position for my armchair, feeling an absurd triumph when I'd finally got it.

'I'm seeing Madeleine,' Boniface was saying. 'I need to ask her to get Dédé to agree to meet me.'

I felt again the pinprick in my stomach from the stiletto. The fears for my son. And now for Dominique. I nodded at him.

'Tell her I'll meet him. And find out if she knows who Henri Lafont is.'

He looked mildly surprised. 'How are you feeling now?'

'I'm all right. Something I ate. Or didn't eat.' He turned to go but I called him back. 'Boniface. Thank you.'

'Right.'

I went to see Dax again.

'The Boulevard Voltaire job. I think Walter le Ricaneur was involved. The witness's description seems to fit with him.'

Dax looked resigned. He took his glasses off and rubbed his eyes. 'Walter le Ricaneur? In which case, there's not a great deal we can do, is there? Whoever's behind his release from Fresnes will make sure he doesn't stay in a cell for very long. Move on, Eddie. Don't waste your time. On this or the prisoners. We choose our battles.'

I studied him as he spoke. He still had his glasses off and was staring myopically at me, so it was impossible to read any reaction on his face. I was no nearer to finding the truth.

'You cut me dead, Eddie. Why should I let you in?'

Dominique wasn't to be swayed. We hadn't spoken since the day by the Jardin du Luxembourg when Capeluche had taken me to meet Hervé. It seemed an age ago.

After talking to Dax, I'd taken extra precautions – although they now seemed second nature – and followed a circuitous Metro ride that had taken in four lines and as many jumps in and out of carriages as the train pulled out of the station, and a hike up and down the slopes and steps of Montmartre. As the effects of the Pervitin began to wear off, the pain in my ankle grew stronger. I felt the tube clamouring for my attention in my pocket and struggled to ignore it. On the landing outside Dominique's building, I'd scanned the streets above and below me. There wasn't a Traction Avant or a Peugeot 202 in sight. I'd hoped it didn't just mean they'd got wise on to how to follow me.

'Can we talk?'

'No, you can come with me.'

She left me at the door while she went back inside her flat to put her coat on and fetch her bag. Downstairs by the door onto the steps outside her building, I could see her steel herself. She led me up the stone flights and turned left, where we went into a small grocer's shop.

'This isn't for you, is it?' the shopkeeper said to her. 'I can't keep on doing this.'

Dominique took out three or four sheets of ration tickets. 'You have to. Please. It's just a couple of things.'

Behind her counter, the owner didn't look happy. I had no idea what was going on. Or why Dominique had left it so late in the day to come shopping.

'I could get into trouble. I don't want problems.'

'You won't. I'll say I lied if anyone asks. I just need some eggs and some flour.'

'No flour. You can have two eggs.'

Dominique looked at the tickets in her hand and sighed. 'That'll be all right. Have you got any cheese?'

'All gone.'

I saw Dominique turn away, frustrated. She paid her money and handed over the right tickets and we took her meagre catch back into her building.

'What was that all about?' I asked her.

'You'll see.'

Upstairs, she went into her flat and picked up a small bag of flour and some milk. She cut a chunk of cheese in half and put it all in a basket, before going back out onto the landing. She knocked on the door opposite hers.

'Madame Goldstein. It's Dominique.'

The door slowly opened and a tiny woman at least in her sixties or seventies opened the door a crack. She saw me and slammed it shut.

'It's all right, Madame Goldstein, he's a friend.' She looked at me wryly and whispered: 'Perhaps.'

The elderly lady opened the door again and peered out at me. Her expression was neutral, but it opened out into a beaming smile when she shifted her gaze to Dominique. An elderly man joined her, standing behind her in the doorway. He was less steady on his feet. Dominique handed over the basket with the food in and asked how they were. They looked cowed.

'We're all right,' the man said. 'Thanks to you.'

'Sorry it's not much. I'll try again tomorrow.'

They closed the door and Dominique led me back across the narrow landing into her apartment.

'What was that about?' I asked her.

'The Goldsteins have been my neighbours for years. But they've been too afraid to go out much since the Germans came. So I do their shopping for them, with their ration tickets. Although I don't know for how much longer. You saw the grocer. She's worried about getting into trouble if I get caught doing their shopping for them.'

'And you give them your own food.'

'You saw what was there. The Nazis have banned Jews from buying food until four in the afternoon. There's nothing left by that time. They'd starve.'

I followed her along the corridor to her living room. She didn't have much more furniture than I did. It just looked better. A table with a crocheted red cloth over it and four solid upright chairs to one side of the room, an ageing but comfortable-looking brown sofa and an armchair around a low table to the other. Plants and ornaments filled the room, the air in it fresh. It smelled better than my place too. She showed me to the armchair and sat on the sofa, as far away from me as

possible before staring at me expectantly. I still wasn't forgiven.
I wasn't sure where to begin.

'I've been back to the Bois d'Eraine.'

She was silent. Whether it was her resentment towards me
or her worry about her son, I didn't know. 'I'm not sure I want
to hear.'

'I think he's a prisoner. Here in France.'

'In France?'

I nodded. I couldn't tell her the reasons that Prochnow gave
me. 'But I'm having problems finding out where exactly. The
Germans aren't giving up the information easily.'

'Will you be able to get it?'

'I think so. I'm not giving up.'

She stared into space for a while. 'Thank you, Eddie.' She
made to stand up, as though she were going to show me out.

'Can we talk now?' I asked her. 'About the other day?'

She sat back again. 'What? When you were too ashamed to
be seen with me.'

'I wasn't ashamed to be seen with you. That wasn't the reason.'

'So what was it if it wasn't shame?'

'It was for your safety.'

She drew back from me even further. 'Why?'

'I can't tell you.' She laughed. I realised she would the
moment I said it. In her position, I'd have laughed too. 'I can't
explain, Dominique, it's police business, but that day in the gardens, I was being followed. There are things happening, things
involving the Germans, that have put me in their crosshairs.'

'You were all right walking with me in the gardens. And
having a coffee.'

'That's my point. If I'd been ashamed or self-conscious, do
you think I'd have done any of that? It was when I came out
of the café that I saw the cars following me. I knew that if

they'd seen me talking to you, it would have brought you to their attention. That's why I had to pretend not to know you.'

'For my safety?'

'Really.' I tried to think of the words to say. It had been a long time. I knew how to talk to Hochstetter, cops and criminals, but I no longer had the terminology of any other form of relationship. Or the skill. 'You have to believe me.'

I think it was the weakness of my last comment that swung it. If I'd been lying, I'd have made a better job of it, but the naivety of my plea seemed to sway her. We sat in silence for some minutes, each with our thoughts.

'Is that something I'm going to have to get used to?' she asked after a time.

I thought of the Nazis in power in the country and felt irretrievably sad. 'I think it is. I'm sorry. Do you want me to go?'

She laughed again, this time more joyful, mischievous. 'Oh, Eddie, don't be any more of an idiot than you have to be.'

'I've been called worse.'

'Stick around and you will be.'

I felt relieved. Sort of. She got up and kissed me on the head before leaving the room and coming back a few moments later with a glass of whisky each. She handed me one and sat down on the end of the sofa nearer my chair. We clinked glasses and drank. It tasted good.

'I've been saving this since before the Germans came,' she explained. 'You're lucky I haven't had any other reason to drink it.'

You know you've been forgiven when you get a kiss on the head and a glass of hoarded whisky. Such was the currency of Occupation.

I raised my glass in a salute. 'Don't take this the wrong way, but I'm glad your life is as sad and empty as mine. I need the whisky.'

She looked at me pityingly. It was only half-mocking. 'Eddie, my life could never be as sad and as empty as yours.'

She laughed gently but I had to look away, my thoughts on the Bois d'Eraine. Other thoughts queued up to kick me while I was down. Boniface, Capeluche, fending off Dax and Hochstetter, taking on the Gestapo and the SD. Jean-Luc.

'I'm fed up. Fed up with the Occupation, of walking on eggshells all day long.'

She reached across and put her hand on my hand, weaving her fingers between mine. The contrast in our skin colour was as harmonious and beautiful as the keys on Ray Ventura's piano. I felt a sudden moment of calm. She smiled at me.

'Now imagine having this to contend with on top of it.' She pointed to her front door. 'And what the Goldsteins have to put up with.'

I pulled my hand away self-consciously. 'I'm sorry.'

'You know, you're not a bad man, Eddie. You just sometimes forget to be a good one.'

Boniface was waiting for me at Thirty-Six with a message.

'Dédé will see you tonight. But only you. Madeleine says he won't talk to anyone else. You've got to meet him at the place where he gave us the slip the last time.'

'What time?'

'Eight o'clock.'

I also had a message on my desk saying that Hochstetter had phoned. I balled up the piece of paper and threw it in the wastepaper basket. Hochstetter could wait. Except he didn't. He rang me barely ten minutes later.

'*Édouard? I have something I want you to see.*'

'It will have to wait until tomorrow. I have work to do.'

'*I'm afraid it won't wait until then. You need to see it now. It is to your benefit.*'

'Now?'

'*I have sent a car for you. It will be with you shortly. I expect you to be here.*'

I checked my watch. I had an hour and a half before I had to see Dédé. 'I can give you half an hour.'

I was talking to a buzzing noise. He'd hung up. I got up and looked out of the window. His car was already downstairs. I told Boniface I had to see Hochstetter.

'But I'll be in Montparnasse in time to meet Dédé.'

He nodded and I went downstairs, hoping that whatever it was Hochstetter wanted me to see was quick. And worth it. A soldier opened the staff car door for me and I got in. He drove off and crossed to the Right Bank.

'What's this about?' I asked him, but he gave no reply.

I stared out of the window and checked my watch. The driver pulled up outside the Palais Garnier. Hochstetter was waiting for me on the steps, his uniform neatly starched and pressed.

'What is it you want me to see?' I asked him impatiently.

He held out both arms expansively. '*Fidelio.*'

38

'It is Beethoven's one and only opera, Édouard. And the fact that it is being staged is a symbol of the unity between our countries.'

'I don't have the time.'

'As I said, a symbol of our unity. And a token of my regard for you. You would be wise to accept it.'

I stood on the opera house steps in frustration. 'You said it would be to my benefit.'

'It is. Culturally.' He caught hold of my elbow, his grasp firm, and guided me up the steps towards the entrance. 'Really, my friend, I will brook no objection. Whatsoever.'

'At least let me make a phone call.'

He looked at his watch in a theatrical gesture. 'If you must.'

We found the manager and he let us into his office. I waited, expecting Hochstetter to leave me to make my call in private, but he simply stood by and looked at me, his eyebrows raised.

'I suggest you make it quick,' he told me.

I rang Thirty-Six and was relieved to be put through to Boniface almost immediately. I checked my own watch. There was little time to spare. Boniface sounded surprised when I spoke to him.

'*Where are you?*'

'At the opera, but that doesn't matter. I need your cooperation on something.'

'*Christ, Eddie, you're supposed to be in Montparnasse.*'

'Yes, that's right.' I glanced at Hochstetter. He was feigning
interest in an oil painting near the desk. 'That request I asked
you to make. I need you to do it this evening.'

'*What the hell are you playing at? I thought you'd pulled yourself
together.*'

'That's the one. On the Rue Madeleine. Can you deal with
it, please?'

'*Dédé won't see me. I told you that. You've got to be there. Christ's
sake, Eddie, not another fuck-up.*'

'That's good. I'll leave it with you, then.'

I hung up and looked across at Hochstetter. 'Just one more.'

I picked up the receiver and got through to the operator. I
asked to be connected to Madeleine's shop. Madeleine answered
and I wondered how I was going to explain it to her in code,
but Hochstetter reached across and placed his fingers on the
phone, cutting the call off.

'I think that's enough, Édouard. You can spare two and a
half hours for the sake of your soul. I do not want to be late.'

'Two and a half hours? Two and a half hours for a woman to
dress as a man and get her husband out of prison?'

'You would do wisely to curb your normal cynicism.'

'Do you have any other information for me at least?' I said in
a lower voice as we approached the auditorium. 'Allow me to
get something worthwhile out of the evening.'

'Nothing tangible, but I would hazard a guess that our
friends are up to something. I suspect that the people behind
these disappearances from Fresnes prison, and I imagine also
the murder of the criminal in the jazz bar, are the responsibility
of the institutions we had expected. I feel this is one occasion

when the SD and the Gestapo are working in harmony. That is not good news for either of us.'

'Would they work with French criminals?'

'At times like these, we all have to compromise. Not all relationships are founded on the trust that ours is, Édouard.'

We took our seats in the dress circle. Hochstetter never did anything by half. I knew that short of feigning illness, I had little for it but to remain as calm as I could and hope that Dédé would agree to see Boniface. Seated on Hochstetter's other side was the Abwehr officer I'd seen with him in the Lutétia, Major Kraus. I hoped they'd engage each other in conversation and leave me to my own thoughts. I felt a tap on my shoulder. Turning, I saw a familiar face in the row behind me. It was Peter, the Wehrmacht officer and jazz lover I'd met the evening Dominique sang.

'Have you been inveigled into coming to the opera too?' he asked me, his tone conspiratorial.

'Is it really two and a half hours?' I asked him.

'I'm sure it will seem a lot longer.'

I felt a huge sadness. I would have given anything to have met a kindred spirit like Peter under any other circumstance than this one. And I didn't mean the opera, although that was pretty bad too.

A commotion to our left distracted us. A man in uniform with a small entourage was making his way to his seat, forcing the other *melomanes* to adopt that curious theatre half-crouch and sideways twist while he squeezed past. I recognised him and willed him not to look in my direction. It was the SD officer who'd had me brought in for questioning about the missing prisoners. In his entourage, I spied the older man who'd been with him the day I paid a social call on the Gestapo.

'Do you know who that is?' I whispered to Peter, nodding at the older man.

'That's Karl Bömelburg, the head of the Gestapo in Paris.'

'And the one finding his seat?'

His voice hushed a notch. 'Helmut Knochen. He's the head of the SD in Paris. Why do you ask? They really aren't people you want to meet.'

'I'll bear that in mind.' Whoops.

'Although the SD and the Gestapo are kept very much in check these days. Here in Paris, I mean. That's largely thanks to General von Stülpnagel, the Military Commander in France. And because the SD is badly undermanned. Badly from their point of view, that is. Knochen there sees his role as mainly information-gathering rather than the sort of thing we've come to expect of them.' He paused to look critically at Knochen before hurriedly looking away and lowering his voice even more. 'Long may it last, for your sake and ours.'

'So you're not a lover of the SD? Or the Gestapo?'

'I'm a lover of every aspect of the Nazi structure. As I'm sure you are of every aspect of French politics over the last twenty years.'

The lights dimmed and the fun started. If only they'd stop all the caterwauling, I thought, as the music was wonderful. Hochstetter's synopsis was accurate, a woman dressed unconvincingly as a man to release a political prisoner. I wondered if there was someone working at the opera who'd decided to push as far as they could and was then surprised to find the Nazi authorities agreeing to the opera being staged. If it wasn't rationed, I'd buy them a drink.

The interval came and I got my eardrums back. I tried ringing Thirty-Six and Madeleine again. Boniface had left, which was good, but there was no reply from Madeleine's shop. Hochstetter remained in the room the whole time.

'I have to go somewhere now that you probably won't want to come,' I told him, heading for the toilets.

I took refuge in one of the cubicles and sat and thought. I wondered what was happening with Boniface and Dédé, but my mind was distracted by the opera. There was one scene that I grudgingly had to admit to liking with a macabre enjoyment. The 'Prisoners' Chorus' that Hochstetter had been listening to on the gramophone at the Lutétia. All the political prisoners were let out of their cells in the belief they were to be set free. They milled around and sang a lot, most of it unnecessary, until their dreams were suddenly burst and they were put back in their cells in a curious distortion of the case that was robbing me of my sleep. I couldn't get the image out of my mind.

I was about to leave my cubicle when I heard voices outside. At least two, and they both rang a bell. I heard the sound of peeing and then water running in the sinks.

'I see Hochstetter is here with his tame policeman,' one of them said.

It clicked. The voice belonged to the man who'd questioned me on Avenue Foch, the one I now knew to be Helmut Knochen, the head of the SD, thanks to Peter. And the other one was the Gestapo chief, Karl Bömelburg. He spoke now.

'We've had a report from the office in Compiègne. A Paris police detective was there, asking about African prisoners. It was Hochstetter's man.'

'African prisoners? I thought it was French prisoners he was asking about.'

'Both, it would appear. Should we be tackling him more vigorously?'

In my cubicle, I couldn't help shaking my head.

'Keep him under surveillance. Should you feel he needs dealing with, do so.' That got another shake of the head, only more so. 'This matter of prisoners going missing is quite perplexing.'

I felt my gun under my jacket. Hochstetter hadn't taken it away from me when I'd arrived. I took it out slowly and put my other hand on the door handle. They were both outside, a door's width away. Two bullets away. Two problems gone. In one stroke. I looked at my pistol and tried to find a reason not to do it.

The outer door opened and the two men stopped talking for a brief moment. It was Knochen who spoke to the newcomer first.

'Hochstetter, we were just discussing you.'

'I'm sure you were,' Hochstetter replied.

Three bullets, I thought. Hochstetter's tame policeman, my arse. I heard the other two men leave and the moment was gone. I put my gun away.

'You can come out now, Édouard. You can't skulk in there forever.'

I flushed the toilet and emerged to wash my hands.

'Did you hear anything of interest?' he asked me.

'They said you had bad breath.'

Back in the auditorium for the second half, I couldn't help looking over at Knochen and Bömelburg. Unfortunately, I caught Knochen's eye and he stared at me before turning to the officer next to him, who looked back and studied me in turn until the lights went down.

Resigned to sitting it out until the end before I could do anything, a moment in the second act struck me. Thanks to Leonore's wholly unrealistic pretence at being a man, she succeeded in releasing her husband. Or she would have if some official hadn't entered stage left and finished the job for them.

When they finally – and mercifully – quit singing, they all applauded themselves and each other and the lights went up. I blinked to get used to it and watched the spectral grey uniforms rise slowly from their seats and drift away to left and right. Next to me, Hochstetter got up and shuffled to the aisle, deep in starry-eyed conversation with Kraus. I sat and pondered, when I felt another tap on my shoulder. It was Peter.

'So how was that for you?' he whispered.

'Truly evil.'

He laughed. 'Spoken like a true jazzman.'

I watched him leave and sat on my own a moment longer. I hadn't been joking. It was truly evil. The rapturous applause at a story of political freedom from the very people who were wilfully and steadfastly removing it from every other country around them. I glanced over at Hochstetter, who was signalling for me to join him. And the cultural arrogance of people like him who saw everything they did as better than everything they replaced. I took a deep breath and left my seat.

'So how was that, Édouard?' a euphoric Hochstetter asked me when I caught up with him. 'Much more enlightening than your jazz, wouldn't you say?'

'You know, I have to agree with you. I learned a valuable lesson this evening. One that will stay with me.'

He gave a half-smile. 'Progress.'

'I hope so.'

I turned to see Knochen throw one last glance in my direction.

Boniface was waiting for me outside. He couldn't hide a look of concern on his face. Signalling him to say nothing, I thanked Hochstetter and excused myself to him.

'Police business,' I told him.

Hochstetter offered help but I declined. Hurrying Boniface away from the building towards his car as fast as my ankle would allow, I asked him what had happened. I saw Knochen and Bömelburg scanning the crowd outside the opera house. I wondered if it was for me.

'I went. I tried the café but it was shut. Dédé wasn't there.'

'And Madeleine?'

'She's out looking for him.'

39

A Traction Avant, its powerful engine growling in the night, cruised past. I ducked back into the doorway. I saw Boniface on the opposite side of the narrow street do the same. He spotted me and grinned. He really had no idea what was going on.

As the car went by, I tried to peer in to see if it was the Gestapo or Capeluche's employers, but it was too dark to tell. It didn't matter, either way. They were both out in force hunting us down in the back streets of Montparnasse.

Boniface and I had driven from the Palais Garnier to the neighbourhood to look for Dédé. Turning back as we'd left the opera house, I'd seen Knochen talking to two men in a Traction Avant, which quickly gunned its engine and set off after us.

'You'd probably better get a bit of a move on,' I told Boniface.

He looked in the mirror. 'I'm on it.'

He lost them in the narrow streets south of the Seine and we'd got to Montparnasse with no other car in sight. Curfew was almost on us. We were cops and allowed to be out but if Dédé or Madeleine were caught by a German patrol, they'd be arrested. And if it were Capeluche's lot that got to Dédé first, his chances were going to be a lot worse. He knew who it was who'd gone through Fresnes, choosing prisoners for impromptu release. I assumed that was Henri Lafont, whoever he was. And whoever he was, he'd be keen on silencing Dédé to make sure we didn't get to know his identity.

Boniface and I had first gone to the café where I'd been supposed to meet Dédé. It was in darkness, as Boniface had said, but we'd banged on the door until the owner had come down to open it. She looked pale as rationed milk.

'I thought you were the Boches,' she'd said, gathering her dressing gown around her chest.

'Have you seen Dédé?' I asked her. 'He was supposed to meet me here.'

'He can't have. We were shut.'

She'd suddenly gone silent and looked over our shoulders. And that's when we'd turned to see the first of the Traction Avants, slowly rumbling towards us. The passenger window wound down and a hand with a pistol emerged from it, like a film slowed down.

'Get back inside,' I told the owner. 'And don't open the door to anyone. Where would we find Dédé?'

She hurriedly retreated inside, gabbling her words as she went. 'He'd go and see Julien.'

'Where?' I asked her, but she'd gone.

Boniface grabbed me and pulled me around the side of the building. The first gunshot of the evening sent splinters of stone from the café wall rattling around our heads and we ran along the narrow alleyway to the left. The car wouldn't be able to follow us down there.

'Who's Julien?' I asked when we drew breath at the end of the lane.

'Who's after us?' Boniface had a question of his own. 'The Gestapo or the Fresnes crowd?'

'Does it matter?'

'If it's French criminals, I'm shooting back. If it's the Gestapo, I'm not.'

I groaned. He was right. Shooting at the Gestapo was not normally known to be a good idea. We had to get away from whichever bunch of lovelies it was that was following us, but we also had to find Dédé. And Madeleine. I took stock of where we were. She lived above the haberdasher's, which was just three streets away.

We went together. Two pairs of eyes peeled for pursuers seemed a better bet than splitting up and taking our chances on finding either Dédé or his mother separately. She wasn't in when we got there. I tried to do the silent knock on her door – enough to get her to open up, not so much anyone else would hear it. She wasn't in either way.

'Who in hell's name is Julien?' I asked again.

'The first café we found Dédé,' Boniface said. 'Would he be there?'

'A few minutes to curfew. We'll try.'

As we got close, though, a Traction Avant came around the corner. This time I saw it was two Gestapo men in the front seats. They'd seen us, so we ran back the way we'd come and cut down a side street. With any luck, the two cars would meet head-on.

'Did you see him in the café?' I asked Boniface. He shook his head.

My ankle was beginning to hurt. In my pocket, I felt the tube of Pervitin. When Boniface turned away, I took it out for the briefest of moments, tempted, but I quickly put it back without opening it. We crouched down in a doorway, listening for sound. A car engine went by a street away, and we both instinctively shrank back.

'Mireille Gourdon,' Boniface suddenly said. 'Calais Jacques' ex. She's friends with Madeleine. She might know.'

'Do you know where she lives?'

I sensed him winking in the dark. 'Got her address.' I heard him rummaging around in his jacket and pull something out. In a brief flash, he lit his lighter and looked quickly at a piece of paper, before flicking the flame off again. 'Got it.'

We ran through the streets, from doorway to doorway. A Wehrmacht patrol car went by, no doubt attracted by all the movement or the gunshot earlier.

'That's all we need.'

Boniface found the apartment block and we broke the downstairs lock to get in. I stayed downstairs in the hallway, keeping an eye out, while Boniface ran upstairs.

'No kissing,' I told him. 'We haven't got time.'

I saw his teeth grin white in the darkened stairwell. He was back down surprisingly quickly.

'Her husband was in,' he explained. 'Madeleine was here earlier. Mireille's told me where I might find her.'

We'd only been out of the door for ten seconds when another gunshot made us run for cover. I hadn't seen where it had come from, so we ran blindly to the nearest shelter.

'This way,' Boniface called by a mews entrance. 'It's up here.'

I turned but couldn't see where the shot had come from. I heard an engine revving somewhere behind me and quickened my pace to catch him up. My ankle was in agony and I half-hobbled, half-ran the final stretch. Boniface was already inside the door of an ancient building and talking to a woman inside.

'Julien?' I heard her whisper when I got there. 'He's dead. He died years ago. He and Dédé were inseparable as kids.' She also told Boniface where we could find Madeleine. 'She was going to the café.' She named the one we'd first gone to.

I groaned. We began to retrace our steps when a thought occurred to me.

'You go back to the café to look for Madeleine,' I told Boniface. 'I think I know where Julien will be.'

'He's dead.'

'Precisely.'

We took off along the same street for a short distance, Boniface on the opposite side to me, ducking back when a Traction Avant cruised slowly past. I turned away from him at the end of the street and hurried as fast as my ankle would allow to the darkened gates of Montparnasse cemetery.

One of the small side gates on the Rue Émile Richard had been forced. Glancing around me, I pushed it and went in. Montparnasse had been dark, but this was another world altogether. The sounds were different. Scuffling and scurrying in the bushes lining the narrow avenues of the dead were in counterpoint to the silence of the graves.

I took my gun out and crept in. The cemetery was huge. I had no idea where Julien would be buried, assuming my supposition was right, but I decided that he'd be most likely to be in the peripheral plots, away from the fine and famous in the central aisles.

A car engine ran along the road outside and I froze. It retreated and I moved on, treading cautiously amid the stones. I kept away from the paths as there was less cover there. Not that there was much among the graves.

For the briefest of moments I saw a flash of light ahead of me and to my right. I stopped again, fixing in my mind where I'd seen it. Edging forward, I heard the car return. This time it stopped behind me. I guessed it was near the entrance where I'd come in. They must have found the broken gate.

Making as little noise as I could, I pressed on. Ahead of me was whoever had flashed a light. Behind me were the occupants of the car. I skirted slightly to the left, hoping to come up on the person ahead from the side, where they wouldn't see me.

I heard a stone scrape under foot. This time a torch shone. A voice shouted in German. As the light traversed, I saw that it was a patrol of uniformed soldiers. There was at least one plain-clothes person with them. Gestapo, I had no doubt.

The stone scratched again and I followed the sound. The soldiers' torch swept and I caught sight of a figure crouching behind a gravestone. The light wouldn't have shone directly on them, so the torch-holder wouldn't have seen them. I only saw them because of the shadow cast by the light. They were a slight build. I hoped it was Dédé.

The Germans moved away, scanning their torches among the graves to my right. I approached the grave where I'd seen the shadow. I heard an intake of breath. It was taken in fear.

'Dédé?' I said in a stage whisper.

'Good to see you, Eddie,' a voice replied.

Only it wasn't Dédé's.

'Calais Jacques,' I cursed.

'Come and join us, *poulet*. See what I've got here.'

He stood up, holding a frightened Dédé in his grip. In his other hand, I saw what looked like a gun. I hid mine by my side and carefully walked towards them. As I drew near, Jacques pulled Dédé with him towards the nearest pathway. In the distance, I heard the Germans sweeping around. It sounded like they were coming back towards us. Their torches began to search the graves nearer and nearer to where we were standing. Jacques looked towards their source. He didn't appear too concerned by their presence.

In one flash of reflected light, I saw that what Jacques was holding was a leather cosh, not a gun. I drew near, one eye on the lights approaching, and raised my pistol.

'Let him go, Jacques.'

He gave a low laugh. 'I reckon you're outnumbered, Eddie.'

The moment he opened his mouth, Dédé took the opportunity to smash his other arm down on Jacques' arm and break away. Jacques made to follow him but I took one step closer and cocked my pistol.

'Don't, Jacques.'

We both listened as Dédé scurried off across the stones, away from the approaching lights. From behind, I heard the pursuers who'd come in through the same gate as me give chase. I guessed Dédé was their target, not me, whoever they were. I'd only managed to give him the smallest of head starts.

'Big mistake, Eddie,' Jacques told me.

'Move out onto the pathway. Into the middle.'

'Company coming. You'd better be prepared.'

'I am.'

Ducking down behind a gravestone, I fired a shot towards the approaching Germans and moved away quickly. The torches came together and focused on Jacques, in the middle of the avenue. The cosh in his hand looked like a gun. He turned to me.

'You bastard, Giral.'

I crept further away into the darkness. I saw him try to drop his weapon, but the soldiers opened fire and he fell under their bullets. His face filled with hate, he turned his head to search for me as he dropped, but I was already retreating into the shadows.

40

Bouchard pushed his semi-lunette glasses up over his forehead and smiled a greeting to me. I let the door close gently behind me.

'With you in a moment, Eddie.'

The smell of the mortuary burrowed into my nostrils and mouth, grubby paws battling the disinfectant to smear and stain. Without wanting to, I shook my head to rid myself of it. It was one place I never got used to. I watched the pathologist remove something from a body on a slab.

'That one mine?' I asked him.

Without looking up from whatever it was that had his attention, he called back to me. 'Outside. This poor soul's a drowning.'

He put it down and washed his hands before joining me. An attendant came in wheeling a trolley and deposited it next to us. A white sheet followed the contours of the body beneath it. With my help, Bouchard positioned the trolley how he wanted it and he went to draw the sheet back. I prepared myself for what I was about to see.

'I've done as much as I can do without further tests,' he told me. 'But things are still slow these days. We've been working with a reduced staff since the Occupation started.'

'I understand. When you can.'

He peeled the sheet back. I looked at the face I recognised and shook my head in anger.

'Heart failure,' Bouchard said. 'Caused, I'm more or less certain, by methamphetamine. I'll know more when I can find someone to run more tests. Don't hold your breath.'

That's all I was doing in his beloved mortuary. I took the tube of Pervitin out of my pocket. 'Could it be down to this?'

He took it from me and examined it. 'Most probably. Not the first time I've seen this stuff. The Germans used it, you know, for their military.'

'I know.'

'Pilot's salt, I heard one of them call it. They give it to the Luftwaffe.'

'And you believe it could have caused this death?'

'It's possible, Eddie. At this stage, I couldn't swear to it. Where did you get this?'

'Drug dealer.' I said it without a moment's hesitation. He made to hand it back to me. 'You keep it. You might need it for comparison.'

He stared into my eyes and placed the tube on the bench near him. 'Thanks. I just might.'

'I know I don't need it,' I added.

He nodded slowly and I took one last look at the body lying on the trolley. The face was soft, gentle.

'So young,' Bouchard commented.

'Yes, she was.'

In front of me was the body of Paulette, the young woman whom Fran had dumped when he felt his club was going up in the world. Fran, who supplied Pervitin.

*

Fran was smooching with another young woman in his office when I went to the Jazz Chaud. The remains of several lines of coke were on the desk. Another pyramid of it was heaped on a piece of paper alongside. I thought of Paulette on a trolley in Bouchard's kingdom and had to stop myself from forcing the white powder down his throat in one go.

'Seen Paulette?' I asked him.

'Who?'

I picked up the pile of cocaine and blew it into the room. He nearly fainted at the waste.

'Paulette. She went with you to Longchamp.'

He smacked his latest victim on the arse and leered at me. 'You're going to have to narrow it down a bit, Eddie.'

'Paulette. Nice kid, lovely face, voice like gravel. You fed her Pervitin and now she's staring at the ceiling from a slab in the forensic institute.'

'Not a clue what you're talking about.'

I reached across and ground the piece of paper into his face, mashing it into his nose and mouth. I screwed it up and threw it at him.

'Remember now?'

He spluttered, half trying to clean his face, half trying to get some of the powder into his mouth. I wish I'd seen it fifteen years ago. I'd never have got hooked.

'Nothing to do with me, Eddie. I haven't seen her in weeks. Is that all you wanted? Because I'm a busy man too.'

'I want a favour.'

He laughed at me. 'You want what?'

'A favour, Fran. In exchange for not arresting you and closing you down again.'

'Arrest me for what?'

I pointed at the remains of the coke. 'That.'

'Sure you want a link between you, me and the white stuff coming out into the public, Eddie?' He licked his finger and dabbed it into the powder and proffered it to me. 'The feeling's still there, isn't it? Go on, try some.'

Slowly, faltering, I reached across the desk and took hold of his finger. I felt the fine grains on the tip and watched the white powder dissolve as I moved my own thumb around in it in a small circle. Sighing, I bent his finger back and sat and watched him howl in pain before I let go. He nursed it, looking aggrieved at me.

'I have to deal,' he said. He shook the pain out of his finger. 'I thought I'd get more people in the club, but they're just not coming. It's Julot. The place is tainted, no one wants to spend an evening in a club where something like that happened.'

'You get into bed with the Devil, Fran, you don't get to be the one to hog the blankets.'

'I tell you, if I ever find who did it, I'd sew their fucking hands together.' He opened a drawer and pulled out his ancient revolver. 'Before I blow their fucking brains out.'

In my mind, I saw the cold certainty of Capeluche. 'I really wouldn't wish for anything you can't handle. Anyway, you don't reckon it's more to do with the way you run the place? You're not going to pull in the jazz-lovers if the place is little more than a drug den.'

He laughed. 'A drug den? When did you grow old?'

I stared coldly at him. 'Every time I saw a young woman lying on a slab. I want a favour, Fran. I pulled the strings to get this place opened. You owe me.'

That got a sneer in return. 'You pulled nothing. I know full well how come this place got reopened. I'm paying them enough for it.'

'Help me and I'll change that.'

He leaned forward across the table and looked at me earnestly. 'You can change nothing. The people protecting me are a fuck of a sight stronger than you or any of your cops.'

'How strong?'

He sat back in triumph. 'As strong as it gets these days. Now, fuck off and don't let the door smack you in the arse on your way out.'

His own line seemed to please him as much as the white ones had.

'Maybe you really are descended from Molière,' I told him, blowing the remains of the coke into his face.

'I told you not to come, Eddie.'

Joe hadn't even sat down, turning to ask the warden to take him back to his cell the moment he saw me in the room. He was more diminished than he had been the last time I saw him.

'Hear me out, Joe. I've got something for you.'

He shook his head and turned to go. Luckily for me, the warden had already left us to go outside and Joe had little choice. Slowly, he walked across the small room and sat down. I guessed that had he not been so depleted, he'd have stayed standing where he was rather than sit facing me.

'I think I've found a way to get you out of here.'

He simply stared at me. 'More promises, Eddie? Haven't you learnt yet?'

'I mean it. Just give me a few days and I'll get you out of here.'

'What you going to do? Take on the Nazis? You reckon that'll work? Or you just going to walk me out of here?'

He looked sideways to see if the warden was coming back. I could see he was impatient to leave.

'I promise, Joe.' I saw his expression. 'I know, I know. I've made promises in the past and I've got it wrong, but I mean it this time. I'll get you out.'

The door opened and the warden came in, buttoning his flies up.

'Can you take me back now?' Joe asked him.

He got up and shuffled slowly away from me. His movements were faltering, failing.

'I mean it, Joe.'

I waited until the warden came back for me to accompany me to the gatehouse.

'I heard what you said,' he told me as we approached the main entrance. 'About getting him out.'

I stopped to look at him. 'I take it you can keep a secret?'

'Oh, I can keep a secret, all right. But you're going to have to hurry. We're handing him over to the Germans tomorrow.'

41

'Have you found my son?' Madeleine demanded over the heads of two old ladies humming and hahing over cotton. There was anger in her voice.

'We were hoping you'd had some news, Madeleine,' Boniface told her, leaning on the counter towards her. I winced at his unwonted confidence.

Boniface and I were looking for Dédé. His trail had gone cold for a couple of days since the night of the opera. We'd been back to the cemetery and found Julien's grave, but nothing to give us a clue where Dédé had gone from there. Just a few stains in the earth where Calais Jacques had been killed. I looked at them and felt nothing. Instead, I recalled the night Jacques had delivered me to Capeluche to have my lips stitched together.

Madeleine looked scornfully at Boniface. 'If I want to talk to the monkey, I will. I'll deal with the organ grinder.' She looked at me. 'Not that you're any better.'

'Has no one said anything, Madeleine?'

'What do you think? I hold you responsible, Eddie Giral. Find my boy.'

'Where should we look for him?' I asked. She didn't like it.

'Well, if you don't know, what are you doing being a cop?'

'I meant do you know of any friends he might be with?'

'You think I haven't asked them?'

I thought of his going to Julien's grave when he was in danger. 'Is there anywhere else like his friend's tomb where he'd go if he was frightened?'

She finally began to cry. 'He'd come to me. If he was in trouble or scared, he'd come to me. Where is he, Eddie?'

'I'll do what I can, Madeleine.' More promises I no longer knew I could fulfil.

We left her being comforted by the two elderly customers and walked back to where Boniface had left his car. My ankle had improved since the night we'd spent running through these streets, but I still had twinges.

We came up against a welcoming committee. Although they didn't look too welcoming and probably couldn't spell committee. Half a dozen of the neighbourhood's lowest common denominators, blocking our exit from the narrow street. I knew them of old, but I didn't recognise any who should have been in Fresnes.

'Morning, boys. Off to the temperance meeting?'

The self-appointed leader, a hard man from the Ardèche with a sun-wizened and lined face and a penchant for holding people's heads in a vice until they paid their debts, folded his arms and spoke.

'We want to know what you're doing for Calais Jacques.'

'Not much we can do, seeing as how he's dead.'

'What are you going to do about it?'

'I plan on having a very stern word with the Gestapo, since they're the ones who killed him.' I indicated the ragtag bunch around him. 'Unless you boys want to take it up with them.'

That got them looking at their feet in embarrassment. Toughness had got redefined since the Nazis had hit town. They began to break up to let us pass, until another committee member wanted one last word. He wasn't someone I associated with Montparnasse and I had to trawl through my memory to remember where I knew him from. It came to me – Henri Chamberlin, a small-time crook who made the likes of Calais Jacques and Walter le Ricaneur look like criminal royalty.

'Calais Jacques is a great loss,' he said.

'He always was.'

Boniface grinned at him as we walked through. Something else occurred to me and I turned back to face them.

'By the way, tell Henri Lafont I've been asking after him.'

'Bit risky,' Boniface said as we retrieved his car.

'Sometimes you need to shake the tree, catch the olives in the net.'

'Spoken like a true southerner.'

I was surprised that his comment didn't irritate me. We drove back to Thirty-Six in relative silence. It gave me time for my thoughts. So much was vying for attention in my head, but uppermost was the news that Joe was to be handed over to the Germans the next day. I recalled the opera. Leonore dressing as Fidelio to release her husband, Florestan. The story had stayed in my mind ever since. I saw out of the window that we were approaching the Île de la Cité.

'If I were to ask you if you'd be able to get hold of some court-headed paper,' I asked Boniface, 'do you reckon you could?'

He looked surprised at my question and then beamed a lustful smile. 'Mathilde. Judge Clément's secretary. She'd let me have some.'

'And a rubber stamp?'

'What's this all about, Eddie?'

We parked outside Thirty-Six.

'Come for a coffee. There's something I want to ask you.'

We chose a table in the Bon Asile as far from the counter as possible. There were no other cops in at this time. Too late for breakfast, too early for mid-morning coffee. I told him about Joe and about his being handed over to the Germans the next day.

'Is this what the paper and stamp are for?' he asked.

'I'm going to fake some release papers for him. Try and get him out before he can be handed over.'

Boniface whistled. 'You like risky, don't you, Eddie?'

'The thing being, they know me in the prison. I can't be the one to hand the papers over and escort him out.'

'You want me to do it?'

'It's a lot to ask.' And I was surprised I was asking him, although a part of me wasn't. Boniface was a twenty-four-carat pain in the arse, but he was a good cop and he'd shown that he could be trusted.

He took a sip of his coffee and stared at the wall behind me. 'What the hell. I'm in.'

'Thank you.'

'Then what do you do? Once you've got him out.'

'I haven't got a clue.'

He laughed, the first time I'd ever seen him give an unguarded reaction.

'I'll go and see the lovely Mathilde now.' He instinctively patted his hair into place, lingering over the Maurice Chevalier quiff, and smiled at the thought. 'I'll see you back in Thirty-Six.'

I checked my watch. 'Somewhere I've got to go first. I'll see you later.'

'Hey, Eddie.' He looked like a puppy with a new ball. 'We make a great team.'

'Don't push it.'

*

A funeral. Me, a priest and a coffin. The service over in minutes, a wartime burial of the lost and displaced under a grey rain. Stout and fatherly, with thick glasses and greying hair, the priest had waited to see if anyone else would show up, but in the end, even he had had to admit defeat and had gone through the motions with a perfunctory devotion.

Seeing the coffin being led away alone to the huge cemetery south of Paris, the last lonely home for the city's poor and unknown, I decided to go with it. My sorrow, not at the person, whom I barely knew, but at their passing and the lack of care for it, turned to a cold anger.

I'd learned that Paulette was newly arrived from the Alsace, no doubt fleeing the Nazis, and she had few friends in Paris. None, at least, who felt it necessary to come to her burial. And that included Fran, the man who'd probably sold her the drugs that had killed her.

I watched the cheap coffin lowered into the ground. A light drizzle fell. By the side of the grave stood a pile of soft earth.

42

Desperation makes for disparate bedfellows.

'Édouard, we will have to set aside an office for you. You spend more time in the Lutétia than you do in your own police station.'

'Got any coffee?'

I needed it. After Paulette's funeral in the rain, I'd felt a sudden exhaustion. I was tired and caffeine-depleted and I was wrestling with what to do next. I had two avenues that were quickly becoming dead ends and I needed to decide if I was willing to open up to Hochstetter to see if he could come up with solutions. I'd decided. It was time for soul searching to become soul selling.

He looked amused as an adjutant brought in a coffee for me. There was a bread roll on the table, most likely from Hochstetter's breakfast. It sat untouched, its light crust golden in the light from his desk. I reached for it. I was hungry.

'May I?' I asked.

'Please do.' He looked at his watch. 'In your own time, Édouard.'

I glanced at mine too. The clock was ticking for Joe too. But that wasn't either of the two blind alleys that had brought me to Hochstetter's door. That one, at least, I had under control.

I wondered how Boniface was faring with his lovely Mathilde.

'I need your help. A name has come up in relation to the missing prisoners. Henri Lafont. It's not one that we know.'

'And now you want my help?' He lit up a cigarette in his usual ritual. It was painfully slow. I'd finished the bread roll, picking up the last crumbs with my fingertips, before he'd flicked the match out into the ashtray. 'And the help you require is what exactly?'

'If you could use your contacts to find out more about this man.'

'Do the French police's job for you, in other words.'

'Assist the French police. I thought that was the point of this relationship.'

'Then you are more naïve than I took you for. Which I know you aren't. But no matter. Leave it with me and I will make some enquiries.'

'You don't want to write the name down?'

'No need. I have a memory that serves me well.' Another point scored to the man in the uniform.

'There's another matter. I'm looking for the whereabouts of a French prisoner. He's being kept in a *Frontstalag* here in France, but no one will tell me where.'

'Is this to do with your investigations into the prisoners missing from Fresnes?'

'No.' I had to weigh up what I was going to say. I wanted to keep Dominique safe from Hochstetter's antennae. 'This is a separate matter.'

'I must say I don't fully understand. I'd understood that French prisoners of war had been sent to Germany.'

'He's from a Senegalese regiment.'

Hochstetter sighed and took a deep drag on his cigarette. 'Oh, Édouard, you do like to complicate matters. Yes, I do believe the colonial prisoners are being kept in France. But what do you think I can achieve?'

'Find out where he is for me.'

'I'm not sure I can.'

'Not sure you can? Or not sure you want to?'

'Both. This is not the type of assistance I am here to give.'

'But if you give me this assistance, I'll be more willing to ask you in other matters.'

He laughed. 'That is not open to negotiation. I'm sorry, but I cannot help. Or will not, if you prefer.' He tapped out his cigarette. 'Did you enjoy your roll?'

I left the Lutétia wanting to see Dominique. I needed a moment of normality in the middle of nonsense and subterfuge.

I took my usual roundabout route to Montmartre and her flat, tired by the time I stood outside her door and knocked. I'd used up the energy Hochstetter's bread roll had given me. I looked at my watch as I waited and knew I really didn't have time for this. I wasn't even sure why I'd come.

She looked exhausted when she finally opened. 'Eddie, I was asleep.'

'Are you all right?' She hadn't asked me in.

'I'm fine. Just one of those days. What is it you wanted?'

'I just came to see you.' I struggled for a reason. 'I've asked Hochstetter for help in looking for Fabrice.' I didn't tell her what his reaction had been.

'Thank you. Listen, can you come back another day? Someone stole my bread and sugar ration tickets this morning and I'm not myself.'

'Did you see who?'

'Please stop being a policeman for two seconds, Eddie. It's pointless. I won't get them back, that's all there is to it.'

'I'll give you some of mine.'

'I'll be fine. I just want to lie down.'

'Shall I come in?'

'Just come back another time. Please, Eddie.'

Boniface wasn't in Thirty-Six when I got there. A ringing phone was. On my desk. It rang off before I got to it.

I went back into the main room to ask if he was in the building. I wanted to know how he'd got on with getting hold of official court paper and a stamp. Even if that meant listening to his love life.

'Gone out,' Tavernier told me. 'He got a call and went straight back out.'

'Who from?'

He shrugged. 'Search me.'

Behind me, my phone started ringing again. This time I got to it before the caller hung up. There was a German voice on the other end.

'*Inspector Giral? We have a message for you. It is waiting for you downstairs.*'

After selling part of my soul – at least the bit of it that I had left – I wasn't in the mood for cryptic phone calls.

'Who is this?'

'*Downstairs. Outside.*'

He rang off. I got up and went to the window to look down at the street three floors below. Just the new normal of bikes and pedestrians replacing cars and buses. I scanned up and down Quai des Orfèvres as far as I could see, but nothing looked out of place. Unless you counted a German army truck trundling by. It disappeared from view. The powers that be in Berlin seemed to like having their soldiers carted here and there around Paris. It reminded me of the idiotic tasks our officers used to have us doing in the last war to stop us from getting bored. Or thinking too much.

'Downstairs it is,' I muttered to my reflection in the window.

I'd crossed the road and was standing by the low wall separating me from the Seine, looking back at Thirty-Six, when I heard the whine of a car engine being over-exerted. From the direction of the Pont Neuf, a Traction Avant appeared.

'Oh good, it's the Gestapo again,' I heard myself say out loud. Strange the words it occurs to you to utter when you're scared.

If I'd tried to make it back to the safety of the building, the bastards would have mowed me down without a moment's hesitation, so I stepped back to the low stone wall and prepared myself for a fight. I hoped Hochstetter's men would join in. On the right side. The Citroën slowed down and the rear door opened. Without the car stopping, a heavy bundle was thrown from the back seat and the driver accelerated away. Looking like an untidy parcel of clothes, the package rolled along the ground towards me.

Shocked, I let out a sigh of relief and turned to make sure the car really was disappearing from view. I didn't trust them not to come back for me.

It was only when I turned my attention back to the bundle and I heard the shouts from a pair of uniformed cops who came running out of Thirty-Six that I registered what the message was.

It was Boniface.

His face thickly layered in blood, he lay motionless in the gutter barely a metre from where I stood.

'I've been worried about you, Eddie.'

Capeluche led me along the corridor to her strange flat on the ground floor. She turned her back on me easily. She either knew she'd reeled me in or she trusted her own ability to protect herself. Inside her apartment, she closed the door behind us and gave me an odd smile, like she knew my thoughts. My face annoyed me with its burning admission of shame. I was already sensing a danger of falling under the spell of the Capeluche myth that had haunted me before meeting her, a narcotic belief in the wraith-like powers the street urchins' song had seemed to ascribe to her. It was more powerful than anything Fran had to sell.

I'd only just come from the hospital and I was still shaken. I didn't want Capeluche to sense that. I'd seen Boniface lying in a bed, paler than the white sheets and pillowcases that seemed to be holding him together. It had been an age before I'd been able to talk to someone and I could only stand and watch his breath shallow and laboured as he lay unconscious.

'He's young, he's tough,' I was finally told by a doctor with white hair and thin cheeks who made Bouchard look a mere slip of a boy. 'He'll be fine.'

'Will he regain consciousness?'

'I just told you. He'll be fine.'

'When?'

'When he's ready.'

I'd had to make do with that. If anything, I'd found the quack's terse demeanour a help. It had to mean Boniface wasn't in any great danger. After leaving the hospital, though, my mind had had to start working, in spite of the guilt I felt about the beating Boniface had taken. He'd been my ally in my plan for Joe. With Boniface out of the game, I had nothing. And the clock was ticking. I'd looked for Mayer in Thirty-Six but had been told he was off duty. I'd thought of Dax but realised I couldn't trust him to help. It was bizarre. I'd trust Hochstetter to look into Fabrice's whereabouts, but not Dax to help me free

Joe. Of course, that might be because what I was planning was ever so slightly illegal.

I'd paced up and down my office, looking for an answer. And here I was. Despite the indoor hiking, my ankle was mending now, so it was just my conscience that pained me. That was by no means a first. So I'd taken to the underworld of the Metro and crossed the Seine – or the Rubicon, as I now liked to think of it – and found myself at Capeluche's door.

'I see your ankle's better,' she added.

'You've been watching me.'

'I told you. I worry about you.'

Hervé was rocking from side to side in his chair, humming the same song from the last war as before. Capeluche shot a concerned glance at him. He seemed calm for the moment.

'You want coffee?' she asked me. For the first time, I noticed the smell of coffee on the stove. It was real stuff, its aroma enough to make me want to weep. Capeluche saw my longing. 'It could be yours.'

It was while she was busy pouring it into the cups that Hervé's humming took on a more urgent tone, his rocking threatening to upend his wheelchair. I got up and hurried over to him. He stared up at me, not understanding. The expression in his eyes brought memories of my own darkness back to me.

'Look at me, Hervé,' I told him.

Holding his face gently in both hands, I slowly lowered my head and rested my own forehead lightly against his, all the time making soothing noises. His rocking slowed, but the humming persisted. I could feel the movement begin to start up again. I held him more firmly.

'It's quiet,' I said. 'Listen.'

Pulling my head back so he could see my eyes, I put one

finger on his lips. Without smiling, I looked into his eyes, concentrating on one then the other, holding his attention.

'Smell the coffee, Hervé. Smell it. Remember the taste.'

'Coffee,' he said to me.

'Coffee,' Capeluche echoed.

She brought us both a cup and knelt down in front of her husband. While I took a sip from mine, she tipped some from his cup into his mouth. His eyes never left me, his actions in swallowing the hot drink mirrored mine.

'Good?' I asked him.

'Good,' he agreed. The humming had stopped.

Capeluche gave him some more and I returned to my chair. I watched them both, but had to look away. I could have had that devotion once, I thought, from Jean-Luc's mother, but I'd chosen not to want it. Only I wanted it now from Dominique. And to give it. At least I think I did.

'So, Eddie,' Capeluche said as she sat down, one hand resting on Hervé's arm to keep him calm, 'the last time you came here, we discussed your future. What have you decided?'

'I need a favour.'

43

'Is it stolen?' I asked Capeluche.

She laughed. 'Hardly.'

She'd picked me up by the Jardin du Luxembourg in a German military lorry. She'd arranged to meet at the corner where she'd forced me to ignore Dominique that Sunday in another show of power. I stored the memory away. I'd looked in at the cab, at all the bells and buttons in German.

'Is it real?'

'It's real, all right. Get used to it, Eddie. You're with us now. This is the strength we have.'

We drove northeast towards Les Tourelles. She and I were alone in the back of the lorry. Walter le Ricaneur and another villain I knew were in the front. I'd been surprised to see the second guy when we'd met up as he wasn't one of the ones who'd been released from Fresnes. With a hangdog expression – and mood to match – he had a slight stoop and a small mole over his left eye, like a bored theatre company had made a half-hearted stab at casting him as the Hunchback of Notre Dame. His real name was Pierre Verzy, but everyone called him Quasi-Quasimodo. Only they'd shortened it to Quasi-Quasi in another show of cut-price apathy. Walter was driving, Quasi-Quasi rode shotgun. They were wearing Wehrmacht uniforms. I didn't even bother asking how they'd got hold of them.

'I've been looking for you,' I'd told Walter when they'd arrived.

'You've found me.'

The absence hadn't improved him any. He still had the lop-sided smirk on his face, like a politician knowing they can't be touched for the latest scandal. There were times I'd have loved to straighten it for him.

'Seen your son?' I asked him.

'What son?'

'I thought I was a bad father.'

We trundled on through the Eleventh, not far from where Capeluche lived. In my pocket, I was aware of an item I'd brought with me from my flat. I made sure it couldn't be seen, without drawing attention.

'Do they speak German?' I asked her. 'They can barely handle French.'

She shook her head. 'I'll be the one doing the talking. They'll keep their mouths shut.'

'I won't be able to go in. The warden knows me.'

'He's been taken off duty today. There'll be no one there who knows you.' She glanced across at me. 'That means you can be involved. A sign of your commitment.'

I looked out of the flap at the rear when it momentarily jolted open over a bump. I caught a glimpse from up high how people in the street looked away at the sight of us. 'If you can have a warden taken off duty, why can't you just get Joe out without all this fuss?'

She laughed. 'Where's the fun in that? Seriously, we have power, but it's not endless. We have to do it this way.'

Inside Les Tourelles, Walter and Quasi-Quasi played their part and accompanied Capeluche and me into the beast's maw. She spoke to the assistant director. The director had been called to a meeting. Capeluche had half-grinned at me when we were told that.

'Here to collect a prisoner for the German authorities,' she told him, a junior functionary with no desire to rock any boats, least of all with two German soldiers present. 'You were informed that we would be collecting him.'

She handed over a wad of official papers, some of them with German eagles and swastikas plastered all over them. They put my court-headed paper and rubber stamp to shame. To his merit, the young guy did check the records and saw that what she was saying was true. He took his time over it, though, and I couldn't help looking up at the clock on the wall, hoping we'd get it done before the real Germans came in to fetch Joe.

'It all seems to be in order,' he said. He began looking at another folder.

Capeluche closed it firmly by placing a finger on it. 'You would do well not to detain us.'

He blanched and asked us to wait while he called for a warden. After what seemed an age, but the clock told me was south of ten minutes, the door opened. My heart was in my throat but Capeluche was enjoying the performance.

Joe was led in. He saw me and sighed angrily.

'What have you done now?' he asked, looking from me to the two German soldiers.

'You will come with us,' Capeluche told him, her voice commanding.

She signed one of the pieces of paper she'd brought with us and left it on the official's desk. He looked uncertain but accepted it. As a final flourish, she asked him to sign another one, waiting until he did. I could have sewn her mouth up right then.

As we led Joe out of the building, a German lorry pulled up

inside the gate. An officer got out of the front, along with half a dozen soldiers from the rear of the beast. Out of the corner of my eye, I saw Walter and Quasi-Quasi nervously heft their rifles and look to Capeluche for a sign. I moved sideways over to them and touched Walter's arm to make sure he didn't do anything stupid. The German officer looked quizzically at our little group and beckoned me over.

'What is going on here?' he demanded.

I showed him my ID, snatching it away before he could take too close a look at my name. 'Special prisoner,' I replied in German. 'He is to be taken to the Avenue Foch. I am seconded to that office.'

'Papers.'

I asked Capeluche for the official documents we'd used to release Joe and hoped they'd cut the mustard. Displaying extraordinary confidence, she handed them over to me and I showed them to the officer. He studied them minutely. Turning around, I could see the assistant director behind us, emerging from the building.

'This is most unusual,' the officer said. He reread the first page before finally folding it over and handing it back. 'But it appears to be in order.'

'Thank you.'

I gave a small cough to hide my relief. Capeluche calmly put them back in her satchel and smiled disarmingly at the German. Behind us, the junior functionary had almost caught up with us. I nodded at Walter and the five of us set off as briskly as we dared to our own waiting lorry. As they placed Joe in the back of the lorry, I half-turned to see the German officer talking to the French official. I hoped our man would dither long enough for us to get away. The officer turned to look at us as the rest of us climbed up into the truck.

'Nice going, Eddie,' Capeluche whispered to me.

She made me sit up front with Walter while she and Quasi-Quasi sat in the back with Joe. After the rush of the encounter with the real party here to take Joe and the other prisoners away, I'd never felt so exposed.

'One more sign of your loyalty,' she told me. 'And we don't want your friend kicking up a fuss with you until we're away from here.'

'Just drive,' I told Walter once we got into the cabin.

To give him his due, he kept his cool and drove off at a moderate speed. I angled my head to look in the mirror. The officer and soldiers were still talking to the assistant director. The gate opened and I let my breath out in a long exhalation.

Outside the gate, Walter and I waited a moment before bursting out laughing. We cried tears of joyous relief as he drove away from Les Tourelles in a roundabout journey. I felt relieved I wasn't the only one to do that. Feeling oddly companionable, we'd calmed by the time he drove us along the Canal Saint-Martin. It brought water and goods to the city centre, but there was a lot less of the bustle of barges and boats you would have seen before the war. We finally pulled up on the banks of the Bassin de la Villette, between the canal and a row of blackened brick warehouses.

'This is where I get out,' Walter told me. He paused at the door. 'Thanks for looking the other way. With the Voltaire bank job. I didn't think you would.'

'I had a choice?'

'Sure you did. And you made it.'

He and Capeluche swapped places. She climbed into the cabin and Walter got into the back of the lorry. I assumed Joe was all right in there.

'Not long now,' Capeluche assured me.

We waited until we saw Walter and Quasi-Quasi, now changed into their civilian clothes, get out of the lorry and cross the road. With the uniforms bundled in canvas bags over their shoulders like sailors home from sea, they went through a half-open gate leading into a warehouse courtyard. I saw another German lorry parked inside. I locked the exact location away in my memory.

When they'd gone, Capeluche turned the truck around and drove us across Paris to the Bois de Boulogne, on the west side of the city. Oddly, there seemed to be more German patrols here than in the centre, but in our lorry, we blended in.

'This bit's not for Walter's eyes,' she explained.

'What happens now? Will Joe be taken to Spain by the same route as my son?'

'The less you know, the better.' She seemed to relent. 'But yes, I can tell you that much.'

She finally turned off the main road into the trees and pulled up. A van was parked off the road, facing us. Not a German one this time, but a French vehicle, advertising a garage down the side. In the shade cast by the thick trunks and wintry branches, I couldn't see inside the cabin.

Capeluche got out and went to the rear of the truck. I followed her. At the back of the lorry, she lowered the tailboard and lifted the flap to one side.

'It's safe, Joe,' she called into the dark interior in a low voice. 'You can come out.'

He emerged cautiously, his movements slow, confused. He climbed down from the lorry and regained his balance on the ground. I hung back, uncertain what his reaction to me would be.

'What's happening?' he asked, his voice unsure.

'We got you out, Joe. Eddie got you out. You're free.'

It took a few moments for her words to have an effect on him. He looked up at the trees overhead and closed his eyes. He began to cry dry tears. 'I thought when you came for me this morning, I was going to be sent to a German camp.'

'So did the Germans,' Capeluche told him.

I still couldn't speak. From our refuge under the trees, we heard a diesel engine rumble past, a German patrol most likely.

'What happens now?' Joe asked. 'I can't stay in Paris. I'll just be interned again.'

'That's where my friends come in,' she told him.

She led us both to the waiting van. As we approached, a man and woman got out of the front and greeted us cautiously. They looked nervous.

'This is Jean and Juliette,' Capeluche told us. 'Or that's how you'll know them. They're going to drive you south. You'll eventually be taken to the Pyrenees. From there, we'll get you across the border into Spain as soon as it's safe.'

Joe looked oddly scared at the thought. 'Are you coming with me, Eddie?' It was the first time he'd spoken to me.

'No, I've got to stay here.'

'You'll be safe,' Capeluche reassured him. 'We've done this dozens of times.'

Joe looked uncertain, but realised it was the only solution he had. He looked at me, his eyes sad. 'I'm sorry we lost touch, Eddie.'

'I'm sorry, too, Joe.'

'We need to go,' Juliette interrupted.

'Can I have two minutes with Joe?' I asked them.

They looked at each other doubtfully but agreed. They left us and walked to the other side of their van. Joe and I looked at each other, uncertain. A trace of a smile creased his face.

'You always were a crazy bastard, Eddie.'

'That wasn't always a good thing, Joe.' I felt irredeemably sad. 'I'm sorry. For the harm I did you.'

'That song's over now.'

We embraced, the way only old friends can.

'I'm sorry,' I repeated.

'Forget it.'

I looked over to make sure the others weren't watching us. 'Can I ask you for something now, Joe?' I took out the item I'd brought from home and showed it to him. It was one of Jean-Luc's baby shoes, from the pair I kept in the tin. I explained what it was.

'Name it,' he told me.

I quickly outlined what I wanted him to do and we embraced again. He hid the shoe in a pocket just as Capeluche and the other two emerged from behind their vehicle.

'You need to go,' she told him. We heard another military vehicle drive past. She showed him into the rear of the van. 'A hidden compartment. You'll be safe from patrols in there.'

I watched him being tucked in behind a panel. He gave me one last wave before it was closed, his arm weak. He smiled but he'd disappeared before I could smile back. We turned and the van was gone before Capeluche and I had returned to the lorry. I felt a heat in my cheeks despite the coolness of the air.

'You said this was nothing to do with your employers?' I asked her.

She laughed. I stood next to her at the rear of the truck as she tied the canvas flap back in place and fastened the catch on the tailboard. Inside, I could make out large wooden crates, with some sort of stencilled marking on them. It was impossible to see them properly in the gloom, but something in what I saw triggered a memory.

'I have an altruistic side left in me. Rather like you do. Look hard enough and it's there. My employers, on the other hand, don't. I'm part of a group that helps people get out of the country. My employers don't know about it.' She finished up and turned to look pointedly at me. 'But you do.'

'Why can't you just do this?'

'You've seen why.'

She drove slowly out of the park and back towards the city. I watched a while in silence as the trees slowly disappear and buildings take their place. The Eiffel Tower came into view on the other side of the river. Like so many parts of the city, it was closed to the public. Someone had cut the lift cables before the Germans had marched into town, and the Occupiers hadn't got around to repairing them yet. There were days when that felt satisfying, others when it felt sad and futile.

She dropped me off in the same place she'd picked me up, by the Jardin du Luxembourg.

'You've made the right choice, Eddie.'

I watched the lorry disappear and waited until it was completely out of view.

'You think so?'

44

An owl. Always a bastard owl.

The echo of its shriek died in the night. It nearly took my heart with it. And me.

'Shut the fuck up, will you?' I hissed as loudly as I dared at the darkened treetops surrounding me.

The waxing gibbous moon that had accompanied me on the drive north had now vanished, swallowed by cloud. The darkness was complete, enveloping. It was my friend but it scared me. But that's friends for you.

The sun had set much earlier than it had the last time I'd been up this way. I'd had an overwhelming need to get out of Paris after Joe's release and Dominique's brusqueness, a need for my own freedom. But that wasn't why I was here. I was here because something I'd seen at Paulette's funeral had resonated with me. Something I didn't want to contemplate. My ankle began to hurt. I'd left Paris in time to get to the Bois d'Eraine before night fell completely, but the darkness had caught up with me before I was ready. It meant fewer farmers around to notice me, but it also meant I had to turn my headlamps on. That was a mixed blessing. The slits cut into the lights were too big to stop me from feeling exposed but too small to see much further than the front of my own car. Any German vehicles coming the other way along the windy forest road would be on me before I had a chance to react.

The door to young Fernand's farmhouse was wide open, but no lights were on. Cautiously, I crossed the threshold and closed the door behind me, making sure to pull the blackout curtain across it. Once my eyes got used to the dark, I saw no one in the small living room, so I went into the kitchen. The stove was still hot, a welcome warmth from the cold of the outside, but the room was just as empty. I tried the other rooms, with the same result, before going back to the kitchen and warming myself by the range. Checking the blackouts were in place, I turned the light on. He at least had electricity, so there was no fiddling with wicks and matches. Quickly, I went outside to check that no light seeped into the dark to give me away. Even in the pitch-black, there was no escaping the fact it was a pig farm.

Back in the kitchen, I was able to look at my surroundings a little more. Young Fernand's gun lay disassembled on the table. He'd obviously been cleaning it, but I wondered what would make him leave it unfinished. My foot crunched on something. I knelt down to find broken crockery, quite a lot of it, strewn on the stone floor. A drawer was partially open, some papers scattered on the dresser. I had no evidence to back it up, but I instinctively knew it was the work of a German patrol. They'd come to question him, or arrest him, for some reason, and had taken him away with them. I wondered if it was anything to do with me. Or if he'd just been caught making moonshine or whatever it was they did up here to relieve the tedium.

'Moonshine,' I echoed in a low voice.

I recalled the cold pantry off the kitchen that I'd seen last time. Opening it, I found none of the sides of pork I'd seen then, but hanging from hooks in the ceiling were two whole pigs. Equal parts horrified and hungry, I walked around them, my thoughts on the rationed lumps of gristle we were used to in Paris. Tentatively, I touched one of them, the skin cold and human to the touch. I recoiled and took a step back, thoughtful. I also knew it was time for me to get on with what I'd come here for.

Turning the kitchen light off and going outside, I felt my way in the dark to a shed and went in. Using my torch cautiously, my hand cupping the end, I spotted a spade in the far corner of the dusty old structure. Everywhere was impregnated with the smell of pig. Grabbing the tool, I went back to the house and looked in a cupboard for a sheet. Instead, I found an old grey blanket and took that.

Overcoming my nausea, I managed to manhandle one of the pigs off its hook and wrap it in the blanket. Half-dragging, half-carrying the dead weight, I got it out to my car and paused to get my breath back. My heart was racing, and that wasn't just the exertion. I listened out intently for any sound in the night.

'Hoot now and I'll shoot the fucking lot of you,' I muttered a general warning to the wood's owl population.

Heaving the pig onto the end of the open boot, I managed to edge it until it reached its fulcrum and tipped more easily into the space. Sweating, I pushed the body to the back of the boot, edging it further in by head and foot. The moon popped out for a moment as the blanket fell away. The slits where the animal's eyes had once been stared at me with a blind malevolence. I pushed the coarse grey material back into place with my fingertips.

'I hope you're worth it,' I told the pig.

I went back into the house and fetched the spade, putting that in the boot and closing the lid gently. In the distance, I heard an engine. At this time of night, it could only be a German patrol, so I hurried back to the kitchen to make sure

I'd left nothing there, before getting into my seat and driving away as quickly and as quietly as I could. Near the end of the long lane from young Fernand's farm, I turned the engine off for a moment to listen. I heard nothing.

Switching the engine back on, I edged out into the road and made for where I remembered the road to the small clearing was. This was the bit I was dreading. I parked as near as I dared and got out.

An owl shrieked. I rejoined my body and tried to stop shaking. The bird's call vanished into the night, its echo remaining only in my head. For some reason, in the loneliness, cold and dark of the Bois d'Eraine, I felt a sudden regret at having found my son again. The thought ran through me like an electric shock and made me go cold. Before Jean-Luc had come back into my life, I'd had no fear for my life. I'd had no fear for my life because I'd had no sense of its worth. But now, I wasn't alone. I had to stay safe for his sake, if not for mine. Safe and me didn't go together well. I immediately felt shame at my regret. And then there was Dominique.

Stowing the thought safely in the depths of my head, I reached into the boot and pulled out the spade. My fingers touched the dead pig and I recoiled. I hoped Albert the butcher would be willing to give me a good price for it.

Not closing the boot for fear of making too much noise, I looked to the trees, searching for the way into the small clearing where I'd stumbled the last time I'd been running scared through the woods. In the dark, a dog barked. I slowly walked towards the tree line, feeling my way for anything that would trip me up.

The owl called again. This time I didn't let it affect me.

'Try again, bird,' I dared it.

Sound carried in the woods, but its source was distorted. A

snuffling that seemed to come from in front of me would turn into a scampering to my right. I just had to keep walking, looking for my goal and not worrying about the noises all around me. That was easy to say.

I found it. The moon chose to stay hidden, but I could tell by the texture of the ground beneath me and the absence of tightly packed trees that I was in the right place. Feeling the earth with my foot, I realised there was a large area that had been dug and filled in again. I saw again the mound of soft earth next to Paulette's grave and my heart sank with the shock that that brought. I just had to choose somewhere to dig and hope I found something. Or hope that I didn't.

Burying the spade in the soft earth, I dug quietly. It was achingly soon that the tool came up against some resistance. Kneeling down, I gently scraped the earth away, first with the tip of the spade, then with my fingers. I had an awful recall of the feel of the pig in the boot of my car and had to stop for a moment to gather courage.

I felt cloth. Coarse and thick, like a military uniform. I let out a breath. There was no prison camp. Just this. Rubbing gently at the ground around the cloth, I knew I was unearthing an arm. The sweet aroma of decay rose up and wormed its way into my throat. The arm in the sleeve had withered, the feel of it amorphous in the dark. I had to force myself to keep going, oblivious to all the sounds in the night air.

Something hard and metallic found its way into my fingers. I shuddered and dropped it. It took me minutes to find it again. It was small and irregular in shape, with a sharp end and a rounded base. I tried to work out what it was without being able to see it when a light flared and I was bathed in white. Startled, I instinctively slipped the object into my right sock before looking up.

More than a dozen German soldiers were surrounding me by the edge of the trees, each one with their rifle trained on me. Two spotlights were pointing at my part of the clearing. In my concentration on the shallow grave, I hadn't heard a thing of what had been happening in the woods.

A face I recognised stood inside the circle of soldiers.

'The policeman,' Hauptmann Prochnow said. 'I wondered when you might be back.'

I was back in the German garrison in Compiègne. My lip was bleeding. I must have fallen down some stairs. Or resisted arrest. I've written reports too, I know how it works. Although the Occupiers probably didn't worry about even those false niceties. The only thing is, all I could think of was having left my car boot open. If some dog made off with my pig, I'd shoot the mangy bastard. Of course, I might not get the chance. Being arrested by the Wehrmacht is seldom a good sign.

Prochnow didn't even bother asking me what I was doing in the Bois d'Eraine. We'd gone past that. He'd even given up on the pretence of the prison camp. And that and the reasons for it had been bad enough. Instead, we were now onto the justifying bit. The bit where it was our fault our troops were executed in cold blood and buried in a mass grave in the woods.

'You fought a French war with African troops. That goes against the grain of civilised warfare.'

'Civilised warfare?' My shocked exclamation opened up the cut on my lip again.

'You will be quiet.' I could feel another punch in the face coming on. That would be to me from the feldwebel to my right. Prochnow was spitting with anger. 'I grew up in the Rhineland. I was an adolescent when the French occupied my home. You used colonial troops to keep us in check. African soldiers sent to watch over German people on German soil. It was a disgrace.'

'Any more than German troops on French soil?'

'It was an insult. The black shame, we called it.'

'If I were you, I wouldn't call it that again.'

He leaned forward. The end of his nose was just within reach. 'The mere presence of these ... these soldiers was an offence against all the laws of European civilisation.'

I was wrong. His nose was just that bit too far away. Either that, or the rifle butt in the back of my shoulders from the gefreiter behind me put me off my aim.

I lay slumped in pain across his desk as he sat back in his chair. I stared up at him, the look of hatred on his face no doubt reflected on my own. Yet one more tiny shift in the spirit of subjugation. A door opened. Prochnow jumped to attention. I almost laughed.

'My prisoner, I think, Hauptmann Prochnow,' a voice said.

I turned to look at the newcomer. 'You took your time.'

'Don't be tiresome, Édouard. I'm not in the mood.'

I looked back at Prochnow and winked. I was suddenly seeing why Boniface saw the appeal in it.

'You are aware that the farmer who gave you this false inform-ation has been arrested?'

'False information?'

There was a lot to unpick in Hochstetter's bold statement. We were in the relative warmth of his staff car, still parked outside the garrison in Compiègne. Hochstetter had made the driver wait outside in the cold night air as he lectured me.

'False information, Édouard. There was no massacre in these woods.'

'The farmer said nothing to me about a massacre. And the fact you all tried to cover it up with stories of prison camps in

France for African prisoners shows you know there was. This is a war crime.'

'The *Frontstalags* are not a fabrication. They exist.'

'And you think that's a justification for anything?'

'There were no executions, Édouard. There was a war. Soldiers die in wars.'

'It depends how they die.'

'Really? Some might dispute that.'

He gathered his greatcoat around himself to keep the cold out. I just had my jacket.

'He has been detained by the Wehrmacht,' Hochstetter went on. 'Your farmer friend. For spreading false rumours. How much further are you willing to go for this, Édouard? Who else are you willing to sacrifice?'

'I'm willing to go as far as others do in trying to hide it.'

Hochstetter let out a wry laugh. 'Very laudable. If stupid. I have secured your release from Hauptmann Prochnow in exchange for your promise to drop this absurd investigation. I can just as easily hand you back.'

I thought of the item in my sock and of my options. Despite my outrage, I knew I had to stay calm. Try as I might, I saw no direction in which I could take what I knew. Or suspected, at least.

'I'll drop it,' I told him.

'Good. If we are to survive, we have to face the fact that there is a need for alliances. Yours and mine is an uneasy one. I would suggest you don't further undermine it with lost causes.'

'Have you got an opera about that too?'

'Don't be flippant. You already have an enemy in the Gestapo, don't extend that to me. I promise you. You won't survive if you do.'

I nodded and looked out of the window at a couple of soldiers standing guard outside the garrison. Their hobnails echoed harshly as they stamped their feet to keep warm. 'So what other uneasy alliances do you have?'

'I'm a major in the Abwehr. My life is a string of uneasy alliances. Although that is mainly a problem for the other party.'

'And the prisoners released from Fresnes? Where do they fit into your uneasy alliances?'

He leaned across me and opened my door. 'I have no idea what you mean and little interest. Now, if you don't mind, I wish to return to Paris. I'm sure you can find your way back to your car.'

At least he returned my pistol. I watched his staff car drive off and contemplated my own hike back into the woods.

'A lift wouldn't have killed you,' I murmured into the night.

The walk nearly killed me. Three hours of owls, dogs and darkness, and never a German patrol when you needed one to drive you back to your car. Not that I imagine they would have anyway. I saw a strip of dawn peer over the tree line as I shut the boot on my intact pig and got into the warmth of the driver's seat. I closed my coat tightly around me to stave off the worst of the cold. Making sure no one was in sight, I reached down and took out the item from my sock that I'd found in the grave. Angling it to the light, I studied it closely. It was a regimental badge. For the Tirailleurs Sénégalais. The 24th Regiment. Fabrice's regiment.

Dropping my hand into my lap, I looked out of the window at the growing dawn and sighed. It was time to go back to Paris.

45

I hadn't slept since the Bois d'Eraine and I was still numbed by what I'd found, but I still looked in a better way than Boniface. His jaw was wired shut so he couldn't speak and his right eye was so swollen, he now had a temporary permanent wink.

'Suits you,' I told him.

He grimaced. At least I think he did. It was hard to tell.

I stifled a yawn. Another sleepless night. I almost wished I hadn't surrendered the Pervitin that Fran had given me to Bouchard.

A young nurse with glossy brown hair that kept falling loose from her crisp white headdress and a retroussé nose came in to check on the patient. Through his cuts and bruises, Boniface turned on a smile. It wasn't much different from the grimace, but the nurse seemed to like it. I will never know how he does it.

He picked up a notepad and pen from the bedside table and wrote on it.

That's Monique, it said. *She's a cutie.*

I tore the sheet out of the pad and threw it into a bin by the bed. 'So the blow to the head didn't do any good, then?'

That got a grin. Or a smile. Or a grimace. It also got a wink from the good eye. I reckoned I could forgive him this once.

He wrote on the notepad again. *What happened with your friend?*

I looked around to make sure no one could hear me. 'It worked. He got away.'

Good, he wrote.

'So what did the Gestapo want? I take it they were the ones behind this.'

He nodded, but then shook his head, and wrote on the pad again.

Gestapo. No questions. Just beating.

'A warning.' I looked at his face. 'I'm sorry I got you involved.'

He shrugged. More scribbling on the pad. *I'm a cop.*

I grabbed hold of the pen and wrote underneath. *I could get used to you like this.*

He laughed and immediately winced with the pain, falling straight into a coughing fit that seemed to tear through him. I reached for a glass of water by the bed and helped him take a sip.

'Good to hear you laughing, Detective Boniface.'

That was a voice from behind me. I turned to see Dax come into the room. The surprise was that he was followed by Hochstetter. I looked to the major.

'Checking up?' I asked him.

'Apologising.'

'You always have the ability to surprise me.'

'I know.'

He and Dax stood at the foot of the bed and studied Boniface's wounds.

'I'll see you get a commendation for this,' Dax told him.

'That should help,' I answered for Boniface.

Hochstetter stood next to me at the side of the bed and looked closely at Boniface. 'I can only apologise for this, Detective

Boniface. You should understand that this is not how we in the Wehrmacht believe we should behave.'

I gave him my best cynical look. 'Mass shallow graves, on the other hand ...'

Dax looked surprised by my comment. Boniface too, I think. Hochstetter remained impassive. 'How many times, Édouard? It is a war. Soldiers die.'

'Eddie,' Dax warned me, aware there was something deeper going on between me and Hochstetter, but not knowing what.

The major gestured to Boniface, the sleeve of his grey uniform neat and sharp as a knife. 'And I think, Édouard, that it is time you heeded my warnings. About the Gestapo and the SD. If not for yourself, then for your colleagues.'

I looked away, knowing I didn't have a leg to stand on. I caught Dax's eye.

'Major Hochstetter is right, Eddie.'

'It is time to forget your feud with these agencies of the Party and move on,' Hochstetter added.

That was me told. I recovered quickly enough. 'Thank you for taking me to the opera.'

Hochstetter looked surprised. 'Very gracious of you, Édouard. Although I wasn't sure you enjoyed it.'

'There was just one thing I'd change.'

'And what would that be?'

'The singing.'

He had the grace to laugh. 'Not to your taste?'

'The music was extraordinary. It's just a pity they spoiled it with all that shrieking. Like angry owls. That aside, it was just what I needed. Although I still think it strange that you allowed a story about political freedom to be staged.'

'Perhaps you will finally see us as enlightened.'

'Perhaps. Extraordinary story, though. The way the political prisoner was freed by the woman posing as something she wasn't. Such a good idea.'

I saw again Joe hiding in the back of the van and his being driven away, I hoped, to freedom, and kept the smile off my face. Boniface gave one of his wink grimaces to show he agreed.

'A German idea.' Hochstetter couldn't hide the smugness in his voice.

'Indeed it was.' I could.

In response, Hochstetter clapped me on the back, between the shoulders, before turning to go. I almost stumbled with the pain. He gave me a knowing look. He always had to have the last word. Even if it was a gesture. I thought again of Joe and felt I could take the ache.

I let Dax accompany Hochstetter out of the door and turned back to see Boniface writing something on his pad. He showed it up to me before tearing it out and throwing it in the bin.

It said, *There goes someone who knows more than he's letting on.*
'Which one?'

He took to his notepad again. This time all he wrote was a giant question mark in the middle of the page.

I smiled ruefully at him. 'You did a good job, Boniface. I'm only telling you this because you can't spoil it all by talking back at me.'

Dax returned. This time, he was accompanied by a woman and two small children, a boy and a girl. He inclined his head to the three newcomers and spoke to me.

'Maybe we should go, Eddie. Give them some privacy.'

I winked at Boniface, a taste of his own medicine, and left with Dax.

'Who's the woman?' I asked him in the corridor.

'Boniface's wife.'

I was puzzled. 'I thought he had three daughters.'

Dax paused and then carried on. 'You're right. That's his mistress then.'

'His what?'

'Surely you've heard about her?'

'I thought it was a myth.'

Dax laughed and shook his head. 'All true, Eddie.' He shook his head in wonder. 'He's got a wife and a mistress and a family with both. What a guy, huh?'

'What a bastard.' I was horrified. 'I'd almost begun to like him for a moment.'

Albert the butcher was waiting for me in the shadowed lane outside the rear of his shop. He emerged from the side of the building, jiggling nervously from one foot to the other.

'Got it?' he whispered urgently.

'No, I was just out for a ride.'

Rolling my eyes, I reversed my car up to as near his back door as I could and got out to open the boot. Luckily, the cold had been my friend, so the load hadn't started smelling. I lifted the blanket off the pig lying across the width of the boot and quickly shone my torch on it, its beam masked. Albert gave out a low whistle. I was the one to feel nervous now, Albert the professional one. I wasn't so much nervous as squeamish.

'Any problems?' he asked me.

'Apart from half the German army, you mean? No, not much.'

He grunted. He was too interested in prodding the contents of my boot.

'The price we agreed?' he finally asked. I nodded.

I helped him lift the dead weight out of the car and into his shop. Cursing in the dark, he guided us to a worktop and we dumped the load onto it. The end I was carrying was wrapped in the blanket, but I still reckoned there'd never be enough soap to wash it out.

'Thanks for this,' I whispered to him. He didn't want us to wake his wife up.

'Funny old business, war.'

I looked at the shape under the thin grey cover. 'Isn't it just?'

In the gloom, I saw him pull back the blanket. I prepared myself. It was lucky for me we didn't dare turn the lights on. He let out another low whistle and slapped the pig appreciatively.

'It's been a long time since I've had anything like this to cut up.'

'I really don't want to know.'

'It's a beauty. If you can get me any more ...'

I looked at the dead meat on his bench and cringed at the thought. I still had the feel of the cold skin on my hands. 'I don't think so somehow, Albert.'

'Pity.' He reached into his pocket and counted out the notes into my hand. 'Wait there.' He went into the front part of the shop and came back again with a small parcel, which he handed to me. 'For you.'

I opened it up to take a look. It was four pork chops wrapped in waxed paper. I smelt them, savouring the aroma. Strange how this didn't make me feel as squeamish as the whole pig I'd just sold to him had done. I looked at them longingly and thought how I could have shared them with Dominique. I hadn't seen meat like it in over a year. Sighing deeply, I handed them back.

'Have you got lamb chops instead, Albert?'

46

'Come in, Eddie. I'm sorry about the other day.'

I followed her into her living room, my little parcel held together with waxed paper and string. In my pocket I had another
smaller, less welcome item. The regimental badge I'd found in
the grave in the forest.

'Not a problem.'

I was the reticent one today. Not because of me or her, but
because I had to tell her what I'd found in the Bois d'Eraine. It
wasn't conclusive, but it was damning, and she had a right to
know. I wished I didn't have to tell her. She stopped to face me
by her sofa.

'Water or water?' It had become our saying, a wartime invitation. I couldn't appreciate it today.

'There's something I have to tell you, Dominique.'

Her face changed, her eyes wary. 'Is it to do with Fabrice?'

'Yes, it is.'

'What's in the parcel?'

'Sorry?'

She pointed at the waxed paper package in my hand. 'The
parcel. What's in it?'

'Meat. Lamb chops.'

'Let's see.'

'I have to tell you something.'

She brushed past me and disappeared down the corridor. 'In the kitchen, Eddie, not the living room, in case it spills.'

I knew what she was doing. In a way, I was happy for her to play for time. It put the moment off for me too. I followed her. She was standing by the stove. I set the package down on the table and opened it.

'Lamb chops,' I repeated. I was stalling as much as she was. 'I thought you could give them to your neighbours. The Goldsteins.'

'That's a nice gesture, thank you.'

'I should have got something for you too. I'm sorry. I didn't think.'

She came nearer and looked at the four chops nestling in the paper. She held them as though they were an injured fledgling, and looked up at me quizzically.

'Where did you get this?'

I cast around for an explanation. 'I'm friends with my butcher.'

Her expression changed to disbelief. 'No one is that much friends with their butcher. What did you have to do to get it? I know you, Eddie.'

'I didn't have to do anything. You don't have to give them to the Goldsteins if you don't want to.'

'These aren't ration portions.'

'I told you, he's a friend.'

'I don't believe you. How come you're suddenly able to get these things? What have you done? Is this to do with Fran?'

I could see her anger rising. But I saw relief there too. It was her chance to avoid hearing what I had to say. I was as guilty as she was. I stoked the argument to put it off.

'It's got nothing to do with him. Christ, Dominique, what is the problem?'

'Nothing, Eddie. I just want to know what's going on.'

I calmed, lowering my voice. 'No, you don't. That's why we're arguing.'

'I want you to leave.'

I tried to touch her but she backed away from me. 'Please sit down, Dominique.'

'Just go, Eddie.' It was her turn to reach for me, but instead of holding me, she pushed me roughly out of the kitchen towards the front door. 'Please just go.'

She opened the door and I allowed her to shepherd me out before closing it on me. From outside on the landing, I heard her lean heavily against the door and start to cry.

'There's something I have to tell you,' I said in a voice low enough for her not to hear.

I waited until evening.

The city had grown dark by the time I got out of my car and I felt the leaves under my shoes. Soaked and dried and soaked again with the rainfall we'd seen over the last month or so, they were crushed slimy and treacherous. In the gloaming, I saw the shadow of skeletal trees reach up into the gloom overhead. The canal glinted deep, the colour of widow's weeds.

I found the gate into the courtyard that I'd seen earlier when Capeluche had dropped Walter and his friend off. I wanted to know what secrets it held. I also really wanted to know if it was the place Capeluche's employers called home. And if that were the case, I might find out who the mysterious Henri Lafont was. The entrance was locked now, its delights tucked up inside. I gently pushed the gate shut behind me and turned to let my vision adjust to the dark. I could have done with a full moon but nature never comes through when you need it. And I didn't dare use a torch. There were apartment blocks surrounding the warehouse and any of them could be home to vigilant neighbours.

The two lorries were parked side by side. I recalled the stencilled boxes I'd seen in the back of one of them the day we'd freed Joe, but instead of trying to take a look inside them, I decided to get into the warehouse itself. I figured that that would have more stories to tell. One of them being how come there were German military lorries inside a French courtyard. Finding the door into the building – a smaller one set into a larger entrance – there was nothing for it but to shine my torch briefly onto the lock to see what I was dealing with. I shielded the beam with my left hand while I made my mind up. Switching the torch off again, I felt the lock picks in my pocket with my fingers and chose the right pair for the job. I was actually quicker opening it than I would have been in daylight. A cat mewed in the dark to celebrate my achievement, although I could have done without the fright it gave me. From the noise the creature was making, I reckoned the yard was one rat fewer.

Inside, I closed the door behind me quietly and rested again to get used to the dark. A ceiling window let in the meagre light from the sliver of moon. That meant I couldn't turn any lights on for fear of them shining out like a beacon. I was surprised that whoever owned the place hadn't put the blackout drapes in place for the night, but as I got used to the dark, I saw that the curtain was in place but had come loose on one side. It was still no help to me.

Shielding the light from my torch and only flashing it in brief bursts to get my bearings, I cautiously ventured further into the room, feeling my way with my left hand stretched out in front of me. From what I could make out, the warehouse was huge. What I took at first to be pillars were stacks of crates, piled high, almost to the ceiling. Lower stacks of smaller wooden boxes stood in serried rows between them.

With a start, I suddenly recognised where I was and had to lean against one of the stacks. I was in the warehouse where I'd been brought the day Capeluche had planned on doing some needlework on my lovely lips. Involuntarily, I clenched my mouth firmly shut until my teeth hurt.

Risking the torch one more time to calm my nerves, I shone the beam directly at one of the shorter piles. I immediately saw what I'd come to find. A marking stencilled onto the coarse wood of the crate. I studied it as long as I dared before turning the torch off. I knew I'd seen it somewhere before, but I couldn't place it. I'd also seen a crowbar. I needed to satisfy my curiosity, so I felt for it in the dark and opened the top box in two different stacks. Despite my doing it as quietly as I could, the sound of the wood cracking seemed to burst through the night. I used the torch one more time to check the contents of the two boxes I'd opened. The first one contained men's shoes, an increasing rarity in Paris and not my size. The second was piled high with tins of sardines. I filled my jacket pockets with as many of the tins as I could and used the crowbar as a hammer to reseal the boxes.

Standing in the darkness again, I was startled by a shadow going across the window that had come uncovered. A small thud echoed with a quiet menace through the vast room. Recoiling into the protection of one of the large pillars of boxes, I listened in the dark for another sound, but I heard nothing. Making as little noise as possible, I transferred the torch to my left hand and took out my gun. I had no idea what I could possibly find to fire at, but it felt marginally safer than nothing.

My eyes had got more used to the dark and I noticed a change in the quality of the blackness at the far end of the room. It was a smaller room built inside the main one, a glass-walled office with a desk and chairs and filing cabinets inside. Ignoring the sound of cat on rat, I felt my way to the area and found a door leading into the space. I was away from the sight of the ceiling window here, and the office itself had its own interior roof. Feeling slightly bolder, and in need of something to take the darkness away, I fumbled with the switch on a desk lamp and angled it down so it would cast as little light as possible.

I quickly opened the drawers on either side of the desk. A sound outside made me glance up. The light in the small office meant the rest of the warehouse was thrown into greater darkness, the shadows beyond the weak glow more menacing than before. I suppressed a shiver and turned back to the drawers. My fears were getting the better of me.

I pulled out a folder from the second drawer down and opened it. It was a pile of invoices. I leafed through them. More invoices. They puzzled me.

This time I did hear a sound from outside. The outer gate into the courtyard being dragged open and a car driving in. It was followed by a second one.

I'd only seen one way in and out of the warehouse, which meant I was trapped inside. The car doors were already slamming shut. Grabbing the first invoice from the pile, I stuffed it into my jacket pocket and shoved the folder back into the drawer before pushing it shut. I switched the desk lamp off and hurried from the little room.

The key was in the lock into the warehouse. I heard it turning.

Finding the towers of crates that I'd seen from the office, I felt my way between two of them and squeezed in as far as a small gap between the first boxes and the next piles. If anyone saw me, I'd be like a duck in a shooting gallery.

The door opened and an overhead light came on. I heard footsteps. Several pairs of them. Two men came into view. I had no idea how many others there were as they were out of my line of vision. I recognised one of the two men I could see as Henri Chamberlin, the low-grade crook who'd been part of the welcoming committee in Montparnasse a few days earlier. Whoever was putting this gang together wasn't exactly going for the best and brightest. Then I remembered Capeluche and qualified that.

I heard a voice speak but couldn't see where it was coming from. A German accent speaking in French. That was one theory ticked, I thought. Evidence of German involvement in whatever was going on. I tried to make out his words. It was about shipments of goods.

'We need to ensure a supply,' he finished. 'I will leave it to you how that is achieved.' He had a harsh, reedy voice, like a cracked clarinet playing out of tune. It was jarring to the ear.

The thought struck me that he must be one of the business-men who'd followed the Occupation. One of the central buying agencies that were snapping up French goods on the cheap – shoes, sardines and who knew what else – fleecing the sellers, and flogging them back home at inflated prices. Just the sort of thing our home-grown mobsters would be getting into. Some of the pieces fell into place, just not the important ones. Not yet.

'I trust I can rely on your organisation to safeguard that,' the German added.

I wondered who he was. He evidently had enough clout to get prisoners released from Fresnes. Greased the right palm, I wondered. Or he had the right connections. I waited in the shadows, uncomfortable amid the piles of crates, and thought that that was more likely. A Nazi Party member calling on his friends in the Gestapo or the SD or whoever was giving him a helping hand. I edged around to try and get a glimpse of him, but I couldn't.

What surprised me was that it was Chamberlin who replied. That stopped me.

'You know you can rely on us,' he told the German. 'We have the contacts and the network. We've already shown that.'

I was confused. I looked more closely. It was definitely Henri Chamberlin talking. He beckoned someone from outside my sightline over. He showed a level of authority I would never have ascribed to him. Standing before him now was Walter le Ricaneur. Walter had another man grasped by the back of the collar. The man looked terrified. His words came out in sobbing gasps.

'You're refusing to sell your goods to my friend here?' Chamberlin said to the man.

'Please,' the man pleaded.

Looking intently at him, Chamberlin slowly pulled something onto his fingers. He adjusted it. It was a knuckleduster. With a crude smile, Chamberlin lashed out at the man, catching him full on the jaw. He hit him a second time, on the cheek, it was all Walter could do to keep hold of the victim.

'How about now?' Chamberlin asked. 'Convinced it's the best deal for you?'

He hit him again, this time in the stomach. I could see a look of pure enjoyment on Chamberlin's face. The man doubled over and struggled for breath. Walter heaved him upright.

'Well, what do you say?' Chamberlin demanded.

'Yes,' the man gasped, his voice weakened.

'Yes, what?'

'Yes, Monsieur Lafont.'

Lafont? I all but rocked on my heels. Henri Chamberlin was Henri Lafont?

'Take him out,' Chamberlin, or Henri Lafont as I now supposed him to be, told Walter. He spoke again, this time to the German. 'I think you can see we are serious businesspeople.'

I heard the German laugh, a shrill sound. I could happily have shoved its echo down his throat.

I stared sightlessly for two seconds and tried to work out what I was witnessing. Had Henri Chamberlin, a petty criminal with the backing of a German businessman, metamorphosed into Henri Lafont, a name already feared in every neighbourhood in the city? If so, I recalled the Henri Chamberlin I knew and tried to equate him with the Henri Lafont he'd become. If it really was the case, it was a fearful reinvention. And then I remembered Capeluche. And I thought of the duumvirate of Lafont and Capeluche – another near-mythical *machine infernale* to punish the people.

As I considered all that I was learning, I heard the men finally making ready to leave the building. I needed to go, not just because of the cramp growing in the confined space. I wanted to be out of the foul place where I'd almost been killed and where I'd seen another part of the new Paris being born, one of Occupation and exploitation.

Only there was one last surprise waiting for me.

I caught a glimpse of the German as he made ready to go. I could only see the back of him, not enough to recognise him even if I had known who he was. But I did glimpse enough to see he was in uniform. But which uniform?

No wonder Henri Lafont was able to get the prisoners released from Fresnes, I realised. This wasn't some businessman borne in on the tide of victory. This was entirely official. The German authorities were using Lafont and the gang they'd

helped him create as enforcers for their own lucrative sideline.
With all the power and all the immunity that that implied.
    I leaned back against the crates and closed my eyes.
    Entirely official and entirely bloody frightening.

47

I was the first detective on the scene the following evening. A uniformed cop let me in. Breathing in the stale air of old bleach and sweat, I had an awful sense of having been here before.

It was a jazz club. In Montparnasse. Another one that had not been allowed to reopen. The same covered drums and dusty tables as I'd seen at the Jazz Chaud the morning Julot le Bavard was found dead. The same state of limbo. The same sense of foreboding.

'Who found it?' I asked the second uniformed cop, a young kid with neat dark hair and a stoop who looked like he'd just got back from the war. I thought of my son. He probably had.

The first cop had stayed at the door to let other detectives and the pathologist in and keep the nosy out. It was an hour before curfew and there were still a few people in the streets, stragglers in search of a drink and a sense of what their life once was.

'The owner,' he told me. 'A Joseph Bartoli. He's over there.'

'What's your name?'

'Rousse, Inspector.'

Instinctively I looked at his dark hair. Rousse. Redhead. That was a gene that had died out somewhere along the way. My mind was focusing on the inconsequential to flee the indescribable.

Rousse pointed to a table in the far corner of the bar, fur-thest from the stage. A middle-aged man was sitting alone at a table, his eyes staring vacantly into the distance. He held a handkerchief over his mouth. I walked over and introduced myself. Bartoli leaned forward and pushed a chair out for me. His one-word greeting told me he was Corsican. I had to stifle my own prejudice. Many of the heads I'd had to knock back in my doorman days in Montmartre were Corsican gangsters, thugs with a finger in every unappetising pie. I gave him the once-over. He wore a suit that was a size too big, but that might just be down to rationing, and had slicked hair and a pencil moustache bookending dark eyes and an aquiline nose. His facial features were doing nothing to ease my prejudgement, but by my reckoning, it wasn't the crooks who were losing weight under rationing.

'You found the body?' I asked him.

He nodded. 'I called the cops straight away. It was the stench.'

I turned to look at the door into the store room next to the bar. The first cop had told me that that was where the body was. I sensed the smell emanating from the open door, its effect fainter this far away, the sound of flies an undertone of frantic rumour.

'Can you tell me what happened?'

'I was away. Visiting my wife's family in Rouen. I got home this afternoon. A cleaner was supposed to have been in while we were away, but she says she lost her key.' He wafted his hand at the far door. 'That's why it's only now I found this.'

I studied him as he spoke. For the moment at least, he seemed to be talking openly to me. Like someone with nothing to hide. Or he was just good, cynical me on my shoulder whispered in my ear.

'How long were you away?'

'Two weeks.'

I looked at the signs of a business going down the drain. 'Has anyone approached you about getting the club reopened? Putting in a word with the Germans?'

He shook his head. 'Nothing. But as I said, I've been away.'

'Let me know if anyone does.'

I left him at the table, staring into space. I guessed that with the club closed, he didn't even have anything to drink in the place for him to take the taste away. As I made for the door, Rousse stepped forward.

'I should warn you, Inspector.'

'No need.'

'It's been a few days,' he insisted.

'Thanks.'

He let me go into the store room on my own. The flies complained but I stayed in the doorway and left them to it. I reckoned it was Bouchard's job to argue the toss with them. Rousse had been right to warn me. Even at three metres away, the smell was overpowering. Just like Julot in the Jazz Chaud, a body was tied to a chair with twine. A man. Young. His mouth was sewn together.

'Capeluche,' I cursed her name in a whisper.

'Two weeks,' Rousse said from behind me. I hadn't realised he was so close.

'Less. Ten days at most.'

I knew because that was the night he went missing. The night I was supposed to meet him here in Montparnasse but Hochstetter had insisted on taking me to see an opera instead. Sitting in the chair was Dédé.

From behind, I heard the sound of people arriving. I heard Bouchard's voice among them. I made ready to move out of the way for him, when I noticed a second chair, just a metre inside the room. It had a jacket on it. I recognised it as the over-sized leather one that Dédé had been wearing the one time I spoke to him. Edging further into the room, I retrieved the jacket and retreated to the door.

Checking the pockets, I felt a small cylinder in one of the inside ones. I emptied it and found it was a tube of tablets. I read the label. Pervitin. I cursed a second name.

'Fran.'

'Bad times, Eddie,' Bouchard said to me, edging past me into the room. He took a deep breath and ventured further in.

'Aren't they just?'

I hefted the Pervitin, feeling the tube's contours and weight, my fingers caressing the edge of the label. All the while, I stared at Dédé's body. And in my other hand, I felt the jacket that had made him look even younger than he was.

I stood outside and failed once more to understand cops who smoked at times like these. Quite apart from my aversion to filling my head with poison, the only thing I would ever want right now was fresh air. I leaned against the wall of the building and sucked in huge lungfuls of the stuff. It might have been city air tainted with fumes and decay, but it was as fresh as it got.

I had a choice. A dilemma.

Capeluche and Fran.

Paulette died because of Fran.

Julot died because of Capeluche.

Young Dédé died because of Capeluche, but Fran could just as easily have been the one to cut the twine with his Pervitin.

Fran has the values of an alley cat.

Capeluche has Hervé.

Fran kills the innocent at random. Capeluche kills her own kind at will. For now.

And more people will die because of both of them.

*

'More favours, Eddie? What's in it for me?'

'The knowledge you've helped a friend.'

Fran snorted. The heiress to Paulette and Cosette was lying face down on the sofa next to him in his office. Her flimsy evening dress had ridden up her thighs. He reached across and slapped her on the arse, a resounding thwack that had to hurt. She yelped in pain.

'Hey you, whatever your name is, pull your knickers up and go and make me a coffee.' He looked up at me. 'You want one too, Eddie?'

'No thanks, Fran.'

The young woman, little older than twenty, adjusted her dress and ran out of the room. She had tears in her eyes, either from Fran's slap or his attitude. I turned back to see him watch her go.

'Nice arse,' he said.

'One day you'll find a woman who hits back,' I told him.

'What was it you wanted again, Eddie? A favour.'

'I just came to see if I can count on you.'

He began cutting some cocaine on the coffee table in front of him.

'As I said, what's in it for me?'

I had to pass by Thirty-Six on my way across town to the Right Bank. For the time being, at least, Dax was off my back, the Boulevard Voltaire robbery and the missing prisoners out of his thoughts.

I wondered again whether he had any involvement in the matter. If he had been, surely he wouldn't have pushed me so much to look into the Voltaire job in the first place. Double bluff? I knew Dax's failings, but I still didn't want to think of him as being involved in the whole Lafont set-up, even if all that meant was turning a blind eye.

'Boniface sends his love,' I told him.

'Have you seen him?'

'No, but I'm sure he does.'

I followed Dax into his office and told him about Dédé's murder, his death the same as Julot's.

'Christ, how's this going to end?' he asked.

'Badly, I'd say.'

We sat in silence for a moment. I had no idea what Dax was thinking, but I was busy trying to convince myself I wasn't just as guilty of looking the other way as I suspected he might have been. For as long as Jean-Luc was within Capeluche's reach, there was nothing I dared do to solve Dédé's death or even prevent more killings like them from happening. I'd sold the price of my soul to protect my son and to free Joe and Dédé had paid for it.

'Armistice Day,' Dax suddenly said, surprising me. His voice was distant. 'The first time I won't have celebrated it since the last war.'

'I hadn't forgotten.' Today was our Armistice Day, November the 11th. Only the Germans were being a bit cagey about allowing us to celebrate it. 'What reminded you?'

'Do you think there'll be any trouble? There are rumours the students are going to kick off.'

'Let's hope so.'

I left Dax and went to my office. There was a message left on my desk. I'd had a phone call. There was a number for me to ring. No name, no mention of what it was about. Mystified, I placed the call with the operator and waited. A southern accent answered. A woman's voice.

'*Café de la Gare?*' she said.

'Who am I talking to?'

I heard some mumbling at the other end and then she spoke again. '*Is this Eddie?*'

'Yes. Who is this?'

'*Wait one moment.*' As I waited, I doodled on the piece of paper. The woman at the other end was gone some time and I considered hanging up. I glanced at the piece of paper and saw I'd written the name 'Dominique' over and over. I screwed it up and threw it in the bin. And then I retrieved it and put it in my jacket to throw away somewhere other than in my office so no one could find it. The love of the adolescent, the paranoia of the old. The phone clicked and I heard someone clearing their voice at the other end.

'*Hello. It's Monsieur Joseph.*'

Joe's voice was still an echo of its old self, but it already sounded stronger. My heart leaped.

'Hello, Monsieur Joseph.'

'*I just wanted to say that the customer has taken receipt of the shoes.*'

I sat up with a jolt. 'He has? You've seen the customer?'

'*I have. He likes the shoes very much. He's wearing them now.*'

'Is he there with you, Joseph?'

'*No, he's gone for a walk in his new shoes. A long walk.*' He paused a moment. '*I have to go.*'

He hung up and I sat holding the phone in my hand for some time before letting it go. Joe had seen Jean-Luc. I'd given him my son's baby shoe the day Capeluche and I had released Joe from Les Tourelles. And he'd passed it on to Jean-Luc as proof that he was who he said he was. And with it he'd passed on my message to get away from the people helping him.

I sat back and breathed out slowly. Jean-Luc had gone for a long walk.

'Who?' Hervé asked me, confused.

He was alone in the ground-floor flat he shared with his wife. He was calm. He'd recognised me when I'd knocked on the door and had led me into the large room at the end of the corridor. I smelt coffee on the stove. I'd come to learn that it was a smell that soothed him. I sat down on one of the chairs next to his wheelchair.

'Capeluche?' I repeated. 'Where is she?'

His look of confusion quickly turned to concern. He began to hum his song. I needed him to stay calm. 'Capeluche? I don't know who that is?'

I twigged. He had no idea of her existence away from this bolt-hole.

'Your wife. Where's your wife?'

He smiled. 'Thérèse? She's out.'

Thérèse. That was Capeluche's name. I felt strangely uncomfortable, like I'd intruded on their life. It was a name I wasn't supposed to know.

'Where is she, Hervé?'

'She's out.'

'I need to find her.'

He glanced at the wall clock above the sink. 'She's not back.'

'No, Hervé, I know. I need to find her. Do you know where she is?'

'She's not back.' He looked at me, his expression one of blank sorrow. 'I like it when she's not back.'

His words stunned me, but he suddenly started humming the tune again. Not gently, but insistent, the sounds tumbling out of his mouth. Getting up quickly, I went over to the stove and poured a cup of coffee from the pot. Sitting down again, I placed it between his hands and cupped them both in mine. He took a deep breath of the aroma and his chant began to slow. I could feel the comfort of the heat from the cup and felt him calm.

'Why do you like it when she's not back?'

He gazed at me, his eyes moving from my right eye to my left and back again. 'She's not happy.'

'Where is she?'

'Saint-Ambroise.'

'The church?' I knew it. It was a short walk from the flat.

He shook his head slowly. 'The garden. In front. She sits there.'

'Do you sit there with her?'

'No. She's happy there.'

He slowly began to cry. I put the coffee cup down and held his face to my own until the crying stopped. I let myself out when he was quiet.

'Never go and see Hervé without my permission.'

Capeluche was on edge. She had been from the moment I found her in the small garden in front of the church. I'd never seen her like it before. I couldn't decide if she was more dangerous like this or when there was a coldness to her.

'I was looking for you. I can't find you unless I go to your home.'

She nodded silently, her mood unchanged. Her eyes flickered at the building opposite from our vantage point in the doorway. She finally spoke.

'You chose wisely, Eddie. Don't make me regret that. I can be your enemy or I can be your friend.'

'As you said, I chose.'

Momentarily turning away from our focus, she studied me. 'I left you no alternative. That doesn't make for loyalty.'

'I know exactly what my alternatives were.'

She gestured at the building. 'This was your request. Another favour. Remember that. You knew the deal you made when you asked for my help with your American friend.'

'I know I did. That's why I'm here now.' I waited a moment before speaking again. 'I also know who Henri Lafont is.'

'You do?'

'Henri Chamberlin.' I still wasn't sure it could be true. Until she turned one more time to look coldly at me.

'What do you want? A pat on the back for working it out?'

We settled in to wait, the silence uneasy. The alliance uneasy. I wondered if I did know what my alternatives were. I had made my choice, but that didn't remove my dilemma. An image of Hochstetter sprang into my mind. Another pact with the devil, another choice made.

I said the one word.

'Dédé.'

She didn't react at first, but then turned to me. 'Is this really the time?'

'This is precisely the time. I need to know.'

Her anger was back. 'Did you think you'd change me? That I'm yours to be changed?'

A figure appeared and I put my finger to my lips.

It was Fran. Turning up at his club in Montparnasse, unaware of our presence in the shadows. Strangely dispassionate, I watched him unlock the front door. Paulette, whose lonely funeral I'd attended, had died because of him. Because of his returning to his source. To the drug peddling that had helped ruin so much of my life. I knew he had to be stopped.

'Let's go,' Capeluche said after Fran had gone in.

She crossed towards the Jazz Chaud. After a few seconds, I followed her.

I questioned whether I'd made the right choice.

48

It was our own cops who led the first baton charge. On school-kids and university students. A couple of boys barely out of shorts had left a floral cross of Lorraine on the tomb of the unknown warrior and the police had had a fit. That might have had something to do with the grey lorries lurking off the Place de l'Étoile, keeping watch on how the cops reacted. Of course, it might also be because there are some nasty bastards among the cops too, who just don't like kids and Communists. We can't blame the Germans for everything.

I watched from my Citroën as the uniforms chased after the schoolkids, but they were too nimble for them and danced away down a side street. In the privacy of my car, I let out a muffled cheer. I was a detective, I wasn't here on duty, but I'd wanted to come and pay my respects. That was as much as I could, of course, since the Nazis had forbidden any commemoration of Armistice Day. Our Armistice Day, that is, the one in 1918, not theirs from the summer. It meant I didn't have to take part in the tense scene acting out in front of me of French cops once again doing the dirty work of the grey shadows in the background. Some cops, I saw, were just too eager to do their bit.

In the vacuum left under the Arc de Triomphe by our home-grown Keystone chase, I saw German soldiers quickly remove the wreath. Some mourners had left tributes through the day on the tomb and at the statue of Clemenceau halfway along the Champs-Élysées, and the Nazis had allowed it to happen, but the presence of the young people as evening drew near had them spooked. After a summer of relative calm since the Occupation had begun, they were the first sign of open dissent any of us had seen.

'It's all kicking off, Eddie,' Dominici, a uniformed cop told me through my car window a short while later. He was one of the good ones, trying to stop other cops from breaking French heads. He nodded at a crowd of young people gathering at the Place de l'Étoile. 'They've just bust up a Fascist bar down the way, Le Tyrol, and they're heading in force up here. And the Nazis are making us the villains by sending us in to sort them out.'

Near the kids, I saw the military lorries gathering in the streets off the square. 'I have a feeling our masters won't be holding back much longer.'

He looked up and gently banged on the car roof. 'I hope you're wrong. Although there's part of me that hopes you're right. They can be the bastards they really are for once.'

He was about to set off for the fray, when we saw the first movement from the sidelines. German lorries and cars raced into the crowd, scattering the students. A Horch pinned a boy and a girl against a railing. Soldiers streamed out of the lorries like lava from an eruption and flowed over the square, burning out protesters in their way. A shot was fired – into the air but it did its damage, panicking the schoolkids.

'They've got fixed bayonets,' I said in awe and anger.

Someone closed the gates to the Metro station as the soldiers worked their way through the crowd, trapping the students in the square, throwing some to the ground, beating others. Some of the French managed to get away, escaping down one of the streets off the Place, but the soldiers were after them immediately. They fired stun grenades, sending shrapnel and confusion through the retreating hordes. The sound of them made me recoil, the aftershock ringing in my ears. Few of the kids got far.

'Christ,' Dominici swore. 'They're much more organised than we are at this.'

'That's why they're here and we're not in Berlin,' I told him.

The pair of us were transfixed. Hesitantly, I got out of the car, but I knew there was little I could do, except cause more confusion. The youngsters wouldn't be looking to me and a uniformed cop for protection and the soldiers would have swept us aside in the cold blink of an eye. Two kids came running past, a boy and a girl, both of them in tears. I tried directing them.

'Get in my car,' I shouted to them, but they swerved to avoid me and ran into the middle of the avenue to get away. Their instinct was that I wasn't to be trusted.

Glancing once at each other, Dominici and I walked purposefully towards the commotion. We couldn't do much, but we couldn't do nothing either. But it was already ending, the French students and schoolkids herded into groups on the Place de l'Étoile, some of them already being forced into the backs of the lorries, arrested not by French cops but by German soldiers. I recalled Hochstetter's comment from over a month ago about getting the French to wield the power as that would be preferable to the Nazis doing it for us. I now knew what he meant.

A noise in one of the streets off the Champs-Élysées caught our attention and we went to look. Some students had been trapped up against a building. One of them was caught in a doorway, a semi-circle of soldiers preventing him from getting out. As we approached, I saw an NCO take his pistol out and point it at the young man.

'French police. Stop,' I shouted to him.

Without turning to look at me, he took aim and fired. The scream from the doorway cut through the air, more chilling than the gunshot. I began to run towards the German NCO, my hand going for my own gun, but Dominici grabbed hold of me and pulled me back.

'Don't, Eddie. There's nothing you can do. You can only make it worse.'

Instead, he went in front of me and looked in the doorway. I caught up with him to find the young man writhing in pain. The NCO had shot him in the thigh. It was one of the most cynical acts I'd seen since the Nazis had come to town.

'French police,' I told him, fighting to keep my rage in check. 'We'll take over.'

Without even throwing a glance at us, the NCO ordered his men to herd us away from the scene. 'No, you won't.'

We were shepherded by half a dozen soldiers with rifles, their bayonets fixed, back to the avenue. Some of them looked flushed with enthusiasm, their first real action after months of inactivity and it was against unarmed kids. It was a moment that I knew would stay with me. Over their shoulders, I saw their colleagues detain the remaining students. Young faces filled with fear. As we retreated, a lorry appeared from the other end of the side street and the trapped protesters were harshly loaded onto the back of it. I lost sight of the boy they'd shot.

'Bastards,' Dominici muttered to the soldiers' backs after they left us helpless on the Champs-Élysées.

It was strangely quiet. I checked my watch. Not yet seven o'clock and it was over. The lorries were leaving, the students arrested or faded away, the streets emptying faster than an impending curfew. Just Dominici and me staring at a now deserted side street and my car standing alone on the avenue.

We looked at each other and shook our heads, both knowing we'd witnessed a change in the fortunes of the wind.

'No one's coming back after this one,' I told him.

We climbed into my car and I drove us back in silence to Quai des Orfèvres. He disappeared without a word, the shock evident on his face, into his part of the building and I waited outside in the car for a moment to gather my thoughts. I had to admit that Hochstetter was right. We had to be the police to stop the Nazis from doing the job for us. All we had to do was make sure we didn't become like them. I glanced up at the windows and thought of some of the people in there and I knew that that was going to be no easy task.

There were days when the climb up the three flights of stairs to my floor made my childhood Pyrenees seem like a gentle slope. This was one of them. Dax was waiting for me outside his office. He wasn't actually waiting for me, but it always seemed like he was. The joys of a guilty conscience, even when I've done nothing wrong. He also had some news for me.

'There's been a killing,' he told me.

I thought of the soldiers' treatment of the protesters. 'I'm not surprised.'

'No, Eddie, you don't understand. There's been another killing. Like Julot le Bavard.'

49

The damp air that had clung to the city all day had turned to rain. A miserable cold drizzle. I stood next to Dax, who'd insisted on coming with me, and felt the rivulets of water run down through my hair and into my eyes. For once, I felt regret at refusing to be like other cops and wear a hat.

The dancing beams of the torches were giving me a slight headache. I watched them play on the scene in front of us, the lights flickering on and over the body kneeling on the floor like a badly lit movie. As the torchlight caught the falling rain, it threw back reflections of needles falling, each one further stabbing the earth. There were no sounds of aircraft in the evening sky, but we still didn't dare illuminate the scene any more than we were doing.

'What a place to choose,' Dax commented. The drips from his hat spattered onto his shoulders and stomach, giving off a curious patting sound as an underscore to the gentle thudding of the raindrops on the compacted wet pathway.

'What a place indeed.'

A torch momentarily picked out the face of the man resting his chin on clenched hands. Below him, the skeletal dark angel seemed to emerge from the stone, glowering and growing in the fulgurating light. At their foot, Baudelaire lay impassive in his mummy's shroud. They were the only witnesses to the death of the fourth figure, left kneeling at the poet's feet as though in prayer.

The cemetery in Montparnasse, where Capeluche had taunted me an age ago. The kneeling figure, a dead body. Not with the lips sewn together this time, but a refinement. This time, a giant needle through the hands, holding them together in false worship.

'Any idea what it means?' Dax asked me.

'None.'

'A bad business.'

The third voice from behind startled me. I turned to find Hochstetter at my shoulder, between me and the commissioner. Standing a short distance away was the Abwehr officer I'd seen with Hochstetter at the Lutétia and at the opera. Major Kraus, a grey man in a grey uniform. For one odd, brief moment, I wondered if I should be more afraid of him than of Hochstetter. I hadn't heard them approaching. Hochstetter held an umbrella over his head. Even the rain couldn't cling to him. I turned to face him.

'What are you doing here?' I asked.

'This whole affair. It is of concern to me. But you know that, Édouard.'

'Yes, I do.'

'The same perpetrator as the previous killings?'

'I think we can assume so.'

We stood in a line and stared at the scene as it faded in and out of vision in the rain curtain and random light.

'A fitting end to an unfortunate day,' Hochstetter judged.

I felt my face burn with anger. I fully expected to see the rain turn to steam in front of me. 'There was nothing unfortunate about the day. Either the Armistice commemorations or this. It was all carefully planned, all of our own making.'

'I apologise, Édouard. You appear to have had a trying time of it.'

He was as calm as he ever was, the rain from his umbrella a threadbare sheet partially shielding his impassive face. 'Trying?'

Dax spoke to defuse the tension. 'Do we know who the victim is?'

From behind Hochstetter, I saw Bouchard arrive along the path. He'd also had the foresight to bring an umbrella, holding it over his head and his bag of tricks. He saw the two Germans and decided not to join us. Instead, he got straight down to examining the body. We nodded a greeting to each other.

'Eddie, do you know who the victim is?' Dax insisted.

'No, I don't,' I lied.

In silence, we watched Bouchard go about his work. The rain continued to fall on immortal stone and mortal flesh. On Baudelaire and on the four of us who stood at his cenotaph – on Dax, Hochstetter, Kraus and me.

It was Hochstetter who decided to bring philosophy to the table.

'If you gaze long enough into the abyss, it will gaze back into you,' he said. It was said with a thoughtful tone. It was said, no doubt, for my benefit.

'And if you fight monsters, you should ensure you don't become a monster in the process.'

His laugh gurgled in the incessant drizzle. 'I often forget you're a man who reads books.'

'Yes, you probably do.' I wasn't much in the mood for his games.

'Nietzsche. A great German.'

'Yep, he's dead.' It was a cheap shot, I know, but sometimes those are the most satisfactory.

'I will let that slide.'

'Christ, Eddie, know when to keep quiet,' Dax admonished me.

'This is regrettable,' Hochstetter continued. 'But I feel that the death of your young man, this Dédé Malin, was more so.'

His frankness shocked me. 'He died the night you took me to the opera.'

He had the grace to look uncomfortable. I took that as a minor victory. They were rare. 'Do you know who killed him?'

I paused a beat. 'No.'

He nodded and turned back to the sight of Bouchard working on the new victim under the torchlit rain.

'A change in the modus operandi,' Hochstetter said, making vague circling motions at his own lips. 'The hands fastened together.'

'A gangland execution,' Dax argued.

'Perhaps.' Hochstetter ignored him and turned to me. 'Do you intend to pursue your investigation into the prisoners released from Fresnes?'

I gestured at the victim. 'Why wouldn't I?'

'Because I feel there is nothing to be achieved by doing so.' He also gestured towards the victim. 'Just this. And your Detective Boniface. The agencies responsible for these acts will only continue to commit them the longer you investigate. More unnecessary deaths. You have to consider a greater good, Édouard.'

'I think the major is right,' Dax chipped in. 'It's time to move on. We don't want to be the reason this escalates.'

I remained silent for a moment, weighing up their words, watching Bouchard at work. There had been enough killings. I still felt guilt at the beating handed out to Boniface. 'All right.'

'I have your assurance?'

'You do.'

That seemed to satisfy both Hochstetter and Dax. They turned to leave.

'Coming, Kraus?' Hochstetter called to the other Abwehr man.

'With you now, Hochstetter,' he replied.

I watched them leave together, my gaze following the route they took along the path long after the rain and the night had swallowed them up. Bouchard still looked a long way from finishing, so I took a step back and sat on a bench facing the light show in front of me. A tree overhead gave me some respite from the weather.

I sat and shook my head in surprise and anger. This was my world now. My job. Private triumphs I could share with no one. I could solve cases, but I could do nothing with the discoveries I made. I couldn't arrest the perpetrators, so I was forced to find other ways to fight back. Ways that were outside the law that I was supposed to be upholding. The Occupation had bred a new amorality. One that I was steadily embracing. I'd assured Hochstetter I'd drop the investigation into the missing prisoners and I would. But not for the reasons he thought. As I said, a new amorality.

I thought of the choice I'd had to make. The dilemma I'd faced. I saw the body kneeling in the rain.

'Eddie,' a voice in front of me said. I looked up to see Bouchard standing between me and the victim. 'We're about to move the body.'

I thanked him and got up. Together, we walked over to the tableau of the poet's cenotaph and the kneeling supplicant. I gazed on the victim.

'You don't know who it is?' Bouchard asked.

'No.'

No longer spiky, her hair was flattened against her head by the rain. The needle holding her hands together was her own stiletto, the one she'd sprung on me that day in Montmartre and then again at the Jardin du Luxembourg. Her eyes were closed, the blood from the gunshot wound to the back of her head washed away.

Unable to summon any emotion, I took one last look at Capeluche and walked away, back along the path taking me out of the cemetery.

50

I was dripping rainwater all over the floor in Dax's office. I didn't much care.

I was alone. It was late and there were only a couple of detectives in the main room, sheltering from the steady rain falling outside. They weren't paying attention to me. I'd driven here straight from the cemetery in Montparnasse and left a trail of rain up the stairs to the third floor. As I said, I didn't much care.

Pulling open the drawer in Dax's desk, I took out the bottle of whisky and one of his glasses. Peering at the murk inside the tumbler, I cleaned it on my wet shirt tail before wiping it dry with my handkerchief. I needed a drink. I poured a healthy slug and drank a small amount, letting the flavour linger in my mouth.

Taking the glass, I stood at the window. I looked past my reflection to the darkness beyond. The night was impenetrable, the rain clouds blotting out any light from the moon or the stars. It felt neither safe nor menacing. I was too lost in my thoughts.

I'd made my choice. I knew that. I just had to be certain I'd made the right one. On the black canvas in front of me, I saw again the figure of Capeluche kneeling in the rain. I'd lost any semblance of religion I might have had a long time ago, but I couldn't help the easy image of her at peace. At a greater peace than I was right now. And I had to ask myself why I'd chosen her. Why I'd decided that she would be the one to die. And, perhaps more importantly, why I'd decided that Fran would be the one to live.

Capeluche had helped me release Joe when Fran had refused. And she'd helped others over the border to safety. Always at a price, but she'd helped. Fran had simply laughed at me. At the thought of helping anyone other than himself. As he always had done.

My dilemma had been that I'd had to enlist the help of one to eliminate the other. They were both too wily for me to have tried to do it alone. And I'd chosen Fran over Capeluche. It was the one time he had helped, and it was purely for his own self-preservation. I tried to convince myself that my choice wasn't solely for mine.

I drank slowly and had to make an admission to myself. I'd liked Capeluche. The thought shocked me. I didn't like Fran. Despite the evil she pursued, Capeluche had a reason, a cause for her actions, one that I understood. One that I'd experienced myself. Fran was none of that. He was a feral cat with the morality and inclinations to match.

The problem was that I knew that Fran was the lesser danger. The lesser of two evils. That was it. Capeluche killed mercilessly to order. Fran killed thoughtlessly to profit. Capeluche would have killed again and again on command, wilfully, with a cruelty I'd rarely seen in all my years as a cop. It didn't matter that I'd come to like her, she was the one I had to stop first.

'Maybe you'll be next, Fran,' I said out loud to the darkness beyond the window.

I took a deep drink, draining the glass.

But Capeluche had Hervé. I let out a deep breath. That was a thought I knew I'd been putting out of my mind. Hervé. Alone in his strange ground-floor world. Thanks to me.

There were other thoughts I was avoiding. Other reasons for my choice that I didn't want to face. I wanted to see a moral dilemma here. That I'd committed no less of a wrong than Capeluche had done to create a right. I'd used evil to destroy evil. I'd taken on the role of the bad to do good. I wanted to see it, but I couldn't. The truth was I could control Fran. It was perhaps as simple as that. I could never have controlled Capeluche. And that had made me afraid of her. Of what she was capable of. Who she would kill. Harmless souls like Julot. Rash kids like Dédé. Me, the moment I ceased to be of use to her or Lafont. Whoever was next on the list given to her. Anyone.

My breath misted the window in front of my face and slowly dissipated.

But most of all, Jean-Luc. My son, whom I'd failed so many times. Even though I knew he was safe for the time being, his continued safety wasn't a given. For as long as Capeluche had lived, he would have been in danger. It would have been her hold over me. I refocused my gaze onto my own reflection and I knew that that had been my reason. Fran posed no threat to Jean-Luc. Capeluche had.

I stood a moment longer at the window, trying in vain to lose sight of myself in the dark. Giving up, I returned to Dax's desk and refilled my glass. Replacing the cap on the bottle, I twisted it around so the label was facing me. With my other hand, I reached into my jacket pocket and pulled out the invoice I'd taken from the warehouse where I'd seen Henri Lafont. The warehouse where Capeluche had been on the point of killing me. The paper was moist but still legible. I compared it with the bottle. The logogram on the two was the same. A pseudo-official Nazi eagle affair with a tiny swastika in its talons. I put the bottle down and returned the invoice to my pocket.

I sat down on Dax's chair and stared at the bottle. A gift from Hochstetter. The light from the lamp cast a small pool of light over the desk, accentuating the dark outside. It was a quiet night, tense after the rioting. No one wanted to be out in the streets, wary after the arrests. The Occupying soldiers had finally shown their cards. Their reaction to schoolchildren and students protesting had been swift and robust. Their law no different from the actions of the Gestapo and the SD in pursuing me, in beating Boniface.

Only the Gestapo and the SD weren't pursuing me to stop my investigation. They were pursuing me as they also had an interest in finding out what was going on. They were no more responsible for the release of the prisoners from Fresnes than they were for the deaths of Julot and Dédé. I knew that now.

That was the Abwehr. Hochstetter's Abwehr.

It was all circumstantial. The whisky, the invoices, the gifts to Dax, Hochstetter's uneasy alliances. Another private triumph I could share with no one and a conclusion I couldn't prove.

Hochstetter had admitted numerous times to his reluctance to work with some of the unpalatable bedfellows he was forced to work with. I knew he was involved. If not actively, then passively in fulfilling the task assigned to him. If anything, I had to be grateful to him. I was certain that he had been the one to step in that night at the warehouse and stop me meeting the same fate as Julot and Dédé. Ultimately, he was the reason why Capeluche had been forced to try and recruit me instead of killing me. I decided I wouldn't thank him for that.

As for Dax, I had no idea what the extent of his involvement was. That was something that I knew would have to wait for another day. One more thing I could probably do nothing about. Nothing legal anyway.

I took a deep drink of the whisky and considered again my own uneasy alliances. First with Capeluche, now with Fran. Fran, who'd promised to sew the killer's hands together. The trap Capeluche thought that she and I were setting for Fran, the loyalty she thought she'd gained with me, was part of her own downfall – the counter-trap I'd set for her with Fran. I wondered how much I'd grow to regret that. I wondered again whether I'd also be forced in the future to bring the alliance with Fran to an end in one way or another.

I sighed and thought of Capeluche and Henri Lafont. Of Julot and Dédé. Of Hochstetter and the Abwehr. It was all circumstantial.

Until Major Kraus had opened his mouth at the cemetery. I recalled the few short words he'd uttered – 'With you now, Hochstetter.'

His voice like a cracked clarinet. A discordant note in the darkness.

Kraus had been the German soldier at the warehouse with Henri Lafont. The Abwehr were the ones that had allowed a French criminal to stroll through Fresnes prison naming the prisoners for release. The ones who'd turned Henri Chamberlin into Henri Lafont. And for what? To buy up essential goods that they could then sell to Germany at preferential rates. French goods that we in France either could not afford or simply could not get at all. A master class in cynicism and opportunism. With an enforcer willing to commit atrocious acts to maintain the mundane secrecy of corporate greed.

The Abwehr – with or without Hochstetter's active involvement – was Lafont's boss. And, in turn, Capeluche's boss. Her employers, as she called them, responsible for the deaths of Julot Le Bavard and Dédé.

I finished Dax's whisky and turned out the light.

I left a fresh trail of rainwater all the slow climb up the stairs to Dominique's apartment. I paused for a moment, dripping onto the landing.

In my hand, the regimental badge I'd been clutching was digging into my flesh. Staring at her front door, I took a deep breath and opened my fist. It lay in the palm of my hand. The badge for the 24th Regiment of the Tirailleurs Sénégalais – Fabrice's regiment – that I'd found in another burial ground next to the sleeve of a dead soldier. A mass grave in a forest of young men we were supposed to forget.

It too was circumstantial. But it too was certain.

I knocked and Dominique let me in. She greeted me with a kiss before disappearing into her bathroom. She came back with a towel and tried drying my hair, but I pulled her hands away.

'You're wet through, Eddie.'

She said it with an affection that was unbearable and an expression that knew. The badge punctured the skin in my closed hand.

'Please sit down, Dominique. There's something I have to tell you.'

51

I walked along an institutional corridor the colour of yesterday's soup and hoped I'd done the right thing. The light bulbs came and went overhead as we passed deeper into the new life I'd created for my companion. His wheelchair squeaked on the tiled floor.

'I'd get that oiled if I were you, Hervé.'

He made a noise. Not a laugh, but not a grunt either.

I'd fetched him that morning. I'd opened the door into his apartment in Folie-Méricourt with the key I'd taken from Capeluche and put the coffee on the stove. He'd hummed his tune at first, his agitation growing, so I'd joined in with him. We'd smiled at each other as the humming got stronger and soon metamorphosed into the words. Raucous and loud, how we'd both remembered it. I was afraid our singing would bring the neighbours to complain, but no one did. We'd raced each other to the end of the song and finished laughing like pack mules in the empty flat. Two old soldiers from a distant war sharing a moment no one else could ever understand.

After we'd got our breath back, Hervé had started humming again, a mischievous look on his face. I'd gone over to the stove and poured two cups.

'No, you don't,' I'd told him. 'Drink your coffee instead. We've got somewhere to go.'

He'd wrapped both hands around the warming cup and taken a sip. 'Thérèse didn't come home last night.'

'I know.'

I'd felt no guilt for her. Only for Hervé.

I'd packed some things while he drank his coffee. He'd watched me the whole time, unsure of what was happening.

'When will she be back?'

I'd stopped to look at him. 'Let's go somewhere new and wait there.'

I pushed him now to a door halfway along the corridor and stopped to open it before manoeuvring his chair inside. It was a bedroom. A bed, a cabinet, a wardrobe, two chairs and French windows overlooking a garden.

'What do you say, Hervé?'

He looked around him, uncertain. 'What's this?'

'Somewhere for you to stay for a while.'

'Where's Thérèse?' He looked scared and started to hum.

A young nurse walked in and I froze for a moment. Blonde and petite, she was so like Sylvie, my ex-wife, Jean-Luc's mother, whom I'd fallen in love with in this same building a quarter of a century ago.

'Good morning, Hervé,' she greeted him, her voice soft like ripples on water.

He stopped humming and looked at her quizzically. 'Thérèse?'

'I'm Marie.'

'Good morning, Marie,' he told her. His voice was calm, but I saw confusion in his eyes.

'Is there anywhere I can get him a cup of coffee, please?' I asked Marie. 'It helps soothe him.'

'I'll go to the kitchen and fetch one.' She turned and left.

'That's a very nice young woman,' Hervé said after she'd gone.

I opened the French windows. 'Why don't we take a look out here?'

I wheeled him through the open doors into the garden and found a bench where I could sit, with his chair next to me. An autumn sun reached into the enclosed space, warming us. We held our faces up to its rays.

At first I thought he was humming. I opened my eyes and wondered where the nurse was with the coffee, but he was softly singing. A lullaby. He got to the end of the song.

'Is Thérèse happy?' he asked. 'She's not happy with me.'

'It's not you she's not happy with, Hervé. You're the closest she knew to what being happy was.'

Marie brought Hervé a coffee and another cup for me. We both thanked her and she left us alone together.

'Am I happy now?'

'I hope so.'

'The war.' He pointed to his legs. 'Thérèse never got over the war. I was worried she never forgave me.'

'She never forgave, Hervé, but it wasn't you.'

He nodded and looked at the gardens. It was bare now, but come spring, it would be luscious and beautiful. I wondered where we'd all be by then.

'It's peaceful here. I haven't felt this since …' He looked thoughtful. 'Since I can't remember when.'

I knew what he meant. 'I felt the same here too. I'll come and sit with you when the flowers bloom.'

After a while, he turned to face me. His voice was calm. 'Thérèse has gone, hasn't she?'

'Yes, she has.'

He twisted back in his chair and stared at the empty

flowerbeds and pots. An insect flitted among the blades of grass opposite where we sat. He sipped his coffee and breathed in its scent before speaking again.

'It's for the best.'

Author's Note

Paris Requiem is a work of fiction, but some of the stories it contains were inspired by real events. There was a massacre at the Bois d'Eraine in early June 1940, during the Battle of France, when a number of French troops were taken prisoner and marched to a farm in the south of the forest. There, the soldiers of the 16th and 24th Régiment de Tirailleurs Sénégalais were separated from the metropolitan French troops and taken away, despite the protests of the French officers. Because of their defence of the African soldiers, six of the officers were taken to a site on the northern edge of the Bois d'Eraine and executed. Their bodies were buried in a mass grave where they fell. Another two bodies were buried nearby – an Ivorian and a Guinean soldier – who had probably been forced to dig the officers' grave before being executed in turn. The African soldiers who had been separated were never seen again, and their graves have never been found. It's thought that sixty-four soldiers were executed in this way. This was one of several known mass killings of French African soldiers during this period of the war.

A memorial was erected in 1992 at the site of the mass grave where the eight bodies were found. A ceremony was held in 2010 to mark the 70th anniversary of the atrocity, and commemorations are now held every year.

Unlike metropolitan French prisoners of war, African and

Arab soldiers who were taken prisoner weren't sent to Germany, but were kept in camps in France – the *Frontstalags*. The argument the Nazis put forward for this practice was to prevent the spread of tropical diseases, although Nazi newspapers claimed that it was also to prevent the 'racial defilement' of German women. The conditions under which they were held were much tougher than for metropolitan French prisoners and the mortality rate was appreciably higher.

Almost all the characters to appear in the story are fictional, but Henri Lafont did exist. A petty criminal who rose to extraordinary power, thanks initially to the Abwehr, he did visit Fresnes prison in August 1940 with the collusion of the Occupier and secured the release of around thirty criminals held there. These men formed the basis of a gang under Lafont's leadership that became known as the Carlingue or the French Gestapo and worked closely with the Germans. I won't go into more detail here as Lafont and his cronies – real or fictional – will feature throughout Eddie's war in future stories, but if you'd like to find out more about him, I recommend *The King of Nazi Paris* by Christopher Othen (Biteback, 2020).

Aside from the part Eddie plays in the story, the events described on Armistice Day are reasonably true to actual events. Fearing demonstrations on 11 November, the German military command initially banned any commemoration from taking place, although, on the day, it is thought that some twenty thousand people laid wreaths at the Tomb of the Unknown Soldier and at the statue to Clemenceau on the Champs-Élysées. This was tolerated by the Occupiers, but in the afternoon and evening, a few thousand schoolchildren and university students marched on the Arc de Triomphe, where they were met with strong opposition from French police and German soldiers. Eventually, Wehrmacht troops charged the crowd with fixed bayonets and fired shots into the air, causing panic. This is seen by many as one of the first turning points in the Occupation, as the initial charm offensive began to give way to more evident repression. The scene with the young man shot in the doorway by a German soldier is based on a real incident.

A forerunner of methamphetamine or crystal meth, Pervitin was Nazi Germany's wonder drug, sold both over the counter and issued to the Wehrmacht in pill form. Known as 'pilot's salt', its effect was to enable soldiers to stay awake for days, function for long periods without rest and withstand pain and hunger. Millions of them were handed out to German soldiers during the Battle of France, and it's been argued that the Ardennes offensive and the invasion of France were made possible thanks to Pervitin. It soon became apparent, though, that the drug could lead to a wide range of health problems, including heart failure, psychosis and addiction, so it was regulated from 1941, although this did little to curb its use among both civilians and military.

Bizarrely, when theatres and opera houses reopened in Paris in autumn 1940, one of the first operas to be staged was *Fidelio*, Beethoven's only opera. A story of political prisoners and political freedom, with its eventual triumph over oppression, it was a strange choice and must have felt like a kick in the teeth for Parisians, if it was the choice of the Occupiers, or a clever and arch thumbing of the nose at the Nazis, if it was a French decision to stage it. The odd nature of its being performed in Paris under the Occupation is highlighted by the fact that after the end of the war and the fall of the Nazis, it became the first opera to be staged in Berlin.

And, finally, the fishing rods. Some Parisians really did walk around the city carrying two fishing rods to show their support for de Gaulle and resistance. By all accounts, the Occupier never saw the significance, which is strangely satisfying.

Acknowledgements

There are always so many people to thank in writing a book, and it's impossible to express just how grateful I am for all the support I've received from everyone around me. The words below are just the tip of the iceberg of how much their help means to me.

I'd like to thank the Society of Authors and the Authors' Foundation for the invaluable work they do in helping authors. While writing this book, I was fortunate enough to receive an Eric Ambler Award, which bought me some much-needed extra time and headspace.

One of the best bits about being an author is getting to meet – in real life or virtually – lots of wonderful readers, bloggers, booksellers and writers. I've been humbled by the way so many people have seen the good in Eddie and enjoyed his story. I'd especially like to thank all the readers who have been kind enough to write to me or post on social media to tell me they enjoyed *The Unwanted Dead*, and all the bloggers and reviewers who have been so supportive of my writing, most particularly Jacky Collins, Jill Doyle, Gordon McGhie and Noel Powell. I also owe a great debt of gratitude to all the crime writers who have been so kind in saying nice things about Eddie – special thanks here must go to Mick Herron, Vaseem Khan, Adrian Magson, Andrew Taylor and David Young.

For people who spend their days dreaming up dastardly deeds and bloody murder, crime writers are one of the nicest bunches of people you could meet, and I'm lucky enough to be a member of Crime Cymru, a collective of Welsh or Wales-based crime fiction writers. This is a big thank-you to all the members and followers, who do so much to promote Welsh crime writing and support each other through thick and thin, with special thanks to Judith Barrow, Mark Ellis, Philip Gwynne Jones, Alis Hawkins, Beverly Jones, Thorne Moore, Louise Mumford, Katherine Stansfield and GB Williams.

I'd like to say a big thank-you to my German and Spanish publishers, who are both an absolute joy to work with and for believing in Eddie. My German editor Thomas Wörtche and translator Andreas Heckmann and everyone at Suhrkamp. My Spanish editor Claudia Casanova and translator Iris Mogollón and all the team at Principal de los Libros. Thank you for your talent, skill and warmth.

The addition of Credits in books is a great idea and one that I really welcome. I would like to say a heartfelt thank-you to everyone who appears in the Credits in this book and everyone at my wonderful publisher, Orion. I am eternally grateful for the talent, dedication and hard work of you all. I am so lucky to work with the best and nicest editors in the business in Emad Akhtar and Celia Killen, whose brilliance and good humour make the whole writing process even more fun. If you've enjoyed this book, they're the ones to thank for their perception, patience and insights – all the other stuff is my fault. My good fortune continues in getting the opportunity to work with an amazing team – my thanks here to Alainna Hadjigeorgiou, Tanjiah Islam and everyone in marketing, promotion and sales, and to Krystyna Kujawinska, Louise Henderson and the whole of the Rights team. I'd also like to thank freelance copy editor

Jon Appleton for the extra dimension he brings, and designer Micaela Alcaino for knocking it out of the park with her amazing covers.

This is the bit where I thank my agent Ella Kahn. I could go on about her talent and insight, her belief in me, her answering my every question with constant good grace and thoughtfulness, and a long et cetera. But, instead, I'll keep it simple and just say a most profound thank-you.

Thank you, too, to friends and family for spreading the word. To my sister Helen and brother-in-law Malcolm for all their support. To Sue Pinfold for cajoling not one, but two book clubs into reading my books.

And, finally, my wife Liz, who is everything. Thank you for all your love and support and for always knowing exactly the right thing to do, the right words to say and the right drink to pour. Thank you with everything I have.